PASSAGGIO

From the Old World to the New

A Novel by

CYNTHIA SGUAZZIN

Book Cover artwork by Cynthia Sguazzin.

Published by Prominence Publishing.

ISBN: 978-1-990830-74-7

Chapter 1

Liliana knelt on the rough stone floor of the church of Santa Maria Immacolata, closed her eyes, and tried to swear at God. *Dio, Dio. Perché? Why? Why does it have to be like this?* She was very angry, so angry she wasn't afraid, even though she was in the second pew, almost directly in front of the altar and God, she knew, was there in the little box with the gold brocade curtain, watching her. *It's not fair! He can't expect me to do this!*

She had come alone to the empty church this Saturday afternoon in early spring after receiving the letter from Carlo. It, with the money order which she hadn't yet told anyone about, was tucked into the zippered pocket of her purse, clutched tightly under her arm. Carlo had sent the money to purchase her airline ticket to go to Canada to marry him, and she was furious. She had come to the church of Santa Maria Immacolata in order to have it out-—with God. Her jaw set grimly, the silk scarf knotted tightly beneath it, she put her elbows on the back of the pew in front and dropped her firm young chin to rest it on her crossed hands. Eyes resolutely shut, she tried to concentrate on letting the anger knotted inside of her dissipate, tried to reason with herself–and with God.

It isn't really Your fault. It's Carlo's. Carlo, so cocky, so sure of himself, so sure of me. How can he think that I would be willing to give up everything I know, my home, my family, even my language, to follow him to some God-forsaken far-away country? She opened her eyes and looked directly at the Tabernacle. You could stop him. You could make him come back for me! Marry me here! Please, God, make him change his mind!

Canada. That was where her Uncle Tony had gone back in 1953, and had come back five years later to the village of San Michele with enough money to build a solid masonry house for himself and his family. But *his* wife, Auntie Silvia, hadn't been expected to go with him. Instead, she and her little boy had stayed with her husband's mother, Liliana's Nonna until her husband came back, laden with presents of *sigarette e cioccolato* for everyone.

It was 1964 now and Liliana was twenty-one years old. But she could clearly remember the day her Uncle had come home, full of stories of the Canadian north, stories of snow and endless forests; of barely civilized towns along the railroad tracks where all the houses were made of wood, he said, and the yards were strewn with litter. Surely wooden houses must be cold, they said. One would think that in *America* they would have progressed beyond wooden houses. But apparently not.

Liliana lifted her head and shifted from her knees so that she was sitting on the cool polished wood of the pew. There was no one else in the church, and she was as close to the altar as she dared be. God was in that little box with the brocade curtain and she knew that He had heard her thoughts. But she was still furious with Him and with Carlo.

Angry at the man she loved who would deprive her of her dearest secret dream—to be married in front of her family and all those girlfriends who had teased her so, to be married with joy in front of this very altar, in the church that her father and all the other men of San Michele had built after the war from the cement of the German airfield. But the war had been over for almost twenty years and her gentle father had been dead for two. He would want her to be married here. She was sure of it.

Picking up her prayer book, Liliana made the sign of the cross and left the pew, still clutching her navy leather purse tightly under her arm. She was aware of it burning into her side. She walked the length of the centre aisle backwards, facing the altar, until she reached the door. It seemed somehow more respectful, perhaps even safer than to turn her back on the God with whom she was so angry. Dipping a finger into the shallow bowl of holy water that sat on the pedestal just inside the door, she genuflected again. Then turning, she stepped out into the blazing sunlight and was struck as always by the contrast—the inside of the church so cool and silent, and outside the heat rising in waves from the pavement and shimmering in the afternoon air as a steady stream of Fiats and people on bicycles sped by in either direction. It was hot for April, but she had worn a light woolen suit and stockings—Nonna wouldn't have let her out of the house otherwise, certainly not to go to the church. It was one of the outfits she wore to her job at the municipal office, and she would have liked not to have to wear it on a Saturday afternoon as well. But Nonna was right, as always. It wouldn't have been proper to enter the church with bare legs and arms. As if anyone ever did. She scuffled at the gravel that lay between the steps and the sidewalk that bordered the road, so that the dust settled on her navy leather shoes. She frowned.

"Hey there, Liliana! What are you up to? Surely you haven't sinned so badly that you have to go to church on Saturday afternoon!"

It was Uncle Tony himself, passing on his bicycle. He crunched to a halt in front of the church and waited while she picked her way over the gravel toward him. *Zio* Tony, her dear uncle, who acted now as *il patriarca della famiglia* since the death of her father.

"Oh, *Zio* Tony, I was only fixing the flowers on the altar! You know how raggedy they get," she lied.

"*Sì*, Liliana, it's true. They do. Are you going home? I'll keep you company part way."

She nodded and reached up to untie her scarf and take it off, stuffing it into a pocket of her navy suit jacket. She walked beside her uncle in companionable silence as he propelled the bicycle with one foot on the road, the other on the sidewalk, matching her progress. They passed in front of *Zio* Arduino's house, where *Zia* Tina was industriously sweeping the front sidewalk. She waved at her niece and her brother-in-law but continued to sweep, the dust circling in eddies around her clog-clad feet.

Finally, Liliana turned her head toward her uncle. "Tell me what Canada was like, *Zio* Tony." She shifted her purse to the other side, feeling guilty that she wasn't telling her uncle about what she had received from Carlo that very morning. The money order. For the ticket she didn't want. For the trip she didn't want to make.

4

"Oh *cara*, I've told you so many times." His eyes were on the sidewalk.

"Please, Zio, tell me again. What was it like?"

"Well," her uncle said, still not looking at her, "I missed my family. And it was terrible hard work on the railroad."

"What did you do, *Zio*?"

"We worked on the tracks—out on the prairie, in the centre of the country—kilometers from any town. Lived like animals in a boxcar. Nearly froze to death." He shook his head.

"But you stayed, *Zio*."

"*Sì, cara,* but only a year. Living like that—a few of us quit. We couldn't stand it any more. And we'd heard about a town where there was a big paper mill."

"Was it Cedar Ridge—where Carlo is?"

"Oh no, *cara,* not on the west coast—we went to northern Quebec."

"Is that far from where Carlo is?"

"Oh, Liliana, you have no idea! It's such a huge country. Quebec is thousands of kilometers from there—thousands!"

They were across the road from *Zio* Ennio's now, the newest and biggest of all her uncles' houses, set well back behind a cream, stuccoed wall. Liliana's youngest cousin, little Maria, called out to them from her perch on the front stoop. *"Ciao, Zio* Tony. *Ciao,* Liliana."* Her reedy voice barely reached them, but they heard and waved at her.

"So you went to Quebec then, *Zio*? But why?"

"Well, my dear, because it meant more money, so I could come home more quickly. But it was hard work in that plant too—and hot. We sweated like pigs in that place. And dangerous—all that machinery—all those fumes." And then,

5

his voice rising almost angrily, he continued. "And the weather—*che brutto*—you can't imagine how much snow, how cold. It's a big cold country. I was so happy to come home."

Danger? Is it dangerous where Carlo is? He works in some sort of plant too.

"But Carlo says he likes it." Her voice quavered. "He wants me to go over there to marry him—to live there!" She could feel her uncle's eyes on her before he turned away again. She felt miserable–guilty that she wasn't telling him the whole truth, that there had been something else in the letter that came today from Carlo, something she was keeping secret.

"Over there? Really?" he replied. She heard her shoes crunching on the gravel, the sound of a child's voice in the distance. She kept her eyes down for fear that he could read her secret.

"Ah—well—it is a beautiful country—beautiful," he said too quickly. "And look, look at the nice house I built for my family," he said proudly, gesturing as they approached it. "I could never have built such a beautiful house if I had not gone to Canada." *It is a beautiful house*, Liliana thought. It was stuccoed in a cream colour with terra-cotta roof tiles and wooden shutters on each window painted a soft blue, sills overflowing with cascading pink-flowered ivy-geraniums.

They moved on without speaking, Liliana chewing on her bottom lip, until Tony turned in at the wrought iron gate set in the apricot-coloured brick wall that surrounded his property. "It'll be all right, you'll see," he said, patting her shoulder. "You'll get used to it once you're there."

She still didn't look up. *But I'm not going,* she thought stubbornly. *I'm not!* She could feel the resentment burning in her chest alongside the guilt for concealing the truth from her uncle. She nodded mutely and walked on slowly, the sun beating on her back as Carlo's face swam before her. She tried to imagine him in his workplace, tried to imagine the machinery, the noise, the heat. But she couldn't. Tried to imagine herself over there, somewhere. But she couldn't.

It wasn't as if Carlo *had* to go, like her uncle. Things weren't that bad now. Back then there had been no industries here on the Adriatic coast north of Venice. And most of the factory jobs in Milan and Turin had been taken by an influx of labourers from Calabria and other southern provinces where there was no industry at all. So when the Canadian National Railway had begun recruiting workers early in 1950, *Zio* Tony had eventually gone, along with many other young men from northern Italy. They were forced to go—*all'estero*—away.

Liliana's memory of that day was dim. He had gone amid much sobbing and hugging and promises to write faithfully, getting on the train with a lunch of salami and cheese, on his way to the port of Genova. He reassured Silvia, who would be living with her widowed mother Maria, Liliana's beloved Nonna, along with his sister Amelia, her husband Pietro and their two daughters, Luisa and Liliana. Assured them all that he would be able to make enough money in a few short years to secure his future; that he would be able to do in four or five years what he would never be able to do if he stayed home and worked the fields for a neighbour. They knew it was true, but it was difficult to see him go. *Zio* Tony, the eldest, was the first son to leave. And for such an unknown land—*Canada*.

Ahead Liliana could see the entrance to the *cortile* where she lived. Her parents, Amelia and Pietro, had always lived with Nonna Maria in the big house. When they married it had been taken for granted that they would live with Amelia's mother, who had been widowed as long as anyone could remember, and raise their family there. She had plenty of room, and Pietro could hardly affford a house for his family. So Liliana and her sister Luisa had known nothing but the warmth and security of living with two generations all their lives. Ruled over by Nonna, who was the final authority in all matters. And deservedly so, everyone said. A wonderful woman. A tower of strength and courage. Wise and loving. And right. Always right.

Still, Liliana reflected, she had grown up in a home full of laughter and conversation, gentle joking and quick hugs. Cousins ran in and out, carrying messages and little gifts of freshly-baked biscotti or a particularly beautiful peach for Nonna.

Her eyes misted, thinking of her father. She still couldn't believe he was gone. So sudden, everyone said. So sad. Now there were only the four women in the house. It was quieter than it had been.

Liliana stopped and stood waiting on the curb until it was safe to venture across the road. A frail old man in a faded black suit, a dusty fedora on his head, wobbled by on his bicycle. He put one knotted hand to the brim of his hat in a wordless salute, and Liliana waved back. It was old man Rovigo, a friend of her father's. She brushed a hand across her eyes and then, looking quickly both ways, hurried across the busy two-lane road to the other side. She slowed and then stopped to admire a vine covered with white flowers, whose name she did not know, that grew up and over an old brick wall. She rubbed her fingertips over the pitted and chalky surfaces of the sun-warmed bricks that formed the wall beside her—as if reading their memories—like a blind person reading braille. Then she frowned. Seeing the old man had reminded her that she and her uncle would have to make another visit to Carlo's parents soon, much as she dreaded the thought.

It had been almost a month since *Zio* Tony had taken her there for one of the obligatory visits following the announcement of her engagement last year, just before Carlo had left for Canada. It was only proper that she go, Nonna had said, and that she be accompanied each time by her uncle. "They will see that you are from a good family, that their son is marrying well."

She didn't like these visits. Carlo's parents were elderly and much poorer than Liliana's family. All his brothers and sisters were married and lived nearby, though Liliana never saw any of them. They never visited their parents, who seemed quite uninterested in Carlo, their youngest son, and even less so in his fiancee. "Carlo?" The old woman had sounded puzzled the first time she and *Zio* Tony visited. "You're Carlo's *fidanzata*?" As though she could barely remember who Carlo was, or where he was, much less that he had a girlfriend, even though Carlo had taken Liliana there to be presented before he left. The old couple in their shabby black clothes sat at the kitchen table in silence, Liliana trying desperately to make conversation, praying that she and her uncle could leave soon. There was a drab hopeless feeling in the house, so unlike what she was used to. Such silence. *No one seems to care about Carlo—to love him. Except me. But that was no reason to go so far away. He could have gone to Switzerland–or France.* But she understood better after that first visit why Carlo was so untalkative, almost mute sometimes, so that she had to coax him to smile, to laugh.

All the sons who had not been mutilated too badly, whose terrors could be kept at bay, looked for work after the war. Some had been able to get jobs at the many construction sites that sprang up, building hotels and apartment blocks at the resort towns on the Adriatic such as Lignano and Bibione, but these were mainly seasonal. Sometimes they got work helping neighbours in their fields, but opportunities were limited and the pay minimal. That was why so many young men had left to work in Switzerland or Germany or France. Or farther. South Africa. Australia. South America.

Liliana thought then of her sister Luisa, whose fiance, Olivo, had gone to South America. That had been eight years ago, and he had not answered any letters for at least four years now. He must have found someone else, they guessed. Many of these men had left fiancees behind, young women who worked in cottage industries making sweaters or shoes, or in offices, living with their parents and dreaming of the return of their loved ones so that they could begin their lives together.

But Olivo had not returned–had stopped writing. And thus Luisa had joined the ranks of the 'White Widows', women whose lives were on hold, their husbands or fiances no longer in contact, whether by accident or on purpose no one could fathom. It was a terrible sorrow, a terrible disgrace. Luisa lived in limbo—a state of unknowable outcome. She, like all the others, like Liliana, dreamed of the day when they would put on the white silk dress and walk up this road lined with ancient plane trees, to be married in the little church Liliana had just left. But it seemed unlikely that Luisa's dream would come true. Carlo said that if Olivo were a good man he would have contacted Luisa–at least to tell her that he would not be coming back–ever. And if he were dead, someone would have told her. Liliana secretly agreed, but she never let on to Luisa that she blamed Olivo for her sister's plight. How could he simply disappear? How cruel! But then, what if he did turn up now? How embarrassing to try to explain it all. Maybe it was better this way. And at the bottom of her heart dwelt the prayer that God would not let her end up like Luisa, bereft of hope. At least her betrothed *would* marry her. Of that she was sure.

But Carlo expected her to follow him to Canada and marry him there, live there, surrounded by strangers speaking an unknown language. She could barely remember the English she had studied in school! How could he ask such a thing of her? And how could the loving God to whom she had always been so devoted betray her this way? For surely it was He who had put this idea into Carlo's head, the idea that she should go to him instead of him coming back home to be married as they had planned. To build a beautiful house like her uncles.

She sighed and shook her head as if to dispel her thoughts, slipping her chalky fingers into her jacket pocket where her hankie lay crisply folded. She took it out, moistened a corner with saliva, and after rubbing her fingers clean, bent down and polished the toes of her good leather shoes. She was almost home. Ahead and to the left of the roadway was the opening in the wall that led to her *cortile*. She turned in and paused.

There was the usual cacophony of screams and chatter from the children playing around the old fig tree which stood in the centre, bicycles leaning against its striated trunk. The roughly rectangular area around it, covered with gravel bleached white from the sun, was bordered on three sides by the houses, the old brick wall that ran along beside the road forming the fourth side. Old women sat on rush-bottomed chairs in the porticos that formed the entryway to each big house, geraniums on every window sill, on every balcony, and hanging in pots overhead. Even now, in April, their tendrils, covered with ivy-shaped leaves, had begun to cascade. Liliana lifted one hand and waved at Nonna, who sat darning in the shade just outside their front door.

These houses, over five hundred years old as near as anyone could tell, were attached to each other in a somewhat haphazard fashion, an indication of how they had grown as the families expanded. Each three-storey house was stuccoed over its fieldstone walls in muted shades of ochre or cream or soft coral, its windows bordered with brightly painted shutters. The living quarters were on the first two floors and the top floor, the *granaio,* a large vacant space under the dark-orange terra-cotta tiled roof, was the storeroom, containing sacks of dried corn and beans and other precious things. A very old wedding portrait in a dark frame. A dusty spinning wheel. A prosthetic limb. A *fogolar.*

The heavy wooden double-doors that led from each portico into the house were folded back and striped or flowered canvas curtains hung in each doorway. Liliana always loved it when the curtain was strung up on its brass rod—a sign that the long languid days of summer had arrived—at last.

She was aware of the eyes of the neighbours, who surely watched her progress from behind their lace curtains as she walked toward her house, still thinking about Carlo—about how it had all begun. He had been gone so long she could barely remember him, the feel of his lips on hers, her hands on the rough wool of his black and white tweed jacket as he pulled her to him in a hasty goodbye. He had been her secret love when they were children, and she still couldn't believe the joy she had felt when she had realized, a few years earlier, that he had always loved her too. It happens like that sometimes, her sister Luisa said. You just know.

He had begun to flirt with her when they met at the open-air market or at a fair, and he would buy her a bag of red candied peanuts and take her for a ride on the roller-coaster. Her girlfriends would hoot and tease her. She didn't care. She would look into his dark eyes and he into her green ones, and they would laugh. He started visiting her on summer evenings, whizzing up on his bicycle, scattering the gravel as he came to a fast stop in front of her house, grinning. Her mother would gather up her darning and Nonna would pick up her knitting, going inside to join Luisa, who was usually sitting at the kitchen table writing one of her interminable letters. But they were just on the other side of the curtain. And Carlo would bend his head close to hers so that she could feel their hair touching as they sat, murmuring softly, surrounded by the musky-smelling geraniums, until Nonna came out, signalling the end of the visit. Liliana would walk across the *cortile* with Carlo through the warm air and he would clasp her hand and accidentally brush against her breast, kissing her lightly on the lips before jumping on his bike and wheeling away with a backward flash of his white teeth in the dark. *Oh God, how she missed him.*

And then her mother would come out onto the portico again, and they would talk of Carlo and how he planned to go to *America* someday soon until, their voices trailing off, they sat silent under the round silver moon, each lost in her own thoughts.

Liliana had dreamt of the day he would come back to claim her, the day she would walk up the road to the church to pledge her love to Carlo. How, after their honeymoon in Rome, where all newly-weds went and also where her parents went, they would come back to San Michele to begin their lives together in the beautiful house he would have built for her. The anger rose again.

"*Dai, Liliana, dai! Muoviti!* Hurry! There's work to be done. Come and help your sister make the pasta for tomorrow," Nonna called out in her cracked old-woman voice, breaking into Liliana's reverie. "You're late. You know we always do this job today, so that we can cook the noon meal as soon as we return from Mass tomorrow. The priest is coming for lunch. Whatever were you thinking?"

Liliana hung her head and hurried past Nonna without speaking. Maybe Nonna would divine her secret if she allowed herself to look into her eyes. She stepped into the large room with its grey-speckled shiny granite floor, like all the downstairs rooms. Pale walls, dark furniture, white venetian blinds on every window covered by immaculate white lace curtains. Family photos and old prints in dark frames. Large rooms, cool in summer, a refuge in winter from the cold winds blowing down from the Dolomites. They were comfortable homes which nurtured and protected those who had been born in them, born in the matrimonial bed upstairs, as she had been–twenty-one years ago.

Liliana loved the upstairs rooms especially, big quiet rooms shaded from the strong sun during the day by their closed shutters which cast a striped pattern over the waxed wooden floors. Each room had a set of matching dark furniture and a huge high bed with a brocade cover, a carpet runner on the floor at either side. It was often her job to polish the furniture in the bedrooms, a task she loved. But she had to hurry now, to change out of her good clothes so that she could help Luisa make the pasta. Poor Luisa.

She placed her navy purse with the offending letter in front of the mirror on the low dressing table, glaring at it for a moment. Then carefully hanging her navy jacket and skirt inside the big wardrobe with the mirrored doors, she took out the cotton skirt and blouse that she had worn for this morning's housework and put them on again. Even though she and Luisa had jobs in offices, she at the Municipio and Luisa at a doctor's office, they were expected to help with the cleaning and cooking, especially on weekends. It was taken for granted.

Liliana sat on the little bench in front of the dressing table, glaring again at her purse sitting innocently behind the crystal perfume atomizer with its pink rubber bulb, above it the reflection of her oval face with its cap of wavy brown hair. *I'm twenty-one, but I look like a child.* She frowned, running both hands over her hair in a vain attempt to achieve the smooth bouffant that was the fashion, Carlo on her mind as always. She opened the top drawer and pulled out a manila envelope, tipping it so that the contents spilled out upon the lace runner. He had sent some grainy black and white pictures of himself and his new friends in Canada, posing in front of high snow banks she could barely believe, backed by a row of sombre black evergreen trees that she knew were cedar because the name of the town was Cedar Ridge. In some pictures the young men, arms linked, were standing in front of a waterfall or by a lake, jaunty and carefree, cigarettes in the corners of their mouths, looking a little drunk. Carlo wrote of fishing and hiking in the mountains, of bears walking into the bar, of men gambling their paychecks away. And then he wrote of his love, of how he longed to hold her and kiss her as he had done only once or twice before, when they had become betrothed and had promised undying fidelity to each other. He wrote of how he was saving every cent he made, planning to buy a little wooden house and furnish it. He would send her the money for a ticket as soon as he was ready for her. She was to trust in him and they would soon be together. She felt the anger again. Quickly she shoved the photos back into the envelope and thrust it into the drawer, closing it with a bang.

Standing, she smoothed her skirt and ran downstairs to the sound of Nonna's voice calling, trying to ignore the knot of fury that sat in her chest. He seemed to be having a glorious time without her, as though he had completely forgotten their plan that he would come back to marry her in

16

the lovely little church in San Michele. Never mind. *She would not be deterred. Surely God will help me, will make him change his mind. Surely.*

Chapter 2

Walking home the next morning after Mass, Liliana lagged behind the cluster of people which included Nonna and Mama and Luisa who were hurrying down the road ahead of her. She had tried again to bargain with God—*I'll be better, I promise. I'll come to pray more often, if only You'll make Carlo come home. We should be getting married here, where we belong!* But she didn't feel at all certain that He had heard. Her body felt heavy, as though she were carrying a great weight, and the purse under her arm, containing the money order for the ticket, burned into her side. She still hadn't told anyone about the contents of that last letter. She walked ever more slowly, turning her head from side to side as if memorizing the scene. But she didn't have to. It was engraved forever in her mind.

Between the houses on either side of the road she caught glimpses of vineyards rolling off toward the hazy horizon; fields of corn or hay dotted here and there with lovely old houses in various stages of disrepair, and beyond, the towns she could not see, towns sprawling along the narrow winding roads just as they had sprawled for hundreds of years. It was home, all of it, and this was where she wanted to be. Always.

Ahead, at the end of what remained of the brick wall to her left, lay a pile of dusty broken shards, pale orange and ochre, and smaller whitish stones and bits of chinking that had fallen from it. The pile had been there as long as she could remember. Probably since the war. Behind the wall stood the façade of an abandoned stone house, its roof missing, its vacant windows and rubble-strewn yard the only remaining evidence along this road of the bombing, but the scars of the war were still raw despite the passage of years. Men still had night terrors, and women too, and there were people walking among them with missing limbs and horrible scars. But out of the wartime horror something good had come.

Behind her was the church of Santa Maria Immacolata, where she had just been praying again for God to change Carlo's mind. It was neither very old nor very beautiful, but a part of the landscape of home. It stood stolidly, its white stuccoed walls and simple *campanile* without ornamentation, but it signified to them all more than a passing stranger might have divined. The story of how it had come to be built made it both beautiful and precious in the eyes of everyone.

These were families who had lived together in the same *cortiles* for hundreds of years, who had rejoiced and suffered together through births and illnesses, weddings and funerals, good fortune and bad, and who had sought comfort and safety in each other's homes through the terrifying days of the war. The railway which ran along behind the village had been a popular target for the bombers, so that the younger children were taken by older sisters and brothers early each morning across the fields to a wooded area beside the river to escape the danger. Though she had been very young,

Luisa had faint memories of the terror of those hot after-noons, listening to the roar of the planes overhead and the distant explosions, wondering if her house would still be standing when they finally went home at dusk.

Liliana's Nonna had told her that twice in her lifetime soldiers—"Our soldiers, their soldiers, it doesn't matter," had burst into her kitchen demanding the gold earrings from her ears and any other valuables she had, on pain of cutting off her children's hands. Toward the end of the war the soldiers had been everywhere, it seemed, having overtaken a nearby villa for their headquarters while they poured concrete to build an aircraft landing strip on farmland close by. Their shouts and curses could be heard from the safety of Nonna's kitchen where the family sat huddled on the benches built into the *fogolar*, the open fireplace in which hung several large cooking pots from an ornate wrought-iron frame.

Once the airstrip had been completed, the roar of the small bombers landing and taking off became the back-ground to all of their activities, their drone like constant malevolent music. The adults would stand in the *cortile,* faces upturned, one hand shading their eyes, watching them approaching, leaving, black shapes like crows high in the sky. When finally the war ended, the relief and joy of the people was great. Liliana had a faint memory of a column of tanks and trucks passing slowly down this very road, the soldiers throwing candy and gum and cigarettes to the people gathered to watch their passing—and of her father holding her up the better to see. And then, blessedly, silence—peace.

Their gratitude to the God to whom they had prayed fervently during all those awful years was immense. They had prayed on their knees beside their beds and they had prayed as families, sitting around their kitchen tables after the evening meal, rosaries in hand. Every Sunday they had arisen at dawn and had walked the two miles into the nearest big town in order to go to church, where they had prayed again. And one of their prayers was that they be shown how they could build a church of their own, in their own community of San Michele. And somehow they devised a way.

Very early one morning several months after the bombing had stopped, Liliana's father and uncles and boy cousins left the *cortile* carrying sturdy implements fashioned from wood, some with heavy metal heads, like sledge-hammers. The younger children followed along behind them to the now-silent airfield. There they watched in amazement as the men, working together with such rudimentary tools, broke sections of the cement tarmac into uneven blocks, each about a foot thick and several feet in diameter. Sweating in the hot sun, they heaved these blocks onto hayracks pulled by donkeys. The loads were taken then to a vacant area beside the road, across and down from Liliana's house, where they were unloaded by another waiting crew of men and boys.

Day after hot spring day they laboured, breaking at noon to eat a meal of pasta, cheese, and wine carried to them where they sat resting in the shade of some upturned blocks. Gradually the form of a building began to grow on the vacant lot, a building made of those uneven thick blocks of cement broken from the airstrip, mortared together to form first the floor and then the four walls of their new church. It was like a miracle, they said. That God should have shown them the way, that they were able to turn the symbol of terror and oppression into a monument to love. And that in doing so, in finding again their wellspring of courage and determination, they had restored their dignity. And they could laugh too. They laughed gently at each other in their raggedness, in their poverty, in the roughness of their church compared to the grandeur of those famous edifices of Venice and Florence and Rome, and they made jokes about how their prayers should go upwards faster, unencumbered by elaborate architecture. It's not San Marco, they said with pride as they stuccoed and sanded and painted, but it's ours. And eventually they had paved the floor with granite and had lovingly placed statues of Mary and Joseph in the niches on either side of the simple altar.

It was a story which always moved Liliana, signifying as it did to her all that was good and courageous and loving about her family and her neighbours. Fearing that she might not be married there after all, that she might have to go, tears welled in her eyes again as she walked home under the huge old plane trees that day. How could she possibly leave such a place where everyone shared this powerful bond? Carlo, too, was part of this. How could he consider not coming back? How could he want to begin a life together away from this place which was so much a part of them, which had formed them and taught them and made them who they were? It was unthinkable.

Don Paolo, the dark haired young priest who had been enticed to become the shepherd of the flock of Santa Maria

Immacolata, stood waiting on the portico of Liliana's house. When he graduated from the seminary, a delegation of men and women had gone to visit him, entreating him with declarations of undying gratitude and promising all the cheese and capicollo he could eat to come to San Michele. And he had agreed. His dusty little Fiat was parked under the fig tree now; he hadn't wasted any time getting there after Mass. Don Paolo was a gentle soul, graceful and ingratiating in manner, and Liliana flushed at the remembrance of the bargaining she had tried to do so forcibly not a half hour before in the church. Surely he couldn't know?

"Liliana, *cara*, hurry along," her mother called out to her as she approached. "Don Paolo is here. Come and talk to him while we prepare the table." Not waiting for an answer, she went on. "And by the way, Liliana, why don't you get your last letter from Carlo. I'm sure *Padre* would be most interested."

Liliana cringed inwardly. The last thing she wanted to do was to share the letter from Carlo with the priest, but she saw that he was waiting for her to do just that. There was no getting around it. But she couldn't let them all know about the money order. She'd take that out and leave it upstairs. Don Paolo lowered himself onto one of the rush-seated chairs surrounded by the pots of red geraniums to wait as Liliana went upstairs to get the letter.

Seating herself a safe distance from the priest, so that he couldn't possibly make out what was written on the thin blue pages, she began to read aloud, editing as she went. Carlo had saved almost enough for the down-payment on a little house. She should begin to make preparations. He couldn't wait to embrace her again. She hadn't meant to read that part aloud. She glanced at the priest, blushing. Carlo had included a photo of himself and another young man holding between them the biggest fish she had ever seen. A salmon, he wrote. The river is alive with them. And a picture of them standing in front of a waterfall. At least she could share all the pictures with Don Paolo. Handing them to him, she continued to read. "And soon you'll be able to see this beautiful waterfall for yourself. I have enclosed a money order for your... ticket." Her voice faded away. Stupid. She had accidentally read the one part she did not want to share with anyone. And she knew that the other women, working quietly inside, had heard. The tears she had been holding back so long spilled down over her cheeks, and a barely stifled sob escaped from her throat. She hadn't meant to tell anyone, but she had. The secret was out. Now she'd never escape her fate.

Just then Liliana's mother, as if driven by some powerful instinct, stepped out through the curtained doorway and pulled her daughter into her arms, holding her tightly as Liliana gave way at last to the scalding, healing tears. "Oh, mama," she sobbed," he's sent the money order. . . for the . . . the ticket! I. . . I don't want to go!"

"There, there, my dear. It will be all right. You'll see!"

"But Mama. . . You don't understand!" Her voice was thick with tears. "I don't want to go. . . I don't want to go at all!"

Don Paolo sat, unmoving, on the low chair, mute in the face of such real drama. Sobbing, Liliana fled inside and ran upstairs, knowing that her mother would tell the priest about her pain, about how she hated Carlo's insistence that she go to Canada to marry him. And of how she, Amelia, widowed now, dreaded the thought of having her youngest daughter leave for a life in such a far-away and rugged—almost uncivilized—place, even though she knew that Liliana had to go.

"The houses are made of wood, *per l'amor di Dio!*" Amelia exclaimed, turning to face the young priest, "and who knows if they even have a church, surrounded there by miles and miles of nothing but trees!"

"Now, now Amelia," murmured the priest consolingly. "She's very young, very adaptable, and you and your husband have given her the greatest gift of all, a strong family and a strong faith. And they will be able to come back for a visit soon, God willing. Give her your blessing. Give her a chance at a better life."

Liliana's mother nodded mutely, but there was rage in her heart. What do you know of losing a daughter, you who live so easily in our midst, wifeless, childless? And what if the life is harder, not better? She thought this, but she did not say it. It wasn't proper to argue with a priest, however young. She wondered again wordlessly at the apparent discrepancy between the pictures and descriptions sent by Carlo and the America they had seen in the Hollywood movies at the Cinema in town. Who could explain it—beautiful women in the latest fashions moving through spacious, sleekly furnished rooms, skyscrapers outside the windows, palm trees lining the boulevards—where was that? Wasn't that America? So where was Carlo?

"*Allora,* are you two coming in for lunch or not? Everything's ready." It was Nonna's voice calling from inside the shadowed room, and Don Paolo rose and went in, taking his place at the head of the table. Amelia followed, silent, and sat. Then she lifted her head and called, "Liliana! Come to the table. Lunch is ready." Almost immediately a silent Liliana came down the stairs and sat opposite her mother, whose pale face was already downturned in antici- pation of the prayer Don Paolo was about to lead.

Chapter 3

Over the next weeks, torn between terror and excitement, Liliana fought always against the knot of anger and resentment she carried in her chest. She still prayed daily to the God who wasn't listening to her, asking him to change Carlo's mind—to intercede. There must be some way to stop the inexorable flow of preparations for that dreaded day when she would have to go. There was still time for things to change. Only He could make that happen. Unless Nonna or her mother or her uncles were to contact Carlo directly and order him to come home and marry her here, in the church their fathers and uncles had built. They could do that. Why were they *not* interceding on her behalf? It was a conspiracy! The knot in her chest tightened and sometimes, lying in the dark, still night, she thought she would suffocate.

As her family swung into action she tried, however unwilling, to join in the preparations for the trip and for her new life. There was much to be done. Her mother and her sister opened drawers and trunks and cupboards, taking out beautiful pieces of embroidered linens and crocheted *centros*, doilies, fine sheets bordered with hand-made lace, dish towels and hand towels and tablecloths which they had made over the years. Each piece had been folded away carefully in tissue against the day when the girls would marry. And the time had come, at least for Liliana. Nonna was determined that she should take with her only the finest things; that it be known by the quality of her possessions the sort of family from which she came. They purchased for her—at who knew what sacrifice—an exquisite set of crystal wineglasses with decanter, and a lovely porcelain demi-tasse set sprinkled with tiny white *stelle alpine*—Mountain Stars. With *Zio* Tony driving, she was taken to the best stores in Udine to be outfitted with a wardrobe of fine wool dresses and sweaters and skirts as befitted a young woman from a good family. And high-necked white nighties made of fine lawn.

"We have known hard times," Amelia said, "but you must not be disgraced. You must have things that are of good quality, tasteful and well-made. You are not a gypsy—a *zingara*, travelling with nothing. You come from a fine old family, and don't you ever forget it."

"But Mama, you're spending too much on me. How can we afford all this?"

"Never you mind. You must make a *bella figura*. It is what your father would have wanted—and Nonna insists."

Carefully, slowly, with tenderness and barely-concealed sorrow, Amelia folded each item and placed it in the big wooden trunk, the *baule,* which would be shipped to *America.* Here and there she tucked in packets of garden seeds, fine linen hankies, a few silver espresso spoons, a photo of her and her husband on their wedding day. But the most beautiful, the most expensive thing, went in last, folded and refolded in tissue, then wrapped in crisp new sheets—the wedding gown. It was simple ivory satin with a slight train, just a virginal column of lustrous fabric which Amelia knew would make Liliana more beautiful than she could guess.

And who knew who would perform the wedding mass? Where? In front of what witnesses? Amelia tried not to visualize the scene from which she had been banned by some cruel stroke of fate. Who would have thought that she would not be present at the wedding of her younger child, her lovely Liliana. Wasn't it enough what had happened to Luisa? There would be no wedding there either for her to attend. But at least her younger daughter would not become a white widow. Softly she closed the lid of the trunk as Liliana came into the room with another pale blue envelope in her hand, tears on her cheeks. "He's still insisting, Mama, that I have to go over there. He refuses to come here." Wordlessly her mother closed her in an embrace.

And then began the saddest days. *Zio* Tony took Liliana and Amelia into Udine to visit the *Agenzia Viaggi* to purchase the ticket. She was to fly from Rome to Toronto, and then to travel the remainder of the way to Cedar Ridge by train. None of them had ever been on an airplane, and the very thought terrified Amelia and Luisa. *Zio* Tony had travelled both ways by boat when he had gone. Imagine, going to *America* in an *apparecchio*! *Not I,* thought Amelia, *I'll never leave this earth.* But Liliana seemed oddly unafraid. In fact, she moved through these last weeks as though in a trance, as though it were someone else who was buying the ticket, buying good new leather shoes and handbag and a beautiful green wool coat with silver buttons, and finally, a set of very good burgundy leather luggage, a gift from her uncles.

Luisa busied herself baking. She, too, was in an inner turmoil which consisted in equal parts of sorrow at her sister's leavetaking and despair at her own sad plight, about which no one ever spoke. What could they say? What could anyone do? So Luisa, silent as always about her own grief, her shame, baked cookies—lovely *biscotti* and tiny almond, *mandorle*, which she arranged in clear glass jars in the big pantry off the main room. It was into this room that one entered via the curtained doorway leading from the portico; the room where the family ate every day. At the opposite end from the pantry was the kitchen itself, the room where the food was prepared. This was not a large room, having been built into the area jutting out from the main room where the open fireplace—the *fogolar*—had been. Nonna had protested when Pietro relegated the *fogolar* to the *granaio* after the war and had the area tiled, replacing the fireplace with both a wood-burning cookstove, which was used primarily in winter and which also provided the heat for the house, and a gas range. These two new appliances now sat side by side along one wall, across from an oilcloth-covered table and two wooden rush-seated chairs, the only other furniture the kitchen contained. It was a room which meant business, and Nonna played the pots and pans on those two stoves like an impressario conducting her orchestra.

One afternoon Nonna, who very rarely made sweets, called the girls to come and pay careful attention while she made an apple *strudel*. "A *strudel!* Really?" It was a momentous occasion, and the sisters sat dutifully at either end of the kitchen table, their eyes on her every move as Nonna rolled out a sheet of dough as large as the tabletop and as transparent as parchment. Over this she spread apple slices, then sprinkled dark sugar and walnuts and raisins over them and spritzed the whole with rum. Then, with the help of the girls, the pastry was rolled up to enclose the filling and transferred to a baking sheet, where it was coaxed into a crescent shape and scored here and there so that the steam could escape. Gently Nonna baptized the *strudel* with brushed-on milk, sprinkled it with sugar, and then slid it carefully into the oven of the pristine white gas range which she had only recently admitted was much more versatile and reliable than even the wood-burning cookstove which sat beside it. Neither Liliana nor Luisa had ever seen Nonna make a *strudel* before, though she had often spoken of the operation in such tones of reverence that it had taken on almost mythical proportions to her two grandaughters, and they were suitably impressed. "*Che bel strudel, Nonna!* How beautiful!"

All these preparations were necessary because, of course, until Liliana left, the house would be filled every night with aunts and uncles and cousins and neighbours from far and wide who came to give their best wishes to the bride-to-be. And many would carry with them a carefully-wrapped parcel containing a lovely salami or a small form of cheese for a son or brother already in *America*. The little pile of parcels to be taken by Liliana grew and grew, and it worried her. "Oh *Dio!* How will I ever find room for all these things in my suitcases? They're going to be too full as it is! What a nuisance! Why don't they just leave me alone!"

"What a thing to say! Shame on you—where are your manners!"

Mortified, Liliana's quick intake of breath betrayed her surprise at Nonna's admonishment. She hadn't realised she had been overheard by her grandmother.

"Now, now," Amelia murmured, knowing that her daughter's outburst wasn't really about a few extra parcels. "Just take them and be gracious. We'll fit them in somehow."

As if I didn't have enough to worry about! Liliana thought as she flounced out of the room. *It's too much, it's all too much! And Nonna doesn't seem to understand.* But she felt ashamed at her outburst and hurried out into the *cortile* as another small car turned in, its passengers smiling broadly and waving at her. She straightened her shoulders and composed her face, lifting her arm to wave in response. She smiled too, but her face felt stiff, as though it might crack.

The visitors were ushered through the main room and into the living-room, the *salotto,* where they were seated on one of the high-backed chairs that surrounded the dark polished table. Pietro had purchased this set for Amelia before the war when things had not been so bad. Plates of the best prosciutto, capicollo, cheese, and crusty rolls were set out, along with decanters of wine that had been made the previous autumn. And then Luisa proudly served her *biscotti* and slices of Nonna's *strudel* along with tiny cups of strong espresso. Nonna brought out the flask of *grappa* then, strong home-made spirits with which to "correct" their coffee— *caffé corretto.*

"Go ahead, have some. Its very good—Pietro made it, and we certainly don't use it," she said proudly, urging it on the men. And they obliged.

Many of the visitors who were received with such graciousness also brought gifts for the young couple, silver serving plates, tiny crystal dishes, plates and jugs of the local pottery hand-decorated with bright flowers. Liliana was going to *America* to live, *America,* where everyone was well-off and set a fine table. *America,* where the sun always shone and everyone was happy. There was much hilarity, gentle teasing and laughter, although the undercurrent of sadness was palpable, and Amelia could often be seen biting her lip to fight back the tears. But Liliana remained impassive. She felt disembodied, as though it were not really happening—as if it were a dream from which they would all awaken, and things would be as they had always been.

The four women went to bed each night exhausted, but Liliana could not sleep. It was not so bad during the days, filled as they were with preparations and visitors, but the nights were hard. The anger came back then, interrupting her sleep, tormenting her in her dreams—the very futility of it adding to her misery. Sometimes she dropped off, only to awake in the midst of an internal argument—a struggle—with someone. *No, don't make me go—this can't be happening! He'll come back for me—I know he will. Wait! Please—wait!* She felt as though she were a pawn in some great conspiracy—betrayed by her own mother—her own grandmother. How could they enter so willingly into this plot to send her off? Yes! It was they who were doing her this great disservice—not Carlo! If her family had not conspired against her, she could have changed Carlo's mind! She was sure. Even *Zio* Tony, whose memories of Canada were so bad, didn't try to stop them from sending her away! Betrayed again. She twisted and turned until her sheets were wrinkled beneath her, her body wet with perspiration, her cheeks wet with tears. *I'm alone, all alone. I have no one to turn to— they're all against me. They're pushing me out—out of my home, away from my family.* Liliana heard a moaning sound and knew that it was her own voice.

She threw back the heavy cotton sheet that covered her and slid out of the high bed, half-staggering across the room to the window. The heavy shutters had been closed since mid-morning to keep out the burning sun, and Nonna insisted that they be kept closed until daylight—the night air was bad for one, she said. But Liliana could not bear the darkness, the stuffiness, and she opened them now, carefully, surreptitiously, hoping they wouldn't squeak as she folded them back part-way back against the outside wall. *Just for a moment, just until I get some air.* She knelt then on the polished wood of the floor, leaning on the sill with her head on her arms. She breathed deeply, trying to calm herself. The sky above was as dark and soft as indigo velvet, punctured here and there by tiny stars that seemed to grow and then recede as she stared at them. The round silver moon hung impassively in the sky, wisps of purple cloud scudding across its surface. Was this the same moon that shone down on Carlo? How could it be?

The comforting sounds of people and animals were stilled now, and the air seemed thick and heavy with their breathing in the dark. If she listened carefully, she became aware of the night music of the crickets, a constant accompaniment through all the nights of her childhood. She felt herself calming, her beating heart quieting as the cool night air moved gently over her body. She turned her head and looked into her room, where she could just make out her own image in the mirrored front of the wardrobe. She stood then and went over to it, peering at herself in the silvery moonlight shining in her window. Her tousled hair seemed darker in the half-light and her luminous eyes larger as they stared back at her from a pale face, her bare young arms at her sides, the white nightie hanging straight to the floor. She had looked exactly like this when she was twelve, she thought, seeing herself framed by the curves of dark wood. How could she be leaving home—getting married? Staring into the mirror, her eyes went slowly, intently, over each object in the room behind her—the narrow bed with its lovely old chintz coverlet, the low dressing table with its blue velvet-covered stool and tall looking-glass, the bedside table with the seashells gathered one summer day from the beach at Lignano arranged now around the feet of the tiny illuminated figure of Mary. *This is where I belong.* This room was all of her, all of the days of her life. She must memorize it so that she could resurrect it in her mind when she was far away. Under the same silver moon. Quietly she rose and closed the shutters once more.

The plan, devised after much discussion between Amelia and her brothers and sisters-in-law, was that the trunk had to be shipped well in advance of Liliana's departure so that it would be there when she arrived. This had been accomplished, and now all that had to be done was to prepare her luggage for the trip. Amelia and Luisa would accompany Liliana to Rome by train, where they would be met by Pietro's only sister, Melania, who would take them in hand. In Toronto she would be met by an Italian immigrant couple who would accompany her on the train for the rest of the journey across Canada to the town near the Pacific Ocean.

This couple would be getting off the train the stop before Liliana, so that she would be entirely alone when she arrived in Cedar Ridge where Carlo would meet her. She was secretly glad of this; that she would be alone when she saw Carlo for the first time after more than a year. When she thought about the feel of his face, how the warmth of his arms had burned into her body when he touched her, she felt weak. Would he have changed? Would she recognize him? Would she still love him?

Even the preparations for the journey to Rome were detailed and fraught with anxiety, for none of them had travelled often, though Amelia had actually been to Rome on her honeymoon many years before. She had been shocked, she told her daughters, at how disinterested the Romans were in the Pope and his frequent appearances on the balcony at St. Peter's, although she remembered the crowds of tourists in St. Peter's square who cheered frantically when he appeared, as though he were a star of the cinema, a matinee idol. And she remembered those sunlit days with her young husband. They had been so sure of the future. This visit to Rome would be very different.

Amid the constant coming and going of family and friends, Amelia and her daughters prepared themselves for the train journey and the visit with Pietro's sister in Rome. Amelia recalled how gracious Melania had been when she had been welcomed into her home as a young bride. She could picture the cool shadowy rooms of Melania's apartment on the ground floor of an ochre-coloured building near the Campo dei Fiori. It was a wonderful location from which to visit the ancient sites of old Rome, the heart of the Eternal City, and Amelia remembered how she and her handsome young husband had enjoyed themselves in their young vitality, never guessing that such hard times would visit them. Never guessing how soon she would lose him. And now, under such different, such sad circumstances, she would visit Rome again, a widow seeing her younger child off to the New World. She shook her head. She mustn't think of it like that. It would turn out to be for the best, she was sure. *Speriamo*—let us hope.

"And of course you must have gifts for your *Zia* Melania," Nonna instructed. "You can't just present your-selves empty-handed."

"*Sì, sì,* of course," Amelia said absent-mindedly. She was used to being offered advice by her mother, hardly noticed any more. She had already organized this, helping the girls to select a few little things like the oil and vinegar cruets on the small silver tray and the tablecloth and napkins purchased in the department store in Udine. But Melania longed for the home made meats and cheeses of her childhood, they knew, and Amelia went to great lengths to find the best salami, the best capicollo, as well as a heavy and large yellow-crusted cheese which had been aged in the pantry for at least a year. These things were wrapped carefully and placed in a basket in the cool storage room in readiness for the trip. And then they had to think about what they would wear that would be not too hot but presentable. And what they would take to eat on the journey for, as Nonna pointed out, they certainly wouldn't be buying food through the train windows when they stopped in Bologna or Firenze, as they knew some would. How undignified!

Liliana's friends from the office where she had worked, the *Municipio*, took her out for lunch one day to an old *osteria* where they sat outside under a *pergola* of vines, eating risotto and delicate fillets of fish, sipping the local white Tocai. And they teased Liliana about her approaching marriage and gave her little gifts and promised to write. But though she never spoke of it, she was never without the tight ball of anger that dwelt in her chest. Anger at Carlo and her family, who had betrayed her–had conspired to force her to leave. Liliana felt as though it were someone else sitting there, watching the August sun making dappled patterns on their faces. Her friends were excited for her, but she felt only a strange numbness and a sense that things were tumbling on without her being a part of them. As though she were a figure in a tableau. Nothing seemed real, and nothing would ever be the same again.

Chapter 4

"*Allora, andiamo.* Well then, let's go," said *Zio* Tony matter-of-factly as he loaded the luggage into the car, struggling to secure the two largest pieces onto the roof rack. He was sweating from the exertion, swiping his forehead and upper lip with his tweed-clad arm, his best jacket contributing in no small measure to his discomfort.

It was the morning of their departure, and Tony had just driven up in the Fiat Sedan which was his pride and joy, parking it on the gravel just outside the portico. Nonna had offered Tony a cup of espresso which he had downed, standing, in one gulp, as the other women adjusted their collars and fixed their hair at the mirror which hung on the wall behind the kitchen door. Liliana hadn't been able to swallow even a mouthful of coffee and she was feeling faintly sick, fighting nausea as she carefully folded her new coat and placed it over her arm. Stepping out through the curtain onto the hot cement, she glanced up to watch her uncle, knowing what he was thinking. *No scene—please God—no scene.* Liliana sensed that the other three women had followed her out onto the portico too and were standing just behind her now.

No one spoke. The dreaded moment had arrived, and Liliana could not bear to look at Nonna. She had never seen her grandmother lose her composure, not even when Liliana's father had died, and she feared above all that she would see her weep now. But she heard her own voice catch as she turned and was enfolded in the older woman's strong embrace. *"Coraggio, figlia mia.* Courage, my grand-daughter," were the words whispered almost fiercely into her ear as Liliana choked back the tears, mumbling *"Sì, Nonna, sì,"* before she quickly got into the car and slammed the door on her side as her mother and sister slammed theirs. But her grandmother's face remained impassive as Liliana, watching her through the car window and waving her hand, was borne out of the cortile and into the rest of her life.

*"Che caldo—*so hot!" *Zio* Tony exclaimed. "It's so hot for so early in the morning—it's going to be a scorcher."

"Sì, it will be miserable on the train," replied Amelia, grateful that her brother had said something, however innocuous. "But we'll be fine, won't we, girls?" She patted Liliana's knee, and Luisa murmured assent, but Liliana remained silent, her face turned toward the window as they passed the houses of her uncles, then the church, then on down the tree-lined road until they turned into San Michele. And so it went until they had almost reached the station— desultory conversation about nothing. Then, in silence, they dismounted and carried their bags along to the foot of the steps leading up into the passenger coach of the *Rapido* which had just come to a stop beside the platform. *Zio* Tony carried Liliana's two largest cases, the new burgundy leather ones, leaving the smallest for Liliana, who walked beside him. Amelia and Luisa, each with her small, slightly scuffed,

black suitcase, followed. *Zio* Tony swung the heavy suitcases up into the train, then took the steps in one bound and hurried in to secure them a compartment. Carrying the smaller bags and struggling to mount the steep steps, the women followed him on board and into an empty compartment whose window overlooked the station. Tony distributed the luggage as best he could about their feet and in the overhead racks, and then, one by one, they were enfolded within his arms, Liliana last. The rough tweed of his jacket scratched as she buried her face on her uncle's shoulder. He held her tightly, this child of his sister. "*Guardati, stai bene,*" he mumbled hoarsely, his voice catching, and then he was gone, closing the compartment door firmly behind him.

At least they were by the window, and Amelia and Luisa sank gratefully down side-by-side into the high-backed blue plush seats. But Liliana folded and re-folded her beautiful new green coat, which was much too hot to wear but which would have become wrinkled if she had packed it—and while she wouldn't need it in Rome, she surely would when she arrived in Canada. Frowning, she placed it carefully on the overhead rack, panting slightly, before she too sat facing Luisa and her mother. She looked out as the train began to move. There was her uncle, standing forlornly on the platform, a huge white handkerchief in one big hand as though he had been wiping his face, the other hand raised in a salute as the train emitted a piercing wail and bore them away.

The morning wore slowly on as the three women sat staring vacantly out the window—speaking only sporadically between long silences, glad to be able to watch the passing countryside without comment. Words might release the wellspring of tears just under the surface, might release the unspoken please ... *don't go ... don't make me go ...* the rhythm of the words in their heads echoing their heartbeats.

Liliana watched the passing scenery without really seeing it, aware always of the shadow of the train itself that lay beside them, moved with them, as they travelled past the cultivated fields, then refracted as the tracks took them past groves of silver-leafed olive trees. Here and there clusters of pale ochre buildings with warm red roofs dotted the hillsides, rows of tall, narrow trees, cypress, she thought, pointing skyward as they surrounded the cemeteries outside each little village.

The train braked to a halt at the larger towns, the faces of the people standing on the platforms a blur as they approached, then coming into focus, then blurring again as the train sped away. Two or three passengers got on at every stop, milling and jostling and talking loudly as they settled themselves and their baggage in the surrounding compartments, though no one tried to enter theirs. Larger groups, correspondingly louder, got on in the cities—*Venezia, Ferrara, Bologna, Firenze.* The countryside became rockier the farther south they travelled, the fields and villages set against a backdrop of craggy hills terraced with vineyards and olive groves and behind these, the sharper barren peaks of the Appenines, the "spine" of Italy.

It was almost noon as they pulled into the busy station in Florence. It was obvious by the number of people pushing to get onto the train that they would soon have company. Amelia rolled her eyes upward when three black-robed nuns bustled in and settled their plump bodies on the plush blue seats next to them, crowding in as best they could. Now the compartment was full and when anyone else attempted to enter they were told in no uncertain terms by the nuns that there was no more room. *"Occupato! È occupato!"*

As soon as they had left the city behind Amelia stood and took down the small cloth bag which contained their lunch of crusty rolls, *mortadella* and cheese, which she offered to share with the nuns. They shook their heads, murmuring, *"No, no, grazie,"* whereupon one of them reached down and picked up a business-like black leather briefcase from the floor which she placed on her knees and clicked open. On top of some papers sat a white napkin which, when unfurled, was seen to contain three raisin-studded sweetbuns which the nuns began to eat with great gusto.

Just then the vendor who plied the aisles between the compartments opened the door and called out his wares. But Amelia shook her head firmly and the nuns glared at him, mouths full, so that he backed meekly out and closed the door gently behind him. Quietly Amelia divided their much plainer food between herself and her daughters while the nuns folded their hands into their habits and slept, snoring softly, their plump faces shiny with perspiration.

As the afternoon wore on and the compartment became more and more stuffy, Amelia talked quietly to her daughters, fanning herself with a piece of pleated paper. She told them again about their *Zia* Melania, their father's sister, who had gone to Rome as a young girl. They had never tired of hearing the story. It was almost like a family myth, like a tale they might have read in a children's storybook, and they listened intently as their mother's voice retold it.

"Tell us, Mama. Tell us again how *Zia* Melania came to be living in Rome."

"Oh my dears, I've told you so often."

"But tell us again, Mama. It's such a lovely story."

"Well, long before the war Melania went to Rome to serve as a domestic in the home of a count."

"How did she know a count?!"

"Through the Bishop of Udine. He was a friend of your father's family, and he recommended Melania to the count. So it was arranged."

"But so far away—Rome! How old was she?"

"I think she was about nineteen," Amelia replied. Her voice took on a dreamlike quality. "Everyone says she was very beautiful, with long red hair and alabaster skin. Like a princess." She fanned herself, perspiration like tiny drops of dew on her forehead and upper lip.

"And how did she meet her husband?"

"I'm not sure. The Gasparini family were quite well off. Probably they came to dinner at the count's home, and the son saw Melania there—and fell in love."

"Oh, how romantic," sighed Luisa. Liliana was silent.

"Yes, it's a very romantic story. But true. So Melania married the Gasparini son and has lived in Rome ever since—over forty years. The family owned a *supermercato*. Maybe more than one. It's sad, though, that they never had children."

"How difficult it must have been for Melania all those years—so far away from home," said Liliana, her voice trailing off. *Not as far away as I am going. But I won't stay away forever.*

44

Her mother's voice stopped short. There was a silence. Then she cleared her throat and again took up the story.

"*Sì*, but she came home every now and then, as often as she could. She and your father were orphans, so they were very close. But forty years in Rome has changed her. She's a city woman now."

My God, forty years away from home! No doubt that would change you. But I'll be back long before that.

Amelia spoke softy as the train shot through the countryside, telling the girls about her memories of the apartment and the surrounding city, trying to prepare her unworldly daughters for what they would see. But she knew that the great mystery, the great adventure that lay ahead was Liliana's to discover alone. With that she could not help.

When at last the train slowed and finally halted beside the platform at the station in Rome, Amelia and her daughters were standing in the aisle between the compartments, loaded down with their luggage, waiting for the conductor, who stood at the head of the line of passengers, to let them off. Despite herself, despite all her fears, Liliana felt a surge of excitement. Rome! And as they finally stepped down from the train, the smell of the city hit her like a slap. It was a smell of hot pavement and diesel fumes and strong cigarettes, and it was so unlike the fresh air of home to which she was accustomed that Liliana thought she would gag. They stood there a moment or two, hesitating, and then Amelia rushed forward into the arms of a slim woman dressed elegantly in black—a black dress and shiny high-heeled black shoes. Liliana was used to seeing women dressed in black, all the old women at home wore only black, including Nonna, but this was something quite different. Her aunt was taller than she remembered, and much more fashionable, like someone in the pages of the magazines that Nonna frowned on. *Zia* Melania had not dressed this way on her trip back home for her brother's funeral two years ago, but perhaps, Liliana thought, trying not to stare, she hadn't noticed through her grief. Melania hugged them each in turn, asking them in her Roman-accented Italian how the journey had been and how everyone at home was. Then she shepherded them through the station and out onto the sidewalk, teeming and noisy with people, the August sun beating down.

Liliana was amazed at the variety she saw—faces of many different colours, women in bright dresses and gold jewellery, girls in tight bluejeans or short skirts and revealing tops, young men walking hand in hand, dark chest hair curling out of open-necked white shirts. Everyone seemed engaged in animated conversation as they hurried along, some smoking, some licking a *gelato* or eating fruit. The hot sun cast sharp shadows on the other side of the street, so that the crowds there seemed bathed in amethyst light, but on the side where she stood the sunlight spotlighted orange and pink and yellow punctuated by the occasional black of a passing priest or nun. It was a street scene of such brilliant colour and movement that Liliana and Luisa stood transfixed.

Laughing and gesturing as she talked with Amelia, their aunt paused to call back over her shoulder, *"Andiamo, andiamo."* "Let's go!" She pushed ahead of them through the crowd outside the station and hailed a taxi from the curb. It came to a screeching halt, scattering pedestrians in every direction, and soon they were careening through the narrow, cobbled side-streets of Rome. Liliana caught a glimpse of the curved wall of pillars around St. Peter's Square, topped with the sculptures of the saints, and she felt her breath catch in her throat. Everywhere she looked she saw buildings and statues she recognized from pictures she had seen in books at school and in the *Famiglia Cristiana,* the magazine Nonna received every week from the Vatican. Was that the Coloseum she was glimpsing at the end of that street? And wasn't this square they were hurtling through the *Campo dei Fiori*? Or was it the *Piazza Navona* with its *Fontana di Trevi*? Yes, she would have known it anywhere!

The streets were dotted with little sidewalk cafes where tanned people sat under umbrellas with bold lettering that said *Cinzano,* sipping espresso or tall pastel drinks, talking and laughing animatedly. It was amazing, it was exciting, it was impossible to believe! She was in Rome, and her heart thudded as her head twisted and turned in an attempt to take it all in.

Suddenly the taxi, without diminishing speed, shot up onto the sidewalk and braked to a violent stop in front of a three-storey apartment building which was apparently their destination. The driver, shaking his fist out the window and cursing loudly at a man who had the temerity to be standing there, leapt out and began unloading the luggage in anticipation of a handsome tip.

Liliana looked up and down the tree-shaded street. It was lined on both sides with buildings which looked very much like this one, some stuccoed in pink, some grey stone, some the familiar pale ochre, but these buildings were more ornate and aged-looking in an elegant way than any she had seen before in San Michele or in Udine. The casements were long and narrow, often with flower-filled wrought-iron balconies outside them, and ornate plaster decorations surrounding them. The doors were painted in contrasting colours, faded and blistered from the sun, with heavy brass knockers. Some were standing ajar just enough to allow a peek into black-and-white, diamond-patterned, marble-tiled entrance foyers, cool and mysterious. Mottled stone urns on either side of the doors held palms looking desperately in need of a drink. A faint sound, rising and falling, puzzled Liliana until she realized that she was hearing a soprano practicing her scales.

It was just such a foyer into which *Zia* Melania ushered them after having paid the taxi driver to his satisfaction, a difficult task which involved a great deal of talking and gesturing. Liliana noticed a discreet brass plaque just outside the door on which was inscribed the name of her aunt, Gasparini, and the family names of the occupants of the other five apartments. Melania opened the door to the left, and they entered another marble-tiled foyer, small, with an elegant gilt-framed oval mirror above a delicate hall table on which they placed their handbags.

"*Madonna, che lusso!*" exclaimed Luisa, for the rooms did indeed give the impression of luxurious gentility. Amelia threw her daughter a withering look. Liliana could only gawk about her, feeling suddenly awkward, as Melania busied herself, helping carry their luggage to the bedrooms, one for Amelia and one to be shared by the sisters. Liliana's eyes roved over the rooms of the apartment, small rooms, but furnished with delicate pieces upholstered in pale velvets, with flowers in crystal vases in front of mirrors over little polished tables. The effect was almost that of the rooms of *palazzos* Liliana had seen in movies, a look—a feeling— of age and faded luxury quite unlike anything in the big old houses at home. Perhaps her mother had been wrong.

Perhaps the *Famiglia Gasparini* had been better off than Amelia knew, and Liliana looked down at her dark blue pleated skirt and white blouse, the sensible navy low-heeled pumps, and for the first time in her life experienced a flash of worry about her appearance. She wondered if she was dressed appropriately, if she would know how to behave. She felt unsure of herself, unsettled—a feeling with which she was not familiar.

Once in their bedroom with the door closed, Luisa and Liliana engaged in a furious whispered conversation. "I had no idea that *Zia* Melania was rich," whispered Liliana. "Just look at all the beautiful things!"

"I know!" replied Luisa. "I can't believe it either. Funny that Mama never told us. Or maybe it's just the impression given by all this old furniture. She probably inherited it from her husband's family, I'm sure she was as poor as Papa when she left home," she said, explaining the unexplainable as an older sister should.

Maybe I'll be able to have a home like this in America someday, Liliana thought, and for the first time felt a pleasant twinge of anticipation.

After they had freshened up in the immaculate little white-tiled bathroom, Melania led them through a door in the sitting room to the *terrazzo* just outside in the narrow space between this building and the one next door, and seated them at a beautifully-set glass table. Anyone could see that this family had lived here for many years, probably for several generations. The vines covering the pergola over-head were old, with thick foliage which provided protection from the sun as well as privacy—an oasis in the city. The *terrazzo* was separated from the street by a high stone wall over which grew more vines, dusty at the top from the constant traffic on the roadway.

Amelia offered to help her sister-in-law serve the supper. Melania had prepared most of it before she went to the station; Liliana had caught a glimpse of plates covered with white cloths on the kitchen counter. *Maybe she even has a maid,* thought Liliana. *I wouldn't know what to do if I had a maid. So I'll always do everything myself, even if Carlo insists.*

It was a simple meal of veal cutlets with lemon, a salad of grilled eggplant, and then cheese and fruit, along with the white wine of *Frascati*. It was delicious, and the gifts they had brought for Melania were presented and received with obviously genuine pleasure. Luisa toyed with her wine glass, listening attentively to the two older women as they talked, and once more, as she had so often over the past few weeks, Liliana felt herself removed, at a distance, as the voices of the other women eddied around her. She sat absolutely still, her eyes on the quietly-rustling leaves of the vines that surrounded them, aware of the sounds of the traffic on the other side of the wall. *In a few days I'll be gone. Who knows if I'll ever see this lovely apartment, this wonderful city again.*

"Run along to bed, my dear, you must be exhausted," Melania said, waving one long hand dismissively. "And don't forget to close your shutters."

Liliana's body was exhausted but her mind was in turmoil, the scents and sounds of the city filling her head as she lay on the high narrow bed. The colours, the noises, it was wonderful. Imagine how exciting to live here! Lucky

Melania. She thought about home, about San Michele, and it seemed drab and poor—and very far away.

She could hear the voices of the other women well into the night, a lulling backdrop, and once, just before she drifted off, she thought she heard someone sobbing, though she wasn't sure. Perhaps she had been dreaming.

Chapter 5

Those few days in Rome, filled with last-minute shopping, sight-seeing, and leisurely suppers under the pergola, moved on inexorably to the day of departure. But they were fascinating, exciting days, and Liliana often forgot about the trip to Canada—and even Carlo—as they moved about the city, usually walking, sometimes taking a horribly crowded bus or, blissfully, a taxi. It was clear that Luisa and their mother were enjoying every moment of it too, though now and then Liliana couldn't help but wonder if Luisa was thinking about the honeymoon trip she would never have. It was she, being the eldest, who should be visiting Rome with her new husband–before Liliana. *Povera Luisa, che disgrazia.* And then the anger would well up in Liliana again. She wasn't visiting Rome for the first time with her new husband either! This was *not* how it was supposed to be!

Zia Melania was a tireless hostess and tour guide, determined to show her visitors the best and most beautiful of the city she had grown to love. She knew it well, and they saw, in those few days, most of its sights. They attended Sunday mass in the square outside St. Peter's with thousands of others, although they were shocked at Melania's opinion that if you had seen one Pope you had seen them all. She seemed somehow hardened, unmoved by the mystery, and while her attitude puzzled the sisters, they were reluctant to query her about it, unable even to voice their shock.

They toured the Vatican museums, they walked through hot piazzas to look at fountains and sculptures, then stopped gratefully to rest in huge cool churches, sitting in the empty pews, heads tipped back the better to see the murals and frescoes that decorated the walls and ceilings. They tramped, along with countless other tourists, through the ancient *Foro Romano* and the Coliseum, through the Baths of Caracalla and all the other well-known sites of ancient Rome. And then they toured the sights of modern Rome, down the *Via Veneto*, noticing in horror the prices of the goods displayed in the windows of the boutiques. Several times, before venturing inside, they were surprised when their aunt admonished them not to speak for fear their obviously non-Roman accents would drive the prices up. They had an espresso, but just one, at a little café in front of one of the famous hotels on the *Via Veneto*, and watched in amazement the foreign tourists passing by, American they guessed, the women stockingless, in bare-shouldered sun dresses, the men in loudly-patterned shirts, draped in cameras. Liliana and Luisa drank it in, devoured it all, and returned each evening to their aunt's lovely apartment as tired as they could ever remember being. It was exhilarating to be in this fascinating city, so unlike the Italy Liliana knew, and she daydreamed of how different her life would have been had she been born here rather than in what she now saw was the much more conservative and dour north.

Whenever Liliana thought of Carlo, it was harder and harder to see his face. Sometimes, when she least expected it, she felt again the anger. She felt cheated. It was he who should have been here with her now! They should have been having their honeymoon together in Rome, like Mama and Papa had done—she was sure she could have talked Carlo into it—instead of her spending these exciting days without him, in the company of women. She slept little, and when she did she dreamed of purple figs and red geraniums, and the feel of Carlo's face against hers, and great black groves of tall trees.

On the appointed day the four women, travelling by taxi, arrived at the airport, a cavernous place full of shouting men and noxious fumes. They endured the line-ups and barked commands of the officious airport employees and Liliana was surprised at this other side of Rome. Gone was the elegance, the sense of ageless refinement, the courtliness. The people at the airport were overwrought, hot and nervous, milling about. But Melania calmly shepherded her charges through the mass of sweaty, noisy people, forging an opening in the crowd so that they could follow behind her. It was almost impossible not to be shoved and elbowed along, and Liliana felt bewildered and frightened as she struggled to keep up with her aunt. There seemed to be no order, no one else seemed calm or purposeful, no one seemed to know where to go. Liliana could feel her heart beating faster. *Oh Dio, what if we can't find the right place! What if I miss the flight?!*

Just then, as if sensing Liliana's rising panic, Melania turned, and pulling the girl up beside her, put an arm about her waist and gave her a squeeze. "Don't worry, my dear, I know where we must go. We're almost there—see—just ahead. Come along, stay with us," she called out to Amelia and Luisa. The four women shuffled along together, Melania and Liliana leading, Amelia and Luisa following closely behind. Grateful for the comforting feel of her aunt's arm about her waist, Liliana listened carefully to her instructions. As they moved slowly forward Melania explained to Liliana what the procedure was, what would happen next, how it would be when she boarded the plane. Apparently, Melania had actually flown once, to Paris with her husband, and thus she was able to help Liliana with the complicated process. After showing the curt official her ticket and her passport she received the important bit of paper, the Boarding Pass, that would allow her entry to the departure lounge, and then to the plane itself. After more jostling and pushing through the crowd, Melania leading, they found the correct departure lounge. They stood there, huddled together, unspeaking. And then, as if frozen in a trance, Liliana was kissed and hugged by her aunt, then by her mother and her sister, her cheeks wet with their mingled tears while the impatient security guard waited, hand outstretched, for her Boarding Pass. Both her mother and her sister were sobbing openly now, their much-prized composure gone as they faced the finality of it all. Liliana's sobs caught in her throat and were stifled as she tore herself from their arms, being borne along by the impatient travellers who had been held up by their goodbyes. The crowd carried her through the lounge and toward the outside door as she struggled to look over her shoulder, trying to catch one last glimpse of her family despite being swept along by the throng, out of the terminal

and into the noisy diesel bus parked just outside. Melania
had already explained that this bus transported the
passengers to the plane itself, and as it careened across the
tarmac Liliana stood, trying desperately to hang onto the
strap with one hand and wipe the tears from her cheeks with
the other, her smallest case on the floor between her feet.
After what seemed like only a minute or two the bus
screeched to a halt at the foot of a set of metal steps leading
up to the glistening white-bodied airplane. Struggling with
her case, which kept knocking against her legs, Liliana was
again swept along by the other passengers, stepping down
off the bus and mounting the stairs. There was no time to
turn back, no time to wave again. They were gone, and she
was being moved inexorably forward. She stepped into the
body of the fat white airplane.

Thanks to Zia Melania's instructions, Liliana knew
enough to hand her Boarding Pass to the Stewardess, who
indicated that her seat was next to the window in the third
row on the left. After Liliana had taken off her green coat
with its silver buttons, folded it carefully, and stowed it in
the overhead bin as she saw the other passengers doing, she
slid across the two empty seats to her own. No sooner had
she accomplished this than a fat elderly priest, breathing
laboriously, plunked himself down in the aisle seat, his belly
filling the space between his seat and the back of the one in
front. He huffed and puffed as he arranged and re-arranged
his bulk in its stained black cassock. He grunted a cursory
greeting to her, then closed his eyes. No one came to claim
the seat between them. Liliana watched carefully as the other
passengers milled about in the aisles, talking and laughing,
opening and closing the overhead bins, then finding their

seats. They were for the most part dressed much more casually than she, even sloppily, and Liliana was amazed that such a thing as a flight to *America* could be taken so lightly. They were acting as though they had done this many times before and that it was something to be enjoyed, like going to a party. No one seemed the least bit nervous or sad. She tried to see the terminal from where she sat, to catch a last glimpse of her family, but the windows of the grimy building looked blank and dark. A wave of anguish washed over her, so powerful that she pressed a hand to her stomach. *What am I doing? Where am I going?* She put her head back and closed her eyes, trying to conjure up the face of Carlo, the reason she was embarking on this frightening experience, but she could see him only faintly and try as she might, he would not come into focus. She concentrated on breathing slowly, deeply, but she could not. Images of the frenetic streets of Rome interspersed with those of the beloved big house and the cortile in San Michele grew and faded behind her closed lids. *I don't have to do this—I don't have to go! What if I get out—now—go back to Zia Melania's—go home! Would it be so bad, being a white widow? At least I'd be at home with all my family.* Before she knew what she had done, she was standing, trying to get past the body of the sleeping priest, trying to get out to the aisle. But she was trapped! As she stood there, breathing quickly, a panicked look on her face, the stewardess came along.

"Please take your seat and fasten your seatbelt. We are preparing for departure," she said calmly, moving on down the aisle. With a sickening feeling of impotence Liliana obediently resumed her seat, turning toward the tiny window and resting her forehead against the cool glass. *Too late. It's too late. I have to go.*

And suddenly she realized that the plane was moving slowly down the runway, then faster and faster, the unbearable screeching noise in her ears, the sense of being borne uncontrollably forward combining to make her heart beat so rapidly she thought she would lose consciousness. And then the sickening sense that they had left the earth, that they were aloft, unsupported, moving through the endless sky.

Her mother and her sister watched through the big dirty windows of the terminal as the plane lifted off, clasping each other's hands. *Not I,* thought Amelia, not for the first time. *I'll never leave this earth.* And then, *Oh God, why have I let her go?*

Chapter 6

The eight-hour flight was beginning to seem interminable, punctuated only by the hostess bringing a tray of inedible food, packaged in little plastic containers. Although Liliana's stomach had settled, the constant droning noise having lulled her somewhat, she ate nothing, only drinking several of the large cups of pale coffee which tasted like dirty water. Soon the stewardess came by to take away their trays, and Liliana was happy to hand hers over to the smartly-uniformed woman. "Tank you," she said gravely, and had a small moment of triumph. Her first words in English, and it had gone all right! Cupping her hands against the glass then, she peered out the window at the colourless sky. She had left the earth and was being born through space to some other earth. She sat back, and resting her head against the little white cover on the headrest, she closed her eyes. The ceaseless chatter of the other passengers continued—snatches of conversation in Italian and what she knew to be English, though of this she understood very little. Would it ever come to her? She worried about how she would manage in Canada, where everyone spoke English.

And then she began to worry about how she would get out of her seat to go to the bathroom, since her only exit was barred by the body of the sleeping priest. But eventually she absolutely had to, and blushingly excusing herself and hiking up her skirt, she stepped over his bulk. Thankfully he didn't open his eyes as she maneuvered her way out nor when she returned.

The cabin lights were dimmed when she returned and the passengers had quieted down considerably, the babble of excited conversation reduced to soft murmurings. To her surprise, soft woollen blankets and little white pillows were passed out by the always-smiling hostess, and again Liliana murmured "Tank you," as she took hers. Though the weight and warmth of the pale green blanket was comforting, she positioned and re-positioned the pillow against the cold glass of the window, trying to find a comfortable place for her head. She thought surely she would never sleep.

Suddenly she felt something—a hand—clutching at her arm where it lay on the armrest, and her eyes flew open. The priest, obviously in some sort of distress but unable to speak, was gesturing frantically with his other pudgy hand at the breast-pocket of his cassock. She stared, unable to make out what he wanted. Finally, wheezing noisily, his face scarlet and his eyes bulging, he was able to extricate from the pocket of his cassock a small bottle containing tiny white pills. Suddenly realizing that he must be having some sort of seizure, probably a heart attack, she rose from her seat, pushing the blanket off her legs. She looked frantically up and down the aisle but saw only the other passengers, heads lolling, asleep. The stewardess was no where in sight. "*Aiuto,* help!" she called out, but in vain. She turned then so that she was looking down at the priest, and her eyes lit on the illuminated buttons on the armrest. On one she saw the drawing of a woman and realized that she must push that button to summon the stewardess. Breathing quickly, her heart pounding, she pressed it, then pressed it again. In the dimness at the far end of the aisle, she saw the uniformed woman rise from her seat and begin to stroll toward her, peering from side to side to determine the source of the call.

"*Calmati,* stay calm," she said to the agitated old man who now held the pill bottle up in one hand, shaking it toward her. It was clear that she would have to help him. Now. The stewardess was still too far away. Her hands shaking, Liliana took the bottle and unscrewed the cap. Then, obeying the ever more frantic gestures of the priest, she placed one tiny white pill on the thick tongue he dangled out of his mouth. He snorted, and with what appeared to be a great effort, retracted his tongue and noisily swallowed. Liliana remained on her feet, bent over him as gradually his breathing became less agitated and he let go of her arm.

At this point, to her great relief, the Italian-speaking stewardess arrived and saw immediately what the situation was. "Thank you—you've done well," she told Liliana. "This happens often, and usually the nearest passengers are terrified." She signalled a steward, then stepped over the priest's body and turned toward him. As Liliana sat on the edge of her seat, the two managed to heave the priest into a more upright position so that the oxygen mask which they released could be attached to his face. He seemed very calm now, and his voice, muffled by the mask, could be heard saying, "*Grazie, grazie*" as he was fussed over and made comfortable.

"Now don't worry, he's going to be fine. You were very helpful." The steward's voice was warm, his dark eyes compassionate as he spoke to Liliana. "Just call if you need anything. Anything at all." They left, but Liliana was not calm now. The incident had unnerved her, and she felt shaky, her breathing rapid and shallow. *What if he dies, right here beside me. Oh, God! Maybe I didn't call for help soon enough! I should have done something sooner. I should have moved faster.* Then faces of Nonna and Mama came into her mind. *But I did help. I did what needed to be done, and I didn't panic.* She had surprised herself. *Maybe I even saved his life! Mama and Nonna would be proud of me.*

She looked at her watch, its face luminous in the half-light of the cabin, and counted off the hours. She realized that they would be landing in Toronto shortly, and who knew what lay ahead? She tried to will herself to breathe slowly and to relax her tense muscles, but she could not. She gripped the armrests with her hands as she felt the plane begin to descend, seemingly forever, until at last it landed with a tremendous thud and Liliana felt herself being plastered against the seatback as the plane roared down the runway. Her heart was absolutely pounding now, so hard that she thought she would choke. Or die.

And then, as the other passengers began to retrieve their hand luggage and coats and jackets in preparation for disembarking, the Italian-speaking stewardess bent over and told Liliana that she could not leave her seat until the priest had been helped off to a waiting ambulance. *Oh God,* she thought, *I'll be the last one off and maybe there'll be no one to meet me! They'll think I haven't come, and I'll be all alone.* But she sat unprotesting, tears glazing her eyes and her legs trembling as she watched everyone else leave the cabin.

Finally, several men in uniform arrived to help the priest. They heaved him onto a stretcher, placed an oxygen mask over his nose and mouth, and, more solicitously than she had expected, carried him off. Now she could leave her seat. Her chest constricted, she stood and retrieved her coat, put it on, and clutching her handbag and carry-on bag, stepped out into the aisle and moved toward the exit where another stewardess, a fixed smile on her face, waited. *Will the couple Carlo has sent to meet me still be waiting? Will they know me? Did Carlo tell them that I am small, with brown hair and green eyes? Of course not.* Despite her resolve, her chin began to quiver and the tears spilled down her cheeks as she stepped out of the plane and found herself in a sort of metal tunnel. She was alone, the other passengers had disappeared already, but ahead she could make out the backs of the paramedics who were wheeling the stretcher on which lay the priest. She hurried then, so as to keep them in sight, her case banging against her leg.

Very quickly she found herself emerging into a large room where the other passengers had formed several long lines. The priest and his entourage were nowhere in sight. Liliana realized that the others had their luggage with them now, and scanning the cavernous room, she saw with a flash of relief where her two burgundy cases sat beside a concrete pillar. She moved stiffly toward them, and struggling mightily, pushing the biggest one along with her foot, she managed to join the end of one of the queues. No one spoke to her. Ahead she could see a frowning uniformed man who was examining the documents of the passengers as, one by one, they stepped up to the window. She opened her purse and took out her passport, clutching it so tightly that its green cover became moist from the perspiration of her hand.

When her turn arrived at last, the official behind the window took her passport and visa and examined them intently, paging slowly through the documents, frowning. Liliana's heart was beating so rapidly she felt faint. It had not occurred to her until this moment that she might get this far and be denied entry. Oh God, what would she do? She didn't have enough money to go back. And she knew no one. But finally, without a word, her documents were passed back to her and she moved past the kiosk to a raised bench onto which she managed to heave her suitcases.

The customs officers were curt and rude, raising their voices and speaking ever more loudly as if that would help her understand the unfamiliar language. They indicated that she open all her luggage, and pawing through it roughly they almost uncannily found and removed each carefully-wrapped salami or bit of prosciutto and threw it into a metal container. She gasped as each package hit the can with a thud—what was going on? Why was this happening. Tentatively, in a quavering voice, she tried to ask. *"Ma perché?* Why?"

The official, intent on his search, didn't even lift his head as he explained in badly-accented Italian. *"È vietato!* It is forbidden to bring meat into Canada!" She swallowed and looked down, trembling, unprotesting, mortified to be seen to be doing something illegal. She hadn't known, but she felt guilty. Would she be detained? Turned back? Fined? Her legs were shaking, her whole body trembling. She was sure she must look as guilty as sin. But the officer went about his business now quite matter-of-factly, expecting to find what

64

he had found, it appeared, unemotionally removing and discarding the offending parcels without comment. It was all so—so impersonal. Eventually her belongings were carelessly stuffed back and the lids closed on her slightly-scuffed burgundy suitcases. It was over.

As she emerged into the terminal on legs that barely held her, disheveled and close to tears again, she heard her name being called. Her eyes roved over the crowd until she realized that the poorly-dressed, middle-aged couple, plump and grey-haired, who stood just behind the rope barrier, were the ones calling her. Relieved, she moved toward them and was enfolded in their arms in an embrace as warm as any she might have received from family. Both talking at once, they explained that their name was Lombardo, and they had been sent by their son, a friend of Carlo's, to accompany her to Cedar Ridge. They were going near there as well by train to visit their son, they said. Now they would take her to their Toronto home and catch the train in the morning. She recognized the accented Italian of the province next to hers, but it was close enough to home for her to be immensely comforted by their presence and their reassurances.

To her great surprise, she was taken to a car which they said was their own, and was driven through tree-lined streets to their home. It was just like all the other houses in the street, small, made of red brick, and Liliana was relieved. So it wasn't true—not all the houses were made of wood! And while the inside of the house, made up of several small rooms stuffed with furniture, was cramped, it was not too unfamiliar. After a supper of familiar cold cuts and a salad, she was delighted to be offered the use of a very modern bathroom where she bathed in unaccustomed luxury in a white ceramic tub. At home there had only been a shower in the bathroom which had recently been installed, attached to the kitchen. But this bathroom with its tub was a vast improvement. The hot water relaxed her, and she very soon drifted into a sound sleep in the small but comfortable bedroom to which her luggage had been taken. She felt safe. She dreamt of water, endless grey water on which she floated in a silver boat, and then nothing.

Early the next morning she was awakened by a soft voice calling. "*Signorina, signorina, buon giorno*," and Liliana sat bolt upright. Where was she? Where was this little room with its shabby furniture? And then she remembered. She was in the hot little red brick house in Toronto, and she had to get ready quickly in order to be on time for the train they were all to take that morning—the train that would take three nights and four days to get to Cedar Ridge, where Carlo was waiting for her. She moved as though in a trance through her preparations, washing herself and dressing in her navy blue suit with the smart navy pumps and matching handbag, before going out into the diminutive dining room where she saw toasted bread on a plate, and a jar of what looked like preserved chopped oranges. *Signora* Lombardo looked surprised at first sight of her, but recovered herself quickly, only admonishing a pale Liliana to eat something. "At least drink a little coffee," said her hostess in a kind voice. Liliana nodded meekly as she sat down at the table which was covered with a flowered plastic cloth. She saw that the label on the jar said MARMALADE, and since *marmellata* in Italian meant jam, she put some sparingly on the toast and took a bite. To her horror it was a bitter orange flavour, not at all what she had expected, and she swallowed it quickly.

Remembering the brown water they had called coffee on the plane, she was relieved when *Signora* Lombardo poured her a tiny cup of espresso. She drank it gratefully, but it didn't help. She felt sick, weak and nauseous as she mentally calculated what time it was at home. Evening. No wonder she felt exhausted, and the day was only beginning.

Her host was busily carrying their luggage out to the car as *Signora* Lombardo explained to Liliana that although there was a dining car on the train, she had prepared food which they could eat in the passenger coach, the dining room being much too expensive. Liliana nodded, though secretly she thought it would have been lovely to eat in a dining car. Then her hostess brought out an enormous valise which bulged with the food she had packed, and handing it to her husband, said briskly, "Well now, let's go." And turning to Liliana, "We still have to buy our tickets when we get to the station. We're not going First Class, you know. We'll have to get on board as fast as we can in order to get good seats." Liliana was puzzled at this but, too unsettled to frame the question, she simply followed the couple out the door and was ushered into the back seat of the car beside her hostess. *Signore* Lombardo sat in the front passenger seat. A neighbour, an elderly gentleman who spoke not a word to Liliana, was to drive them to the station and then return the car to the Lombardo's garage.

Liliana felt disembodied as she sat silently in the back seat, uncomfortably hot in her good clothes, the green coat folded over her arm. Mrs. Lombardo was wearing a floral dress of some light material. Several strings of pink plastic pearls were wound around her chubby neck, and she was stockingless, her calloused feet crammed into white plastic sandals. *Not very elegant,* Liliana thought, *but she's probably a good deal more comfortable than I am.* Besides her bright pink purse, she carried a paper bag with handles which appeared to contain things she would require on the journey. A ball of purple wool and some knitting needles sat on top, and Liliana could see a deck of playing cards.

The Lombardos talked and laughed in English with the neighbour, ignoring Liliana, whose head was turned as she watched the houses go by. Where were the luxurious homes, the mansions she had expected to see in this big city? Surely in Toronto not everyone lived in little red and yellow brick houses? And then, up ahead, she saw for the first time the tall silver skyscrapers, somehow familiar, that rose into the endless blue sky, and she felt a twinge of excitement. Here was the big modern city she had expected. And now they were driving between the towers in a busy downtown area with a great deal of traffic, everyone obeying the lights and stop signs with quiet placidity. Everything was grey and dull and not silver at all. Although Liliana knew that the sun was shining, the tall buildings cast such deep shadows here that the streets were in semi-darkness, and the people on the sidewalks were grey too, not at all the colourful noisy crowds of Rome but dressed rather drably and moving purposefully along, eyes down, waiting meekly in little clusters for the light to change at the corner. Going to work, she supposed. But joylessly, silently. Or so it seemed to Liliana that August morning, the first day of her new life.

Chapter 7

The cavernous train station was cool, its high ceiling and shadowy arched alcoves full of people standing about in clusters, surrounded by cardboard suitcases and brown paper shopping bags and various other shabby bundles. They were standing talking quietly, some smoking or chewing gum as slightly dirty children dressed in very little ran in and out between them. No one was shouting, no voices could be heard raised, either in argument or in happiness, only the occasional tearful face or quick embrace betrayed any emotion. No one seemed in a hurry or nervous, yet there was a repressed undercurrent of excitement that Liliana could feel as she stood waiting with the Lombardos in the line-up in front of the ticket window.

These were the first Canadians Liliana had seen at close quarters. These people were either meeting someone or travelling themselves, yet they were dressed extremely casually. Now she understood why Mrs. Lombardo had looked surprised when she had appeared that morning in her good navy suit. She saw that the women had bare legs and carried huge white plastic handbags with matching white sandals. A few of the men wore ties, but with short-sleeved shirts. Not a dark jacket, not a suit to be seen. Young girls wore brightly-patterned sundresses, or old-looking blue jeans. Some wore short pants, their slim legs exposed!

The line she was in moved gradually forward and Liliana realized that each person kept a respectful distance from the person ahead. There was no touching of bodies, no shoving.

It all seemed so very different, so subdued and—she couldn't think of the word—somehow disappointing. Everyone was dressed differently, the language was unknown—she was indeed in a new country. Where were the elegant, well-dressed people of this wealthy land? A faint understanding began to dawn on Liliana—the wealthy and elegant did not travel by train on hot summer afternoons. In her fine wool suit, carrying her green coat over her arm, Lilana felt as though she had landed on another planet. She could feel herself wilting. They shuffled on, picking up and moving their suitcases ahead each time someone at the front of the line successfully purchased a ticket.

Suddenly a voice boomed from overhead in indecipherable words, startling Liliana from her contemplation of the scene, and she remembered that she, too, was travelling. She wondered what the voice had said. Surely her two companions would understand and would not make some mistake and miss the train. It was too important. Still, she had no choice but to rely on them, she thought dispiritedly. Soon the three of them stood before the wicket, and a shirt-sleeved man wearing a tie sold the Lombardos their tickets—two for Mountain View. Liliana had a moment of horror as it occurred to her that she might not have enough Canadian money. *Zia* Melania had taken her to a bank in Rome to exchange some *lira,* but who knew how much the ticket would cost. Patiently *Signore* Lombardo took the right amount from her hand and passed it over to the clerk, who shoved the ticket through to him. One for Cedar Ridge. *Signore* Lombardo turned and presented Liliana with the small piece of cardboard, and as she held it in her hand she realized that there was truly no turning back. Her journey was half over. *I'm coming, Carlo, I'm coming to you because I have to, because you wouldn't come to me,* she thought, and the anger rose in her again. But try as she might she could not see his face, and her eyes filled with tears. She felt utterly alone, utterly desolate, and incredibly furious at the twist of fate that brought her here.

Blinking back the tears and getting a fresh grip on her handbag, she followed the Lombardos as they hurried out onto the platform and alongside the train which had CN written on the sides of the cars in bold letters. She was somehow comforted by the thought of *Zio* Tony and how he had come to Canada to work for this company. They stopped and, after showing their tickets to a uniformed black man who surprised her by holding out his hand to assist the ladies, stepped up into the coach. There were several other groups already seated, but the three quickly settled on seats facing each other toward the far end of the coach. There were no compartments. It was like a bus, completely open, and everyone watched them as they arranged themselves and their belongings. Liliana felt embarrassed. She thought people were staring at her, as though they knew that she had just arrived from Italy, that she could neither understand nor speak their language, and that in fact she had no idea where she was going. But of course her companions were speaking Italian to her and to each other, she realized, and that must be why people were staring.

The two women sat side by side, Liliana being given the window seat, and *Signore* Lombardo sat across from her. The train was dirty, she thought, noticing with distaste the bits of paper and cigarette butts on the floor, and the rather stained and well-worn seats. Once again she noted that the other passengers were very casually dressed, some looking quite disheveled. One plump woman with three young children must have been travelling for a very long time, judging by the books and toys and half-eaten sandwiches strewn about their seats. The children were unruly, whining and quarreling and teasing each other while the woman smoked a cigarette, her nose in a magazine. Liliana's eyes roved over the other passengers who were in various degrees untidy, hot and tired. There was an elderly couple sitting across the aisle, playing cards at a table attached under the window. The woman, who must have been much older than her Nonna, had white hair tortured into tiny curls all over her head, with blue eyeshadow on her lids and a startling slash of bright red lipstick on her mouth. Her scrawny bare arms and legs poked out of a flowered dress with red buttons all the way down the front. She wore matching round red discs on her ears, and her feet were encased in bright red sandals. Liliana was shocked. It was unseemly that such an old woman should be so colourful, so immodest in public. She couldn't imagine what her family would have said had they seen such a sight. The old man, scrawny as his wife, wore blue jeans, a white T-shirt pulled tightly over his little paunch, and a blue peaked cap. They played without speaking, the cards slapping down on the plasticized surface. They were both smoking, the blue fumes swirling about their heads as they absent-mindedly squashed out one cigarette in the overflowing ashtray between them and lit the next. Liliana became aware that she was staring and forced herself to look once more out the window. *Madonna,* she thought, *I can't believe what I'm seeing—these people don't know how to dress, how to comport themselves in public.* But she said nothing.

There were several other groups in the coach, among them some young people seated together reading books or talking quietly. Liliana guessed them to be students. One of them had a guitar which he strummed tunelessly. The girls wore colourful ankle-length skirts of some wrinkled fabric and all of them, both boys and girls, had long straight hair centre-parted and held back by a rolled piece of cloth tied around their foreheads. Liliana averted her eyes, only to find herself looking at them over and over again. She couldn't help it. She had never in all her life seen anyone dressed this way. Then she remembered the article she had read in the *Famiglia Cristiana* about the hippies in America and their lives of sin—free love and drugs, and her amazement grew. She was seeing some of them in the flesh and though they were dressed oddly, outlandishly, at least they were behaving better than groups of young students she had seen at home who gestured and talked loudly, intent on gaining the attention of everyone. Despite what she knew of their sinful lifestyle, she thought these students actually seemed quite thoughtful, studious even, as they paged through their books. She was perplexed. They didn't seem evil. Only young and rather serious. Perhaps the Vatican publication hadn't told the whole story. Perhaps the writer hadn't known the whole story.

In the seats behind her were two middle-aged women reading from small black books, who looked almost out-of-place in their dark blue dresses, dark stockings, and shiny black oxfords. Was that a tiny silver cross she saw pinned on each collar? Puzzling. She knew they couldn't be nuns, dressed as they were.

It was late morning and the August sun beat through the windows. *Signora* Lombardo stood up to pull the dusty blind down part-way, and Liliana was glad that she was still able to see out. The platform was almost empty now, littered with scraps of paper and cigarette packages and melting blobs of who knew what substances. Beyond the front of the station with its huge black windows she could just make out the tops of the silver skyscrapers pointing up. *Gratta-cieli,* she thought. Sky graters. The train jerked once, twice, hissed, and started off, gaining speed gradually as Liliana watched the squat brown buildings pass by, hung with signs she couldn't decipher. They began to pick up speed now, but the view changed little—unkempt buildings with broken windows, occasionally vacant weed-filled areas strewn with debris, then more and smaller buildings, until at last they seemed to have left the city. Her companions had been silent, staring out the window as well, but now *Signore* Lombardo unhooked the table from underneath the window and pulled it up. This surface filled the space between the seats, and as the older couple began to play cards too, Liliana felt trapped. The image of the fat priest on the airplane flashed into her mind. Not again!

But she soon forgot about the table as her attention turned to the countryside through which they were passing. Never had she seen anything so green, so lush, so indescribably rich and complex as this maze of trees and bushes with the occasional glint of water between them. And it went on forever, to the horizon, at times without a building in sight. As her eyes took in the beauty of it under the endless blue sky her thoughts turned again to the man who was waiting for her under this same sky. Carlo. But try as she might—trying again and again until she gave up—she still could not conjure up his face, and this frightened her. *I'm just tired—it will come back to me when I'm more rested*, she comforted herself. But what if it didn't. *Damn you, Carlo!* And the anger washed over her again. Her lips pressed tightly together, she closed her eyes and willed herself to remain calm, to think about the good things that lay ahead, she hoped. The train rumbled on.

She must have slept a little, for suddenly she was aware of activity around her, and her eyes snapped open. "Time to have a little lunch, dear," said *Signora* Lombardo, busily putting plates and glasses and paper napkins out. The cards had disappeared, and her husband was smoking a cigarette. Rustling in her valise, the older woman produced rolls, some hard-boiled eggs, a fat salami, and a vicious-looking knife with which to cut it. This accomplished, she gave them each several pieces, exhorting them to eat. Next she produced a bottle of home-made wine, pouring a little into each glass. Just then a white-jacketed black man walked through the coach, calling out something in a sing-song voice, and several people stood and followed him out. As Mrs. Lombardo explained that he had announced that lunch was being served in the dining car, Liliana realized that they had the attention of everyone in the coach. No one else had actually set a table, though some were munching on delicate-looking sandwiches or apples, but no one seemed to have the sort of full-blown meal that her hostess was serving. For out of the valise now came a jar of home-made pickles, *giardiniera,* and several chunks of roasted chicken. Followed by pieces of cake. And *biscotti.* And fruit. Liliana was mortified, but she sat well back in her seat in the shadow of S*ignora* Lombardo and ate. She was quite hungry after all.

The lunch finished and the food put away, the older woman took Liliana with her to the washroom, showing her where things were and how to operate them. As soon as they returned to their seats the Lombardos, in an unspoken pact, folded their hands over their stomachs, closed their eyes, and soon were emitting little puffing noises from between their lips. The coach was quiet, even the unruly children had fallen asleep, and Liliana sat staring out the window. She had never seen so many shades of green. Forest green and moss green and fern green and leaf green, celadon and emerald and olive. *Terra verde.* She slept and dreamt of waterfalls and flying through the endless sky, and little houses with many rooms like rabbit warrens.

The rest of that first day and the evening passed slowly, the movements and voices of her fellow passengers muffled by the constant racketing of the train. Liliana had become accustomed to the people in the seats around her and had stopped staring, but she caught herself listening hard as snatches of conversation eddied about. She *had* studied a little English in school after all, and admitting grudgingly to herself a feeling of isolation, strained to understand what was being said, but to no avail. They spoke too quickly and slurred one word into another. She would never learn, she was sure. She would have to rely totally on Carlo, she thought, and a new fear settled on her. Would she always feel this sense of isolation? Would she never feel at home again? *Damn you, Carlo, you'll have to help me. This is what you wanted, and now you'll have to help me.* But not a trace of this new fear showed on her face. Not any more. She was becoming stoic. She sat motionless, watching the scene both inside and out. There was no turning back.

The combination of the constant sound of the wheels on the tracks and her weariness lulled her—she felt as though she were watching herself from a great height. Every now and then she tried to concentrate on what lay ahead, but she couldn't seem to focus. It was all so unclear, so vague, so terrifying. There would be a wedding, there would be a house, and that was really all she knew. She allowed herself to fall into a reverie, images of home, her Nonna's house with its geranium-filled window sills, the big fig tree by the door, the faces of her mother and sister, her lovely cool bedroom with its dark furniture—and scenes of Rome, all intermingling in her mind. But Carlo did not appear. As the evening wore on, the other passengers arranged themselves in various positions for sleeping and the Lombardos showed Liliana how to lower her seat-back for greater comfort. The porter had come by offering little white pillows for rent, but that seemed an unnecessary luxury which they declined. Soon the coach was filled with the night sounds of people, little puffs and snorts and buzzes and the occasional mumbled phrase of a dreamer. Rustles and moans. Sighs and groans. Liliana slept.

Chapter 8

The second day began to Liliana's surprise with *Signora* Lombardo purchasing three cups of coffee from the vendor who passed down the aisle with his wares. They sipped slowly, balancing the hot paper cups on the upturned palms of their hands, their eyes on the passing countryside. After the other passengers returned from breakfast in the dining car, they occupied themselves with reading or sleeping or talking as the never-ending greenness rolled by outside the dirty windows. But Liliana was as interested now in the people inside the coach as she was in the view outside.

The old couple across the aisle, somewhat more rumpled now but still playing cards, astounded Liliana when they produced a narrow piece of wood like a ruler with a groove running down its centre, a package of long thin papers, and a blue can of what she realized was tobacco. Carefully they laid a piece of the paper onto the wood, indented it into the groove, stuffed the groove with tobacco, performed some intricate move, and rolled a long lumpy cigarette. Then they produced a razor blade and quickly cut this into normal-length cigarettes which they carefully placed in a crumpled blue package. All this was accomplished without a word between them.

The train had passed through several quite large towns by now, always with the same untidy debris-filled yards surrounding shabby wooden buildings—larger in size near the train station, then decreasing as they moved through and out of the town. On several occasions when the conductor passed by announcing a stop of ten minutes or so, Liliana joined the other passengers in taking a walk along the platform to stretch her legs. She was by this time quite uncomfortable in her good wool suit, wrinkled and hot and feeling very unclean. But she smoothed her skirt and made an effort to stand up straight and stride along, her purse primly over her arm. Posture was important, Nonna always said. How she longed to be able to bathe and shampoo her hair, to change into clean clothes. She began to understand the apparent custom of comfort over appearance which she had noticed both on the train and among the people on the station platforms, a concept new to her. *Back home one dressed according to the importance of the occasion—or was it for effect—or to impress others?* She sighed. *And how many more days in this limbo? If I spent this long on the train at home I'd be somewhere in Russia by now—and I wouldn't be wearing this. Why didn't somebody tell me how hot it gets here in summer?* The now-familiar anger wrenched her again. No one had helped her. *Signora* Lombardo could have suggested that she change into something more appropriate for train travel here, but she hadn't. No one had told her the truth. And what other unpleasant surprises were in store for her? A cynicism quite foreign to Liliana crept over her. She would have to be strong, because she was truly alone now. She could trust no one.

Liliana sat unmoving, her face turned toward the window. They had been travelling alongside an enormous body of dark green water which continued to the horizon, fringed on the edge nearest the tracks and as far along as she could see with trees like the ones in the pictures Carlo had sent, trees which seemed to grow out of buff and apricot-coloured rocks jutting over the water. It was a lake, *Signora* Lombardo told her, but Liliana was sceptical. It looked like a sea. An inland sea. The tracks eventually veered away from the water's edge and entered a sort of tunnel of trees through which they sped until Liliana noticed the forest changing gradually. The trees thinned out and the impression now was of more light, more lightness, pale trunks topped by clouds of paler green leaves under an azure sky that soared above. She could make out the individual trees now, with low bushes growing between them and in some areas nothing between the slender trunks with the black markings except tufts of yellow grass. She thought she would like to be able to get off this train and to run, unhindered, through those trees until she disappeared. But the strange thing was that there were no buildings for kilometer after kilometer, no sign of human habitation. Had no one ever walked in these woods? Hunted? Fished? Built a home? Liliana was amazed at this apparent lack of any sign of man's presence as far as the eye could see. So much land—untouched by humans. It was incredible! Would she ever be able to explain the vastness of it when she wrote to her family? They simply wouldn't believe her.

At each stop one or two people could be seen leaving the train, but no one from their car got off, although they were joined by several new passengers. One of these was a man who sat alone in his rumpled light-coloured suit. *At least he's wearing a suit.* He seemed to be drinking something out of a container which was still encased in a brown paper bag. When he stood up and moved down the aisle past her, Liliana saw that he was swaying more than the movement of the train necessitated, and she realized that the drink in the bag must be something alcoholic. This swaying progression up and down was repeated numerous times over the hours, and each time he heralded his arrival by the fumes which preceded him. No one paid him the slightest attention, and eventually, as the second night approached, he fell asleep, snoring loudly.

As Liliana twisted and turned in her seat, at one point standing up and turning around like a dog before he lies down, she noticed the two quiet women in the seat behind her making the sign of the cross and bowing their heads, their lips moving as they fingered the black beads in their hands. They were saying the rosary! They *were* nuns! Nuns in short dresses, without wimples! *Oh God, what next?* she thought, ducking back into her seat. But then she, too, tried to pray. She tried to pray for serenity, for peace in her heart, for her lost sense of optimism. She remembered herself as a young child—how everyone said she was like a ray of sunshine—how she had always been sure that everything would turn out well. Did all children have that sense of joy—and did all girls lose it when they became women? She felt only profound sadness as she drifted off, to sleep away the second night of her journey to Cedar Ridge. She dreamt of the simple church built from the cement of the airstrip, and she was there with Carlo, in it. When she woke, there were tears on her cheeks, but she couldn't remember why.

The train began to slow again and the whistle sounded. They entered a town which, although spread out over quite a large area, consisted almost exclusively of low painted wooden buildings, some extremely unkempt-looking. The station was as usual dark and shabby, mottled here and there with unknown words painted helter-skelter on its sides. She saw that there were people sitting on the platform in the shade of the ugly building, leaning against it, while others stood about surrounded by the usual assortment of bundles and bags. She made a move to stand up, intending to get out and stretch her legs, but an almost imperceptible nod and a quick frown from *Signora* Lombardo stopped her. No one got off.

She became aware that they were being joined in their coach by a family which settled very quietly in seats just behind the skinny old couple still playing cards, so that Liliana could watch with interest the father, the mother, and the two long-legged boys as they arranged themselves without speaking, placing their lumpy-looking bag on the floor between them. The boys wore short pants, and Liliana saw that their legs were tanned a nut brown. And so were their hands and arms and faces and necks. And then she saw the two adults. The man wore a shirt of faded plaid, neatly pressed. She could see the crease down the arms to the neatly-buttoned frayed cuffs over his thin brown wrists. Then she noticed the thick braid of jet black hair hanging down to the middle of his back. He spoke softly to the boys, whose huge black eyes studied Liliana, then he sat back and stared straight ahead. The woman, in a clean but faded cotton dress, did the same. And from some forgotten part of Liliana's brain came the word *Indians. They're Canadian Indians.* And she could see in her mind's eye the picture in her school textbook of people dressed in fringed animal hides posed in front of a tent with poles sticking out of the top. *But these people don't look like that.* Quickly she averted her eyes. She must remember her manners. She was struck by the dignity of their demeanour. Imagine, their people had always lived here. They had not come from somewhere else across the ocean as she and everyone else in the coach had at one time or another. A startling new thought. These were in truth the native people of this land, just as she was a native of Europe. *I wonder what they're thinking about us? Are they wondering too? Wondering where we've come from, where we're going? And why?*

As she dozed off, it occurred to her how she would like to be able to talk to the woman, to ask her about her life, about where she lived and why she was travelling. About how she had come to be married to this man. About what she thought, what she felt.

Periodically *Signora* Lombardo had decided another mealtime had arrived, usually prompted by the passage through the carriage of the dining-car steward announcing a meal, and Liliana would endure once more the embarrassment of the elaborate production of the lunch. Secretly she hoped they would soon run out of food and have to go to the dining car as most of the others were doing, but there seemed to be an endless supply of cheese and bread and meat. And wine to drink.

Time passed in segments of waking and sleeping as the train rumbled across the land, and Liliana was often not sure when she opened her eyes whether it was night or day, whether it was the second day or the third. The hours were punctuated by the occasional stroll along a platform or by the offering of increasingly stale food by *Signora* Lombardo, and Liliana became almost desperate in her boredom, in her anxiety to get off the train. "Just a little longer, dear. Be patient," said the older woman in an effort to comfort her.

Liliana closed her eyes, willing herself to sleep in order to escape, trying to conjure up the faces of her loved ones. By sleeping, or at least by daydreaming, more of the endless time would slip away. But by now Liliana could only remember Carlo's name. His face had long since deserted her. Even the beloved faces of Mama and Nonna and Luisa were fading—as though her life back home had been a dream—vague, distant—and in her fretful sleep she saw only dark-skinned strangers peering from behind white-trunked trees and the sound of distant thunder. Or was it drums?

Brilliant sunlight burning a streak across her face woke her sometime on the third day, and she saw that they had left the forest behind—who knew how long ago? She looked at her watch—it was almost noon. Outside were only undulating waves of bright yellow grain disappearing to the horizon where the endless blue sky cupped down to meet the yellow, and she almost stopped breathing. How beautiful, with the bright sun pouring down.

"Where are we?" She rubbed her eyes and yawned behind her hand.

"These are the famous great plains of Canada," explained the Lombardos, happy to be able to answer her questions. "We're in Saskatchewan. Think about it! All that pasta we ate back home—all made from this grain."

She had never quite believed what she had been taught about these endless fields of grain, but it was true. The scene was breathtaking. *Madonna, if only Zio Ennio could see this! How many times would his little fields fit into this immensity?* She was transfixed by the strangeness and brilliance of the scene and she stared out the window until her eyes burned. She had to close them. And though she knew she had been dozing, every time she opened her eyes she saw the same thing, fields and fields of grain, punctuated here and there by little towns with tall orange towers which she was told were for the storage of the grain. *Granai.* They looked a bit like the turrets and towers of Tuscany glimpsed here and there, but brighter, glowing warmly in the clear light. She couldn't imagine how much grain each one must hold. Rivers of grain.

Sometimes they stopped at very little towns where old men with suspenders holding up baggy pants stood motionless on the platform, watches in hand. Often no one got on or off, but there always seemed to be bulging grey canvas sacks being transferred. "What's in those dirty bags?"

"Mail—letters and parcels. The sacks are probably really old—probably been thrown down on the platform, rain or shine, for years."

At one of these seemingly deserted prairie towns a group of women, dressed identically, got on and sat at the far end of the coach. Liliana could not help but stare in amazement. There were two grown women and three teen-aged girls, each wearing an ankle-length dress, black with small white polka dots. Their heads were covered by kerchiefs of the same dotted fabric, knotted securely under their chins. Their faces were solemn and pale. They seemed ill-at-ease, lowering themselves self-consciously into their seats with downcast eyes, carefully distributing their cloth bundles about their feet and then sitting very still, their hands folded quietly in their laps. They did not speak, and they did not look about.

Liliana leaned forward so as not to be overheard, but she couldn't resist remarking on their unusual appearance. She had never seen anything like it. "Look, look at those women all dressed alike, and so oddly. Who in the world are they?"

"Hutterites," whispered *Signora* Lombardo, cupping her hand around her mouth. "They have some kind of religion that keeps them apart from others—you can see that they still dress as people did in the old days."

"Buy why all the same?"

"Well, I imagine they must have to make their dresses from whatever cheap fabric the men bring home in bolts. That's why they're all dressed alike. Poor creatures, those women, completely under the thumbs of the men," and she cast a fierce look at the sleeping and docile figure of her husband. "They come from Russia or Germany or some place like that—they still don't speak English anyway," she went on earnestly, "and they live all together on big farms. Those ones must be going to another colony to help out."

Liliana's gaze was turned now from the panorama that swept by the train to the assortment of people who surrounded her. For the first time she became consciously aware of the variety of ages and races and religions that made up her travelling companions, and she understood that here in the dirty coach rocketing through the countryside was a microcosm of society in this new world. A world of which she was now a part whether she liked it or not, just as much an oddity in the eyes of these people as they were in hers. A country made up of strangers—except for *them.* Her eyes went to the native family, sitting so silently, and she wondered what the woman was thinking. Did she love the man she sat beside? At least she hadn't been expected to leave her homeland and travel to God knows where to be with him.

"Jas—per, Jas—per," intoned the conductor in his now-familiar sing-song, passing through the coach as Liliana watched the sheer mauve and pinkish-grey rock faces pass by, interspersed with the dark green of cedar and pine. They had been travelling through these craggy mountains for many hours now, and she knew these were the famous Rockies. They had entered them quite unexpectedly, one minute on the plains (or so it seemed to her), the next into the soft blue of the foothills, their gentle slopes giving rise quickly to the soaring peaks mottled with areas of snow. The rock surfaces near the tracks changed colour almost imperceptibly, merging from cream to ochre to rose, covered here and there with intricate growth, silvery lichen and soft green moss, then stands of dark trees farther back from the tracks. Rivers of white stones ran along beside them, and her companions had several times shouted and pointed out some wild creature gravely watching the train pass by.

The Lombardos and Liliana, along with several of the other groups in their coach, were busy now organizing their belongings in preparation for changing trains in Jasper. Those who were travelling north and west toward the Pacific Ocean would have to take a different line, while those who were going on to Vancouver would be able to stay on the train, they explained to her. Liliana didn't care. She only wanted the journey to be over by whatever means, and if they had to struggle off with their bags and bundles, and then onto another train, so be it.

She had never felt so filthy and miserable in her life as she followed her companions onto the platform. The sharp-peaked mountains soared all around them, dark blue with rivers of white ice flowing down from their peaks, but Liliana barely lifted her head.

Chapter 9

Jasper was far behind them, and Liliana was enduring another uncomfortable night. She had often felt herself rocking quite severely from side to side, the train swaying as it rounded sharp curves, slowing as it climbed, gathering speed on the downward slope. The terrain must be rougher and wilder, she thought. *Where in God's name am I going?* Her head rolled back and forth on the plush seatback and she caught glimpses of her white visage in the dark glass of the window—or was it her? Liliana cupped her hands on either side of her face so as to see into the darkness outside. They were travelling now on a high trestle built over a deep gorge. Far below she could make out a narrow channel of dark blue water edged with white tracery, disappearing between cliffs that looked as though they had been sheared off by some giant knife. And that same giant knife had seemingly sliced through the rocks to allow the passage of the train as it rumbled along in its inexorable journey to Cedar Ridge.

Liliana knew she was very near her destination now, and she felt her insides constrict each time she allowed herself to think about her reunion with Carlo. It was as though she were travelling to an assignation with a stranger, someone she had heard of once, who had written her letters once, but not someone she had ever touched, had ever been held by. *Why* couldn't she see his face?

"Where are we—are we near Cedar Ridge? Will it be much longer?"

"No, not too much longer—maybe another four hours. We'll arrive at our stop in the late afternoon, and then you'll get to Cedar Ridge an hour or so after that."

The mountains had receded now, were softer in contour, their tops disappearing into low-lying cloud. Tall dark trees, cedars she guessed, pressed in upon the tracks which seemed to have been laid through a tunnel of these trees which formed an impenetrable wall on either side. Wisps of mist rolled by between the train-window and the trees, and in some patches their tops were obscured by fog. Grey rain lashed silently at the windows. Liliana shivered.

And then they arrived at the stop before hers, where the only two people in this world who were her friends, the Lombardos, were to leave. They stood and turned toward her and she read the unspoken concern in their eyes as she allowed herself to be muffled in the sweaty but earnest embrace of first one and then the other. Her tears spilled down her cheeks but she made no attempt to wipe them as she was hugged and patted consolingly. She nodded wordlessly as *Signora* Lombardo assured her that Carlo would be waiting at the next stop. "You'll see, my dear, you'll see. He'll be there and everything will be fine. Everything will be just as it should be. It's not so bad here.

You'll get used to it. I did." And in a flurry of bundles and waves, they left her. *"Ciao, Liliana. Arrividerci. Ciao, Ciao."*

Liliana sank back into the seat by the window, alone now. Almost everyone else had left their coach, only the two elderly card-players remained, their interminable game over. They had collected their bags and bundles and were sitting quietly, faces toward the window, watching the interminable wall of trees on either side of the tracks, softened only by occasional patches of wispy mist. The coach was silent.

It seemed like an eternity, but it couldn't have been more than half-an-hour before Liliana heard the conductor's voice approaching as he chanted "Ce—dar Ri—idge, Ce—dar Ri—idge," and she was overcome with a fit of trembling so deep and fierce she thought she would never be able to get to her feet. But she did, and as she retrieved her luggage and her wrinkled green coat she could hear her own breath coming in little gasps. *Soon. Soon. Try to be calm. Breathe slowly. Surely, he is out there, waiting, and surely, I'll know him the moment I set eyes on him. It will be all right.*

And she was off the train and a dark bristly cheek was pressed against hers, and she was in a grip so tight she could barely breathe, her arms around his neck, her hands feeling the familiar tweed of his back. "Liliana, Liliana, *cara*," he murmured into her hair, "I've missed you so much. *Ti amo*— I love you."

At last, the comforting sound of the language of home, the familiar beloved phrases. Her hands pressed against his chest and she pushed him back just far enough so that she could look into his face, and he into hers.

"Oh Carlo, my sweet Carlo! Oh God, how long I've waited for this day—and now you see me like this—so dirty and rumpled—don't look at me, don't look," she said, burying her face in his shoulder. But he turned her face back to his and kissed her on the mouth, a hard long kiss that startled her, and she pushed him away again, gasping, the sobs in her throat strangling her as she tried to tell him how angry she was. She felt it, deep in her body, but she could not get it out. Furious. Wanting to be in his arms, but furious. Wanting him to know, but wanting to be held, to be comforted. Even by this stranger with the familiar face.

"Oh Liliana, I've waited so long to hold you, to kiss you. You are as beautiful to me as ever. Don't worry, you'll soon have a chance to get cleaned up. You're just overtired," he went on, as he saw the tears coursing down her cheeks. "Come along, dearest. Come along," and putting a protective arm around her waist, he hurried her off the platform and through the station. "I've borrowed a car from one of the guys. He's away on holidays. I've got it for a month. Let's go home." And before Liliana could properly take in the scene, the low, stuccoed, grey building crouched in front of the dark mountain, she was in the car and Carlo was wheeling out of the parking lot. Liliana was aware of the dark mountain looming up just behind the station and its surrounding buildings, a mountain which looked as though it had been burned in a terrible fire; the trees on its flanks reduced to skeletons as they pointed skyward from the powdery earth. "No, not a fire," Carlo said as her head swivelled back to look at it. "It's some dreadful disease that has struck only this mountain. Or so the company says." He gestured toward the right, and she could see clouds of grey smoke puffing up into the already-grey sky beyond the fringe of dark green trees which stood behind the buildings.

"The smoke's coming from the mill over there where we work," he said, pointing at the darkest concentration of clouds. "It's like dying and going to Hell, working in there with the fumes and the smoke." He was silent for a moment. "But the money's good, very good."

It was raining, the wipers beating their insistent rhythm as Liliana peered around her. This rain was a relentless drizzle, fine and invisible, not at all like the unmistakable rain of home. She felt bewildered and faintly sick at her stomach. "Where is everything? Is this the town? Where are the shops? Where are you taking me? And what is that awful stench?"

"Relax, darling, relax," Carlo said. "What you smell is the plant. Sometimes it's like this when the clouds are low. But not always, and not up where the houses are. I'm taking you to a nice house, the home of friends. Tomorrow I'll take you around the town and out to the plant, so that you can get your bearings. But for today, just let me look after you. I feel as though we've been apart for a thousand years."

She felt more than saw him beside her, his hands with the silky black hairs on the backs of the slender fingers gripping the steering wheel as he talked. "How was the trip? How is everyone at home? Look, there's the hotel over there, where the bear walked into the bar, like I told you in the letter . . . . are you tired? Hungry? We'll soon be there."

Suddenly they were driving over a steel bridge, its rough grid-like surface causing the tires to emit a horrible screeching sound as they passed under its gaudy orange girders. "That's the Cedar River," Carlo shouted over the noise. "It empties into the Pacific Ocean, out beyond the plant. I'll take you to see everything tomorrow." Liliana stared down at the fast-moving brown water that ran between banks of white pebbles bordered by the same dark trees. Farther along the bank she saw two men in hip waders standing knee-deep in the river, their lines arcing out over the water as they cast. The silhouettes of the trees wavered and rippled through the rivulets of rain that ran down the side window, and she thought of the time that she and her girlfriends had gone into a Fun House at the fair and had laughed at their images rippling like this in the trick mirrors. So long ago. And then they had burst out of the tent and Carlo had been waiting for her, grinning.

She turned and looked hard at Carlo's profile as he drove on, talking quietly now, telling her that he had bought a little house as he had promised, that he had furnished it and supplied it with the necessities for housekeeping. "Nothing beautiful or fine, you know, just whatever I could find. People gave me bits of furniture and so on, and I know that we can make do until we can afford better things."

Liliana did not reply, though inside she was seething. *"Until we can afford. . . No, no, not that long,"* she thought, *"We won't be here that long."*

"But where will I stay?" she asked, and out burst all the questions at once in a torrent of words. "We can't stay together yet! Where will I go? And the marriage, what about the wedding? Is it arranged? Is there a church? A priest?" She had been so silent for so long, she couldn't stop them now, all those unasked questions. And she was not afraid to let him know how she felt, though she had promised herself on the train that she would keep quiet, that by her silence he would know of her suffering and be sorry. "Oh Carlo, I'm frightened and so tired. I didn't want to come here at all, you know. Don't you understand? I had no idea how far away it would turn out to be!" She heard the anger, the desperation in her own voice, but she couldn't stop herself. "Why? Why didn't you come home?"

"I couldn't," he said, looking straight ahead. "I couldn't afford two tickets and besides, I couldn't get the time off. After all, it would only be for a wedding."

"But no one told me anything! I had no idea! Here I am, all wrinkled and dirty. Just look at my poor green coat!" Her tears caught in her throat. "*Madonna*, what a long, long trip. I just want to wash myself and go to bed. Where are you taking me?" She knew that she sounded like a child, bewildered and exhausted. And that, she realized, was exactly how she felt. Young and alone and frightened. Well, she thought, momentarily defiant, Carlo would just have to put up with her. He had wanted her to come, and here she was, tears and grime and all. *Comfort me, you idiot, don't just stare straight ahead as if I'm not really here. I came, like you insisted, and now it's up to you to make it all right.*

But, "*Dai, dai, cara, tu sei troppo stanca*–you're just over-tired," was all he said, and she turned her head to stare out the window through the drizzle at the cluster of low buildings, barely glimpsed through the smoky pall, that huddled alongside the road. The sky, laden with black clouds, pressed down upon the little town, the buildings seemingly flattened by its weight.

"Those are the shops over there, not too many, but you can find what you need. Not like back home, but passable. You'll get used to it."

Now Carlo had come to an intersection and up ahead was a large pink stuccoed building, perhaps five stories high, the tallest building she had seen so far. As they turned left and drove past it, Carlo told her that it was the hospital. And it did look somewhat comforting and solid, though not at all like a hospital. It seemed to be made of concrete, in a spare, modern design quite unlike what she had seen of the other buildings in Cedar Ridge. Across the road from it was a dense wall of dark green trees, and as she tried and failed to see through them and between them for some sign of habitation, Carlo told her again that he was taking her to the home of friends, a married couple, where she would stay until the wedding. "You'll like Gina and Mario. They're from our province, not too far from San Michele. I feel as though I've known them forever. There are so few of us here that we stick together. *Brava gente*—good people. Gina came to marry Mario last year, so she knows how you feel. Mario and I work together, and we go fishing sometimes. You'll like them, and they'll be good to you. Please don't cry, Liliana. Don't cry. It will be all right. *Non piangere, cara, non piangere. Ti amo.*" And he reached out his hand and caressed her cheek as, with the other, he drove the car down a street of identical houses with wooden siding and pitched roofs. Each house was painted a different pastel colour with contrasting trim, each one with a tidy patch of bright green grass on either side of the cement walkway going up to the door. They reminded Liliana of the houses children draw, a pointed roof with one window under it, then the front door with a window on either side, coloured pink or yellow or pale green. Colours dulled by the smoky pall, they huddled under the heavy, dark sky that loomed overhead.

As the car turned into the driveway of one of these houses, Liliana saw a smiling, dark-haired woman, obviously pregnant, step out of the doorway. And in a flurry of activity of which Liliana was barely aware, she was presented to Gina and folded into a warm embrace while Carlo carried her three burgundy leather bags, looking oddly out-of-place, into the house. Carlo was constantly touching her now, a hand on the small of her back, a caress of her hair, a touch on her hand, as he and Gina sat her on the sofa and Gina offered her a cup of espresso.

"You must eat something, my dear," said Gina warmly. "I have some *brodo* on the stove. Won't you please have a little?" And without waiting for an answer, she went into the kitchen and returned with a tray on which sat a bowl of the warm broth with *tortellini*, a slice of crusty bread, and some cheese. It was exactly what her mother would have offered her after such a long journey, and Liliana ate it all with murmurings of gratitude between each bite. As she ate, Gina talked, answering her unasked questions with simple directness. "Don't worry about a thing now. We've made all the arrangements for your wedding next Saturday. Father Haber will perform the ceremony, and then we'll go to a small reception room in the hotel for a dinner in the evening. And dancing. That's what they do here. You'll see, it will be lovely. We've arranged for the nuptial mass, and then we'll come back here for lunch, just a few of us. Oh, and Carlo has asked Mario and I to stand up for you, to be the witnesses— I hope that's all right. So soon we'll be *comare* and *compare!*" Liliana nodded mutely as she chewed on the delicious *tortellini*. It hadn't even occurred to her that there would have to be witnesses to sign the register. But Carlo had thought of everything, it seemed. "We've invited all the other Italian families for the reception in the evening. There'll be about fifty people. Yes, fifty," she went on, noticing Liliana's glance of surprise.

"We'll have antipasto and then vegetables and roast chicken, and I've ordered a big cake. It will be lovely, you'll see. Not as elegant as you would have had in a restaurant at home, but everyone knows that's the best we can do in Cedar Ridge. Many of the other young women here have had the same sort of wedding. One friend of mine, who was the first Italian woman to come to Cedar Ridge, was the only woman at her own wedding. Imagine! The only woman! At least you'll have all Carlo's friends and their wives. And you'll get to meet them all starting tomorrow. You'll see, you'll get along very well." And then Gina stopped talking as she saw the tears rolling down Liliana's cheeks. Liliana couldn't help it. A *stranger—telling me about my own wedding. I can't bear it. It shouldn't be like this, strangers deciding about my wedding day, about my life. Not even Carlo has that right.*

"Don't cry, my dear," said Gina. "You're just overtired. Carlo! Go now! Can't you see the poor girl is exhausted. She needs to get some rest."

"Your're right, Gina. I'll come for her tomorrow morning. She's had enough for today," said Carlo, tipping his wine glass and draining it. He kissed Liliana gently on the forehead and looking once fiercely into her green eyes, strode out of the room, leaving her limp against the rough cushions of the sofa, watching his retreating back.

As Gina, whose husband was apparently at work on the afternoon shift, stood to pick up the tray and turned to walk to the kitchen, she caught Liliana looking intently at her legs.

Gina was wearing pants! "Yes, Liliana, *cara*, we all wear pants here. And mark my word, you'll soon do the same. It's the damp, the perpetual rain. Skirts are just too cold and uncomfortable in this climate. Even though it's only August, you can smell the autumn in the air already and the days are getting very short. Soon the snow will start to fall, and you too will need pants!" Liliana smiled and ducked her head, embarrassed at having been caught staring, but secretly she thought that she would never succumb to this aberration— pants indeed! Not her. What would Nonna say? She would be shocked at the very suggestion, and Mama would be equally horrified. She hadn't even been allowed to go out to the little grocery store on the corner without putting on stockings, no matter how hot it was. Pants indeed! How immodest! But Gina only laughed at the shocked expression on Liliana's face as she picked up the tray and carried it out.

Liliana sighed and looked around her, registering for the first time her surroundings. The rooms seemed to be very small, opening one into another. In fact, they had entered into the kitchen from the outside door, passing through it into this room. She could see that there were several other rooms off a corridor, and a flight of bare stairs with brown rubber treads led up. She felt as though she were in a cave, a small, dim cave. The ceilings seemed so low, the walls so thin, the floors so bare. This room was painted a pale green, the floor covered in mustard-coloured linoleum tiles, some of their corners slightly upturned. The sofa on which she sat, and its matching armchair, were covered in some sort of bristly maroon fabric, worn and frayed on the arms. There were no pictures on the walls, only a few straggly green plants here and there. The curtains on the row of three windows were thin, a patterned fabric that shone where the light caught it. The ugliness of this barren little room, its shabby makeshift air, shocked Liliana. She thought she had never seen a room so ugly. It looked temporary, without history, without personality. It was as if no one really lived here, only visited, camped. *Oh God, what have I come to?!*

Everything seemed to be disconnected now, unreal. She closed her eyes, leaning against the rough sofa back, only faintly aware of the clattering of dishes in the kitchen. There was an insistent buzzing noise in her head—tiredness, she knew. It was only early evening, not really bedtime yet, but there was nothing she wanted more than to be able to wash herself and get into a clean bed. Would she ever feel normal again?

"*Povera* Liliana, *povera ragazza*," lamented Gina as she re-entered the room. "You, poor girl, come with me. I'll take you to your bedroom. You really must get some sleep. Now don't worry, I'll call you in the morning before Carlo arrives. He's been beside himself these past few days, knowing you were en route but not hearing anything from you. He was really worried." Surprised to hear that Carlo had worried about her, Liliana was secretly, guiltily glad. It served him right to have a little misery too. She stood on shaky legs and followed Gina up the stairs, relieved to be leaving the ugly room, hoping where she was going would be more comfortable, would feel less strange. At least she would be alone at last, free to give vent to her misery and the anger which boiled just beneath the surface. It was so unfair, that she should be expected to do this—to come here, to marry here, to live here. And it was even worse than she had imagined. It was all so—so barren, so raw and uncivilized.

She wondered how Gina could be so unembarrassed, unaware of the shabbiness of it all. Didn't she see? But then Gina had not likely come from as well-appointed a home as hers. She knew how much the standard of living from home to home had varied, even within the same cortile. Not every family put equal emphasis on having finer things, on having as gracious and well-ordered a life as their poverty would allow. Carlo's parents, seated at their bare kitchen table, flashed into her head. Perhaps Gina was better-off now than she had been at home.

At the top of the stairs Liliana turned and looked into the bedroom which Gina indicated was to be hers. She caught her breath. There, under the window, stood her shiny blue trunk, the one Mama and Nonna had packed so carefully all those weeks before. At last, something familiar. She ran and knelt beside it, caressing its smooth surface as memory flooded over her and she saw clearly each beautiful, each precious thing that was packed in it. And she saw her mother's hands carefully laying in her wedding dress last of all. "My dress, oh my poor dress," she gasped, turning to Gina. "Do you think we could take it out now?"

So Gina got a hanger, a pretty one, padded with pale blue satin, and carefully hung the wedding dress on the curtain rod in front of the window above the trunk. Its pale white silhouette hung, disembodied, in front of the dark glass, and Liliana felt a wave of emotion wash over her.

The wedding will be in August.

Her wedding dress. Her wedding! She shouldn't be here in this ugly little house, with this strange woman fussing over the folds of the dress. It should be her mother and her Nonna and her sister with her, and she should be happy. It should be a time of shared joy, a time for the women of her family to envelop her in their love, giving her advice, giving her courage. She would be married next Saturday—in five days. But she felt no joy. Only a great tiredness, and that knot of anger that was always there. She was trembling, and the skin of her face felt taut.

Finally Gina had the great good sense, after showing her where the bathroom was and admonishing her to sleep well and not to worry, to leave her.

Liliana sat on the edge of the bed for a long time, looking about her at the sloping ceiling over the barren little room with the pale yellow walls. The bed was covered with a thin yellow coverlet, there was a chipped brown chest, and on the small painted table that passed for a bedside stand—the only nod toward a gracious touch—a few white daisies in a glass. She took one and held it to her face, but it had no perfume. Slowly she picked up her smallest travel case and extracted one of her fine, high-necked nighties, laying it out on the bed. Then she placed her silver-backed comb and brush on the chipped and stained brown chest. These lovely things looked incongruous in the barren room, but as she continued to find and take out her toiletries, her robe and slippers, she felt somehow comforted. These things were hers, they reminded her of the home she had left, of her family, of who she was. But she had never felt so alone in her life. Slowly, as though sleepwalking, she went down the stairs to the bathroom.

Liliana was glad to see that, while small, it was quite modern, much like the one in *Signora* Lombardo's house in Toronto. The hot water would be plentiful, she knew, and the towels were soft and clean. After she had bathed and shampooed her hair she caught a glimpse of herself in the misted mirror, and saw that her face was pale and her large green eyes looked back at her worriedly. There were little frown lines between her eyes, like her mother's, and she thought with a start that she looked much older. Sighing, she put on her new nightie and robe and moving quietly back up the stairs to her room, became faintly aware of music coming from down below. There was no television in this town. Reception was impossible because of the distances and the mountains, they had explained to her. What she was hearing was a scratchy recording of an old song. *Torna a Sorrento.* The plaintive notes of the tenor filled her with such sadness she could hardly bear it. Gina was waiting for her husband to come home. "*Buona notte,*" she called out when she heard Liliana going back upstairs. "Sleep well."

As Liliana entered her bedroom and closed the door to shut out the nostalgic refrain, the sight of the wedding dress hanging starkly in front of the window startled her for a moment. She had almost forgotten why she was here. She turned back the yellow coverlet and then knelt on the cold linoleum floor. She folded her hands on the edge of the bed and closed her eyes. She needed to pray. She needed to pray for courage, for acceptance, for peace. But she felt no inner calm, no peace. *Why? Why was I chosen for this unwelcome adventure? Why me? It's so unfair!* She knelt there for a long time, half-dreaming, half-praying, until at last she crossed herself and got into bed. Eyes closed, she saw Carlo's face floating above hers, and behind him, the smoky mountains. She fell asleep to the sound of the rain drumming on the thin roof just above her head, and dreamt of red geraniums and girls in white dresses dancing among them.

Chapter 10

Several times during that first night in Gina and Mario's house, Liliana awoke to the sound of the rain drumming on the roof just over her head and stared, puzzled, into the darkness until she made out the dress silhouetted against the window and remembered where she was—and why. But sleep came again each time, until she awoke fully to the realization of voices and laughter and the smell of coffee. She lay there for a while, thinking about what lay ahead, then, remembering the tears of the night before, felt embarrassed. She must maintain her dignity, there would be no more tears. She could hear Nonna's voice in her head, telling her to be strong, to be calm. *You are a woman now, you must act like one.* She arose and went quietly downstairs to the bathroom. Then she dressed in one of her new skirts and a white blouse with fine embroidery on the collar. She had taken her navy *impermeabile*—her raincoat—out of her trunk last night so that the creases would have a chance to fall out, and she placed it now over her arm. She would need it. Today was the first day of her new life in Cedar Ridge, and she squared her shoulders and moved toward the stairs, scarcely betraying the trembling she felt inside.

Downstairs, Carlo sat at the kitchen table with another man, shorter, with darker hair, who rose quickly to his feet when she entered the room, then sat again when he had been introduced as Mario, Gina's husband. Gina moved over to stand behind Mario's chair, her hands massaging his shoulders in a gesture of such matter-of-fact tenderness that Liliana felt a lump in her throat. Would she and Carlo ever attain this easy sensuality, this companionship? Carlo had risen too when he saw her in the doorway, and the smile on his face as he moved toward her was so open, so genuinely full of love, that again her throat constricted. She was glad when he put his arms around her, pulling her face to his shoulder so that she didn't have to speak just yet. She stood calmly in his embrace, conscious of the eyes of the other two on them, but oddly unembarrassed. Gently she placed a kiss on Carlo's sweet-smelling cheek before sitting on the chair that Gina gestured toward.

The men took up where they had left off, discussing the details of the wedding reception, who would pick up what, when, their voices droning on, and Liliana felt herself tuning them out.

As Gina moved about the kitchen with its painted cupboards and simple wooden table and chairs, Liliana's gaze followed her. Gina's pregnancy was in its early stages, her stomach only slightly swollen under the loose sweater she wore, but Liliana saw that every now and then she would place her hand on the bump, almost caressing the unseen baby. And that Mario would sometimes reach out and touch her stomach as well, as though reassuring the child that he was there too. Liliana had never seen a young couple act this way, open and completely unselfconscious in front of others, and it discomfited her somewhat while at the same time she liked what she saw. It occurred to her that they would not likely have acted quite this way back home, that their removal from all that was familiar had somehow freed them—freed them to act unselfconsciously, according to their true feelings, in a way that would not have been possible before. Would this begin to happen for them too—for her and Carlo?

Gina served her a cup of *espresso* and some *biscotti*, touching her shoulder lightly as she placed them in front of her. "*Mangia, stella*, eat, you need to be careful not to get sick after such a long trip," she said warmly, and then moved on about her tasks. She appeared to be making bread, something Liliana had never seen done back home, where crusty rolls were delivered to the door each morning, as if by magic. "We have to make our own bread here. You wouldn't believe the white fluffy stuff they call bread. We can't eat it," Gina explained over her shoulder. "I had to learn, and you will too."

"Don't worry about Liliana, I know she'll do just fine," said Carlo, placing a reassuring hand over hers. "I know she's going to be a wonderful wife." Liliana threw him a glance of gratitude—Carlo seemed to understand how any admonition of Gina's would be somewhat overwhelming, and it surprised her that he knew how she was feeling. Gina laughed easily and went on kneading the dough, picking it up and turning it, then slapping it down on the counter. There was a smear of flour across her abdomen but she seemed not to care.

Gratefully Liliana realized that their attention was at least momentarily diverted from her, and she took the opportunity to have a good look around. She saw that the kitchen was more modern than she had expected from her impression of the house last night, with an electric stove standing beside a white electric refrigerator. There was a grey-coloured metal sink, rather grimy, set in the yellow countertop, and above it a wide curtainless window. It was a businesslike kitchen, lacking any sense of warmth or character, but Liliana saw that it had all the amenities. In fact, it would certainly be easier to work in than the kitchen at home. And surely it could be made more attractive than this. She caught herself mentally putting up some flowered curtains.

Quietly sipping her coffee, she listened to the conversation ebb around her, nodding and smiling occasionally as Gina and Mario and Carlo once more went over certain details of the impending events as though they hardly concerned her. Everything was well in hand. It was as though they were discussing someone else's wedding, the conversation hardly interesting to her as she nibbled on the *biscotti*. It was as though she were living someone else's life. And finally, Carlo said, "*Ben, cara, andiamo*. Let's go and see our house. And then I'll take you to meet some of your new friends. Everyone is anxious to meet you."

Liliana was glad she had dressed carefully as Carlo held her navy raincoat so that she could slip her arms into the sleeves. Then he reached out and proprietarily turned up her collar so that it framed her face, kissing her quickly on the forehead. Her cheeks flamed as she stepped out and walked down the driveway to the car. Carlo held the car door open for her and then got in behind the wheel. She turned to look at him, taking in again the silky brown hair and the dark hazel eyes, the long fingers on the steering wheel. He was beginning to feel familiar. She remembered how she had felt when he had come whizzing into the cortile on his bicycle—he had always made her stomach feel like butterflies. Still, he seemed much more serious now—he had filled out in the way boys do when they become men. But when he turned to speak to her, smiling into her eyes, she saw that he was the same Carlo she had loved. But different. Why did she feel so remote? She wanted to throw her arms around his neck and press her mouth to his, and cry and scream at him, and be comforted. But she couldn't—she mustn't. She was a woman now.

They had been in the car only a few minutes when he wheeled around the corner and up another driveway on the street behind Gina's, stopping in front of a house painted in a soft pink colour. She turned and looked at him quizzically. It was exactly the same as Gina's: the pitched roof with one window under it, the door set in the middle with a window on either side, the patch of green grass bisected by the sidewalk leading to it. And as she glanced up and down the street, she saw that all the houses were the same, distinguishable only by the different colours of paint on their wooden sides. She saw no one. She wondered for the first time who lived behind those dark windows, who lived in those houses glimpsed through the slanting drizzle? Could anyone else have experienced what she was living these days—this terrifying aloneness? Her eyes went from window to window, hoping to see some evidence of family life in this dismal, isolated town. But she saw none. Or did she see a curtain move slightly in the front window of the house across the street? Was someone watching her?

"Yes, *cara*, this is it. Our house, our very own. This is your new home," Carlo said proudly, jumping out and running around the car to open the door on her side. "*Andiamo, Liliana*—come and see," and laughing and talking excitedly at the same time, he rushed her out of the car and up the driveway, pausing only a second while he unlocked the door before ushering her into the kitchen. She saw instantly that the floorplan inside was also exactly the same as Gina's, with an opening straight ahead into the living-room. The lino-tiled floor was mercifully blue, a soft mottled blue rather than the hideous mustard colour in Gina's house, but otherwise there was little difference. Her eyes travelled to the table and chairs in the kitchen. They were pink plastic with chrome legs and trim, in a once-fashionable style which she recognized from American movies. They looked so insubstantial, so cheap. There was a vase in the middle of the table, with two floppy red dahlias leaning out of it. Her eyes filled with tears. He had done that, in a pitiful effort to make it all seem more homey, more welcoming, and she thought she could have borne it better, could have held back her tears, but for this sad, brave little touch. Carlo had become silent. She looked over at him and saw the stricken look on his face as he watched the tears coursing down her cheeks. *Damn,* she thought, *why do I have to cry?! I want him to see me as strong and brave, but I've been snivelling ever since I got here. I want him to know I'm angry and disappointed, but I'm acting like a little girl. I can't even control my emotions.* She fumbled in her purse for her handkerchief, and as quickly as she could she wiped her eyes and nose. She felt silly. Silly, but miserable. Her fury rose again. *I have every right to be furious! After all, he's dragged me here halfway around the world with promises of God-knows what, and I'm supposed to be grateful for this pitiful little house in the middle of nowhere—doesn't he see how awful it is? He knows I came from much better than this! How dare he try to pawn this off as something wonderful! How can he expect me to be happy here? If Mama saw this, she'd be furious too. God knows she wouldn't want me to have to make a life in such a place. And he must know that! He must!*

"But Carlo," she said through clenched teeth, trying with all her might not to sob, "it's so—so shabby—so barren. How can I—how can we ever live here?" and the suppressed sobs burst out.

"Don't cry, Liliana," Carlo said beseechingly, moving toward her. "It's all right. This is our new home. It'll be fine. It'll be beautiful, you'll see. Come, let's look at the other rooms. Look how big it is! It's big for just the two of us, don't you think? And we can make it attractive and comfortable, you'll see." A note of desperation was in his voice now. "Please, don't cry, Liliana, please. Come, I have a surprise for you."

And he took her hand and pulled her after him through the living room, which she barely saw, and down the corridor past the bathroom to the bedroom at the back. There he stopped, and her glance quickly took in the blue floor and the pale blue of the walls and curtains, thinking that this wasn't too bad, not too bad at all compared to the bedroom she had been given at Gina's. Then her eyes fell on the furniture. She stood silently beside Carlo, their shoulders touching as they looked at the double bed which took up most of the floor space. The bed had been made up and was covered with a pale blue chenille spread. Suddenly it dawned on Liliana that the furniture was new, the headboard and the matching bureau and dresser made of some pale golden wood which gleamed softly in the dull light. "Look, darling," he said. "Look. This is my surprise, my wedding gift to you, a new bedroom set, a matrimonial suite." He waited.

She was mute with astonishment, riveted to the spot. She hadn't expected this. Carlo had done the right thing, the proper thing, as would have been done had they been back home. He had somehow managed to purchase and set up this brand-new matrimonial suite, his first gift to his bride. And he had apparently also purchased new linens for the bed and had made it up, a bit askew, a bit lumpy, but made up—for her. He was trying so hard—so hard to please her. She saw him anew. Her heart melted. She felt it melting as she turned toward him.

"Oh Carlo, oh *Madonna*. It's beautiful. *Guarda che bella*! Look how beautiful! Wherever did you get it in this God-forsaken place? I can't believe my eyes. Oh, thank you, thank you," she said, choking on her tears, and without another word she moved into his arms. The man smell of him overwhelmed her, and she felt her knees trembling as she leaned into him. He held her tightly, moaning. *"Ti amo, ti amo,* I love you," was all he said, over and over, until at last she pulled away and, stepping back, straightened her skirt. She was shaking, but she smiled brightly and walked out toward the living room, calling back, "But I want to have another look at the *salotto*. Come on."

He followed her back down the corridor to the living room, which she took in now at a glance. It was not nearly as finished-looking as the bedroom, furnished as it was with mis-matched pieces; a sofa and matching arm-chairs, a scarred brown wooden coffee table covered with pale rings, a matching end table, and other bits and pieces. She instantly hated the thin shiny curtains with their blue geometric pattern which hung limply on either side of the three close-set windows. The only saving grace in the otherwise graceless room was the pale mottled blue of the linoleum-tiled floor which by some stroke of luck had been laid throughout the downstairs of this little house. Its soft, clear hue reminded Liliana of the colour of the sky at home in autumn. She caught herself thinking how she might accent that tint, how she might make the room more liveable—cushions perhaps. Then, suddenly, visions of the lovely dark rooms of home swam before her eyes: the polished granite floors, the white lace curtains over white Venetian shades on the windows diffusing the sunlight, causing lovely patterns to dance in the rooms. But the sight of the rain lashing greyly against the glass where the curtains did not quite cover them, the sound of its drumming, told her she was not at home.

"I used to live down in the camp with the other single men, but since I bought the house I've been sleeping in the upstairs room, like the one you're in at Gina's," Carlo said, coming up behind her, quite unaware of her momentary vision of home. "I've been cooking for myself here, but not very well—just a bit of pasta and the occasional cutlet—I'm not a very good cook. But people are so kind, they've had me for meals so many times. It's not like at home, where we only have meals with our relatives. Here, it's almost as if we have become each other's family. So we'll have to begin inviting people back as soon as we can," he went on, "as soon as we're married and you've settled in. Won't that be great? You'll see, we Italians are few, but we stick together. We have a great time."

Liliana smiled, but she felt a momentary surge again of that anger she thought she had defeated. He was so sure of her, so sure that she would react as he expected. But no one would ever take the place of her family. She wouldn't let them. And she had no desire to entertain total strangers. Besides, she had never been responsible for the preparation of an entire meal in her life. Would she be able to carry it off? What would she cook? Where did one shop? Were there any decent pots? Any dishes? But she said nothing. She would cross that bridge when she came to it, she thought, as she caught sight again of the ghastly pink chrome set in the kitchen and gave an inadvertent shiver.

"Are you chilly, *cara*? It's the rain, it makes the rooms so damp. But look here, I'll fix that in no time," and reaching up to a small circular glass-covered dial on the wall which Liliana hadn't noticed, he turned it slightly. "It's a thermostat," he said in answer to her unspoken question. "It regulates the temperature in the rooms. The oil furnace is just down the hallway behind those louvred doors, and since I've just turned up the heat, we'll feel a difference in a few minutes. Come on, I'll show you." He turned her, guiding her by her shoulders so that she faced the door as he opened it to expose the furnace, a sleek metal box taller than he was. "It burns oil," he went on proudly. "See, the heat will be blown out of those metal grates in the floor." And sure enough, Liliana was aware of a sudden faintly roaring noise and the warm air as it blew up through the registers. *My God,* she thought, *so that's how these flimsy wooden houses are heated. Maybe it will be more comfortable than I expected.*

At least I won't have to always be chilled to the bone in this damp climate. Wouldn't it be wonderful if Mama and Nonna had something like this to take the chill off, instead of having to rely on the cookstove for heat! But to Carlo she only said, "That's nice. That's much better."

"We should go," Carlo said, taking her hand again and pulling her toward the door. "That's enough of your new house for now. We've been invited to Anna and Tony's for lunch, and then to Lena and Claudio's for dinner. I know," he said when he saw the look of apprehension on her face, "I know, *cara*, you don't know these people at all, but believe me, they are great, good friends who want to meet you and make you feel welcome. You'll see, you'll like them. But first, we'll go for a little drive and I'll show you the town." And pulling the door of her new house firmly shut behind them, he rushed her down the driveway and into the car once more.

She felt hollow, strangely empty, and yet excited, but she said nothing as he got in behind the wheel. As he backed down the driveway and drove out onto the main road, she lifted her eyes to the smoky blue-grey mountains that lay like hump-backed beasts just behind the dark trees. They made her feel enclosed, surrounded. Inadvertently she heaved a great sigh, and Carlo turned his head quickly toward her at the sound of it. She caught his worried look and smiled at him, then reached over and put one hand on his arm, hard and muscled under his jacket, and patted it reassuringly. "The house is fine, just fine," she lied. "You'll see, we'll make it into a lovely home," and was gratified at the smile he flashed. She realized for the first time that he didn't seem to notice the greyness of the day, the dismal little houses glimpsed through the rain, the smoky mountains circling them. He glanced over at her every now and then as he drove, his voice droning on as he explained about the town and how it had come to be.

He really doesn't see all this as I do, at least not any more. He thinks this awful town is pretty, the surroundings beautiful. He must. It isn't dismal to him, nor strange. Only to me. Will I ever see it differently? Will I ever feel at home again?

For the next two hours Liliana and Carlo were cocooned in the car, its wipers swishing back and forth in the relentless rain as Carlo's voice droned on. He drove up and down the streets, telling her how the company had built here because of the natural setting; the deep-sea port, the plentiful timber, the hydro-electric power, and that in fact no town had existed here before, only a small settlement of indigenous people nearby. "Real Indians?" she asked in amazement. No one had mentioned this possibility before, though she remembered now the silent family on the train. "Yes, native people," he answered. "My friend Aldo fell in love with a native woman, a beautiful young widow. I'll take you to meet them one day. They just got married a few months ago. She's very nice, his wife." Liliana only nodded, not wanting him to see her puzzlement—how could such a union work? How could they even communicate? There was so much for her to learn about this place.

Not noticing her reaction, his voice went on, telling her how all the houses had been pre-fabricated, brought in by barge, piles of walls and roofs and windows ready to be assembled. She had never heard of such a thing as pre-fabricated houses. No wonder they all looked the same, or nearly so. There seemed to be two basic styles; one like hers and Gina's with the pitched roof and another style where the living area was upstairs under a flat roof with only an open area underneath which Carlo explained was to protect the car, and what looked like one small room on the ground floor which was where the furnace was, he explained.

Peering through the rain-streaked windshield as they moved along, she saw that there were two areas for shopping, one within easy walking distance from her house—she caught herself thinking of it as *her* house, even though she hated it—and another larger shopping area down the hill past the pink hospital, to which Carlo would have to drive her. There was a *cinema*, and a long, low building with a rounded roof which Carlo explained was a place where the locals played a game called curling, which she had never heard of. There were a few low, spread-out buildings he said were schools, and the occasional service station. And that was it. The townsite was surrounded by a wall of evergreens, dripping in the rain, and behind them the smoky blue-grey mountains. And the heavy, dark clouds overhead. There was one road out, leading to the town where Mr. and Mrs. Lombardo had gotten off the train so long ago. Or was it only yesterday?

She began to see a map of the town in her head—the train station across the river where the small one-storey houses clustered near the larger shopping centre, then the long hill up to the neighbourhood where her house was, with the cinema and smaller shopping area nearby. She saw that when Carlo drove down the hill, across the orange bridge, and turned left, travelling a newly-paved road bounded on both sides by the never-ending evergreens, he came eventually to the plantsite on the shore of a long meandering finger of the Pacific. When he stopped at last she saw the ocean's choppy grey water, angry-looking in the lashing rain where it lapped at the edges of the squat grey buildings under their smoky pall. "There it is," said Carlo sardonically, gesturing toward the plant buildings, "the reason why we're all here so far from home." Liliana heard for the first time a hard note in his voice. She said nothing. She was thinking of pictures of the beautiful blue Pacific, white sandy beaches shaded by palm trees, that she remembered from books and magazines, from movies and postcards. Surely not the same Pacific as this expanse of oily-looking water with its angry waves rocking the small wooden shacks on floats dotted here and there amid the loose logs. It looked as though the sun had never shone here and never would. She was glad when Carlo turned the car back toward the town.

"Carlo," she said, her voice small, "is it dangerous in the plant? Is it dangerous work you do? It looks like it would be awful in there."

He drove silently, staring straight ahead, not answering. Perhaps he hadn't heard. She asked again.

"Carlo? Is it dangerous in there?"

"No, not really," he said at last. "Not if you're careful."

Lunch at Anna and Tony's was pleasant enough, though Liliana still felt as though she were in a dream. It was all happening too abruptly. She felt as though some sort of violence had been done to her, albeit inadvertently. She felt bruised.

They had welcomed her warmly enough, with hugs and exclamations about how small and pretty she was, and how tired she must be, fussing over her so that she was spared the necessity of speaking more than a word or two. To her surprise, Gina and Mario were also there, and Liliana realized that she was glad to see their familiar faces. Apparently, the other men were working the afternoon shift, though Carlo had two weeks off. They all sat immediately at the table in the kitchen, and Liliana saw that she was again in a house exactly like Gina's—and her own. Again, the table in the kitchen was the only table. There was no dining room in these houses. They would always have to eat in the kitchen. But the meal was comprised of familiar food, pasta with meat sauce followed by cutlets and salad, and the easy camaraderie of Carlo and the others allowed Liliana to relax. She wasn't expected to take part in the conversation, she realized. She was being allowed to sit in silence and get the feel of their relationship. She was perfectly aware, but apart. *Even though I understand every word that's being said, it's as though they're speaking a foreign language. This whole scene is like a tableau on a stage, and I'm the audience. Like it's not really about me at all. It wouldn't have been like this if I were at home, laughing with Luisa and Mama as we planned my wedding. It would have been such a joyous time for all of us. I've been cheated of something I've looked forward to all my life.*

Carlo was more open, more animated and talkative than she had ever seen him, laughing and gesturing as the discussion went on. He acted as if he were at home with his brothers. Then she thought with a start, *He is at home. He has made this his home and he has made these people his family. He has come to this in less than a year. Will it ever happen for me?* And then, *Do I want this? Do I want these people to take the place of my family? I can't imagine ever being as unguarded, as intimate, with people who are not of my blood.* But she smiled as they joked and laughed about the upcoming wedding. She didn't want them to see that she felt bruised. She didn't want them to think she was stiff, like a child at a grown-up's party. But that was how she felt. Like a child, like a bewildered, frightened child who was trying with all her might to appear grown up.

As soon as they had left Anna and Tony's, with Gina and Mario's car following them, she began to pepper Carlo with the questions, long harbored in her mind, that she could no longer hold back. "What about the priest? Did you say his name was Father Haber? What sort of name is that? And won't I get to meet him before the ceremony? Is he really a Catholic priest? And the church—where is the church?"

"*Dai, dai, cara,*" soothed Carlo, "there *is* a church, and Father Haber *is* a catholic priest. In fact, we have an appointment to meet with him later this afternoon in the rectory. You'll see, he's a gentle man. He knows that you can't speak English, he's used to that—there are people here from all over Europe," he explained, catching her glance of surprise. "But I'll help you. I'll translate. I'm not very good, but we'll manage. He understands. Now don't worry. All the documents are in order. We *will* be married properly. Everything will be fine." Grasping the steering wheel with his left hand and reaching out with the other, he touched her face, stroking her cheek as you would a bird's wing, or the soft fuzz of a kitten. She didn't resist, but she felt a twinge of the anger again. *He's patronizing me, as though I were a*

child, to be cajoled and soothed. Is that how he thinks of me?
Then she thought, *Is that how I've been acting?*

Turning in to the driveway at Gina's and Mario's, Liliana
looked up and saw with a start the flat white shape of her
wedding dress in the upstairs window, like a flag for all the
world to see. Here in this house is a girl about to be married.

Upstairs, Liliana changed into her best tailored wool suit,
the navy one, while Carlo had a glass of wine with Mario,
sitting companionably at the kitchen table like brothers. She
could hear their voices and occasional laughter as she
readied herself to meet Father Haber. She fastened the top
button at the neck of her white blouse—she certainly
wouldn't want the priest to think she was not of good family,
that she didn't know how to dress properly for such an
important meeting. She realized that at the back of her mind
always was the voice of her Nonna, advising, admonishing,
and she felt comforted. Nonna's voice. Mama's voice.
Always there.

Chapter 11

It turned out that the Catholic church was simply one large room under one of the schools she had gone by earlier in the day—the Catholic school, Carlo explained as they parked the car and walked over to the small wooden house which stood just behind it, the rectory. Apparently not all the schools were Catholic, some, he went on, were secular—no religion was taught in them at all. She took in this news without comment.

The square building which housed the church on the ground floor, with the school above it, was painted a soft grey colour with white trim. It loomed eerily in the rain and mist, and Liliana could barely make out the simple white cross above the door when Carlo pointed it out to her. The newer-looking rectory was painted yellow, and lights were on inside, glowing almost warmly in the fast-darkening afternoon. Carlo knocked at the door, and it was opened, not by a black-uniformed maid as would have been the case had they been going to see Don Paolo (how she wished it were Don Paolo they were about to meet to discuss the details of the marriage ceremony), but by Father Haber himself, a young blond fellow in a faded cassock, who clasped her hand warmly with his small soft one and invited them in.

To her amazement, though she couldn't think why she was surprised—she should have expected this—Carlo introduced her in English, and continued to converse with the priest in the unknown language. This was the first time in her life that Liliana had ever been completely shut out of the conversation. She caught the odd word, the odd phrase, but they spoke too quickly for her to follow. She was surprised at Carlo's seeming fluency. It was almost like a betrayal. *I hate this. I hate not knowing what's being said, as though I'm a naughty child and the adults are talking about me in a language I don't understand, as an intentional way of leaving me out. This is about my marriage, for God's sake. About the most important thing in a girl's life—don't they understand that?* The priest murmured intently to Carlo, casting warm glances at her through gold-rimmed lenses on which she could plainly see fingerprints. But though she sat up very straight and looked intently at first one face and then the other, she had no idea what was going on, and the anger made her face flush hotly, her legs tremble. She hoped that the priest didn't notice. She hoped that what he saw was a well-mannered and no-doubt devout young woman who was well-versed in the Catholic ritual. Sometimes Carlo translated, and she could nod her head, "*Sì*" or "*No*", but other than that whatever transpired remained a mystery. She tried by an effort of will to make Carlo understand her sense of isolation, of being…demeaned. Her eyes bore into the side of his face as he spoke to the priest. She felt mute. Yet she trusted Carlo. Despite her anger, she knew that he would make sure that everything was in order. They would be married in a proper nuptial mass the following Saturday. In three days. She couldn't think beyond that.

As the voices of the two men droned on, question, answer, question, answer, her thoughts drifted to her wedding day. For the first time she saw herself in her mind's eye dressed in the ivory satin gown that hung now in front of the window in the ugly little room, saw herself walking toward Carlo, who waited at the altar in a dark suit, and she was aware of a faint quaking sensation deep inside.

When the conversation was over, details having been settled to the satisfaction of the two men, they stood and shook hands. Liliana stood up as well, adjusting her skirt and touching quickly the neck of her white blouse. It was securely fastened. Gesturing to them to follow, the priest walked out of the house and across the gravelled parking area to the grey building, opening the door and leading them in. Liliana stared. There, at the front of a large gloomy auditorium was what was unmistakably an altar, dressed as it was in a stiff white lace cloth topped with tall candles on either side of the tabernacle. It stood on a raised dais carpeted in dark red, and there was a slim metal cross suspended on the wall above it. There were rows of rough benches facing the altar, and the walls of the room were panelled in mottled brown wood, cheap wood finished with some sort of shiny lacquer. Liliana hated it. There were rows of brown wooden pillars, holding up the low roof, she supposed, and the whole effect was that of a cavernous underground chamber, chilly, empty. Father Haber flicked a switch inside the door and a row of lights directly overhead came on, though the altar was still barely visible in the gloom. There were no windows except for one on either side of the door. Their footfalls echoed as they walked up the aisle between the rows of brown benches toward the altar, where Liliana genuflected hastily and sat in the front bench. *Well God, here I am. I've come to marry Carlo in this cold wooden church, and I will. But You know it's not how I wanted it to be. Help me to be brave and not to disgrace myself. Oh God, help me through this.* And in a flash, she saw the altar of the simple, beloved church back home a million miles away, the rounded pink granite pillars on either side, and for a moment she felt as though she couldn't breathe.

Liliana walked trancelike through the next three days, the lunches and dinners at the kitchen tables of soon-to-be-friends, their carefully-prepared food and their welcoming warmth all that stood between her and total isolation. She tried to shake this sense of separation, but she couldn't. She knew they were all trying desperately to make her feel that she would come to enjoy her life among them, that this new world and all its strangeness would come to feel like home, as it seemed to do for Carlo, who remained at the centre of it all. He loved her. She almost felt sorry for him sometimes, seeing the beseeching glances he cast her way, wanting her to be happy, to be excited to know—as he seemed to—that everything would be all right. Everyone was trying so hard, and while she found herself increasingly able to join in the light-hearted conversation, it felt as though it were someone else talking and laughing. Sometimes she rose up and out of her body, hovering just above the room, looking down at herself sitting there among these strangers, before she shook her head and returned. She was there, but she was still apart.

Friday, August 28, 1964

Carissime:

Tomorrow is my wedding day, and I cannot get to sleep. My heart is full, so full I think it will burst, so I will pass an hour writing to you all whom I miss so very much. You cannot imagine how I feel tonight, so far away, without family. Everyone here has been very good to me, and Carlo is so thoughtful and sweet, but I miss your dear faces and cannot stop thinking about you. I never imagined that I would be married so far from home, from my dear San Michele. And I never imagined that I would be married without you to help me dress, dear Mama, without you to stand up with me, dear Luisa, without you to pray for me, dear Nonna. The priest is very nice, but it is so difficult not to be able to understand his words. And the church is not beautiful at all. It is very plain, almost ugly, but they tell me it is only temporary, and that they will build a proper church when they can. But it will never be as dear to my heart as S. Maria Immacolata. This building doesn't feel like a church at all. But I don't mean to complain. I am grateful to you for all you have done for me, and I shall try to be happy. Please don't worry, Carlo is very good to me, and we do love each other. I will write again soon and tell you all about my wedding.

Love, Liliana

Sealed in its pale blue envelope, her letter sat propped against the mirror on the dresser. Placing it there, she had been stopped by her pale reflection staring back at her, green eyes clouded, the little frown lines between them making her look so astonishingly like her mother. But she had her Nonna's grit, too, she thought, and she would not let this feeling of sadness overwhelm her. She should be happy. Tomorrow should be a day of joy. She turned and knelt by the side of the bed as she had done every night of her life, and closing her eyes and clenching her jaw, she asked again for strength, for joy. But she felt none, only determination and a certainty that she must do this. The unstoppable ritual must proceed. She got up and lay on the narrow bed, staring she knew not how long at the white wedding dress where it hung ghostlike in the window. Until at last she slept and dreamt again of pots of red geraniums on sun-drenched window sills, and Carlo whizzing toward her on his bicycle.

Chapter 12

And then it was her wedding day. She knew it as soon as she rose to consciousness. It was her wedding day and she was here, in this shabby little room in this barren little house, so far from her family. But she had to get through it, so that she and Carlo, her beloved Carlo, could begin their life together. At least it didn't seem to be raining today. A ray of weak late-August sunlight was illuminating her dress where it hung in the window. She rose and bathed and laid out her clothes, the new silk underthings, the lace cap and sheer veil, the satin shoes. And as she slowly began to dress, she remembered buying each thing, looking, choosing, discussing each purchase with Mama and Luisa in the big department store in Udine.

She was startled from her reverie by a knock on her bedroom door. "*Buongiorno*, Liliana," called Gina, "May I come in?" And as she opened the door, "I can't bring you any coffee today. We must fast until we take Communion, but please let me help you dress. Oh, I see you have a letter to post. Don't worry, I'll do that for you tomorrow morning." And then, allowing herself to be hugged and patted, Liliana succumbed to Gina's ministrations, letting her lift the dress over her head and guide it down over her shoulders. "Don't

look, don't look yet 'till I've fixed your hair and veil
properly," said a suddenly matronly Gina, and Liliana
allowed her to brush and comb her hair and affix the cap and
veil to it. "And now, a little colour," said Gina, producing
from her pocket a tube of pink lipstick and a small red case
which contained mascara and a stiff little brush. Liliana did
not protest, though she had never used cosmetics before. She
knew that, with her pale colouring, she needed help, and
after all, when could she use cosmetics if not on this day?
She wanted them to see her as beautiful, even though she
knew she was not. She wanted them to see her as composed,
strong and sure, even though she was not. So Gina fussed
over her, murmuring softly, Liliana answering, the two of
them smiling into each other's faces. It was a special time,
just before she was to be married, and Liliana was conscious
of this, knowing that she would think often of this scene and
wish it had been her mother with her. But that could not be.

At last Gina pronounced Liliana ready, and she turned
and looked at herself in the mirror above the pale blue
envelope, and gasped. She *was* beautiful. She was a beautiful
bride, as beautiful as she had ever imagined she might be.
The lustrous satin gleamed in the light, the veil fell smoothly
on either side of her face, and she felt a quaking inside
herself when she thought of what Carlo would do when he
saw her. Surely, he would faint. Or she would.

But they neither of them fainted. As she paused in the
entrance to the church she looked ahead and saw Gina in a
simple blue dress—the first time she had seen her in
anything but trousers—and Carlo in a dark suit with Mario
beside him. Then she was walking up the aisle alone,
conscious of the eyes upon her, the bouquet of white lilies—

which had appeared miraculously that morning on the kitchen table—trembling visibly in her hands. *I must remember this, every detail, because I will want to relive it, to tell my family and some day my children about our wedding day. I must concentrate.* She lifted her eyes from her trembling bouquet and looked up, surprised to hear the strains of organ music, a melody she could not name, but familiar from weddings she had attended. Carefully she matched her steps to its cadences. Then she became aware of the faces turned toward her, the smiles, the odd glittering of tears in eyes that took in her white beauty. She looked ahead and was astonished to see the transformation that her new friends had wrought. The stark altar was alive with clusters of late-summer flowers, asters in shades of gold and rose, backed by tall white gladioli, and at the foot of the altar on either side, a tall arrangement of gladioli repeating the golds and roses and whites, the blooms punctuated by the dark spikes of the leaves. Her eyes filled, and she blinked hard. She wanted to see so that she would remember. Two pretty little white chairs sat side by side, facing the altar, for them to sit on during the Mass, and there were bows of white tulle on the ends of the pews marking her path toward the front where Carlo waited. He had turned to watch her as she walked slowly, solemnly, toward him, and she saw the glitter of tears in his eyes too. Now she was beside him, and she could feel the faint trembling of Carlo's body through the sleeve of his suit where it touched her satin-covered arm, conscious of the eyes on their backs. They both stared straight ahead as the priest began to speak. Liliana knew the Mass by heart, and genuflected and knelt at the proper times, but her eyes never left the altar as the strange sounds came out of the priest's mouth.

God was there, in the tabernacle, watching her. She had kept her end of the bargain. She looked up momentarily at the silver cross above the altar, plain except for the anguished body hung upon it. The music stopped, and she could feel God's eyes on her. On and on went the voice of Father Haber as they sat on the little white chairs, then rose, then knelt, then rose again. Suddenly she heard her name pronounced, Liliana Manon, and turned to find Carlo looking at her, his dark eyes burning into hers. She saw that his face was fine-boned and gentle. "*Sì*," she whispered. And then she heard his name, Carlo Pellegrino. "*Sì*, yes," he replied in a strong, clear voice. And they were married. Carlo placed one hand gently under her chin and pulled her face toward his until their lips met in a solemn and chaste sealing of the pact.

Then the four of them followed the priest as he walked to a small room off to the side while the organ played the opening strains of that most beautiful of all songs, *Ave Maria*, and she heard the soaring tenor of the unknown soloist. *Oh, how perfect, how absolutely perfect. Carlo knew. He must have arranged this.* And then, *I must remember all this, all the details. I must find out who is singing and thank him. It's so beautiful.* Then all four signed their names on the lines indicated by Father Haber, followed by a flurry of hugging and hand-shaking which included the priest, who, she saw, seemed genuinely moved by the moment. They re-entered the church and stood side by side on the slightly raised dais in front of the altar, facing the grinning crowd. The priest said a few words and to her astonishment they broke into resounding applause, something she had never heard in a church before, as the organist played the joyous Triumphant March from Aida. *I must find out who the organist is too and thank her.*

Back down the aisle they walked, arm in arm, and in the pictures, she is smiling radiantly, but she was to have no memory of that walk, filled as she was with such emotion. Then they were out on the steps of the church and were being crushed in the centre of a crowd of well-wishers hugging her, shaking Carlo's hand, slapping him on the back, and suddenly, in the midst of all the excitement, she realized that joy had touched her at last. She felt her husband's arm around her waist, holding her tightly as they accepted the congratulations of the handful of people, and Liliana was aware of a rush of emotion sweeter that anything she had ever known. It filled her, it suffused her, and she flushed with happiness. Glad that a number of the faces were familiar, she called them by name as she thanked them for their good wishes and submitted to their kisses and hugs and exclamations at her beauty.

Then she felt Carlo pulling her away, and they ran and got into the back seat of Gina and Mario's car, freshly washed and waxed for the occasion, with coloured paper streamers tied to its bumper. But she was surprised to find that instead of going directly back to Gina's house for picture-taking and a light lunch before going to the reception, they were driving up and down the streets of the town, followed by several other cars, all with horns honking loudly. "It's the custom here, *cara*," laughed Carlo. "They always do this. To let everyone know that we're newly-weds." And then he turned and pulled her to him, kissing her longer and harder than he ever had before. She couldn't breathe, and laughing, pushed him away. "I love you, Liliana," Carlo said, looking into her face. "I love you too, Carlo," she replied, and knew that it was true. She loved this man she barely knew.

The afternoon passed in a blur—Gina and Mario, Anna and Tony taking pictures, posing them this way and that in the living room, then outside in front of a big Blue Spruce. Inside again, Liliana perched on the edge of the bristly sofa in her white satin dress, being very careful not to wrinkle it or stain it with the food and drink that Gina passed around— cold cuts and cheese, glasses of white wine, delicate home- made sweets. Toasts were proposed, little self-conscious speeches were made, and through it all Liliana was aware, for the first time in a long time, of a sense of happiness. She felt happiness and she felt sadness. How could one be happy and sad at the same time? But she was. She glanced at Carlo's profile, felt his hand on the small of her back and was happy. Her husband. But every now and then she would feel a surge of sadness wash over her—of longing for the dear faces of her family who should be sharing this precious day with her. She wondered if Carlo was thinking about his family too. Once, quite clearly, she saw herself in her mind's eye walking back down the aisle on Carlo's arm, smiling, but she was in her beloved church back home with its smooth rounded pillars and shiny granite floor, and there was sunlight streaming in the opened door toward which they walked.

At last it was time to get back into the cars and drive down the long hill to the hotel. It was, as usual, a shabby wooden building painted brown, the gutters which ran along beside it filled with bits of paper and empty bottles and cans. The row of darkened windows on the second floor indicated that no one was staying there tonight, but the large room on the main floor into which she entered on Carlo's arm was surprisingly spacious. The walls, she saw instantly, were panelled in the ever-present brown wood, but the floor was carpeted in a colourful floral pattern and rows of bright lights shone down on several long tables in the centre of the room, set for dinner. All the people who had been at the church seemed to be here, standing in little clusters about the room, holding glasses, and a general cheer went up as the bridal party entered.

A receiving line was formed just inside the door, and one by one the guests went down the line, introducing themselves to her even if they had already met, kissing her first on one cheek and then on the other, shaking Carlo's hand and telling him what a beautiful bride he had, what a lucky fellow he was. There was a buzzing noise inside Liliana's head. She would never remember all those names. But everyone seemed so happy for them, so welcoming. She was grateful. She even felt beautiful.

Finally, they were ushered to the head table and sat down in front of a three-tiered cake decorated with voluptuous red icing-roses. She wondered whose idea that was. She was wishing that the icing roses had been white when suddenly there was a cacophony of noise—glasses being hit with cutlery, an ungodly din, and she knew what that meant. She turned, laughing, to Carlo, who pulled her to him and kissed her soundly to the ongoing clatter. She had forgotten about this custom, glad that it was being observed here too. This was as it should be. And then the dinner was served, course by course, accompanied by wine. The meal was not nearly as elaborate as it had been at weddings she had attended at home in elegant hotels with large rooms just for such occasions, but it was adequate—plates of olives and cheese and *prosciutto* first, followed by a salad of tasteless pale lettuce and then roast chicken and tiny roast potatoes.

The din in the room was incredible, everyone laughing and talking loudly, gesturing broadly, clinking glasses and shouting out, *"Viva gli sposi!"* The guests were much less restrained than she remembered from similar occasions back home, but these people were from various provinces of Italy, she reminded herself, and while each area had its own customs and mannerisms, it seemed to Liliana that here, thrown together by fate as they were, they had somehow melded these variations together into a new form of social-ization. Ancient rivalries forgotten, they were enjoying themselves immensely, and it occurred to her that other than the occasional wedding, there would not likely be any opportunities to be out together like this. The women were all wearing vividly-coloured dresses, and frequently patted their freshly-done hair. Many were festooned with every golden ring and bracelet and necklace they owned. She took it as a compliment, that everyone had dressed in their very best. And the men certainly did look different in their dark suits, with their hair slicked down. Some even looked handsome, she thought.

After dinner, when the tables had been cleared except for the wineglasses, Mario rose and made a charming toast to the newlyweds, and then from his pocket produced a crumpled telegram, which he proceeded to read aloud. Liliana could barely hear him over the din, but she knew that it was from all her family, and the beautiful words of love made her tears spill over and run down her cheeks. Carlo reached over and gently wiped them away with the rough paper napkin, and she smiled at him. He knew. But there was no telegram from his family.

Then, with Gina coaching—whispering into her ear what to do—she and Carlo rose and did a ceremonial cutting of the florid cake, which was then whisked away so that it could be cut and served to everyone. Liliana saw that the snow-white pieces of cake were smeared with streaks of scarlet from the icing roses.

After the cake had been consumed, she was surprised to see the crowd rise to its feet as though at some unseen command, the women clustering around the door to the powder room while the men manhandled the tables into a rough semi-circle on either side of the head table, exposing a square wooden dance floor. Liliana had never seen dancing at a wedding, but only course after elaborate course served until the bride and groom left, signalling the end of the festivities. First, she and Carlo danced sedately to a Viennese waltz the name of which she did not know, and then Gina and Mario, then she and Mario along with Carlo and Gina, swaying to the old-fashioned music of an accordian played with gusto by Tony and a guitar and drums played by two other shirt-sleeved men. Soon everyone had joined in the dancing. Liliana thought it odd that the tunes were so out-of-date, many of them old folk songs that she hadn't heard since her school days—certainly nothing from San Remo, the annual Popular music competition back home. She guessed that some of these people had left Italy before the San Remo festival had begun. But she managed to remember how to polka and waltz, first with her husband, then with every other man in the room. She was whirled and passed from partner to partner until she was dizzy and panting, begging laughingly to be allowed to sit down.

From her vantage point behind the head table she watched as the women, all of them married, danced one by one with Carlo, pulling him up from his chair if he happened to sit down for a second. She saw him then through their eyes, saw that he was tallish and slender, with a graceful and sweetly attentive manner that made the other men seem coarse by comparison. And she smiled at him whenever he glanced over at her. Her husband.

She had been taken aback at first to learn that here in "America" a woman forfeited the right to use her own surname when she married, that she would forever after be known as *Signora* whatever her husband's name was. Not so back home. Her mother was Amelia Urban from her birth to her death, though she had married Pietro Manon and her children bore his name. But she, Liliana Manon, would now and forever be Liliana Pellegrino. *Signora* Pellegrino.

The dancing went on and on. There were no disapproving older women here, no young children as there would have been back home, and Liliana realized that she was seeing for the first time unfettered gaiety, almost delirium. The guests partied with a sort of frenzy which Liliana had never seen before, as though they were desperate to forget who they were. Or was it where they were? As Liliana watched, the noise grew louder and louder. She knew that most of the men were in some stage of drunkenness now. It made her sad, their desperate gaiety, but she smiled as she was pulled to her feet again, laughing as she too was whirled from one man to another, trying desperately to catch a glimpse of Carlo through the moving crowd.

Liliana was very tired. Her face felt drawn, her mouth stretched in a fixed smile, her hand covering her frequent yawns. Her beautiful ivory satin shoes were ruined, and she knew that the makeup so carefully applied by Gina had long since disappeared, leaving her face naked, shiny with perspiration. At last, blessedly, Carlo whispered they could leave. Linking arms, they ran the gauntlet of guests who lined up on either side of the door to send them off amid much hugging and slaps on the back. Finally, they were out in the parking lot, running toward their car and jumping in, slamming the doors as hard as they could. They collapsed into each other's arms, laughing, exhausted. "Oh Carlo, it was wonderful. Everything was wonderful," she said to him. "Thank you. You thought of everything. But I'm so tired now. Let's go home." She didn't notice that she had said *home*.

"Yes, darling, it was wonderful, wasn't it, but I'm really glad it's over. I was beginning to think they'd never let us go. We can go home, but first..," and he pulled her to him, wrapping his arms completely around her and pulling her body against his. He kissed her, long and deeply, and she responded with the first stirrings of passion. This was her husband, and she loved him and trusted him. "Stop, Carlo, stop, darling," she gasped at last and pulled away. He said nothing, starting the car and driving with one hand on the wheel and the other on her satin-covered thigh, and soon they were turning up their driveway. He must have left a light on, for the windows were glowing warmly as they approached and Liliana was glad for the first time to be there.

It had begun to rain again, and they laughed as they ran in, colliding in the doorway and falling into each other's arms as soon as Carlo had closed and locked the door. This kiss was longer and more passionate than the one in the car, and Liliana was trembling so hard she could barely stand. *I've had too much wine. No, it isn't the wine. It's Carlo. I'm alone with him at last, and I am his wife. I am his.* And all rational thought left her as he guided her into the bedroom and slowly and reverently undressed her, so that she had no time even to put on one of the lovely high-necked nighties before they were on the bed, limbs entwined, and she understood how much he loved her, and she him. Once she heard a voice call out and knew it was hers.

Sometime later, much later, Liliana woke and lay for a long time watching Carlo as he slept, his fine features in repose, spent. *Oh God, you who sent me here, thank you for my love. I will truly try to be a good and deserving wife, and I will not blame him for my own shortcomings. I will try to make the best of whatever comes. I will try not to be ungrateful.*

She rose and went to the window, drawing aside the pale blue curtains to look up at the dark sky. The rain had stopped and she saw the silver moon, round and full, shining down on her hands and glinting off the gold band on her finger. Was that the same moon that had looked down on her so often as she knelt in front of her bedroom window at home? It couldn't be. Dark purple clouds scudded across the sky and just above the smoky mountains she saw the first glimmer of dawn.

Chapter 13

Monday, September 14, 1964

Carrisime:

I hope this finds you all in good health. Thank you so much for sending us the telegram on our wedding day. It was read aloud at the reception and gave me much comfort.

I cannot believe that I have been married for two weeks already. I'm sorry I didn't write sooner, but it has been a very busy time. All of Carlo's friends have been so kind to us, inviting us for dinners every night. I haven't prepared a dinner yet, but I will have to do so, so that I can return their hospitality. How I wish you were closer. I should have paid more attention to how you cooked, Nonna.

About the wedding—everything went off very well. The new friends that I have made here were very kind and helpful. I will be sending you some pictures that were taken, and you will see that while the church is nothing special, my friends had decorated it with bouquets of garden flowers so that it was quite pretty.

Everyone said my dress was beautiful, and Carlo looked very handsome in his dark suit.

After the ceremony we had a nice dinner at the hotel with all the other Italians here, about fifty in all, and Carlo and his friends had seen to it that there was a proper wedding cake. After dinner there was dancing. That is the custom here and I must confess that I rather enjoyed that part, although my beautiful satin shoes are ruined. I think everyone had a good time. It wasn't as elegant as it would have been at home, and I missed you all more than I can say, but all in all it wasn't too bad.

My little house requires a great deal of attention, but it is adequate. The rooms are quite large, though sparsely furnished. The kitchen is very convenient, and the bathroom has lots of running hot water. *Cara Mama*, I am enclosing a money order for you to buy me some nice white curtains with a cutwork border, like the ones in the *salotto* at home. I hope you can do that for me. They would make such a difference. But don't worry about me, although the house is made of wood, it is nice and warm, and we are very comfortable.

Cara Mama, I wish we could talk, it is so hard to say in a letter what is in my heart. Please write to me soon. I am all right, but I miss you very much. I am so anxious to hear from you. Although we do have a telephone, I know it would be very expensive for you to call. Carlo sends his best to you all. If you see his mother, tell her we are fine. I'm sure he will write to his family soon, but he is very busy.

Love, Liliana

She put the pen down and folded her letter, placing it in the pale blue envelope. Carlo would post it on his way to work tomorrow. She sat at the kitchen table, the ugly pink formica top covered now by one of the beautiful white embroidered cloths that she had taken from her blue trunk. Her eyes traced the intricate pattern of vines and leaves, roses and daisies, that bordered it, remembering the long hot afternoons when she and Luisa had sat on the shady portico, learning to embroider under the watchful eye of Nonna. Heady with the scent of the red geraniums, thirsty from the heat, she would catch herself dozing off until the tinkling of ice would rouse her, Nonna bringing them drinks in tall glasses, almond-flavoured syrup, *orzata,* stirred into fizzy-water. So delicious. And they would lay aside their embroidery and sip at the cool drinks, dabbing at their foreheads with the fine lawn hankies they always carried in their apron pockets. Mama would come out and sit with them, and she and Nonna would talk quietly, reminiscing about the days of their girlhoods, gossiping kindly about the neighbours, wondering, wishing, hoping. And she and Luisa would listen, and learn—learn how women thought, how women talked, what women worried about and prayed for.

And now here she was, a married woman, living in Canada. She could hardly believe it. And she was at home alone in her own house. Her husband, like all the other husbands, had gone off to work this morning as he would do every day, in his car. Imagine, owning a car! She had been skeptical when Carlo had first mentioned the idea of buying one, but she had been easily persuaded.

"Just think, Lili. I'll be able to take you shopping and for drives all around the town. Won't that be great? And I won't have to ride to work and home again with Mario. I'll be free."

"But Carlo, how will we pay for it?"

"Don't worry, darling. I'm sure the bank where I cash my paycheque will loan me the money. They know me now. And then we'll pay them back a little each month until it's paid for."

"Really? I didn't know you could do that!"

"Oh yes, that's what all the guys do. And I can easily find a car that's not new, and in good shape. I'll start asking around."

And so it was decided. A few days later he said he'd found the perfect car for them, and that all he had to do now was make the arrangements at the bank. He would look after that next payday, before bringing her money to run the household. As her father had done. They would share the responsibility as her parents had always done, a joint effort for the good of the family. No secrets. Liliana knew that not all the women had this sort of open relationship when it came to money. Some didn't even know how much their husbands made!

A week later he came driving up in the little black car, honking the horn as he turned into the driveway, and Liliana dropped the pot she was holding into the sink and went running out, as happy and excited as she could remember being. "Hop in!" he cried, grinning broadly. And hop in she did, rolling down her window and laughing aloud as he drove around the neighbourhood.

The sound of the black telephone mounted by the kitchen door startled her. She couldn't get used to the idea that anyone could call, that she could call anyone, at any time. Telephones had been scarce back home, only one or two in the whole cortile, and using one was an event reserved for the sending and receiving of important messages, not for passing the time of day.

She picked up the receiver and said *"Pronto,"* a little tremble in her voice. This was the first time she had answered the phone. Carlo had always done so, assuming rightly that the caller would want to talk to him. And Liliana had only been alone in her house for a few hours, her husband having gone to work that day for the first time since their wedding.

"Liliana? It's me, Gina. What are you doing?"

"Just finishing a letter home, that's all," she replied, wondering why Gina wanted to know.

"Well, what if I come over to your house, and we can go shopping. Don't you need anything at the store? You've been closeted in that house for weeks now," she said teasingly. "Time to get out!"

"*Sì*, that's true. I do need to get out, and I do need things from the store, but I'm not even sure where it is. Carlo's been driving me. And my English is so poor, you know. I do need some help. Please, I'd be happy if you would come over, and we could walk over to the *supermercato* together. I'll be ready in five minutes."

The two women walked up and down the aisles of the huge store pushing their buggies, Liliana trying to decipher the labels on the packages and cans, trying to become familiarized with the idea of finding whatever she needed and placing it in the buggy to be paid for at the check-out at the front. At home, whenever she had gone shopping with her mother or her grandmother, they had to ask for each item, bulk goods carefully weighed out and wrapped by the grocer before being handed over the counter. Here, she marvelled at the freedom of being able to handle each piece of fruit she chose, each vegetable, to choose from the assortment of wrapped meats, pieces of cheese, bottled juices, canned goods, condiments—the list was endless. She marvelled at the variety of choice, the availability of Mediterranean vegetables and tropical fruits in this remote corner of the world. Eggplants. Bananas. Pineapple. Dried dates and figs. It was luxurious, it was almost sinful, this over-abundance, and she thought that she would probably never purchase any of these things. She would be a careful shopper, running her household as frugally as she could.

On this, her first shopping trip without Carlo, she caught herself staring at a man who propelled himself up and down the aisles in his wheelchair, piling his purchases in his lap. She saw with horror that he had no legs, just empty pantlegs folded underneath his body. She had seen men back home who had been maimed in the war, older men, but she was shocked to see it here. And this was a much younger man. Gina saw her staring at him.

"That man was hurt at work," she whispered, turning her head aside. "He was caught in some machinery–almost killed. *Povero uomo*."

"You mean where Carlo and Mario work?"

"*Sì*," replied Gina, steering Liliana past the wheelchair and up the next aisle. "At the plant. I guess it can be quite dangerous—if they're not careful."

Liliana averted her gaze. It didn't bear thinking about.

At last, her shopping completed, the dreaded check-out stand loomed before her. It was a struggle to learn to handle the strange currency and she felt flustered as she examined and re-examined the bills and coins in her damp hand, shifting her weight first to one foot and then the other in front of the cashier. Finally, impatient, the girl reached over and took the necessary money out of Liliana's hand as though she were a child sent shopping by her mother. Liliana hated that. But then the cashier made some innocuous and friendly-sounding remark which Liliana thought was about the weather, and she smiled widely and tried her very best to reply, pleased that she had been mistaken for someone who belonged.

As they approached her door, laden with the bags of groceries, Liliana invited Gina to stop off for coffee, hoping her efforts to alleviate the barrenness of her house, to make it look as though a woman of taste lived there, would be noticed.

After Gina helped her put her purchases away, they sat at the table having a cup of *espresso*. As she put out a plate of the *biscotti* she had made the day before, she noticed the other woman's eyes looking appraisingly around. "You've done wonders with this place," Gina said. "This is a lovely table cloth, and the new cushions in the living room make such a difference."

"Yes," replied Liliana, flushing with pleasure, "I made the cushions by hand from some fabric I had in my trunk. I enjoy sewing, and there are more things I could do, but I don't have a sewing machine. Carlo says he'll buy me one soon. I used to make most of my own clothes and most of my sister's. I really miss not being able to make things on a machine."

"And I love those pretty little curtains at the window above the sink," Gina went on. "Wherever did you get them?"

"Well," said Liliana, ducking her head in embarrassment, "I had a tablecloth that I had embroidered with those yellow and blue flowers when I was a young girl, and I just cut it in half and hemmed the edges by hand. I didn't know what else to do."

"For God's sake, Liliana," exclaimed Gina, "hasn't that man of yours even taken you downtown yet? There's a big department store there, the Hudson's Bay Company, and several smaller stores, and then there's always the Eaton's catalogue. I can't believe you've never been down there yet."

Liliana was very embarrassed. She felt that she had somehow betrayed Carlo and she hadn't meant to demean him like this. She found herself leaping to his defence. "Oh yes," she lied, "we've driven down there often, but we've been so busy re-arranging things, getting the things out of my trunk, that I haven't even mentioned going shopping."

Gina looked at her skeptically, and Liliana knew she was blushing. They had been busy all right, but not entirely due to rearranging the household. "By the way," she said, trying desperately to change the subject, "how are things with your pregnancy, Gina? You seem to be blooming. When is the baby due?"

"Not for five months, but I'm in no hurry. I'm scared. Everybody tells me it hurts so much, I don't know if I will be able to bear it. But I guess I'll have to."

"Oh, it can't be that bad," comforted Liliana. She didn't know what to say. No one had ever told her the truth about childbirth, and she too was afraid, afraid even to discuss it.

"Do you and Carlo plan to have a family?"

"Oh yes, we plan to have a family, but not for a while. We need to get on our feet first," she went on, not wanting to admit that she and Carlo had never even talked about it. She knew that this was a subject which she would have to broach to him at the first opportunity, but she didn't know how. *Later. I'll bring it up later. We've barely been married a month.*

"Yes, that's what Mario and I said too, but now look at me. It happens, and there's nothing you can do about it. But we're happy," she added quickly, "and we're hoping for a boy."

But it was that very night, after they had made love, that Carlo brought up the subject as she lay in his arms. "Do you want to start a family, *cara*? What do you think about having children?"

"Oh yes, Carlo, I do want to have a family. I would love to have a little boy just like you. But not yet. Let's wait a while. Everything is so new to me, so strange."

"I know, my love, I know. It's true, it's too soon. But we must be careful, or we will be starting a family whether you want to or not."

"What can we do? Is there anything we can do? Gina told me about a pill, but that's not right, is it? Besides, I don't even know if it's available here."

"No, I don't think so, but Liliana, there is something I can do. We can do together."

Later, when she told Gina about their worry, and what they had decided to do, she laughed. "Oh yes, I know all about that. Mario says it's called Vatican Roulette. That's what the men at the plant call it. Just look at me. I'm a fine example of what happens when you do that!"

"Well, what else can we do? Even if the pill were available, we don't think it would be right. That's what the church says. But we really don't want to start a family yet. Not for a while," wailed Liliana, covering her face with her hands as much to hide her furious blush as to silence her wail. "What can we do?"

"Not much, I guess. Look at me. But after all, I was married for almost two years before I got pregnant. Sometimes it works for a while. And if it does happen, it isn't so bad," she went on, as much to comfort herself as Liliana.

The meals she had so far prepared for Carlo had been rudimentary—salads, *minestrone*, cutlets and potatoes, stews, *polenta*, pasta—but never more than one or two dishes per meal. He seemed to appreciate her every effort and was generous with his praise, but she knew that her offerings fell far short of the meals prepared by Mama and Nonna. Or for that matter, those prepared by her new friends who seemed to have effortlessly mastered the intricacies of *straciatella* and *tortellini*, of *arrosto arrotolato* and *vitello tonnato*. She determined to branch out. She knew she would not be able to delay much longer the inevitable reciprocation of meals enjoyed in the homes of their friends, but she was afraid. She so much wanted Carlo to be proud of her efforts. Besides, their dinnerware consisted only of a few thick white plates and cups that Carlo had accumulated she knew not where. They simply wouldn't do, and those few lovely things that she had packed in her trunk couldn't fill the gap. She had pretty little serving plates, espresso sets, silver condiment sets, a crystal decanter and liqueur glasses, things that looked incongruous in these surroundings, things she rarely used. Whatever had she been thinking, to bring these frivolous pretty things and not the practical necessities? She knew why. It was because she had no idea how rudimentary her home would be. So now she didn't have a complete set of dinnerware. She worried about that—a little.

One evening, finishing their meal of p*asta al forno,* Liliana looked again with distaste at the ugly thick plates on which she was forced to serve the meals she so laboriously produced. "Could you bring me home a catalogue one of these days, Carlo?"

"Sure, but what for?" he asked through a mouthful of pasta, fork waving.

"Oh, just to see one. Gina says they're full of pictures of everything under the sun," she replied, not wanting to be too specific just yet. "But I would like to look at things for the house, maybe some new dishes. We really do need a decent set of china, you know, so that we can have people over. We can't put it off forever," *though I wish I could.*

"I'll bring one home tomorrow. You'll find it has absolutely everything in it."

"I wonder why we don't have catalogues back home," she said, carrying their plates to the sink.

"Well," Carlo replied, bringing the dirty glasses over, "that's a huge company, that Eatons. I guess they have to have a catalogue because so many people here in Canada are far away from stores."

And then, as she began washing the plates, "Just don't break the bank," he said. She laughed. She knew exactly how much they could afford, better than he. She took her responsibilities very seriously, with pride.

The next evening, she was able to look with astonishment at the brightly-coloured photos of clothes and shoes and furniture, toys and skis and drapes and dishes. Page after page. It was unbelievable. Apparently, all you did was fill out the enclosed order form and mail it off. You paid when your parcel arrived down at the store, Carlo explained. C.O.D. Cash On Delivery.

She was beginning to understand quite a number of English words and phrases, and Carlo was endearingly patient with her, anxious that she become fluent to lessen her sense of isolation, to make her feel more at home, he said. *And probably to make her less dependent on him.* Sometimes she even engaged in a rudimentary conversation with a clerk in the supermarket where she went almost daily with Gina now, enjoying the sense of independence it gave her to choose her groceries, pay for them, and carry them home. She prided herself that she didn't have to pester Carlo for every little need as she knew some women pestered their husbands.

Often, standing at the kitchen sink, she would notice the woman from the house across the street coming and going in her car. Liliana envied her. It must be wonderful to be so self-sufficient. And there seemed to be children, two of them, a long-legged sandy-haired boy about ten years old she guessed, and a little girl with curly red hair. She watched the children in their colourful clothes playing in the yard or out on the road, heard them calling out to each other, and wished she understood what they were saying. They spoke so quickly in incomplete sentences, running the words together. Sometimes, surprisingly, the woman came out and played too, something she had never seen back home, laughing and chasing the squealing children.

There were also two other children who played on the street, sometimes alone, sometimes with the two from the house right across, but Liliana couldn't figure out which house they lived in. These children had darker skin and very black, glossy hair, the boy's cut straight across his forehead, the girl's in pigtails down her back. She would have to ask Carlo about them.

"Those two with the black hair are Aldo and Loretta's. They live just around the corner."

"Where are they from?"

"Loretta comes from the village just across the bay–she's from the Native community over there. I told you that."

"But you said they'd only been married a few months. How could those be their children?"

"Well actually, they belong to Loretta. Her first husband was killed and she was left a widow with those two children. But Aldo married her anyway. He's crazy about her."

"He must be a good man," Liliana said, "to have taken on a ready-made family."

"Yes. And she's a good person too. He says she's a good mother."

"How was her husband killed, Carlo?"

No answer.

"Was it in the plant, Carlo?"

Still no answer.

"Carlo, was he killed in the plant?"

"No, no," he murmured comfortingly. "Never mind about that," he said, reaching for her.

But she was troubled. This was not the first time she'd heard references to people getting hurt–even being killed–in the plant. She remembered the man in the supermarket with no legs. "Please–tell me, Carlo! Is it dangerous where you work? Is it? How did he die, the father of those children?"

But Carlo did not reply, only drawing her closer, more insistently, so that her head was buried in his shoulder.

There was almost enough housework to keep her occupied, what with the waxing and polishing of the lino floors, the dusting and sweeping, the cooking and the laundry. There was an electric washing machine with rubber wringers in the kitchen, and a long line outside on which to hang the clothes to dry, a time-consuming task but not as bad as washing by hand as they had done at home. And a good thing too, Liliana thought. Carlo brought his work-clothes home every Friday night and she had never in her life seen such filthy garments. And they stank of the plant. Carlo didn't talk much about work, and she wondered again what he did to get himself so dirty. The dirt and the smell seemed ingrained into the rough fabric, grey woolen pants, grey underwear, and a black and red checked shirt. She always washed them as soon as she could, and hung them out on the line to dry. If it was raining, she had to festoon them over chairs above the hot-air vents in the second small bedroom. Then she would bathe and put on some pretty scent. She hoped she didn't smell like the plant when Carlo crept up behind her and enclosed her in an encompassing embrace, nuzzling the back of her neck and sending shivers down her spine.

Chapter 14

The days were getting ever shorter as the winter solstice approached. It rained every day and every night. She went to bed to the sound of the rain drumming on the roof and woke to the same drumming, a persistent background noise to which she would never become accustomed. No one had mentioned this, no one had told her that it would rain throughout the autumn months, that she would rarely be able to venture outdoors without a raincoat and boots, carrying an umbrella at an angle in front of her as she walked to prevent the slanting rain from hitting her face. It chilled her to the bone, and she thanked God daily for the luxury of the hot-air furnace when she arrived home and turned up the thermostat again.

Carlo was going to work at the same time as he always did each morning, but she began to stay in bed as he quietly made coffee and let himself out. It was so dark. When she finally did leave her warm bed, she walked through the little house turning on all the lights, creating a warm bright cocoon in which to function. It was the only way she knew of to fend off the dark.

In her mind's eye the sun had always been shining back home, shining in the doorway and through the slats of the blinds on the windows so that they had to stop their work and have a cool glass of *orzata*. But the sun couldn't have been shining all the time, could it? It must have rained sometimes, she thought, looking at the rivulets of water

155

running down the windows. And the anger came again, stealthily, knowing it had not visited her for some time. *How did I end up here, a prisoner in this house with the everlasting rain outside? Carlo's gone all day, and the other women have their families. But I am alone. I miss talking things over with my sister, my mother, even my nonna. I need them. I need their support and advice and love now more than ever. Oh God, I'm so lonely. Help me.*

And then there were the times when she was surprised to recognize a deep sense of well-being, a feeling such as she had never expected to experience. Sometimes in the afternoons when her little house was in order, the feeble light reflecting the shapes of the windows on the blue tiles of the floor, she thought she might even say she was happy. Carlo loved her. Their lovemaking was something so wonderful, so mystical, that she was constantly surprised at its power. She tried not to think about it during the day.

Her home was as attractive as she could make it, the starched curtains over the yellow countertop framing the view of the big mountain ash outside. She loved to polish her matrimonial suite until it gleamed, and she would stand transfixed by her own image in the big mirror over the dresser. She looked pale and small, older, like her mother had in old snaps, when her father had been alive. Pretty, her grave green eyes preoccupied.

Soon all the leaves had fallen from the mountain ash, and occasionally the rain stopped long enough for her to enjoy her walk with Gina to the grocery store, their feet scuffling through the piles of fallen leaves on the sidewalk. Sometimes the sky cleared briefly and she caught her breath at the sight of the sparkling snow-tipped mountains in the distance, their peaks outlined clearly against the cerulean sky. And then the rain would begin again, interspersed now with flakes of snow. And then, just snow. She had rarely seen snow, and its appearance delighted her at first as it fell softly, covering the yards and walkways with its pristine white mantle. It brightened the grey days as it fell, creating beautiful patterns where it covered each branch and twig of the bushes and trees, softening the contours of the houses and drifting up against them in soft pillows. It lay like a silent white coverlet on the mountains, putting into sudden sharp contrast the indigo trees diminishing upward into tiny dots.

Sometimes in the afternoons while the thick snowflakes fell like a lacey curtain outside the windows, she spent hours daydreaming over the pages of the Eaton's catalogue. So much to choose from. There were some very attractive sets of bone china dishes, some quite tasteful, but she simply hadn't been able to decide yet which set to order.

The women would sometimes visit each other during the afternoons while their husbands were at work, tramping through the snow, laughing, and Liliana soaked up their conversations. She had so much to learn. These were the conversations she wanted to be having with her mother and her sister. They talked about things like how to make *osso-buco* and how to get the sheets as white as back home, and where to find the best chicken, and who was pregnant, and they talked about their husbands, their quarrels, their dreams, their disappointments. And Liliana listened, and learned that women had to be smart, forgiving, tough and brave and resourceful. She learned that she was not alone in her homesickness. Anna and Lena and Gina were lonely too, missed their families and the familiar surroundings of home as much as she did. But they had toughened themselves. Sometimes she told them how hard she found it to be isolated by the unfamiliar language, the unknown customs, how diminished she felt, how angry at her inability to express herself. We know, they said laughingly, we know that all too well. But it will come, they assured her, it will come. And she was comforted for a time.

One night in mid-November, just as Liliana was draining the pasta at the sink and thinking that Carlo was late for supper for the first time, he came struggling through the doorway carrying a huge brown-paper wrapped parcel. "Surprise!" he yelled, "a surprise, Liliana, for you! Come on, make room on the table so I can put it down."

"What is it, Carlo? What in the world? What have you done?" she squealed, his obvious excitement infecting her as she moved the thick white plates and bowls aside to make room for the box. "Open it! Let's see!"

Grabbing a tableknife, Carlo made short work of the wrapping paper and soon exposed a large shiny white box imprinted with florid magenta and yellow roses. "Open it, *cara*, open it," he said, barely containing his excitement. Tentatively she opened the flaps on either end and lifted the lid, feeling Carlo's eyes on her every move. She stared. She was speechless. Struck dumb. The box contained a set of bone china dishes, dinner plates standing up in little slots and beside them breakfast plates, bread and butter plates and soup bowls, with cups and saucers nestled at either end of the row. She recognized it immediately as the service for twelve that she had stared at so often in the catalogue. The one she had hated. The one with the garish, florid magenta and yellow roses, the one that she had long-ago decided was the ugliest, the most tasteless set of china she had ever seen or could imagine. She felt Carlo's eyes on her face, waiting for her reaction, completely innocent of his transgression. Her heart beating so loudly she was sure he could hear it, a rushing noise in her ears, she turned to face him. "Oh Carlo, it's beautiful," she breathed, not trusting herself to speak out loud. "Just what I've wanted. Just what we need. Oh, it is absolutely perfect. Perfect." And not daring to speak another word, she stepped into Carlo's embrace, pressing her face into his shoulder to keep her mouth closed, willing the threatening tears to go away. "Thank you. Oh, thank you, Carlo," was all she said, and he tightened his embrace as his mouth sought hers.

A week later she sat proudly at one end of the table with Carlo at the other, flanked on her right by Gina and Mario across from Anna and Tony. The table, covered by a stiffly-starched white cloth which Liliana had hoped would tone down the total effect, was nevertheless a riot of colour with the brightly-patterned dishes set out around it. Her friends had exclaimed appropriately at the elegantly-set table as Carlo beamed, but Liliana wondered if they weren't secretly amazed at her dramatic taste in china.

"Ma che bei piatti! Guarda, che belli!" exclaimed Gina in genuine admiration, and Liliana smiled secretly as Carlo basked in her admiration.

The antipasto, over which she had anguished, had been served, consisting of a large platter of olives, anchovies, sliced hard-boiled eggs, artichoke hearts and roasted red peppers, exquisitely arranged, the whole glistening with a drizzle of olive oil. *So far so good,* she thought as she took away the little plates and served each person some of the clear chicken broth dotted with the star-shaped pasta her mother had always favoured. She passed the little silver bowl of *parmigiano* which Carlo had proudly grated earlier, his only contribution to this debut meal over which she had slaved for two stressful days. But she hadn't expected him to do more; she had never seen a man in the kitchen. *Will it ever become easy,* she wondered, *as effortless as it seemed to be for Mama and Nonna?*

And then, with more than a little trepidation, she rose to remove the soup plates and to serve the main course. She had struggled mightily to produce these little *involtini*; thin cutlets rolled up with *prosciutto cotto* (thinly-sliced ham) and batons of *provolone*. Each roll had been closed with toothpicks, devilishly difficult to do. Next, they had been browned and then simmered in a light tomato sauce. Of course, some rolls had leaked their cheese so that the sauce was dotted with unsightly white lumps and strings of *provolone* which she had fished out, one by one. When the rolls were cooked, she had carefully removed the toothpicks. She hated those damned *involtini*, cursing herself for having settled on this as her entrée. But she served them, alongside the little potatoes roasted with rosemary, with a gracious smile. All seemed well so far, and Carlo was grinning foolishly as the others complimented her on the food when suddenly, in the midst of it all, Anna gave a piercing shriek. Their heads swivelled with one accord to stare, transfixed, at Anna's red face and bulging, terror-filled eyes. Gagging, her open mouth filled with half-chewed *involtini*, she inserted one ringed finger and laboriously fished out a toothpick, which she held up and glared at accusingly. By this time everyone was gathered around her, clapping her on the back and exclaiming with concern.

"Don't swallow! Make sure there isn't another one!"

"Be careful, that happened to my cousin once and she had to go to the hospital!"

Liliana held her breath. I knew it! It was going too well. Oh God, how mortifying!

And then Gina began to laugh, and after a brief moment of silence they all joined in. They laughed as though they were insane, at first Carlo and then Liliana too. They hooted and screamed, describing to each other over and over what everyone had seen, laughing until the tears ran down their faces. The ice was broken, well and truly broken, and the rest of the meal was eaten amid much hilarity. Wine was poured, and poured again, so that by the time the *zuppa inglese* and coffee with brandy had been consumed, the carefully-set table was a shamble of glasses and dishes and spills and drops, and Liliana knew that she had arrived. She was flushed with success as she and Carlo finally bid farewell to their guests, standing with their arms around each other in the open doorway as the snowflakes drifted in.

Chapter 15

Midnight Mass that Christmas was the most moving she could remember, its sacred mystery enhanced by the silence and isolation enforced by the snowy surroundings. The nativity scene outside the church was set in a creche of cedar boughs with little white lights interspersed among them, drifts of snow on the shoulders of the silent figures. As Liliana sat in the rough brown pew beside Carlo, inhaling the smell of the incense and the hot wax from the tall white candles ranged behind the pots of red poinsettias, she felt at peace.

After Mass they all went outside onto the steps, their breath floating in little plumes from their mouths as they smiled and hugged and wished each other a Merry Christmas, then turned up collars and pulled up hoods as they walked through the falling snow toward their cars. *"Buon Natale, Buon Natale,"* they called out as they stood brushing off the white mounds, engines running, wipers labouring to keep up with the mounting flakes. Carlo drove slowly, careful to keep the wheels in the faint ruts, knowing that the slightest deviation would leave them stranded in the rapidly-mounting drifts on either side of the road. "Oh *Dio*! Be careful. We don't want to get stuck!"

"Don't worry. I know how to drive," he said calmly, concentrating hard on the tracks illuminated by the headlights. "But this is really something, it's coming down hard. I hope we make it home safely."

The town was transformed, its dark streets lit by the soft glow of the strings of lights on the houses, their greens and blues and reds diffused by the falling snow. Liliana had never seen Christmas lights before. She thought the way they dispelled the gloom of the bleak winter streets, at least for a time, was wonderful.

There was silence as they inched along in the caravan of cars, each one with mounds of snow on its roof and hood and trunk. Liliana let out a sigh of relief when finally they turned off into their street. She knew Carlo was as anxious to get home as she was. It was hard work, driving in such a storm. Her own house, the light glowing in the kitchen window, welcomed them. "Next year I want to have lights on our house too."

"You want what?" he said absentmindedly, concentrating on turning the car into their driveway.

"Lights. Outside lights on the house. Look how pretty they are."

"I know, we should have done it this year. I like them too. Next year."

In the living room stood their Christmas tree, a real tree, festooned with tinsel ropes and coloured lights which Carlo and she had purchased at 'the Bay.' She had heard of this custom, though it was unknown back home—wherever would they have gotten an evergreen tree? But she had never seen a decorated Christmas tree until this year. It was so cozy to sit in the room with all the other lights out, she and Carlo on the sofa sipping a glass of wine while the soft colours danced and rippled on the tinsel.

Under the tree were two parcels, and now, standing inside the kitchen door taking off their snowy boots on the mat and hanging their damp coats on the backs of the kitchen chairs to dry, she could hardly wait to turn on the lights and exchange gifts. She had ordered Carlo's from the catalogue, a handsome woolen sweater in a cable stitch which she knew he would look wonderful in. His parcel for her was large and rectangular, clumsily wrapped. It touched her that he had done this, bought something and wrapped it himself. She wouldn't have thought he would bother to wrap it at all.

"Oh Lili, it's beautiful, just beautiful, and it looks so nice and warm. Just what I need!" And pulling the dark green sweater on over the shirt and tie he wore, he grabbed her in a bear hug, dancing her around in a circle. "Now open yours. Go on. Pick it up and open it!"

She bent to retrieve her gift from where it had been pushed back under the bottom boughs, but to her surprise she couldn't budge it. Not at all. It was impossibly heavy. She looked up questioningly at Carlo, who was watching her with a grin on his face, obviously enjoying her surprise. "Oh all right, I'll get it. Stand aside," he said laughingly in a fake muscle-man sort of voice, and dragged it further out so that she could tear off the wrapping paper.

"No! No! Not really!" she screamed. "A sewing machine! An electric sewing machine!" Tearing the paper completely off, she threw herself down onto the floor to examine it more closely. "Kenmore Portable," she read laboriously, unclicking the clasps and lifting off the cover. "Look at it! It does everything. Oh thank you, thank you, Carlo. You knew!" And visions of the pages and pages of fabric in the catalogue, bolts and bolts of it up on the third floor of 'the Bay' danced through her head.

During that Christmas season, punctuated by evenings with friends in her home or in theirs, eating chestnuts roasted in the oven, exchanging small gifts, Liliana felt almost settled. She missed her family as much as ever, but these informal times with friends provided a new and unexpected sort of casual pleasure that had been unknown back home. There, men gathered in bars in the evenings but rarely were women seen out with them. They were at home with their children and often their mothers and sisters. This, she had to admit, was much better, much more modern and somehow more grown-up. She was a person with a life among adults, independent. She had never thought she would feel this way, proud of her ability to function outside the bosom of her family. No one she had ever known back home had been called upon to do this, but she, Liliana Manon, was doing it.

The snow that had replaced the rain continued to fall steadily, large soft wet flakes that clung to her hair, melting slowly. When it had first begun to snow she would stick out her tongue to feel the flakes landing gently, marvelling at their beauty as they lay on her arms and shoulders. Now the town lay thickly blanketed, the windowsills covered with miniature mountains, the undulating white forms outside burying who-knew-what secrets. The boughs of the giant cedars were weighed down, sagging almost to the ground.

"No, Lili, I can't have supper until I've cleared the roof."

"What do you mean, cleared the roof? You've just finished the driveway and you're soaking wet. Can't you stop now?" She saw that Carlo was panting, rivulets of sweat running down his face from under his toque. He had been working all day at the plant, and then he had shovelled snow for at least an hour already.

"No, I can't stop. The snow has built up on the roof, and the guys told me today that the Fire Department has issued a snow-load warning. Everybody is supposed to clear their roof—there's such a weight that it might collapse." He wiped his face with one snow-encrusted glove and heaving a great sigh, turned and went back outside.

Liliana put the supper in the oven to keep warm, feeling faintly chagrined. Carlo was working so hard, willing to put up with so much to keep her comfortable. She ought to show more gratitude. She would make a special effort to be nice to him when he came in, would make sure he had a good hot meal. But when Carlo finally entered the kitchen, exhausted, he threw his wet jacket on the chairback and went straight to the sofa, where he lay down and fell immediately into a deep sleep.

Soon there was no place to put the snow cleared from the pathways or driveways except out onto the street, and Liliana was awakened every night for weeks on end by the roar of the snowblower as it rumbled by, streaming out a blast of snow onto the tops of the banks, first on one side of the street and then on the other.

She would rise from the bed where Carlo slumbered peacefully, worn out from working at the plant and then shovelling for several hours, to watch its cumbersome progress, like some huge blinking roaring beast. The reality of the endlessly falling snow was overwhelming—its depth, its cold, its imprisonment of the people in the houses. She couldn't believe that no one, not even Uncle Tony, had mentioned the snow. Or had they? Had she been too self-engrossed to hear? The snow, the never-ending snow, was more than a mere detail. It created a totally new, all-encompassing environment. The world had shrunk to a white universe, a cold, colourless world outside her little house. She stood motionless in her nightgown at the bedroom window night after night, staring out at the whiteness and silence of this world, and saw with pleasure the occasional glow of light in the windows across the street. She began to leave a small light on in her kitchen all night, telling herself that anyone looking out into the night would see it and be comforted. She wished she knew the people who lived there, in the house exactly like hers across the street.

She had often watched the comings and goings of the woman, a little older than she, and a man who went to work each morning carrying a silver-coloured metal lunch box like Carlo's. The children often played out in the street, regard-less of the snow, their shrill voices like distant birds until their mother called to them from the doorway. It was a family life so unlike hers.

Before the snow came and isolated her she had tried to think of a way to approach this woman. She must be Canadian, and Liliana wanted badly to make friends with a woman who was at home here, comfortable in her own country, in her own language. But she didn't know how.

Sometimes as she stood at the kitchen sink, leaning on her elbows and staring absently out the window, she allowed herself a fantasy—she was laughing and talking animatedly in English with her new friend as they walked home together from the market. And then they were huddled over cups of coffee at her table, brushing the drops of water off their foreheads as the snow that had caught in their hair melted. On the mat just inside the door their heavy wet boots sat dripping, their damp jackets draped over the backs of the chairs.

And then she would shake her head and see again through the curtain of lacy flakes the silent street, the pristine trackless road.

The dark days and the enforced isolation made the days go by slowly, and she knew she had been going around with a long face lately. She had been feeling morose, and she realized, though she tried to hide it from him, that Carlo had sensed it and was worried. Once or twice he had asked her if something was wrong, and she had put him off, saying only "Oh. It's nothing, *caro*, nothing. I'm just a little down—*un po' giù*—I guess it's the weather. I'll be fine." She hated to seem whiney. She had thought she might be pregnant, a worry she endured silently each month. But she wasn't.

It was a Saturday morning in mid-February and Liliana was making pasta, the kitchen table covered with flour and strips of drying noodles, when the phone rang. It didn't startle her anymore. Her friends often called just to chat, unable to get out when the snow-blower couldn't keep up with the downfall and the roads and paths were drifted in— sometimes over their waists.

"Oh Liliana, help me! It's me, Gina. The pains have started, they're very strong now! I didn't tell Mario before he left for work—I didn't know for sure. But they're getting closer together and I'm scared—I tried to phone Anna, but she's not answering—I don't know what to do!" Gina's voice ended in a wail as another pain overtook her.

"I'll be right over. Just sit down and wait for me. I'll be right there. Don't worry." But Liliana was quaking with fear. *My God, I don't know what to do. I don't know anything about childbirth. What should I do? It sounds like she's in such terrible pain. Oh God.* She felt total panic, but her movements were rapid and precise as she grabbed a damp tea towel and wrapped up her ball of pasta—too bad if it's ruined—and threw on her coat. *I've got to get there somehow, as fast as I can. I'll figure out what to do when I'm there.* Pulling on her heavy boots and taking a last glance around the kitchen, she hurried out and shut the door firmly behind her. They never bothered to lock it.

Down the path and out into the roadway she went, lifting each leg high in order to make more rapid progress through the snow. It was well above her knees and each step left a deep hole in its unmarked surface, but she ploughed on. *God, God, I don't know what I'll be able to do when I get there, but I'll think of something. Babies don't come out that fast—or do they?*

As she approached the door, panting, she distinctly heard Gina's voice moaning, keening. And then silence. *Oh God, maybe she's dead.* And as she burst through the door in a flurry of snow, "Gina, Gina, it's all right. I'm here." She immediately saw Gina in front of the kitchen sink, her enormous belly forcing her to stand well back, her arms held straight out, stiffly, on either side as she grasped the counter edge with her hands. Drops of sweat beaded her forehead and tears ran down her cheeks. Liliana's first instinct was to turn and run, but then she knew with a sinking feeling that she was it—she was the woman who would have to assist Gina in her trial. And suddenly she remembered the elderly priest on the airplane—how she had done what had to be done despite her terror—and she knew that she would not fail Gina. She would figure out what to do. As the pain passed and Gina's arms fell to her sides, she turned toward Liliana, helplessly crying as Liliana patted her and murmured comforting words.

Carefully she guided Gina to the sofa in the living room, the same sofa where she, Liliana, had sat so stiffly on her wedding day so long ago. Gently, feeling in one tiny corner of her mind proud that she was able to hide her fear, to comfort Gina, she covered her with a throw and with hardly a conscious thought heard herself saying, "I'm going for help. I'll be right back. I'll be right back. Just don't move. Everything is going to be fine." And without answering Gina's whimpered pleas not to leave her, she turned and went back out the door, heedless of the puddles of water that lay on the floor where she had walked in her snow-caked boots.

Half-running, stumbling and falling and getting up again, she arrived finally at the door of the woman in the house across from hers, the Canadian woman with whom she had never exchanged a word. Frantically she pounded on the door, which was opened immediately by the little girl with the red hair whose eyes widened as she called out in a high voice, "Mama, Mama," followed by words that Liliana could not understand. But when the woman came running, drying her hands on her apron, Liliana managed by dint of gestures, a few words, and the urgency on her face to convince the woman to put on her coat and boots and come with her. Calling to the boy and obviously admonishing him sternly to look after his little sister, she hurried out after Liliana.

Through the deep snowy ruts of the road they ran together, helping each other up as they stumbled and fell, lurching forward in their urgency to get to Gina. *She must have seen Gina, so obviously pregnant. She has passed by often on her way to my house. She must understand what's happening now. She'll know what to do.*

Later, Liliana was to wonder many times at her own brashness, knocking on Margie's door without a moment's hesitation, to wonder at Margie's instant understanding and willingness to help. They had acted as one, Lili bending over Gina as she lay twisting and moaning on the sofa, Margie at the telephone summoning help, both comforting and assisting Gina into the ambulance when it arrived, siren screaming, red lights flashing, Gina calling out, "Call Mario, please, call Mario! Tell him to come to the hospital!" And then, summoning a faint smile, "Thank you. Thank you."

Somehow Margie had understood and had known how to call the plant and get Mario on the phone to tell him what had happened, which she did in a clear, firm voice, reassuring him, Lili supposed, that everything would be fine. Suddenly Gina's house was quiet, the two pairs of boots standing in pools of water inside the kitchen door, the two jackets thrown carelessly over the kitchen chair-backs. The women turned and looked searchingly into each other's faces. "My name is Liliana," she said as carefully and clearly as she could, and the other replied, "My name is Margie," in the same clear and stilted way. They shook hands, laughing sheepishly, knowing it was a meaningless gesture, knowing that their bond in womanhood was firm. They were friends already.

"Come, come to my house for coffee," said Margie, miming the lifting of a cup to her mouth, but Liliana had understood perfectly. She nodded her head in assent as they both turned to the task of straightening Gina's house, folding the throw which lay now on the floor, setting the kitchen chairs back in place and straightening the cloth on the table. Then they bent to pull on their wet boots, wiped up the puddles on the floor as best they could with the dishcloth, then put on their heavy damp jackets.

The two women closed Gina's door firmly and locked it—*surely Mario would have the key, and who knew how late he'd get home tonight*—then stood for a moment on the doorstep as they pulled on their mittens and put up their hoods. The snow was falling thickly and they could barely see the tracks of the ambulance where it had turned up the driveway, so quickly had the ruts filled with snow. They started off, walking slowly arm in arm toward Margie's house, laughing gently as first one stumbled and then the other. Margie was talking to her, slowly, in a warm and friendly tone of voice that put Liliana at her ease, so that she was able to understand almost everything, and to reply hesitatingly. And Margie seemed to understand her replies.

"Cold?"

"No, No. Not cold. *Difficile a camminare.* Hard to walk!"

"Yah, it is. It's very hard to walk. But we'll make it. We need some hot coffee."

"*Sì*, yes. Some coffee. Good. You cold?"

"No, I'm fine Lili. I'm O.K. Those are great pants you're wearing. Keep your legs warm, huh?"

"Sì, yes. Me—I do. I make."

"You *made* those? You mean you sewed them yourself?"

Liliana looked down to where the tops of her carefully-pressed slacks, which she had just finished making the day before, were tucked unceremoniously into her boots and caked now with snow. She had made several pairs in different colours, all of fine wool. She was so pleased that Margie had noticed.

"Yes, I make. Carlo—*mio marito*—give me *macchina*—*per Natale*."

"Your husband is Carlo?"

"Yes, Carlo."

"And he gave you a sewing machine for Christmas? Well, you sure do know how to use it! I wish I could sew like that. Make things for the kids."

"Yes, I know. *Mia Mama* –my mother show—teach me. I sew many things." *I could make clothes for her children. I have lots of time. I could do that for her.*

"That's great. Well, here we are. Come on in."

Entering Margie's house, they took off their boots and hung their wet jackets on the backs of the chairs, and Margie indicated that Lili should sit. Once she had made sure that the children were playing happily, she turned to the business of making coffee. Lili seized the opportunity, while Margie's back was turned, to have a good look around. Margie's house, identical in plan to her own, but somehow much more finished-looking. Some of the walls had been painted in quite strong colours, a dark peacock blue in the living room, with a wall-to-wall rug of the same colour on the floor and new-looking furniture of dark shiny wood. The kitchen floor had been tiled, and the cupboards had been replaced with better-looking ones in a soft vanilla tone. The table at which she sat was quite substantial, with matching chairs of the same wood. This house had a permanence about it that Lili thought was sadly lacking in hers, and she realized that for all her attempts to improve things, it still looked as though its inhabitants were only there for a brief stay. Makeshift. She silently vowed to change things. They were not so poor.

And then she stole a look out the window above the sink. There was her little house across the street, its roof covered with a thick layer of startlingly white snow which hung down in a wave-like valance covering the tops of the windows, the bottom halves buried behind the undulating mounds. A thin line of blue-grey smoke was spiralling out of the red brick chimney, and Lili could see the light glowing through her kitchen window behind the snow-traced Mountain Ash. She always left the light on these days to ward off the perpetual twilight of winter. Such long dark days. *It looks so familiar, my little house, just like the illustrations of villages in winter from my childhood picture books. It's as though I've seen that house buried in snow before.* And she felt a surge of warmth for it, perhaps even of love.

"Coffee's ready. Can I pour you some? Milk? Sugar?" half-said, half-gestured Margie as she approached the table with the pot in her hand. Lili smiled and nodded. She was surprised at the size of the big aluminum coffee pot with its little glass dome in the centre of the lid, and at the size of the huge cups with big thick handles, no saucers, which Margie had set out and had filled with the pale brown liquid. She copied Margie, who added plenty of milk and sugar and stirred vigorously, hoping her surprise wasn't too evident. The coffee was quite pleasant, hot and sweet, but much too weak. And suddenly she was back on the airplane, her stomach queasy as she had tried to drink the tasteless liquid. But this was better, much better than that.

"Mmm. Good coffee. Hot. Your *bambini*—what names?" asked Lili, wanting to know everything.

"You mean my children?"

"Yes. Your children," she said, ducking her head as she stumbled over the word. "What names?"

"My boy is Jack, and my little girl is Terry. It's hard for them now, the snow is so high they can't play outside. But they're good kids."

"*Sì*, yes. Good children. And your *marito*?"

"My husband? His name is Mike. He works at the plant. On day shift this week."

"Yes, my—husband—work at plant. He at work today, but never he work night shift."

"Well, that's a blessing. Tell me, where are you from, Lili? Tell me about yourself."

"*Italia*—Italy. I come from Italy," replied Liliana, so happy to finally be able to tell her new friend about her beloved homeland, and of how she missed it. "I have mother, and grandmother, and sister—Luisa. I—I," and she felt the tears forming in the corners of her eyes. She hadn't cried in a long time.

"Yah, yah, I know, I know," said Margie comfortingly. "I have a sister too—Monica. I know how you feel. I miss my Mom and Dad too. We come from Nova Scotia, from the other coast of Canada. It's hard, it's hard to be so far away. Everything is so different out here."

They talked on, Margie's manner animated and warm, and though Lili was far from able to understand word for word, to her surprise she was getting the gist of it. She smiled and gestured and spoke haltingly in return, grateful for Margie's earnest and compassionate efforts, hoping that some of what she was saying in return was intelligible, that she didn't sound too stupid, too childlike. She had sometimes caught the ridicule in the voices of the clerks in the supermarket, caught their arch glances as she had struggled to ask a question or reply to a remark. Aware that she sounded like a backward child, she would seeth at her inability to make herself understood. But more than that—at the thought that she was being mistaken for some sort of inferior being. Feeling demeaned beyond words. But Margie was not demeaning her, not making her feel stupid and childish, and Liliana would be forever grateful to her newfound friend for her mighty efforts to understand and to be understood that day.

The coffee sat cooling in the mugs while the two women talked, looking carefully into each other's faces. They talked about poor Gina, about her fear, and about their terror while they were waiting for the ambulance. "Oh *Dio*, I—*paura, molto paura!*" Liliana confessed, seeing now that Margie would understand and not think less of her for it. She clenched her hands in front of her heart, a frown on her face, trying to indicate to Margie what she meant.

"Yes, I know. Scared. You were scared. Me too."

"*Sì*, yes. Scar-red. I—very scar-red. Never—I not know," struggled Liliana.

"I understand. You've never been with a woman in labour, and it really scared you. Me too. It's always scary. I thought that ambulance would never come."

"Yes, yes," said Liliana, nodding her head vehemently. "I too think never. But she be all right?"

"Oh I think so. I think so. She'll be all right. Don't worry," said Margie, reaching out and patting Liliana's hands as they lay twisting on the table. And to Liliana's surprise, though Margie had two children, she said that she too had been afraid.

"You never know, things can happen very quickly, and it's never the same twice. Poor Mario, he sounded so frightened too. I'm sure she'll be all right. It's a good little hospital, but I'll be glad to hear when it's all over."

"Oh yes, *anche io*—me too. I ask Carlo to phone the hospital—talk Mario. Soon he get home."

That settled, Liliana and Margie talked on, persevering despite the difficulty of the language, each asking the other the questions that were foremost in their minds—about their husbands, about their far-away homes.

"I guess you were pretty hard-up over there, huh?" Margie asked.

"What. . . hard-up? Sorry?"

"I mean poor—you were very poor—you came here to Canada because you were very poor."

"*Pauvero?* Poor? Oh, no, my family was not poor! We lived in a big house, much bigger than these. . . with beautiful furniture. I had everything."

"But why then?" Margie asked. "Why did you come here?"

177

Liliana struggled to find the words. She very much wanted Margie to know that she came from a good family, from a well-appointed home, and that she had only come to this isolated town of little houses because of Carlo.

"I come here because. . . because Carlo *insiste!*"

"He insisted? Why?"

"Because. . ." She didn't know how to explain. "Because–he *insiste* that we–marry– here–he has good job. No jobs back home."

"Oh, I get it!" Margie said, visibly relieved to have understood at last. "Same here. We came all this way across the country because there were no jobs back home. But we were poor, no doubt about it. No big fancy house back home. Not us."

They spoke then of how they missed their homes, their sisters, their parents, until Liliana realized with a start that it was beginning to darken outside.

When Carlo came home that evening, he found Liliana humming in the kitchen, her cheeks flushed, as the water for the pasta boiled vigorously on the stove. But he soon realized it wasn't only the heat of the kitchen that was causing the sparkle in her eyes, the high colour. Excitedly she told him about her day, about Gina, about finally meeting Margie, about what a wonderful person she was. The ringing of the telephone interrupted her.

"Wonderful, that's wonderful—a boy! Good. Good. Everything's O.K. then? Good. Yes, I'll tell her. Our congratulations to you both."

"Mario thanks you both for all your help today. He says Gina would have been in serious trouble if you hadn't known what to do. And he asks you to thank that other woman too."

"Margie–her name is Margie, and she is my new friend."

"Well, he says to thank you both."

"Oh, it was nothing—we just phoned for an ambulance. Anyone could have done as much," she said, pouring the pasta and water into the colander in the sink, the window above it fogging up from the heat so that she couldn't see Margie's kitchen window across the street. But she knew her friend was there, the light from her window glowing onto the top of the snowbank.

Chapter 16

In the few months since Carlo had surprised her with a television, just after Christmas, it had become their habit to spend Saturday evenings in front of it, Lili working on a piece of embroidery or leafing through a magazine, puzzling over the text, while Carlo watched the hockey game. He often lamented the lack of soccer games to watch or even European Soccer League scores about which he was passionate, but she could tell that he was beginning to understand this new game and she was glad of that. It helped to pass the time on long winter evenings, gave him something to look forward to on Saturday nights. It was a cozy feeling, just the two of them sitting close together on the sofa, shoulders touching, rarely speaking. It was good to establish rituals different than the ones back home, but rituals nevertheless. She pictured them years later, a loving family gathered together in the flickering light cast by the TV screen, children lying on the rug on their stomachs, feet in the air, as she had seen Margie's children in their living room across the street. Often, she would prepare a little snack and serve it on the coffee table like a picnic, and there was a tiny delicious sense of the forbidden in this. Meals were to be eaten at the table—and only at the table—she had always been taught.

After the hockey game, a big blonde woman named Juliette came on, performing songs that were for the most part unfamiliar to them, her black and white image filling the screen, her wide-open mouth outlined in black lipstick. But they enjoyed the music, however unfamiliar, and the intricately choreographed dancing was fascinating. On Sunday evenings Ed Sullivan would come on, and they enjoyed the singers and dancers and laughed out loud at the variety acts. She thought she understood every word that came out of Ed's stony face. This evening, though, after the excitement of the baby coming Lili and Carlo were quieter than usual, deep in their own thoughts as they watched the hockey game–Danny Gallivan's voice calling the plays.

Gina and Mario named their son Nello, and Liliana and Carlo were asked to be his godparents as soon as the baby and his mother, pale and teary, arrived home from the hospital. They were there at the house to help Mario get his wife and tiny son settled in, and Liliana thought that it seemed like much longer than a week since she and Margie had comforted the moaning Gina as she was helped into the ambulance. Who knew what torture she had endured before her baby finally came?

Liliana looked at Gina curiously. She was like a stranger. Someone who had been to a different place. Weak and trembling, she seemed relieved to find Liliana waiting for her at home and after lowering herself gingerly onto the bed, unprotestingly allowed herself to be covered with a comforter, the baby nestled beside her.

"*Dio,* I've been lying in that hospital for almost ten days. No wonder I feel so weak," she said, her voice faint. "And I had so many stitches too." She sounded apologetic.

"Don't worry, Gina. You'll soon be strong again," replied Liliana, not at all sure of the truth of what she said. Gina began immediately to nurse the baby, who kneaded her breast with one tiny fist as he suckled greedily. Liliana watched, fascinated. She had never seen this, and she felt a little embarrassed at the first sight of Gina's breast with its dark engorged nipple. Even slightly disgusted. *Stupida, don't be so silly. This is perfectly natural. There's nothing wrong. We're only women in this room.*

Gina's eyes were focused on her baby, a plump little creature cocooned in layers of flannette and wool, his red face barely visible as he nursed. With one finger she stroked his blotchy cheeks and his sparse dark hair, making little cooing sounds. Liliana sat helplessly on the edge of the bed, watching.

"Here, Lili, don't you want to hold him?" she said when the baby was finally sated. "Isn't he beautiful? My beautiful little Nello!"

"Oh no, not yet! I-I'm sure he doesn't want anyone else to hold him so soon," she said, hoping to delay the inevitable. But Gina insisted and reverently passed the bundle over to Liliana, who took it apprehensively. It had an unexpected weight, and automatically one hand went under his firm round little rump as the other supported his head. He continued to stretch and yawn, opening and closing his tiny pink fists tipped with transparent little nails, quite oblivious to who held him, and Liliana peered into his dark unfocused eyes and was smitten. The warmth of his tiny body spread through her chest and arms and her heart beat just a little faster as she involuntarily began to rock. She glanced over at Gina, asleep now, her long dark lashes feathered on her pale cheeks. Liliana stood and walked slowly through the house, swaying and rocking as she went, back and forth, until she lost track of time.

"Hey there, Lili, you've stolen my son." Startled, she realized that Mario was calling out to her from the kitchen, and sheepishly she walked to where the two men were sitting at the table having a glass of wine.

"No, No. I'm just giving Gina a break. She needs her rest." And she felt Carlo's eyes on her, appraisingly. *I know what he's thinking. Maybe it's time.*

"Here, let's have a look," said Carlo, and she walked over and bent at the knees so as not to disturb the baby. There was silence as he peered into the bundle, and then one finger, looking large and hairy, crept out and stroked the baby's cheek.

"*Che bello*," he said. "You have a beautiful son, Mario. *Bello.*"

"*Sì*," nodded Mario matter-of-factly, "I know. Beautiful. *Mio figlio Nello*," he went on as he gazed adoringly into the little face with its roving eyes.

"I'd better get him back to his mother now. Enough admiration," Lili announced, standing up straight and walking carefully and slowly back toward the bedroom, calling softly over her shoulder to Carlo, "We should go now. These two need some peace and quiet."

On a snowy Saturday morning two weeks later, Liliana and Carlo, dressed in their finest, drove to Gina and Mario's house. There were last-minute preparations to be done for the baptism party which would be held later in the afternoon when they returned from the church.

The baptism of a child called for a great celebration, which meant in actuality a huge meal to be prepared and served by the two women. About a dozen of their mutual friends, who anticipated nothing less than a feast, had been invited to the ceremony and for dinner afterward, and Liliana had been helping Gina for several days already so that they wouldn't have too much to do when they returned from the church. These preparations had meant that Gina had no choice but to throw herself into the work, and she was much stronger now as a result.

"Don't forget the table, Carlo. We promised to get it over here," reminded Liliana as soon as they entered the house, redolent with its smells of cooking and baking and spotlessly clean, though as starkly furnished as the day Liliana had arrived so many months before.

"Sì, we'll walk over and pick it up now. It's not heavy," replied Carlo, and he and Mario struck out, walking carefully down the road, arms held out from their sides for balance, slipping now and then in their good black shoes. Liliana paused a moment at the window to watch their progress down the snow-rutted road, their bodies in the dark suits outlined starkly against the snow banks.

We're like pioneers, inventing new rituals, finding ways to adapt the old traditions to new surroundings.

The women put on aprons and began to work, talking quietly as they slid pans of *pasta al forno,* or *lasagna* as some called it, into the oven to warm, arranged cold cuts and cheeses, made salads, piled up plates of fruit and and buns and *crostoli.* Liliana had made these delicate fried ribbon cookies, sprinkled with powdered sugar, and she was pleased at the lovely tower she had arranged so carefully on a big blue plate.

In the midst of the bustle the door opened, letting in a blast of cold air, and Mario and Carlo entered carrying Liliana's much-hated pink formica table. Stamping their feet on the mat inside the door, they carried the table over to place it end to end with Gina's, pushing the two together to form one longer table. Then they left again to collect the kitchen chairs.

When the men returned they arranged all the kitchen chairs around the living room. This meal was going to be served buffet-style, something they would never have done at home. But the small houses and minimal furniture here made it impossible to serve that many people sitting down at the table, so this makeshift arrangement was the best they could come up with. It would have to do. Finished, they removed their suit jackets and, loosening their ties, settled themselves on the sofa, their contribution to the preparations at an end.

As Liliana passed the doorway into the living room she glanced in at them sitting, heads together, intent on their conversation. She saw again that they were very much alike—Carlo a little taller, his hair a little lighter than Mario's, but both slim, with fine features and a courtly manner. Each inclined his head slightly as he spoke, Mario's black eyes meeting Carlo's hazel ones, each with a similar engaging smile. Mario's darker hair and slightly darker complexion stood out now, more than she had noticed before, in contrast to the whiteness of his shirt. They were both fine looking men, she saw, men of good character, men you could rely on. Carlo, looking up, caught her eye and flashed her a grin. She smiled back and gave him a wink. She was lucky indeed.

Gina told Lili where to find table linens and dishes and cutlery, and she busied herself arranging them on the long table as Gina answered the cries of her child, who needed to be nursed. Gina did not possess many nice things, Liliana saw, not nearly as nice as hers. There were odds and ends of dishes and serving plates, some chipped, nothing matching. She felt a twinge of sorrow for Gina, who seemed unaware of any lack. Liliana thought that she could have lent her some things, dishes and trays, if Gina had only asked.

Liliana's task now was to take care of the arrangement of the platters of food on the table and she did her utmost to make it attractive. She felt Carlo's eyes on her, watching her fondly as she fussed. Despite her best efforts, however, something was missing. The table looked makeshift and simple. No centrepiece. She could use the big potted begonia covered in tiny white blooms that sat in front of the window in the living room. Carlo jumped up and helped her to carry it over. *"Bravo! Bravo!"* cried Mario mockingly. Carlo grinned sheepishly and sat back down, watching as Liliana turned the big plant this way and that until its best side was showing. There, that was better!

"Oh Lili, you're so clever," exclaimed Gina, re-entering the kitchen with the baby in her arms. "I'd never have thought of that." And then, "Look, look at Nello. Isn't he beautiful?"

Liliana turned. There stood Gina proudly holding up the baby, who was imprisoned now in an elaborate white gown stiff with embroidery, its long lace-edged skirt hanging well down over Gina's arm. His round little head was encased in a ruffled embroidered bonnet, quite ridiculous really—but proper. Gina's mother had sent this outfit months before.

"Oh yes," Liliana squealed. "Look, Carlo. Look at Nello!"

"Yes, I see. He's very pretty," Carlo replied, glancing mischievously at Mario.

"Now just a minute—that's my son you're talking about," Mario growled, faking anger.

"All right, that's enough. Time to go now. We mustn't be late," ordered Gina.

Laughing, Mario and Carlo stood then, straightening their ties and buttoning their suit jackets. Mario caressed his son's cheek with one finger as he passed by, then followed Carlo outside to brush the snow off the car and start the motor so that it would be warm inside. They would leave Carlo's vehicle behind.

Checking the oven and surveying the table one last time, the two women flashed a smile of satisfaction at each other, then took turns holding the baby as they put on their coats and boots. Gingerly Gina carried her son down the two steps, out onto the driveway and over to the car, Liliana following closely behind to steady her if she slipped. Then she tucked in the end of Nello's long white gown before slamming the car door. Getting into the back seat beside Carlo, she slid over so as to be nearer to him. The last time she had ridden in the back seat of this car, her husband beside her, she had been wearing her beautiful wedding dress and her satin shoes, and life with its unknown passages had stretched ahead.

Their footfalls echoed in the empty church as they entered and automatically they found themselves whispering. The baptismal font, of some pale stone—or was it fake?—holding a tiny pool of holy water, was just inside the main door of the church, to the right, so there were no lights on elsewhere in the cavernous building. They were the only ones there. They shuffled their feet uncomfortably, waiting, Gina jiggling a squirming Nello. This was a momentous occasion, and Liliana and Carlo were taking very seriously their new responsibility. If anything ever happened to Gina and Mario, they would be responsible for seeing to the religious education of this child, and they would certainly do so.

They clustered together around the font and were soon joined by Anna and Tony, Lena and Claudio, and several other couples who had been invited to witness this important ceremony. Each woman wore her very best tailored woolen suit over a pale blouse—Liliana had made hers that week. The other men wore heavy jackets over their carefully pressed pants. The women had taken off their coats, intending to put them in the back pew, but the church was chilly and they wore them now draped over their shoulders.

Finally, Father Haber appeared, hurrying down the centre aisle toward them, his youthful face flushed. "Sorry, so sorry. Had to go to the hospital. One of our parishioners just died. In the arms of God now," he went on matter-of-factly.

He sees the beginning. He sees the end. Doesn't seem to affect him much.

As soon as the brief but solemn ceremony was over and Father Haber had blessed them all and been thanked, they left the church, Liliana and Carlo in Mario's car, the others following in a caravan. Again, Liliana flashed back to her wedding day. She had felt so alone then. Now she was part of a family of friends. She reached over to place her hand on Carlo's, the gold band glinting on her hand. He responded by curling his fingers up over hers as Mario called out jovially, "*Bene. Andiamo tutti!*"

Liliana helped Gina and the fussing baby out of the car and into the warm house, perfumed with the rich smell of the lasagna warming in the oven. Mario waited in the doorway to usher the others in as Gina hurried down the hall toward the bedroom. She would have to nurse Nello before bringing him out for the picture-taking.

Liliana stood just inside the kitchen, arms out to receive the heavy coats and jackets of the guests as they moved past her into the living room, laughing and talking. A decanter of wine, a bottle of sweet liqueur for the ladies and some glasses sat on the coffee table, a crocheted *centro* from Liliana's trunk under them covering the worst of the scars on the brown wood. A suddenly gregarious Mario busied himself offering drinks to his guests, beaming, his cheeks flushed.

"*Cin cin. A vostro figlio.*" Carlo, the proud godfather, lifted his glass toward Mario in a toast as the others followed suit. "To Nello! To the new baby!" they cried, lifting their glasses and clinking in every direction before tossing down the liquid. The women, seated on the chairs about the room, sipped more demurely, while the men stood in a cluster in the centre, some with their arms about each other's shoulders, talking loudly.

"Liliana, where's Gina? We want to have a better look at the baby," Lena called out as Liliana staggered by under the load of coats and jackets.

"They'll be along in a moment," she puffed. "She's just feeding him. They'll be back out for pictures as soon as she's finished."

Just then she heard a sharp rap on the kitchen door, and knowingly immediately that it would be Margie and Mike from across the street, she hurried to open it. She was glad that they had been invited, though originally it didn't seem to have occurred to Gina. But Liliana thought they should be–after all, hadn't Margie really been the one to make the important decisions that day? She had gently inferred as much to Gina, who had then asked Liliana to invite them. Now, Liliana wanted to be sure they felt welcome and comfortable. She seated them in the middle of the Italians, who seemed somewhat nonplussed at first to have these non-Italians among them. But soon Lili saw that they were making valiant efforts at conversation, and she caught Margie's eye and smiled broadly.

Liliana picked up another heavy pile of garments as she had been about to do, and carried it down to the bedroom to deposit them on the foot of the wide bed where Gina sat nursing Nello. His stiff bonnet was off, his sparse dark hair plastered to his damp head as he sucked urgently at his mother's breast, oblivious to the commotion which his presence had created. Liliana stood a moment gazing down at him, aware of the crescendo of noise at the other end of the house signalling the arrival of more guests. Sweet little face. Innocent. Her little godson. Strange to think she would be linked to him forever.

Chapter 17

One April morning when the street ran with water like the Tagliamento, sheets of liquid pouring off the snow-laden rooftops as the sun hit them, Liliana stood at the kitchen sink washing the pots and pans that she hadn't bothered with the night before. Absentmindedly polishing the shiny metal with her tea towel, she gazed across the street. There was Margie's house, a place where she felt increasingly welcome and at home. Beside it stood another house, exactly the same but for the colour—Margie's was yellow, the one beside it green. No children lived there, only a middle-aged couple. Margie said that the man, Steve, worked in the front office at the plant, and Lili often saw him coming and going in his car, though he never lifted his head or looked about as he went in and out. The woman, Darlene, was from down south somewhere, near Vancouver, Margie said. A Native Canadian. She had stopped by Margie's for coffee a few times. Once, last February, Liliana had been sitting companionably with Margie at her kitchen table when a knock had come at the door, and there was Darlene, not even wearing a coat and seemingly unaware of a little pile of snow on top of her head and more on her shoulders. She had sat awkwardly at the table beside Lili, obviously ill at ease to find a stranger there, though Margie had done her best to include them both in the conversation. But she spoke little, sipping her coffee, answering questions, keeping her eyes down. She smiled warmly when she stood to go, but Lili felt a sadness in her.

As soon as Darlene had closed the door behind her, Lili and Margie looked at each other quizzically.

"She's alone so much," said Margie. "Her husband is always at work, and he seems to have to go away on business every so often. Sometimes he's gone for a few weeks. That's usually when she visits."

"That's too bad. Why don't you bring her over to visit me some time?"

Margie nodded. "Yes, I'll try. I worry about being too pushy, too much for her. She's very private."

It was almost ten o'clock and though Liliana had seen Margie drive off to her dental appointment she was, she knew, waiting for her knock on the kitchen door. She didn't come over every morning, just once in a while "when I need some company". Liliana looked forward to these morning sessions more than she cared to admit—her blossoming friendship with Margie had been the beginning of her real life in Canada. She felt just a little guilty about these feelings, as though she were betraying her Italian friends, but she was learning so much. It was as though she had been in a darkened room before meeting Margie, and now she was lifting her eyes and looking around her. She saw that there was life outside her little home to be experienced—and Margie could teach her how.

There was no school today for some reason, and Lili had happily agreed to keep an eye on Margie's two kids while she went to the dentist. Lili could hear their voices outside and sometimes, as she stood at the kitchen counter, caught a glimpse of them out on the road where they played with their friends. She knew they'd never leave the street, and she intended to call them in soon for a mid-morning snack.

When the knock came, Lili called out, "Come in," as she quickly tidied the sink, then turned toward the door. But it wasn't the children standing there. It was Darlene who walked unsteadily over to a chair and sat, uttering only a low "Hi," as she took a package of cigarettes from her sweater pocket. She lit one, drawing the smoke in deeply and then exhaling a plume of blue into the air. Quickly Lili mentally reviewed everything she knew about Darlene. Not much.

"Hello Darlene," she said. "Nice to see you. Coffee?"

"Yes please," was all the other woman replied, continuing to pull on her cigarette.

Liliana felt guilty at the feeling of dread she was experiencing. How could she manage a conversation if the other woman didn't talk? But she must have come for a reason. Must have wanted some companionship. And Margie wasn't home. Liliana felt nervous. *Well, why not? I'm a grown woman. I should be able to listen as well as Margie does.* Quickly she got out an ashtray and set it down in front of Darlene. She poured a cup of coffee and placed it on the table, then the sugar bowl and a little pitcher of milk as she'd learned to do from Margie. Liliana seated herself across the table from Darlene, who remained silent. With great difficulty Liliana, too, stayed silent. Apparently, this woman didn't speak needlessly. Her soft brown eyes were

194

downcast, her entire body still. Liliana waited. She could hear the voices of the children out on the street. The sounds of normalcy.

At last, heaving a sigh, Darlene raised her eyes and looked up, and Liliana saw that they were filled with tears. Reaching out, Lili placed a hand on Darlene's where it lay motionless on the table.

"What?" she said softly. "What is it?"

"Today is. . ." There was a pause, then an indrawn breath–a sob. "Today is my son's birthday."

Liliana said nothing, only thinking *Her son? What son? I've never seen a child over there. And Margie never mentioned one.*

"Your son?" she said at last.

"Yah. Howie. He's 30 years old today. He lives with his wife and children in Vancouver." Another long pause. "I ... I never see them," Darlene said so softly that Lili had to bend forward to hear her.

There was another silence. Liliana knew better than to speak.

"I lost him when he was a baby. Had to give him to my mother to bring up. So he doesn't want to see me." Tears coursed down her brown cheeks and Liliana felt her own eyes misting.

"But why, Darlene? Why ... you lose him?" She wasn't sure what that meant, only that it was something so painful that Darlene could barely speak of it. And yet she was obviously compelled to do so.

Darlene withdrew her hand from beneath Liliana's. Then she drew a deep breath and the words began to flow, haltingly, softly, her eyes now downcast, now seeking Liliana's as though beseeching her to understand.

"When I was a little girl I was happy. We were a big family—six brothers and five sisters. We had lots of good times. We'd never been into the city. Didn't know how lucky we were." Darlene's voice went on, describing sun-filled summers playing in the fields, swimming in the river, fishing, attending family feasts with aunts and uncles and cousins. How all the men fished for salmon, and how important the oolichan run was in the spring ... candlefish, she explained. But always she spoke with such an under-current of sadness in her voice that Liliana was aware of a sense of foreboding—an uneasy feeling at the turn the story was about to take.

Darlene lit another cigarette and looked off into space beyond Lili's shoulder. She inhaled, drawing the smoke in deeply, then heaved a great sigh. "But we had to leave home. There was nothing for us there. No jobs."

Just like Carlo and all my uncles back home. Had to leave. Displaced. Like us. Like Margie.

"So I left ... went into the big city. But that turned out to be worse than anything I had imagined. I didn't realize ... It turned out nobody wanted to hire any of us. Shiftless, they said. Couldn't be trusted."

Liliana said nothing, faintly aware of the ongoing sounds of the children. Sheepishly she hoped they wouldn't choose this moment to come bursting in. Darlene's monologue was not for children's ears. Though Lili didn't know all the words that Darlene was using, she got the general idea ... Darlene was talking about racism. Something she knew nothing about, coming as she did from a place where everyone was the same colour, same religion, with the same customs and background. But she knew that it was wrong … and very hurtful. That much was clear. *But then*, *we've never been tested. Would we have been the same?* And then, *What can I say? How can I tell her I'm sorry?* Wordlessly she reached out again to cover Darlene's hand with her own, patting it, hoping that Darlene would know that she was sorry. *But why? Why was she treated that way–and by Canadians! Wasn't Darlene Canadian too?*

"So I started taking drugs … heroin." Darlene went on. Liliana gasped … just a little.

"And then I started selling the stuff."

The tears were pouring down her cheeks now, dripping onto their hands where they lay intertwined on the table, and every now and then Darlene was convulsed with a wracking sob, her shoulders shaking.

"So the police caught me … I was arrested–across the line … in the States. I did eight years in the penitentiary down there. That's how I lost my son … my little boy."

By this time the tears were coursing down Liliana's cheeks as well, though part of her brain was trained on the sounds of the children, praying that they wouldn't burst in and see this raw emotion, at the same time feeling guilty at her reaction. She didn't know why she didn't want the children to see or hear this scene, or why she would have given anything to escape it herself. But she couldn't help but be transfixed by the pain so evident on Darlene's face and in her voice. Liliana was beginning to understand. *She went to prison … that's how she lost her son. Oh, poor, poor woman. No wonder she rarely speaks.*

"When I knew I'd be going to prison, I gave my baby to my mother ... to take care of. I thought about him all the time. I knew he was safe. That's the only thing that got me through. But after eight years, when I went to get him, he didn't know me. And my mother wouldn't give him to me ... said I couldn't look after him."

Darlene was crying open-mouthed now, and Liliana thought her heart would break. What awful misery. She had never before seen such a display of grief, and there was nothing she could do about it. *Oh God, why doesn't Margie come now? I need her. Maybe* she *can comfort this poor woman.*

"She said he'd be better off with her, that I couldn't bring him up properly. And I believed her. I thought I didn't deserve him. So I left him there." Her sobs caught in her throat. "Howie, my Howie."

She lifted her head then, her body limp. Looking across the table into Liliana's eyes, she said, "I'm sorry. But I can't talk about this with my husband. Steve doesn't want to hear about it any more. And I don't want to make him mad. He's so good to me."

"It's okay, it's okay," was all Liliana could think of to say or had the vocabulary for. But she guessed that Darlene didn't really expect her to say anything, didn't expect anyone to be able to heal her pain. Just to listen compassionately was all she asked. And Liliana wondered at the courage of the other woman, carrying this great misery in her heart day in and day out, this guilt, this sorrow, never mentioning it, never letting on to anyone the pain she carried. Like her, Liliana thought with a flash. Like her. The pain always there, just under the surface. And then she felt guilty—Darlene's pain was much greater than hers. No comparison, really.

Darlene stood then, pushing her chair back from the table. "Well, thanks for the coffee. Steve's away on a business trip but he'll phone. He phones me every morning. And every night. He worries." She walked to the door and let herself out just as Margie's two kids appeared, calling out, "We're hungry, Auntie Lili. We're hungry!"

One morning a few weeks later as they sat in Margie's kitchen Liliana's eyes fell on a framed photo on the wall above the table that she hadn't noticed before.

"That's my family, my Mom and Dad and my sister." Margie's voice cracked. "I miss them so much."

And then Margie began to talk about her family and about her life both past and present in words that Liliana was increasingly able to understand. Margie, too, suffered from homesickness and battled the depression brought on by the forced isolation and the weather. The long dark days were hard on all the women, Margie explained, and that was why it was so important to get out, to make friends, to become part of the community. Liliana nodded. And Margie was unfailingly patient and compassionate in encouraging Liliana's ability to express herself in English without those feelings of self-consciousness that had often left her tongue-tied. Sometimes she was surprised at the sound of her own voice speaking in this new language. But it felt so good to have the words to express her feelings out loud and to be unafraid of doing so.

Occasionally Margie sat quietly, not interrupting, as Liliana talked on and on—about back home, the trip, the wedding, her first impressions, her homesickness. The pent-up anger and loneliness had at last found a safe egress.

"Oh *Dio*, I did not want to go—to say goodbye to my family. That day—that day at the airport in *Roma*—it was so hard."

"I know. I'll never forget the day we got on that plane in Halifax. I couldn't even see where I was going I was crying so hard."

"I did not understand anything—*niente, niente*! I did not really know where Canada was, and I was so—so—*furiosa*!"

"Furious? Why were you furious?"

"I furious—I was furious because I did not want to get married in Canada! I want Carlo to come home! To marry me in my church! I was really mad! I feel—I felt cheat!"

"Cheated? Yah, I see what you mean. You felt cheated out of a wedding in your own church, with all your family around you. I don't blame you. At least I had that."

"*Sì*, and also you speak English!" replied Liliana in a strangled voice, choking back the tears.

"Well, that's true. I *do* speak a little English," said Margie, and they both laughed gently, so that Liliana was able to recover, surreptitiously wiping her eyes with the back of her hand. She felt better. She had said it. And Margie had understood and didn't think less of her for it. She had much more to say, she thought, but she would save it for another time. *Be careful. Don't frighten her with your outbursts. Don't tell her yet how angry you still feel sometimes. And lost. Odd how one can feel lonely even in the intimacy of marriage. Does Carlo? Does he ever feel lonely or nostalgic?*

And suddenly she was ashamed. She had never even asked Carlo if he felt these things. Saying them out loud to Margie had normalized the feelings that she had so long hidden and made it possible for her to imagine a similar conversation with her husband. She would ask him—later.

Sometimes they laughed at Liliana's efforts when something was particularly difficult to get out. "You did what— you washed the chicken floor today? Oh, you mean the kitchen floor!" And they'd laugh until the tears ran down their cheeks and they rested their heads helplessly on the table.

Margie often talked about her mother and her sister back home in Nova Scotia, and once or twice *she* had cried. Liliana understood that she wasn't the only one missing her family, missing her girlhood home, and it gave her a good feeling to be able to comfort Margie when nostalgia got the better of her. *Nostalgia, no-stal-gi-a. A beautiful word for a miserable feeling.* Still, Margie had created a full life here. It had a richness that Liliana could only observe. Margie drove the car whenever the roads were cleared and Mike didn't have it, taking her children to school or going out shopping or visiting. Sometimes, as Liliana stood working at the sink, she would see women drive up in cars and go inside the house, and she envied Margie her circle of friends and their freedom. Through her children and her activities Margie was part of the community while she, Liliana, remained on the outside. Suddenly, for the first time in months, she thought of herself as she had been in San Michele, buzzing off to work on her little red Mo-ped, fashionably dressed, confident, her hair flying. She shook her head.

She had been pleased to find out that her neighbours went to church too, though somewhat nonplussed to learn that they were not Catholic. What would Nonna say? But then, would she ever know? No. And it was clear that Margie and her family were no closer to Hell than any number of other people she knew.

Margie and Mike often went out together, though she almost never saw Darlene and Steve leaving their house. He came and went to work, but she appeared only rarely. Poor thing, Liliana thought. She's so sad. She dwells on her past, on her losses, but then who could blame her? Her losses were worse than anyone else's. Worse than Loretta's. Worse than Margie's. Worse than hers even. She was distanced from her family. Her son had been stolen from her and there was nothing she could do. *I should try to get her out, even if it's only to come here once in a while for coffee with Margie and me.*

Sometimes Margie and Mike went out in the evenings without their children, paying a young girl from down the street to come and look after them. A babysitter, Margie called her. Something unheard of back home. She said that a husband and wife needed time together, that it was good for the marriage. Liliana listened carefully. Margie pointed out that without any relatives nearby, paying someone to watch the children was the only option. Liliana saw the sense in that, though she thought that Nonna and Mama would be scandalized. Mike and Margie went out to the homes of friends and to dances and dinners at the Curling Club. Margie had tried to explain to Liliana what curling was, reducing them both to helpless laughter as she demonstrated throwing the rock and sweeping frantically on Liliana's kitchen floor. They also belonged to a plant-worker's social club that took them out to events held in a big hall down town. Margie had urged Liliana and Carlo to join them at the club when something was going on, but so far they had both felt too shy. After all, who would they know there? But Liliana felt envious of her neighbour's life, though she would never say so. She would have loved to get dressed up to go dancing. If Carlo would agree, then I would go. But he doesn't seem to want to do anything other than be with his Italian friends. We'll never break away from them. And then the guilt would come. Who do you think you are? Your old friends aren't good enough for you any more?

The Italian-Canadian club, which had been formed several years before Liliana's arrival in Cedar Ridge, had organized a pre-Christmas party which every man, woman, and child in the Italian community had attended, with nuts and oranges and candy given out to the children and drinks for the adults. Liliana remembered that it had been warm and boisterous, very informal, and she and Carlo had enjoyed themselves. She wondered aloud why they had never before attended anything organized by the club. Carlo said he guessed there hadn't been anything else since she had arrived. And there had been nothing since the Christmas party.

Thinking about the fullness of Margie's life in contrast to hers, a surge of sadness was just beginning to creep over her when there was a rapid-fire knock on the door and Margie burst through, carrying in her arms what appeared to be a plastic-wrapped length of fabric.

"Oh Lili, I really need some help!" she exclaimed, throwing the parcel onto the table and sitting down with a thump. "We're going to a party tonight, a dressy affair at the Curling Club, and I thought I could wear this," she wailed, unwrapping a long silver-grey dress with a large beaded collar. "But I can't! I've lost weight since I wore it last, and it looks awful on me. Do you think you could fix it?"

Liliana picked up the dress and turned it partially inside out to examine the seams.

"*Sì*, yes, I think—I think I can. Let's go into the bedroom so you can try it on."

"I knew you could help me! I saw those beautifully-tailored slacks and that jacket you made for yourself last month. You must have been taught really well. And those professional-looking slipcovers on the sofa," Margie went on as they passed through the living room on their way to the bedroom.

"Try it on first. Here, let me help you."

Quickly and unselfconsciously Margie shed her jeans and sweater and obediently lifted her arms above her head so that Lili could slide the dress down over her shoulders. Adjusting its folds, she couldn't help but laugh. Her friend had almost disappeared inside the heavy taffeta dress. Margie turned to look at herself in the mirror and caught sight of Liliana's grin. Their eyes met in the mirror and they were off, doubled over in a fit of laughter.

"*Basta!* Stand still or I'll pin you!" ordered Liliana as she started fitting the garment, bunching the excess fabric along the seams between her fingers and pinning it, extra pins in her mouth. It was an elegant long dress, something she had never owned, and she wished she needed one too. She could make something really beautiful, a green silk with little fabric roses around the neckline, she thought, but for what? She shook her head. *Don't be silly, you don't need a long dress. Stupida.* "Don't worry, I can do this in few hours.

Come back this afternoon and I should have it ready," Liliana said as she handed Margie her clothes.

So Margie bustled off, calling her thanks over her shoulder as she hurried out the door. Jack and Terry were due home from school any minute for lunch, and she made a point of always having something hot ready for them when they returned. *She's a good mother and such a good person. I wish I could do something more for her. She's helped me so much,* reflected Liliana as she carried the dress and her box of pins into the smaller downstairs bedroom where she had set up her sewing room. She had been working on a little outfit for her godson, Nello, but she set it aside and got busy with the alterations. She loved sewing, not so much the act of using the machine, though she counted her blessings every time she sat down at it, but the creative part—getting an idea for a garment or something for the house, then choosing the pattern—or even making a pattern if she had to—selecting the fabric, the trim, seeing how it all went together. She was fascinated by the textures and colours of the materials and spent hours poring over the pages of the catalogue, creating garments in her mind. She enjoyed making soft tailored shirts for Carlo in the muted blue or brown tones that suited him so well. And she felt so good when she saw his pleasure, his obvious pride each time he put one on.

"Come in, come in." She walked rapidly toward the kitchen door in answer to Margie's knock that afternoon. "It's all ready," she replied to Margie's unasked question as she opened the door. "Hope it fits. Come and see."

The two women hurried to the bedroom, where Liliana had hung the dress in the window. Its silhouette startled her just for a moment as she entered. Where had she—oh yes, her wedding dress had hung like that in Gina's upstairs window. A long time ago.

"Oh, thanks so much, Lili. It looks terrific. You've even pressed it," said Margie, hurriedly shedding her blue jeans. Liliana helped her to ease the heavy dress over her head, then pulled it down over her shoulders and hips as she smoothed and adjusted its folds. Standing side by side, they turned in unison and gazed for a moment at themselves in the big mirror. Both women broke into wide smiles. "Margie, you look—you look *bellissima!*" exclaimed Liliana, pleased at what she had wrought.

"Oh Lili, you've done a wonderful job!" grinned Margie, her eyes sparkling. "I do look *bellissima.* Oh, thank you. You're wonderful!"

Liliana ducked her head, smiling and shrugging her shoulders in an oh-it-was-nothing-really sort of way.

"I wish you could come with us tonight," Margie said, shedding the dress. "But I guess it's too late." And with a swift hug and a smack on the cheek, she was gone.

I wish I were too. I'd love to be able to get dressed up in something fancy. And I'd like to see Carlo dressed up again. But then, Anna said I wouldn't like it at the Curling Club. Said none of the Italians ever go. Sighing, she walked back into the sewing room, turning her attention once more to the little outfit she was making for Nello. Blue and white checks, with a little bow tie. It lay on the cutting table just under the high window, and lifting her eyes she glanced out and realized with a start that the sun was shining this afternoon and the sky, studded with puffy white clouds, was the truest blue she had seen in many months. She had been so intent on fixing Margie's dress that she hadn't even looked outside today. Spring really must be here at last. Humming, she began to sew on the tiny garment.

"Lili, Lili," called Margie, sticking her head into the kitchen unannounced. "What are you up to today?"

"*Niente.* Nothing, just taking a break," replied Liliana from the living room, hastily turning off the TV. She didn't want Margie or anyone else to know that she still watched— or at least listened to—children's programs in the mornings. Sometimes she even answered Mr. Dressup out loud, practicing her pronunciation. "Come in, come in." She was glad to have a visit from Margie. Gina's whole life revolved now around her baby, his feeding time, his bath time, his nap time. They hardly ever walked to the market together any more, though Liliana continued to go herself or with Anna or Lena. Sometimes Margie took her downtown in her car and they would walk through the stores together. Once, Liliana had been shocked to see a man whose entire face was a mass of ugly, red scars criss-crossing it this way and that. She turned away, but not before Margie had seen the look of horror.

"He was burned—in the plant. Happened before we got here. Poor guy."

Liliana didn't reply, could think of nothing to say. It must be a very dangerous place—though Carlo never gave any hint of that. In fact, any time she brought up her concerns about the danger in the plant he managed to avoid replying —to divert her attention somehow. As if she were a child who needed to be protected.

"Come on," Margie called, "Let's go up to the fabrics." It was Liliana's favorite place, up on the third floor of The Bay, strolling between the rows and rows of bolts of material. It was great to have a companion who could speak English fluently, who knew where things were or at least how to ask for them. Sometimes they would go to a restaurant and have coffee and a piece of cake. There were always other women there doing the same thing, though never any of the Italian women.

"Now listen," said Margie conspiratorially as they sat at the table this morning. "Next Saturday night there's a May dance at the club. Nothing fancy, just couples getting together to have a few drinks and do some dancing. I've already lined up a sitter, and Mike and I were talking. Please, why don't you two join us?"

"Oh Margie, I would like—very much—I would love to! But I don't know—about Carlo."

"Well, that's exactly what I told Mike, and he's going to talk to him tonight. He sees him out working in the yard all the time, so he's just going to come over and talk him into it. You'll see, it'll work!"

And work it did. Standing at the sink washing the dishes that evening after Carlo had gone out to dig up the ground for their first vegetable garden, she watched Mike coming casually across the street and disappearing around the corner of her house. She waited, trying to keep busy, fiddling at this and that. She felt just the tiniest bit uneasy at this manipulation. Later, when Carlo came in and stood washing his hands at the sink, he turned his head to speak to her over his shoulder. "How would you feel about going to the dance at the Curling Club on Saturday night? With Mike and Margie? He just came over and asked us."

"Oh Carlo, I'd love to! I'd just love to! It's time we started to get to know other people. I'm sure some of the men you work with will be there. We'll have fun." And she grabbed him from behind, her arms encircling his waist, laying her cheek against his back as he continued to lather his hands. It was a beginning.

"But what will I wear, Margie? I don't have anything but my wedding dress!"

"Well, you *could* chop it off, I suppose. But why don't you make something? There's time. Come on, let's go downtown and look at fabric."

She chose a pattern for a dress unlike any she had ever owned, and she made it up in only two days. Putting it on now, she turned this way and that in front of the mirror in her bedroom, at one point kicking off her shoes and standing on her bed the better to check the hem. Satisfied, she phoned Margie and asked her to come over, anxious that she approve the finished garment though she had been running in and out for the past two days, watching every step of the process. The dress was periwinkle blue shot taffeta, with a scoop neck and short sleeves, the princess line emphasizing her small waist, the gored skirt hanging in folds to just above her knees. She was wearing it when Margie opened the kitchen door without knocking, as Liliana would never do at her house. Darlene was with her.

"Oh, my God! Look, Darlene! Did you ever...?" Margie exclaimed. "You look like a million bucks!"

"What?" Liliana wasn't sure if this was good or bad.

"Lili, you are absolutely *bellissima!*"

"Oh yes, you did a really great job," Darlene echoed. "I can't believe you made that!"

"Just wait till Carlo sees you in that!" Margie went on.

And they looked into each other's eyes and smiled broadly. *The delightful conspiracy of seduction.*

"But Darlene," Liliana said, suddenly worrying that she would feel left out–slighted. "Why don't you and Steve come with us?"

There was an uncomfortable silence, broken finally by Darlene's quiet voice.

"Oh no, that's okay. Don't worry. Steve doesn't like dancing. . . and I . . ." Her voice trailed off.

The party was wonderful, beyond her wildest expectations. *Like an enchanted evening*, she thought as she undressed and prepared for bed. Mike and Margie had been great, introducing them to other couples and shepherding them through the evening. She and Carlo had danced in a way they had never danced before—not waltzes and polkas, like at her wedding, but this new modern way where you faced each other, not touching, and moved to the beat. It was marvellous. After the first few dances she got the hang of it. Carlo had looked a little shocked the first time as he watched her move but eventually he had loosened up too. She felt freed to allow her body to respond to the rhythm. Everyone was joining in, the sounds of the music and the crowd swelling and roaring around them. She was exhausted now, her feet burning, her legs aching, but she felt exhilarated. She had done it!

"Carlo, come to bed!" she called out, bathed in the shaft of silver moonlight where it crept through the window and lay like a molten ribbon across the bed. "Carlo!" And when he came, he found her lying naked, smiling up at him, her eyes luminous, her skin glowing in the moonlight.

Chapter 18

The days grew longer, the sun rose higher and higher in the azure sky, and the smoky mountains gradually lost their white patches on all but the highest peaks. Carlo, she was learning, loved to work in the soil, planting and tending his vegetable garden in the back yard. He built up the beds and bordered them with planks, cutting and trimming twigs for the green beans to climb on, carefully transplanting the *radicchio* seedlings, setting out the tomato plants that he had started indoors on the window sills. He tended them lovingly, going out first thing every morning before work, coffee in hand, to examine the rows intently, bending down and cupping each tiny plant in his palm—looking for she knew not what. It was not at all surprising, she reflected, remembering how every family back home had planted a vegetable garden each spring. But it was the women and sometimes an old man who tended them through the hot summer months, carrying water in buckets, thinning and weeding, until it was time to harvest their bounty—baskets of tomatoes smelling of the sun, onions, braided bunches of garlic.

From her vantage point at the kitchen sink Liliana surveyed the green lawn stretching between the front of the house and the street. It was odd how the houses were positioned so that the kitchen window faced the street and the living room windows faced the back yard. But she was glad—she wouldn't have liked to be facing away from the road when she stood at the kitchen sink.

How fortunate, she reflected, that a few trees and shrubs had been planted in each yard after the town had been built. It must have been very difficult to carve the townsite out of the old-growth forest—to build a town where none had stood before. She had seen some pictures in the local newspaper, photos of the area being logged. There were tall metal poles with long heavy cables attached, which Carlo explained was the method used to drag the trees away to be transported via water to the city. Then there were huge treaded machines which crawled over the rough terrain, levelling it, contouring it to make way for the streets. Sometimes a machine had disappeared into the mud, sinking out of sight—or so someone had told her. Very little of the natural growth in what was now the townsite remained except for a few small stands where the suddenly exposed trees, spindly and unprotected by others, were in danger of toppling over. The first boardwalks had been placed over this rough muddy terrain once the streets had been laid out and the first pre-fabricated houses erected. Her friend Antonietta, the one who had been the only woman at her own wedding, had described how she would venture out wearing rubber boots, slipping and sliding on the wet boards in her efforts to get to a friend's house or to the store. But it had been a great adventure, she said, learning to live in Cedar Ridge. A planned community. One of a kind. So different from back home—so raw. Difficult, but exciting.

Building this town with its curving boulevards and long, straight roads joining the neighbourhoods had been a marvel of modern engineering. This new town, that is. Liliana knew that somewhere in the surrounding forest was the ancient village where the native people had always lived. She wondered sometimes about that place which must be hidden in the shadows of the tangled growth, wondered where it was, what it looked like. She must ask Carlo.

From the kitchen window she could see a shrub that was a blaze of tiny yellow flowers up and down each branch. It had surprised her with its blooms even before all the snow had melted, its brave bright colour lighting up a corner of the yard, its feet still buried in a patch of crystallized snow. Forsythia, Margie said. Its brilliance announced that summer was almost here. Sun, at last.

Liliana had watched the mountain ash outside her window throughout the autumn when it had been laden with clusters of red berries, then with its bare branches traced with snow, and now, at last, bursting with green. It had been a delight to find that someone, probably a woman, had planted bulbs in a bed around its trunk, their green tips pushing up through the last of the snow. Now, at the end of May, some of the more delicate flowers were already finished. She had recognized the tulips and daffodils immediately, but some Margie had to name for her—narcissus, crocuses, tiny snow-drops. Liliana had delighted in them, falling to her knees and burying her nose in their delicate blooms.

The cuttings of rhododendron and other perennial shrubs transplanted from Margie's bushes would one day border the walkway along the front of the yard and even, Margie assured her, grow into a hedge, but so far they remained sparse. The flowerbeds were planted with tiny seedlings that Margie and some of her friends so kindly supplied, sweet william, pansies, marigolds. They had planted a lilac just beside the step, "close enough that you'll smell its fragrance from inside," Margie promised.

It was all so different here, the climate, the names of the plants, which ones would thrive, but the biggest difference was that she, Liliana, was experiencing the triumph of imagination that all gardeners know. Though she had never gardened before she found that she quite enjoyed this kneeling on the coarse grass in her oldest pants, digging and turning up the soil with the yellow-handled trowel, imagining how the beds would look in a few months. And more— she liked the sense that she and Carlo were building something together—for their future.

The back yard was more Carlo's domain, vegetable beds ranged across the back and along either side. The afternoon sun burned already, so he had placed a wooden table and several chairs in the shade of the big birch which stood in the middle of the yard, casting its dappled markings onto the grass. In each of the back corners stood three tall blue spruce, their thick branches alive with tiny chattering birds. Starlings, he said.

Sitting back on her heels, Liliana stretched her arms up over her head. The roar of the lawn mower Carlo was pushing nearly drowned out the voices of Margie's kids playing with their friends on the road. They had been housebound for so long by the snow and then by the river of running water in the roadway as the snow melted and the spring rains came. "What a country!" Margie said, as if it was a strange land even to her. The children played now with a sort of frenzy, rushing back outside after supper to use up every minute of daylight before Margie called them in, which she would soon do.

As Liliana stood, thinking she would go in and run a nice warm bath before bed, the world shifted—just for a moment, but it definitely shifted beneath her feet. She staggered. She felt dizzy. She had been kneeling on the grass too long—not used to this gardening business.

Sitting in the tub with the soapy bubbles foaming around her shoulders, she leaned back and breathed in the perfumed steamy air. How luxurious. It was almost sinful, this leisurely freedom. She could do whatever she liked, whenever she liked. A twinge of guilt crept over her—Carlo worked so hard. It was thanks to him that she enjoyed this leisure. And then she thought of her poor sister Luisa at home with her mother and grandmother, subject to their whims and commands, their restrictions—without luxury, without independence. And with no hope of change. *I'm the lucky one, after all.*

As she stepped out of the tub she could still hear the buzz of a lawnmower, but it might not be Carlo's. He might be bent over his garden beds again. Slowly, savoring the moment, she dried herself on the big absorbent towel and putting on a clean nightgown, lay down on her bed to the sounds of the birds who sang every evening as the sun sank lower in the sky toward the indigo mountains. The birds— they must be nesting, she thought drowsily.

And then she is flying, her long white nightie flowing out behind her. She flies over the town and over the mountains and over the bottle-green sea. On and on she flies—through the fluffy clouds, through the soft golden-pink light of the sunset—toward home.

"Lili, Lili, wake up." Carlo stood beside the bed in his pajamas. "You're on top of the covers and I can't get in."

"Oh, sorry. Sorry, Carlo," she mumbled, shaking her head sleepily as she swung her legs over the edge of the bed and sat up. "I didn't mean to go to sleep. I don't know what came over me. I was just lying listening to the birds when the next thing I knew, I was gone." She laughed sheepishly, turning down the bedspread and smoothing the sheet over its top edge. "I guess I've been gardening too much." They got into the bed and Liliana knew by the sound of his slow, even breathing that Carlo had fallen asleep almost instantly. The sun had set, the birds had quieted for the night, and the moonlight shone in upon them.

She is flying again, and then she is standing on a speckled granite rock. There is coloured light all around her wavering in bands like a huge enveloping rainbow, a scented rainbow. She feels the colours moving on her body like tinted water, golds and corals and mauves, as she stands motion-less, breathing in the perfumed air.

And when she woke, toward morning, she knew. She turned to her husband as he lay quietly beside her, listening perhaps to the birds which had just begun their daylight songs. "Carlo? Why don't we ever go down to the beach? We live on an arm of the Pacific Ocean but you'd never know. Now that the snow is gone we could go down there, couldn't we? I want to see the water again."

"*Sì*, we could," he said, one brown arm thrusting under her back and pulling her to him. "I just never think of it. But we could, now that it has warmed up. I'll take you on the weekend."

She had not been on the paved highway that led around the town to the ocean's edge since Carlo had taken her before they were married. She couldn't think why, though Carlo drove it every day of the week on his way to work. Now they were speeding toward the smokestacks of the plant in the distance, the dense green trees on her right as impenetrable as she remembered them. But it wasn't raining today as it had been the last time, and the green of the trees seemed brighter, the sky higher, the ocean glinting silver in the distance. She remembered how angry, how cold and dark grey it had looked when she had first seen it—and how angry she had been, how despairing. She had thought she would never be happy again.

At last Carlo turned down a narrow road and stopped the car under the branches of a huge evergreen. Ahead was a narrow strip of sandy beach dotted with large rocks and gnarled, bleached pieces of driftwood. Farther down toward the plant a lone woman sat on a big white log while several children wearing rubber boots splashed at the water's edge and called out to her in thin voices hardly distinguishable from the calls of the gulls that wheeled and soared overhead.

"Oh, it's so green and calm. Look, there are even little boats out on the water. I can't believe you've never brought me here before!" And hurriedly getting out of the car, Liliana took off her sandals and carried them in one hand as she ran down to the water, which was dotted and speckled with tiny brown sticks and bits of bark where it lapped onto the coarse sand.

"We couldn't have gotten down here to the beach as long as there was snow on the ground," Carlo called out to her retreating back, his voice disappearing into the wind as he hurried to catch up to her.

"Oh *Dio*, it's cold," Liliana screamed, dipping one bare foot into the clear foamy water. Then she stopped short. There across the choppy inlet and slightly to her right on the far shore was a little town. She could plainly see the small marina filled with boats, the white houses with their multi-coloured roofs hugging the shoreline and rising in steps above it. "What's that, Carlo?" she asked in amazement. She had thought Cedar Ridge was the only town for hundreds, even thousands of kilometers, yet plainly there was a settlement on the far shore.

"That's where the native people live," he replied. "They've always lived there. Some of the men work with me in the plant. Most of them are fishermen, though. Look, you can see their fishboats."

So their village isn't hidden somewhere in the forest, as I imagined. I wonder why I thought that?

"But why didn't I see that little town when we drove to the plant the first time?"

"The rain. Probably foggy too. Not every day is as clear as this. That's where Aldo's wife, Loretta, is from." Carlo stood shading his eyes with one brown hand as he gazed across the inlet to the little village on the far shore.

Liliana thought of Darlene, whom she saw so rarely even though she lived across the street. But then, she remembered, she wasn't from here. Liliana had seen Native people on her excursions downtown—beautiful women who stood in groups in the stores, visiting, their musical laughter rippling around them, or sometimes a couple of teenagers on the street. Though she would have liked to, she had never spoken with them, except for Darlene. Liliana was very curious. She thought of the quiet family she had seen on the train, remembering how she had wondered what they were thinking. She hadn't been able to read their faces at all. And they had looked very different from these people, with high cheekbones and sharp noses. It puzzled her.

"Why don't you invite Aldo and his wife over? I would love to meet Loretta. Imagine, she's always lived here–all her life." She paused, lifting her head and turning to look in all directions. "On the edge of the forest, surrounded by mountains—for generations and generations. I wonder what it was like before Cedar Ridge was built. Wild and beautiful. No cities, no towns, nothing. Imagine never having lived anywhere else, never having seen a city, a train, an airplane. I can't. . . I can't imagine."

"Oh, I don't know," Carlo replied, eyes still fixed on the soft reds and blues of the distant rooftops. "It's a different culture. I don't know if you'd get along with Loretta."

Of course I will. Darlene and Margie and I are friends. We get along just fine. But Liliana stayed silent. Carlo didn't really know that. He'd never been around when they were together. Hadn't witnessed their easy companionship. But I want to meet Loretta. I want to find out for myself what she's like. After all, our child will be born here, just as she was.

"Well, I've often seen their children playing with Margie's out on the road. I think it's about time we met, don't you?

Ask him," she said. "Tell him your wife wants to meet his. Tell him I get lonely. Tell him I want to meet Loretta."

They got back into the car, Liliana brushing the sand off her feet and putting her sandals on before closing the door. She swiveled her head to look again at the village across the water as Carlo started the car and turned it back up the road that led from the beach toward the highway.

"And now," he said, trumpeting as though he were a tour guide, "for our next attraction—close your eyes and don't open them until I tell you." He drove a short distance up the narrow road and then along the highway until she heard the tires crunching on the gravel of the shoulder. "All right. You can look now." Obediently opening her eyes, Liliana gasped. She must have passed by here that other time. She must have, but she had missed it. A waterfall! You could only see it from this very spot, she realized, and only if your head was at the right angle, but there it was! It cascaded down in a roaring, foaming stream, not wide, but from a great height, pouring over jagged shiny granite rocks, the spray flying up wherever it touched them on its downward journey. She got out of the car and stood mesmerized on the rocky ledge. The dark pool into which the water roared was far below her, the spray splashing up onto its border of glistening black rocks, the air filled with the smell of the water. How beautiful! How powerful. And then she saw it. A rainbow, arcing through the spray as if putting on a special performance for her, and she remembered her dream, the dream about the scented rainbow.

Carlo came and stood behind her, his arms around her waist, resting his chin on the top of her head. They stood there motionless for a long time, their bodies fitted together, the sound of the roaring filling their heads. *I must tell him. Tonight. I'll tell him that we're going to have a baby.*

She was down on her knees, weeding the bed under the mountain ash as her mind went back to that moment when she had told Carlo about her pregnancy. She had never seen such happiness on his face before, such clear joy. She smiled to herself, remembering. The sun's rays warmed her back, she felt its warmth right through to her heart. The days were long now, she knew it would be several more hours before the soft golden ball disappeared behind the mountains. It was only the end of May, still time to set out new plants. Carlo was digging another flowerbed for her on the other side of the walk, glancing over every now and then to flash her a smile. Their yard was beginning to look quite lovely, she thought proprietarily, almost as good as Margie and Mike's, despite the fact they had been working on theirs for several years now. Her neighbours had many varieties of shrubs and flowering bushes, but they didn't seem to be much interested in growing vegetables. Not like Carlo. His garden beds were lush now with the promise of harvest.

"*Buona sera*, Lili, b*uona sera.* Time to take a break." It was Gina's voice, and Liliana looked over her shoulder from where she knelt and saw Gina and Mario approaching, pushing Nello in a shiny new stroller. "We were just out for a walk and thought we'd drop in," Gina called out as she pushed the stroller up the walkway and stopped close to where Liliana still knelt. Carlo had risen to his feet and he and Mario were already on their way around to the back yard to check out the garden.

"Oh Gina, I'm really glad to see you. It's been too long. And look at Nello." Standing, she felt dizzy again just for a second before she bent over the baby as he lay looking up at her. "And how is my little godson today?" she cooed. He had grown so much it was hard to believe. He was wearing the blue and white checked outfit she had made for him, and she realized that it only now fit him. She resisted the urge to pick him up and snuggle his warm little head into her neck. Her hands were too dirty from working in the soil. But she had something to tell Gina.

When Carlo and Mario rounded the corner of the house and came toward them, having completed their examination of the garden, they found the two women sitting companionably on the cement step in front of the door, Liliana's sandy head and Gina's dark one almost touching as they bent toward each other, deep in conversation. Gina was holding both of Liliana's hands in hers.

"Hey there, *donne*!" called Mario. "We've just had a great idea. Let's get Anna and Tony over here. We can have a game of bocce now that the lawn is dry."

"Oh *Dio*, I forgot all about it. You gave us that set of bocce balls last fall and we've never used them. Great idea! Do it," said Liliana excitedly, jumping to her feet. "I'll go over and ask Mike and Margie to join us." *I should knock on Darlene and Steve's door and ask them too. But I'm sure she'd say no. Maybe next time.*

The sun had almost disappeared behind the mountains, and they were still playing in the back yard, the baby asleep in the stroller. Anna and Tony had been happy to come by and join in, and so had Margie and Mike, for whom the game was new, but they soon caught on and joined in with gusto. Liliana realized that they had all seamlessly switched to English when Mike and Margie arrived, and everyone seemed to be feeling comfortable and relaxed. Tony and Anna's two children played happily in the street with Jack and Terry. As Liliana returned to the back yard from the kitchen where she had taken the dirty plates and glasses, she stopped and surveyed the scene. She had thought it would never happen. Her closest friends gathered together in her backyard, laughing and calling out to each other to hurry and finish the game. It was getting chilly, the last of the sun's rays slanting across the yard. Such an ordinary scene. But extraordinary. Something that would never have happened back home. For one thing, only men played bocce. And not at home, but at a public *campo di bocce* from which women and children were banished. Not really, but it simply would never have occurred to any of them to go. They had their own pursuits. Perhaps the women were glad of the temporary reprieve. This was so much better, the husbands and wives ribbing each other companionably, laughing and touching each other quite unselfconsciously. And just for a moment, as she tidied the table and put out the plates of food, she pictured other children, their children, playing on the grass in a last frenzy of joy before she called them in to go to bed.

Red geraniums filled the terra-cotta pots, their scalloped, veined leaves tumbling down the sides, the heavy red blooms with the little spikes in the centres drooping ever so slightly in the afternoon heat, giving off their musky perfume. It was a cloying, heavy scent of which she never tired, and her first task each sunny July morning when she and Carlo went outside was to bend and examine each bloom carefully, breaking off the dead flowers and leaves before watering the pots. She could hardly believe they had been able to grow such lush, strong plants here in this mountain valley beside the grey Pacific.

They had started the geraniums from cuttings that Daria and Anna had given them, planting them in small black plastic pots lined up close together in the warmest spot, next to the house. Now the pots of geraniums sat on either side of the cement step in front of the door, and others were lined up partway down the walk so that when the door was left open in the heat of the day, Liliana could smell them as she worked in the kitchen.

Sometimes, when she had finished preparing the evening meal and was waiting for Carlo to come home, she sat on the step in the open doorway in the midst of the scarlet blooms, breathing in their dusky scent. Her elbows on her drawn-up knees, her hands cupping her face as she turned it up to the sun whose warmth penetrated to her very soul, she was back on the stoop with Mama and Nonna and Luisa. They were working on their embroidery, long silences punctuated periodically by languid conversation. She could hear the clink of the ice in the tall glasses, hear the footsteps of some-one approaching across the gravelled courtyard. She would stay like that, motionless, far away, until she heard the crunch of the tires in the driveway signalling Carlo's arrival. And then, and only then, she would open her eyes slowly, savouring the quiet. Looking around at her stoop, her geraniums, her husband coming up the walk toward her, she would shake her head as if to re-arrange the images in it. And then, getting to her feet, she would stand in the shade of the doorway, smiling, until he folded her into his arms—in spite of his dirty work clothes.

Chapter 19

The Cedar River flowed splashing green and turquoise and brown over its rocky bed in its rush toward the Pacific. It hurried past the town and under the bright orange bridge over which Carlo and the other men drove to work each day. It separated the residential and shopping areas from the plant site, from the smokier industrial area, a natural barrier between the two. It was a beautiful river. Liliana looked forward to seeing it when they crossed the bridge on the evenings when Carlo drove her down to the beach. They went fairly often now after an evening of gardening, arriving just in time to watch from their perch on the big rock the changing, flowing colours on the ocean cast by the setting of the sun. They sat in silence, watching, listening to the sound of the waves washing up onto the rocks, the world darkening around them. She felt as though they were the only two people inhabiting this place of sky and water and rocks. Nothing else, no one else existed.

And in the twilight, she could just make out the pale shapes of the houses and boats across the water where Loretta's mother and all her family lived. Now and then a light twinkled as people came indoors for the evening, but not a sound carried across to where they sat.

"Lili, I'm home," called Carlo, returning from work one evening in mid-July. "I've got some good news." Liliana had been working in her sewing room, the roast and potatoes for dinner warming in the oven, the table set. She was making a sundress for Terry from some left-over fabric. She had already learned that Margie would never have accepted it if she thought Liliana had purchased the yardgoods new. She enjoyed making simple clothes for Margie's children, shorts and tops and little dresses for Terry. She had lots of time and she loved to watch them running and playing in the street wearing her creations. It was the least she could do for Margie, who had been so good to her.

"What is it?" She came into the kitchen, her tape measure draped around her neck.

"I saw Aldo at work today. He and Loretta are coming over for coffee tonight."

"Oh I'm so glad," replied Liliana, suppressing a faint flutter of trepidation. "Good thing I made those *biscotti* yesterday." She busied herself getting the food onto the table, not wanting him to see her sudden nervousness. After all, this was her idea. He had invited them to please her. *I hope I'll be able to talk to her. Will she know English? Don't be silly, what else could she and Aldo be speaking? She surely wouldn't have learned Italian. I wonder what she thinks of us all, living here on her people's land. Angry? Resentful? Resigned?*

The four of them sat rather rigidly in the living room, Aldo and Loretta on the sofa and she and Carlo flanking them in the two matching armchairs. The room was looking much nicer these days, with new wall-to-wall carpet in a soft grey-blue tone which went very well, Liliana thought, with the smart navy and grey striped slipcovers she had sewn for the sofa and chairs. Her houseplants had grown, creating a small green oasis in the room, and the rose throw cushions added a warm note. The off-white curtains with their wide cutwork borders that Mama had sent so many months ago hung at the windows, the only slightly formal touch. Liliana loved the way they filtered the sunlight so that it bathed the room in a warm glow, the cutouts creating intricate patterns on the carpet. The days were so much longer now that the sun often shone into the room until well after dinner.

The plate of *biscotti* sat on the coffee table along with the empty coffee cups and the bottle of Brandy with which the men had "corrected" their coffee. But Liliana saw that Loretta was not relaxed. She sat bolt upright, her hands folded in her lap, her gaze travelling from one to the other as they spoke, though she herself said nothing. She was, thought Liliana, one of the most beautiful women she had ever seen, tall and slender, her brown skin set off by the white sweater she wore, her straight raven hair cut in a smart asymmetrical style. Beautiful silver earrings with intricate engraved designs on them dangled from her ears, the silver ovals glinting in the diffused light. Liliana felt dowdy. She wished she had worn something a bit better than slacks and a blouse. One hand went up to smooth her hair. Loretta was not at all what she had expected. Liliana had commented earlier on the lovely earrings, and Loretta had said that they had been made by her brother. That he was an artist, a carver.

"Oh, maybe I see—I saw some of his carvings—some jewellery—in a shop in the mall. Did I?"

"Yes, probably. Sam, his name is, and he does have some small carvings and some earrings and bracelets down there."

"Very beautiful. Very beautiful." She was trying to think of something else to say. "How did he learn to carve?"

"Our people have always carved." She paused, then after a moment added, "We have always been settled, always had abundant food. We've had time to make art."

Liliana was pondering this when Carlo broke in. "Come on, Aldo. Come and see my *radicchio*," he said, and the two men rose and left the room, talking animatedly about gardening. Loretta's eyes followed them. Did she look a little frightened?

Liliana thought of the things they had been taught in school about the 'Indians' of North America, how they were nomadic, travelling by horseback, following the buffalo. How they lived in skin tents and wore feathered headdresses and beaded and fringed clothing made of animal hides. How they danced around their fires at night to the beat of drums. Obviously, her schoolbooks were mistaken or there had been a great deal left out. She had never been taught about these people who had always lived here on the Pacific coast, sustained by fish, not buffalo. And somehow this settled lifestyle had enabled the people to develop their art. Liliana puzzled over this. She felt enormously ignorant, ashamed. She didn't know much at all about this culture so unlike anything she had known in Europe. She did not want Loretta ever to see the depth of her ignorance. But perhaps she had guessed.

The women turned back to face each other. Liliana felt herself trembling as Loretta's dark eyes, impenetrable, held hers. She searched her mind anxiously for something to say. The right thing—something that would help her make a connection with Loretta. She couldn't have explained why it was so important for her to make this connection, it simply was. Carlo had known that. Maybe it had something to do with the baby that was coming—or maybe she was simply too curious for her own good. She thought again of the silent family on the train.

"It is very beautiful, your—your country—your land," said Liliana haltingly, correcting herself, struggling, wanting the words to be right. "I am very—I feel so *fortunata*— fortunate to be living here. It is so different from Italy. I see—I *feel* the mountains around me."

Loretta said nothing for a long moment, only looking into Liliana's eyes. The silence dragged on. *Oh Dio, what have I said? Have I offended her? I only meant to tell her that I know—that I understand—about her people being here first, about this being their homeland.*

"Thank you," replied Loretta at last. "Yes, it is very beautiful, our land. My people have been here in our village at the mouth of the channel for a very long time—forever." She paused. There was another silence. Liliana waited. "My mother's eldest son, my brother John, is the hereditary chief."

"The chief! You mean your *brother* is the chief?"

"Yes, he's the chief. The line passes through her."

A chief—that's like a king. So she is a princess. Yes, there is something regal about her.

"I have several other brothers besides those two. And four sisters. We are a large family. And close. At least we were close. But my mother was not happy when I married Aldo," Loretta went on. "None of my family was. So I haven't seen them since I moved here to the new town to live with him."

"Oh-h-h, it is very—*triste*—sad—for you, and for them." Liliana took a deep breath. "I also have left my mother. It is very hard." She struggled to find the words to enable her to make a connection with this proud woman whose eyes glistened now with tears. Impulsively she reached out and took one hand in hers. "It is hard—hard to be a woman. Always." Loretta nodded, and Liliana wondered if she had noticed the tears in her own eyes.

Just then the back door opened. The two women smiled quickly at each other and turned their heads toward the men as they entered, brushing the dirt from their pants where they had obviously been kneeling to examine the plants. Carlo held several heads of *radicchio* in his hand and fussed about finding a paper bag to put them in for Aldo. The women rose and walked toward the kitchen, seeing that the visit was over. As the men walked ahead out to the car, Loretta turned solemnly to Liliana.

"We must meet again. I could show you some beautiful places. I'd like you to see them."

"Oh yes, I would love that. I would love to go with you."

"Good. I'll call you. Bye for now."

As Aldo and Loretta got in their car and drove away, Liliana and Carlo watched and waved. Then they closed the kitchen door and turned toward each other. Liliana sighed. Lovingly Carlo put his two tanned hands on her front, where no baby was as yet visible, and patted her.

"How are you feeling, my sweet?" he asked. "Is everything all right?"

"Oh I'm fine, perfectly fine. But I was just thinking how much I want to be Loretta's friend. It seems right, somehow, to have at least one friend who was actually born right here, don't you think? I hope she liked me."

"Of course she liked you, silly. I could tell. Would she have asked you to go out with her if she didn't like you?"

One morning several days later when the men were at work, Loretta phoned just as she had promised, saying that she would pick up Liliana in half-an-hour. *It hadn't occurred to me, but she must drive. What freedom comes with that! I must learn. Carlo will teach me. Or I could ask Margie. I should have started by now.*

Without explanation Loretta began driving, and Liliana saw they were following the same way Carlo had driven when they went to see the waterfall. As the women talked, Loretta answered with a quiet matter-of-factness Liliana's questions about her people and about the changes the coming of the plant had wrought in their lives. There had been changes, difficult changes, more jobs for the young men, but more disruption, more trouble. There were long silences between the sentences. Liliana was learning not to interrupt—to wait for the next thought. It occurred to her that

Loretta was translating in her head from her own language to English. Her admiration grew.

Loretta stopped the car at almost exactly the same spot on the edge of the pavement where Carlo had. Without speaking, she got out of the car and walked behind a screen of tall trees. A sloping series of rocks rose upward, bordering the waterfall, and Loretta began to climb up from ledge to ledge. Liliana followed, carefully placing her feet in exactly the same position as Loretta's, on exactly the same narrow ledge, the spray hitting them sometimes as they climbed, the air laden with moisture. Every now and then Liliana was able to help herself up by catching hold of the branches of one of the stunted evergreens that miraculously grew from crevasses between the pinky-beige rocks. Finally, Loretta stopped. They were not too high, perhaps as high as the roof of her house, Liliana thought. But she knew that they could not be seen from the road.

"There," Loretta said quietly, though Liliana could hear her voice above the roar, "Look carefully and you will see it."

"What?" said Liliana, "I don't see anything. What?"

"There," repeated Loretta, pointing. And with a start, Liliana realized that she was looking at a painting on a rock face just above their heads. She had been looking right at it, but she hadn't seen it. She could clearly make out its form, though it was not large. It appeared to be an animal of some sort, perhaps a frog, painted with thick curved lines in red and white and a little black. *It's been there forever, like her ancestors. Looking down on us. And she wanted me to know.* Suddenly Liliana felt very small, like a tiny creature flattened there against the rock under the moving sky, the water roaring down beside her as it had been forever. They clung there, suspended between heaven and earth, for quite some time, until Liliana's hands grew numb where she clutched the rock, her legs trembling. Then, without speaking, Loretta began to slowly back down, forcing Liliana to do the same.

Liliana felt as though she had silently been given a gift, a very important gift. She couldn't think what to say—the whole experience had been so unexpected. She wanted to ask Loretta about the painting. What did it mean? But she remained silent.

They reached the base of the rock and stood side by side in silence, watching the water as it thundered and foamed on its frantic downward course.

"I'm going to have a baby," Liliana said quietly, not sure she could be heard above the roar of the falls.

"I know," replied Loretta. "Are you tired? Maybe we'd better be getting back now."

They turned in silence and got into the car.

"Did Carlo tell Aldo?"

"No. I just knew," replied Loretta as she started the engine and turned the car on the shoulder, heading back toward town. "That's our village, over there across the water," she said. There was a long silence. Then she went on, "Someday I'll take you." Liliana thought how she would like to meet Loretta's family, but she said nothing.

"It was so strange, Carlo. I can't explain it," Liliana told him when he returned from work that night and asked her how her day had gone. "We just hit it off. And she showed me the most amazing sight—a rock painting, high up beside the waterfall. We must have been looking right at it when we were there, but you have to know where it is before you can see it. It's something very important, to her and to her people, but I don't understand. What was it? Why was it there?"

"Don't ask me! I have no idea. Maybe something religious."

"I don't know. Maybe. Maybe someday I can ask her—or she will tell me. But I know it was important. Something powerful."

"You see, Lili," he replied, "I told you she liked you."

"And that's not all. She said she knew I was pregnant. How could she know?"

"Well, I haven't told Aldo, but maybe Mario did. Or maybe she just saw it in your face. You've changed, you know, Lili. Your face is softer, prettier even than before."

"Oh Carlo, I can't wait. I can't wait to find out. Do you think it will be a girl or a boy?"

"Don't know," he said as he moved toward the bedroom to change his clothes before dinner, "but it doesn't matter to me. Long as it's healthy."

I don't care either, though I can't help but be afraid of the birth, knowing what Gina went through. But Margie and Gina will help me, they said they would. I'll make it, just like every other woman does. Just like Nonna did, and Mama. And they had theirs at home! Surely, I can do it here with all this help.

Each morning that July dawned bright and glorious, and Liliana and Carlo rejoiced in the warmth of the summer sun which shone in upon them so early in the morning that they couldn't sleep. Rising and making a pot of espresso, they filled their cups and went out into the garden before any of their neighbours were moving about. Liliana would tend her geraniums, pot by pot, savouring the task as the birds sang their morning devotions, until Carlo went reluctantly into the kitchen to pick up his lunch box. Time to go to work.

Waving goodbye from the walkway, Liliana looked around at the lushness of the summer. The trees that had stood bare-branched for so many months, darkened by the rain and then traced along each bough by the snow, were covered now in bright leathery leaves that twisted and turned up their undersides to the breeze. Even the tall dark evergreens had lightened, the sunlight lying along their boughs in patches of bright new growth. The sap that lay in rivulets on their trunks gave off a pungent clean scent, mixed with the overpowering smell of freshly-cut grass.

She loved the summer weekends. She and Carlo would linger over coffee in the mornings, talking, planning, until he went outside. At home the main meal was always served at midday, but here they could only do that on the weekends. She would begin to make a *sugo* as soon as the morning coffee cups were washed, filling the house with the rich dark tomatoey aroma of the sauce. Leaving it to simmer and with the kitchen door open so that she could smell it as she worked in her flowerbeds while Carlo tended his vegetables, she would lose herself in the images of her childhood evoked by the scent. The sun shone hotter on her back as it rose in the high blue sky, and she could not stop herself from singing in her clear soprano. She hoped no one was listening, but then, what if they were? She was happy. She rubbed her hand across her abdomen, disappointed that she could not yet feel any change. She must write home and tell them about the baby. She could just imagine their excitement, how they would get out the pattern books and begin immediately to knit and crochet tiny garments, as she had seen them do for her younger aunties. She frowned. This would be hard on Luisa, who lived in perpetual sorrow. No baby for her. No home of her own. She would grow old in that house of women.

Loretta had brought her a number of plants that she had dug up in her mother's yard, she said, wild violas and foxgloves. She had driven up one afternoon when Liliana was hard at work in her sewing room, running up little white flannelette nighties open down the back for the baby. Margie said you could never have enough of these. She had hurried to answer the knock at the door, wondering who it could be, and there was Loretta carrying a battered blue enamel basin filled with the tiny plants, the aroma of the freshly-dug earth filling the air between them as she held out the container. Liliana had been so touched at this offering and pleased too to hear that Loretta and her mother had made peace. Loretta told her about this as they knelt companionably side by side, putting the tiny wilted plants into the warm soil and watering them gently.

"She doesn't like it. She's angry, but she can't turn me away any longer." There was another of Loretta's long pauses. Liliana was beginning to know instinctively when there was more coming. But this time, though she waited, Loretta was silent. Liliana kept her eyes down, noticing the reddish colour of the moist earth as she dug.

"Why? Why is she angry, Loretta?"

There was another long silence while Loretta continued to dig. Then, lifting her head and looking off toward the low hump of dark blue mountains beyond the rooftops she said, "She doesn't like it that I've married a white man."

Chapter 20

July and August were always the best months for sun, though Margie said sometimes even the summers in Cedar Ridge were rainy. This one, however, was proving to be unexpectedly hot, so that the women took shelter in the shade of the trees in Liliana's back yard in the afternoons, the children playing noisily nearby. Gina and Margie and Anna, Silvia and Loretta, Darlene—she recited their names in her mind like the beads of a rosary. These were her friends, and she was proud that they gathered at her home. It wasn't much trouble. She frowned, remembering the long silent days of winter.

Her friends often turned up unexpectedly in the afternoons, sometimes at the same time. She thought they probably congregated at her place because she didn't have any children, and therefore wasn't as busy as they were. Or perhaps it was to keep her company, to be sure she didn't succumb to melancholy now that she was pregnant. Whatever the reason, she was very glad. They told her about their pregnancies and deliveries, about their depression when the rains came and they were alone. They were trying to comfort her, to prepare her, she knew, though sometimes they frightened her, however innocently.

At first, Gina and Anna had obviously been uncomfortable when Loretta and Darlene were there, but that had dissipated. Loretta had a silent, seemingly haughty manner, and to some of the women she kept herself too aloof. "Who does she think she is?" Gina commented. Liliana stayed quiet, silencing her instinct to defend Loretta. She didn't need any defending. Eventually, the women had come to realize that beneath that cool exterior lay an intelligent and compassionate woman with a quiet sense of humour. "I'm going to have a hard time keeping up this tan when winter comes," she had said one day, and there had been a silence until they saw her broad smile and burst into laughter. Darlene, too, was often quiet for long stretches as the conversation of the other women flowed around her, and Liliana would remember the pain that she bore so silently, and wonder at her ability to keep it hidden. Both of them. As much as she, perhaps more, and yet they never let on.

Once, watching her friends together, it occurred to Liliana that neither her mother nor her grandmother had ever *met* anyone of a different race, never mind having a friend who was a different race. It pleased her to think that she did. It was only right. This, after all, was Canada—the *new* world–where things were different, as they should be. Different traditions, different beliefs–different people.

Liliana would carry a tray of glasses and a pitcher of something refreshing out to the table in the shade of the tall birch tree whose silver leaves rustled at the slightest breeze. Sometimes it was lemonade with slices of lemon swirling in it, sometimes *orzata*, the almond-flavoured syrup which clouded the water in which it was dissolved, making it look milky. Always, she had plenty of ice cubes. The tinkling noise they made when she stirred the pitcher never failed to remind her of the summers of her childhood.

In the back of her mind she was always aware of her mother watching her as she served her friends, passing out pretty paper napkins and refilling their glasses. She felt her mother's presence and Nonna's always. Sometimes she had a green melon in the fridge, *Honeydew* it said on the round sticker. Although she might have intended it for Carlo when he came home, she would slice it and pile it high on her cobalt-blue plate, loving the look of the dewy arcs of palest green overlapping each other. She knew her mother would approve of this gracious gesture. Nello would have his afternoon nap on a blanket beside them while the older children played on the grass or out on the street, shouting and running in an endless game of tag or hide-and-go-seek.

The women talked quietly, their usually desultory conversations punctuated periodically by gentle laughter. Sometimes, though, they would lean forward in their chairs, heads close, voices lowered, intense, talking about the men. They were worried. Their husbands were suffering in the plant. It was awful, they said, the heat and the noxious fumes were making them sick. Silvia said her husband threw up repeatedly every night when he got home. They nodded. Loretta said that Aldo suffered from a miserable red rash that came and went all over his body. The doctor had said he should change jobs, but how could he? They were silent. "I know a man who developed bladder cancer. The first thing the doctors asked him was where he worked. Must be some connection," said Margie. "And several men Mike knows have developed lung cancer." Another silence. It wasn't right. It was dangerous, and someone should do something.

There must be something that could be done to improve conditions for the workers. It wasn't like they could move to another job here. The women would stop talking and stare off at the ridge of smoky blue mountains, hazy in the heat, that lay just beyond the town. Plumes of dark grey smoke, or was it fumes, rose from the smoke stacks in front of the mountains and dissipated into the blue sky. "Look at it," they said, "How can that be good for anyone?"

"It's not. Not a bit." Loretta spoke curtly, looking off into the distance, and the others sensed the held-in anger. "My people are beginning to have asthma and lung problems. Never happened before."

"Well, at least the money's good." Margie the peace-maker, always trying to make things right. Loretta didn't reply. No one did.

When Carlo came home, exhausted, his clothes wet with perspiration and stinking of the plant, he would run a cool bath, piling his dirty clothes on the floor beside the tub. She would bring him a tall glass of lemonade, the slices of lemon pink now from an added dash of wine, ice cubes tinkling as she walked down the corridor. A spritz, he called it.

"How much longer will you have to work like this—in these awful conditions?" she would ask him sometimes, seeing the grimy ring in the bathtub. "How many more years before we can go home?" But he never answered. He always managed to change the subject or somehow to divert her attention to something happy, to make a joke or tell her a story about someone else.

"Mario says he and Gina want to have another baby—soon!"

"God, not already—Nello's not even a year old!"

"Well, that's only what *he* says—who knows how Gina feels? I'll bet she's not so anxious."

"Well, she's never mentioned it," she replied, bending and scooping up the filthy workclothes, averting her nose as she carried them out of the bathroom and down the corridor into the kitchen where she put them immediately into the washing machine, for which she thanked God every day.

She and her friends talked about money sometimes, about how much one needed to have saved before it would be possible to make a life back home again, but they never decided. Margie too talked about going home, about how hard it was to be so far away, about how difficult it would be to live well if Mike took a lesser-paying job back east. And Gina would agree. Mario talked often about how much longer they would need to stay, she said, but they didn't have enough saved yet. Loretta only listened, nodding sympathetically. "If I ask Carlo he changes the subject," Liliana said quietly. "He just refuses to talk about it. Makes me so mad."

"Well, they're sort of torn, I guess," Margie offered. "They want to go, and they want to stay. Me, too."

"Hmmmm, uh-huh," they replied, nodding. That was how it was, all right. And then the conversations would veer off inevitably into discussions about how great it would be to go back just for a visit, then about houses and new furniture they wanted, how the car needed to be fixed or changed, how a child needed orthodontic work.

"Maybe next year," said Gina. "Mario and I talk about it all the time. We'd really like to go in the summertime when the weather is at its best. But then it's at its best here too. I'd hate to miss the summer here."

"I know," Liliana nodded. "It's so beautiful. Does Mario talk about going back for good?"

"Yes," Gina replied. "He talks about it more now that we have Nello. We were just saying last night that if we wait until Nello goes to school here, then it will be much harder. Because of the language. He wouldn't know how to write or read Italian when we go back."

"Hmmm. Uh-huh." They all nodded. "It's hard to know what to do."

"We worry about it all the time too," Margie offered. "For us there's no problem with language or schooling, but the kids are growing up without knowing their families, their grandparents and aunties and uncles—and cousins. Lord, so many cousins! It's not right, to keep them so far away."

The women were silent, pensive. They looked into their glasses, swishing half-dissolved ice cubes, then down at their feet, flexing bare toes in sandals, and up and over to the blue mountains shimmering in the heat. The air lay heavy between them.

"Time to go." Loretta, who had been silent, rose, uncrossing long legs and tucking her blouse neatly into her shorts. "Time to think about fixing supper. Talk to you soon."

Tomorrow, a Sunday, would be Liliana's birthday. Her twenty-third birthday. The first she had ever celebrated without her family, and she had no intention of marking the day in any special way. Well, perhaps a simple cake to share with the friends who were expected to come over tonight for an evening of bocce. This, too, had become something of a regular ritual, this gathering in her back yard on Saturday evenings, as long as the club had nothing planned. It was good, she reflected, to have developed these traditions. The young couples—all but she and Carlo with small children— had few options for a social life and yet they were very sociable, having grown up in the intimacy of *cortiles* like Liliana's where they had interacted daily with extended family and old friends. Now, they needed this companion- ship—this sense of family—like they needed food. It, too, was a form of sustenance. Liliana reflected that this was true even for Loretta, whose large family lived across the water. She, too, was exiled. While the women had nurtured their friendship during the languid summer after-noons, the husbands had been working together, sharing the bond of the hardships of the plant with its smoke and heat, its officious foremen, its regimentation of punching timeclocks in and out. They, too, had grown up and worked in much more relaxed and intimate environments before they came here.

Liliana could see that these men liked Carlo, gravitated to him naturally. She could see that he took delight in playing the part of the expansive host, pressing food and drinks on the men, bragging about his garden, about her cooking. And when their conversation turned to complaining about work—about the conditions or about the behaviour of some particularly rude foreman who had demeaned them in some way—Carlo listened and nodded sympathetically. That made her proud. He *was* a good man. The men joked and laughed with each other in a brotherly way, she thought, and suddenly realized that they *were* his surrogate brothers. She remembered that he had grown up in a family of four boys and that he missed the camaraderie and replaced it with this. Spirits ran high. In these long cloudless evenings, she sensed again that undercurrent of frenzy—as she had at her wedding. They laughed too loudly sometimes, too long. *Are they worrying about never being able to go home again? Or do they know they never will? Will I?*

For their evenings of bocce, the women took turns bringing something over for a snack. Tonight, Gina would probably bring a tray of hot freshly-baked pizza, balanced on the handle of Nello's stroller, and Daria a plate of meats and cheeses. So she *could* bake a cake. It wouldn't kill her.

Although she had received a card with a loving message in it from her family back home, she hadn't told anyone here about her birthday. Her last one had fallen in the middle of all the preparations for coming to Canada, and while her family as always had purchased a cake at the *pasticceria* for the occasion, there hadn't otherwise been any special celebration. She remembered those dreamlike days and herself moving through them as if they were a series of tableaus in which her body only had been present.

She didn't know whether or not Carlo had remembered. He hadn't said anything, she thought, getting out the pans and oiling and flouring them. His family had never been much for birthdays he had told her when she surprised him last February with a present and a cake. Maybe he had been hinting that they shouldn't make a fuss over hers either. Not a fuss, she thought, pouring the batter into the pans and sliding them into the oven, but some small gesture. After all, they would certainly be celebrating the baby's birthday each year from now on. Carlo might as well get used to the idea. The baby. Their little Canadian baby.

The cake was cooling on the counter, the air filled with its warm vanilla scent. Loretta had said she was beginning to show, though she couldn't see it herself as she turned this way and that in front of the mirror in the bedroom after combing her hair. She heard the kitchen door open and Carlo calling her name.

"I'm in the bedroom," she answered in a singsong voice, and continued to primp, taking her time. After all, he had gone out without explanation and had been gone for half-an-hour.

"There you are," he said, coming up behind her and putting one arm around her waist, perhaps ever so slightly thicker now. She smiled at him in the mirror as with the other hand he brought a small white box up to her face. It took her a minute to realize—he was giving her a present. He had remembered, and she turned and snatched the box with both hands.

"What is it? Let me see," she squealed as he pretended to keep it from her for just a moment before relinquishing it.

She sat down on the bed, the ends of the silver ribbon on the little box trembling in her hand. He had brought home a set of dishes, and a TV, and other things for the house, but she could tell that this was a piece of jewellery and that it was therefore a special gift, fraught with intent. With meaning. She opened it. Inside, cushioned on their bed of white fluff, lay a pair of oval-shaped silver earrings hung on long silver hooks. They were intricately engraved with curved lines in the shape of fish, each one embellished with finely-wrought cross-hatching. Killer whales, she thought. Earrings like the ones she had so admired in the little shop down town, earrings like Loretta's. She gasped and jumped to her feet. Without a word he picked them up, one at a time, and put them in her ears, cupping her face with the other hand as he did so. When he had finished, he kissed her lovingly on her forehead and then on her lips.

"Thank you, thank you, my love. They are beautiful. How did you know?"

He smiled, and they turned shoulder-to-shoulder and looked gravely at themselves in the mirror, her small face with its luminous green eyes and sandy hair lightened now by the sun, the earrings glinting silver on either side of her face, and his tanned face with the serious dark eyes looking back at her. They stood there, not moving, for what seemed like a very long time. Liliana broke the spell.

"I have so much to be thankful for. Grateful for." She turned to face him and kissed him on the lips. "Come on, Carlo. Let's go. I'd better make supper before everybody comes over for bocce." Moving out of the room, she called back over her shoulder, "And I've made a cake."

It was a hot afternoon, the sun blazing down from a cloudless sky, and Carlo only watered his garden in the cool of the evening. So he had taken his newspaper and gone to sit in the shade of the big tree in the back yard while Liliana cooked, humming to herself, lost in thought.

She jerked suddenly at the loud and unexpected jangling of the telephone.

"Hello?" she said, sounding slightly out of breath.

"Liliana? It's me, Gina. What are you up to?"

"Not much, I was just starting to fix supper."

"Well, I'm sorry to bother you," Gina went on, "but I'm right in the middle of baking something and I've run out of sugar. Could I run over and borrow a cup?"

"Of course you can. We'll be here."

"Great. I'll be right over. *Ciao*."

Just as she hung up the phone Carlo came in, folding his newspaper. "Who was that?" he asked.

"It was Gina. She's coming over to borrow something. Hope you're not starving."

"Oh no, I can wait," he replied, reaching out to tuck a strand of her hair behind one ear.

Just then there was a rapid-fire knock on the kitchen door and before either of them could reach it, it burst open and Gina entered. Liliana gasped. Gina was bearing a huge pan of steaming lasagna, followed closely by Mario, and then Anna and Tony and Margie and Mike and Loretta and Aldo, and last of all Darlene and even Steve. They streamed in, each one carrying a platter or casserole of food or a bottle of champagne, all laughing and talking at once as they set their burdens down on the kitchen table. "Happy Birthday! *Buon compleanno!*" they shouted, grabbing Liliana and kissing her soundly on both cheeks. Between hugs Liliana glanced over at Carlo and saw him grinning from ear to ear.

"Carlo, you told them!" she exclaimed. "You gave away my secret!" But she was more than a little pleased. It was the right thing to do, after all.

Loretta carried a huge bouquet of mixed garden flowers, gladiolas, asters, mums, wrapped loosely in white tissue. She knew where the vases were kept and immediately arranged the flowers in one before placing it on the table. Liliana saw her doing this out of the corner of her eye, but there was so much confusion that she wasn't able to thank her just then.

"So! Did you really think you could get away with not having a birthday party?"

"We just decided we'd have a party for you whether you liked it or not!"

"And in *your* house!" It was Gina's voice, rising above the others. "You've always been so hospitable, we thought this time *we'd* supply everything!"

"Oh, you shouldn't have. It's too much!" replied Liliana. "However did you get it all planned so secretly? I never suspected a thing!"

"Never mind how we did it," laughed Margie. "We're starving! Here, let me set out some plates and cutlery."

Working quickly, the women set out the plates and glasses and cutlery, putting serving spoons in the dishes of hot food, and then, before calling the men who were congregated by now in the living room, took Liliana on a quick tour of the buffet table. She was amazed at the variety and totally overcome with surprise.

"It's too much!" she exclaimed as her eyes went over the steaming dishes on the table. Beside Gina's lasagna, Anna had labored over her offering—*vitello tonnato*—knowing it was a favorite of Liliana's. Margie had produced a huge platter of fried chicken and a big bowl of potato salad, and Darlene had a plate of smoked salmon. Loretta explained that her casserole, steaming hot, consisted of clams and crabmeat and chunks of bright pink salmon dotted with kernels of corn, all enveloped in a creamy sauce. No one said a word about the corn, even though it was something they had never eaten back home, not like that. But the seafood smelled delicious. Everything smelled delicious. What a feast! They set to, filling and re-filling their plates amid much loud laughter and gentle teasing, their voices rising and falling, then rising again to a crescendo of laughter.

It was a wonderful evening. They played bocce after supper, laughing and teasing one another until the sun disappeared behind the mountains and the chilly air drove them in. Then they gathered around the kitchen table while Liliana served the cake she had made, along with coffee.

As the sun dropped behind the mountains and the room began to darken, Liliana took the opportunity in the half-light to look around unobserved. So much had changed in almost a year. She had changed. Carlo had changed. Their marriage had grown solid, their child was on the way. And they had acquired these wonderful friends, each one different, each one treasured. Margie, her mentor, her guide through the vagaries of this strange place, her constant source of sensible advice. Anna and Gina, her touchstones, the ones who knew better than anyone how much she had to learn, to change. And Loretta, her connection to this new land, this land where she had thought she would never feel at home. And Carlo, her rock. Quickly, feeling the tears start up in her eyes, she stood and moved from lamp to lamp, turning them on so that their soft light glowed on the faces of her friends, softening their features and making their eyes shine.

"To Liliana! *Buon compleanno!* Happy birthday, Happy birthday," they cried, taking turns hugging her, lifting their glasses and clinking them, then tossing the bubbly wine down. It made her feel warm, loved and appreciated, and she had a flash of herself at her wedding, alone, while everyone else had a good time.

"To you, Lili. All the best to you. And to the baby!" It was Mario who had risen to his feet and was lifting his glass toward her as he spoke. Then, turning his head and lifting his glass toward Carlo, he went on. "To you both. Our dear friends. All the best—*ogni bene*—now and in the future. May all your dreams come true! And thank you for so many happy times here in your home!" And looking around at the full table, "It's almost like you already have a big family!"

Liliana and Carlo looked at each other for a moment, laughing, and Liliana saw that there were tears glittering at the corners of his eyes. She rose to her feet then, and picking up her glass, turned and looked gravely from face to face.

"Thank you, all of you, for sharing my birthday with me. And thank you for your friendship, which Carlo and I will always treasure." She couldn't believe she was doing it, making a speech, but she was. She sat down quickly, overcome, as their shouts of *Salute!* and *Buon compleanno!* went on, accompanied by the noisy clicking of glasses. She knew that there were tears in her eyes, too. And she didn't care who saw them. Grinning foolishly, she wiped at the corners of her eyes with the paper napkin. "Cake—who'll have more cake?" she called out and began to put the thick wedges, oozing their liqueur-laden cream filling, onto the plates that were being thrust toward her.

Liliana was dreaming. She was standing on a beach, her silver earrings, long and heavy, resting on her shoulders, the foam-flecked green water lapping at her bare toes, when a shrill but distant noise brought her to sudden consciousness. The phone! Groggily she half sat up and looked at the luminous dial of the clock on the bedside table. Three o'clock in the morning! Her stomach gave a lurch of fear. No one ever phoned in the middle of the night. Carlo was beginning to make little mumbling sounds, but she had already swung her legs over the edge of the bed and was on her way down the corridor, half running, stumbling, her hand on the wall to guide her in the dark. Panting, she grabbed the black receiver from its cradle on the wall beside the back door.

"*Pronto*. Hello? Hello?"

"Liliana? Is that you, Liliana?"

"*Sì. Sì*. This is Liliana. Who is it? Who's speaking?"

"It's me, Luisa! Your sister!"

"Luisa?" she said incredulously. "Luisa? Is it really you?" Liliana could feel her legs trembling, her breath coming in little gasps. "What's wrong?"

"Nothing's wrong. Really, nothing's wrong."

"Then why—what—there must be something. Mama? Nonna? Are you all right?" She knew she was shouting, how else could her sister hear her from such a great distance?

"Yes, Liliana, we're all just fine."

"But it's the middle of the night," Liliana shouted. "Why are you calling?"

"It's eleven o'clock here and we are getting ready for lunch. I have some good news!"

"Good news? What?" said Liliana, still struggling to comprehend, her voice croaking.

"Oh Liliana, you'll never believe it. It's Olivo, he's coming home to San Michele to marry me!"

"But when—how did you find him?"

"Don Paolo had a friend in Argentina, a priest he went to the seminary with, and he wrote and asked him to look for Olivo. And he found him! He found him!"

"And he's coming home? Why didn't he write?" She turned her head toward Carlo, who had just come into the kitchen and turned on the light. "It's Luisa," she said. "It's Luisa calling—they've found Olivo and he's coming home!"

Carlo just stood there, struck dumb.

"He's finally saved enough, and if I'll still have him, he'll come home. He sent a letter via Don Paolo's friend. I'm not sure exactly when he'll arrive. I'm sorry to call you in the middle of the night," Luisa went on, "but I just couldn't wait to tell you."

"Oh Luisa, I'm so happy for you. Write and tell me all the details. I'm so glad you called. You'd better hang up now, this is costing you money. But write soon!"

"Oh Liliana, I almost forgot! Happy Birthday. Mama says she sends her best. Nonna's fine, we're all just fine. We'll write soon. Bye. Bye." Her voice trailed off, and Liliana had an image of their voices arcing across the endless stretch of dark water over which she had flown almost a year ago. So far away.

Slowly replacing the receiver in its cradle, she turned and looked at Carlo seeing her own amazement reflected in his face. But no joy. He looked serious, in fact, and worried.

"It was so wonderful to hear Luisa's voice again," she said quickly, "but I can't believe that Olivo could have turned up after all this time. Whatever has he been doing until now, I wonder. And not writing all that time. It's terrible how Luisa has suffered. And now she has to wait again. Poor Luisa."

Carlo was surprisingly quiet. "Well, he'd better be serious this time. She's waited long enough," he finally mumbled in a gravelly voice. "Let's hope she's not disappointed again. I never liked him, you know. Never trusted him. Well, enough for now. You go on ahead. I'll turn out the light."

He could be a little more happy for her, thought Liliana, walking slowly down the corridor, instead of reacting like a stern father. Poor Luisa, living in purgatory all these years, and now with a few words all is forgiven. Oh, I hope it works out for her this time. She got into the bed and settled on her left side, remembering her dream, hoping it would continue, wanting to be standing again with her toes in the clear green water. Not wanting to have to deal with this turn of events. Maybe Luisa would be able to escape from the house of women after all. She closed her eyes and waited. And when sleep finally came, she did not dream of flying over the clear green water. She did not dream.

Chapter 21

They were sitting on the big rock down by the beach again, watching the colours from the setting sun rippling and moving in bands across the water. They had spent most of the day putting their house and yard in order after the birthday party, gathering stray plates, crumpled paper napkins and plastic glasses from their hiding places under chairs and shrubs. After a light meal of leftovers, they had driven down to the beach, empty now of sunbathers and picnickers. They had been sitting silently for a long time, their eyes on the water. Then Carlo spoke.

"I couldn't believe that Mario, making such a nice speech last night. Made me cry."

"*Sì*, me too. He really meant it. He loves you like a brother, Carlo."

"I know. And I feel the same way." He paused. "But I miss my real brothers."

"Do you, Carlo? You hardly ever mention them. I know how much I miss Luisa. When do you think we can go home? Another year? Two?"

"Don't know. Don't know. . ." His voice trailed off. There was another long silence, each lost in thought. "You know, sometimes I don't think about home for days and days. And then, sometimes, it just hits me in the stomach.

Like a fist." Carlo's eyes were on the distant horizon, the line, barely visible, where the dark water met the glowing sky.

"But when, Carlo? When can we go?" Liliana implored, ignoring his admission of pain, of homesickness. "How much longer?"

He held up one hand, palm toward her. "*Basta*," he said. "Enough. No more." His voice was cold, like ice.

She felt the fury rising in her. He was speaking to her now in that paternalistic tone he adopted sometimes, as if she were a wheedling child. How dare he? Refusing as always to discuss things like two adults. Refusing to be engaged in a debate—as though his was the final word. She refused to accept that. But she hated confrontation as much as he, and she said nothing. *He'll change his mind—I'll make him.* She had been brought up in a family where voices were rarely raised, where the loud shouting and arguing that she some-times heard coming from other houses in the cortile were unknown, where calm reason prevailed, and dissent was kept for the most part internal. She huffed then, wordless, and turned away from him. He was so stubborn she couldn't stand it. Why wouldn't he at least talk about going home? So they could make plans. He had, after all, just admitted how homesick he was. Liliana watched as lights flickered on in Loretta's village on the far shore. Those people had no such quandary. They *were* home.

After a long time, slowly and still without speaking, they slid down off the rock and walked back to the car. She got in behind the wheel. Carlo made no comment. She had been practicing in the afternoons with Margie. As there was hardly any traffic at this time of night, she had perfect confidence in herself and in him, knowing that he would save them if she made a mistake. Carefully she guided the car up onto the highway and turned back toward the town. Finally, as they approached the bridge with its ugly orange girders, Carlo spoke.

"Oh, that reminds me. There's a picnic coming up this weekend at the Cedar River park. I almost forgot. It's being organized by the Italian Club."

"Our club? When?"

"Next Sunday afternoon. Each family brings its own food and whatever they'd like to cook. I went last year, just before you came. It was great! The club had a huge firepit filled with hot coals, covered by a grill, and we stood around it cooking our food. There are tables and benches there too."

Later that week Liliana had to phone Gina, and—just to be sure—Anna, to ask what was appropriate to take. She had never been to a picnic before. She had heard of them, though, back home and had pictured a fine cloth set out on the lawn under a tree in a manicured park, with ladies in large hats, their full skirts spread out on the grass around them. She wondered just how much fun it could be eating somewhere in the wilderness beside the river. She imagined the air filled with bugs and ashes. But early on Sunday afternoon she got out her laundry basket and packed it with dishes (the old cracked ones, not the ones with the roses) and cutlery, as her friends had advised. Then she wrapped a piece of good cheese, some fruit, a bottle of wine and several glasses, a bowl of potato salad made with strong *giardiniera* and tuna, the way Nonna liked it, and a big bag of fresh radicchio.

Carlo had gone out to pick it and had washed it and dried it too. She could tell that he planned to offer it proudly around. Bragging. Into a screw-top jar she poured some oil and vinegar, to dress the salad at the last minute. Then she carefully wrapped several steaks, a cut of meat that she had only recently begun to purchase, feeling just a little guilty each time she did so. She had never seen such slabs of meat served back home, and she hadn't quite developed a taste for them yet, though Carlo thoroughly enjoyed one every so often. With plenty of salad from his garden.

Walking back and forth in the kitchen, placing first one thing and then another carefully into the oval wicker basket, she was suddenly reminded of the endless supply of food Mrs. Lombardo had packed for the train trip from Toronto. She flushed, thinking how silly she had been to be so embarrassed about eating in front of everyone on the train. Silly and ungrateful. Only now did she realize how much thought and work had gone into that lunch, which had lasted them for days and days.

When everything was packed into the basket and she had placed a neatly-pressed but older tablecloth on the top, Carlo carried it out to the car. She followed with some warm sweaters, a blanket, a magazine to look at and a change of shoes. Then they were off, backing down the driveway and waving at Margie and Mike who were working in their front yard. No sign of Darlene. There rarely was. Liliana felt a twinge of regret. It would have been nice if they had invited her neighbours along. She just hadn't thought of it. But it was an Italian Club event, Carlo had said. He seemed to be really looking forward to the day. Excited even. She felt the familiar twinge of trepidation. This was another new experience and she didn't know quite what to expect, but at least her other friends would be there. She could handle it.

Carlo drove through the town and approached the orange girders of the bridge which crossed the Cedar River.

"God, this is an ugly bridge. An awful colour. I'll never forget the first time I saw it," she remarked as they approached the span. "Who in their right mind would paint a bridge this colour? Look how it jumps out at you."

"Yes, it is awful. But this way you can't miss it, even if its foggy or snowing."

"Oh, is that why? Because it makes it safer?" she queried, looking up into the clumsy girders as Carlo drove over its humming metal bed.

"I'm not sure," he replied. "Maybe it has something to do with rust resistance."

"Well, it's a pity. Look how it sticks out against the blue and green of those mountains."

He didn't answer, and she saw that he was concentrating hard on his driving, peering off to the right into the thick forest that bordered the road.

"Here we go," Carlo said. "I hope we can find the place."

Turning the car to the right, he followed a narrow dirt road between tall dark evergreens. Large-leafed plants covered the ground between their trunks as far in as she could make out in the darkness and shadow under the trees. She could see glimpses of the river to their right, glinting through the trees and undergrowth. They must be driving parallel to its path, away from the town, deeper into the forest where she had never been. Its mysterious darkness frightened her.

"When I went last year, Mario drove and I didn't pay much attention to where we were going. But he said the road doesn't go anywhere else, so let's just follow it." Carlo sounded excited, as though they were embarking on some great adventure. Then he became silent, intent on following the winding road, the lower branches of the trees sometimes scraping along the roof of the car or flattening themselves against the windshield, only to be let loose with a swoosh as the car pressed on. Liliana rolled her window part-way down. Instantly, she was assailed by the overpowering scent of the forest, the piney dank green-ness of it, the air heavy with its redolence. It took her breath away, this powerful smell of old forest, of rotted stumps and cedar, and the faint almost sweet perfume of skunk. It was as though no one had ever been here before them. And she could hear the river roaring in the background as it raced over the rocks on its way to the ocean. They drove farther and farther into the forest. She peered through the trees on her side of the car, between the mammoth striated trunks sticky with rivulets of white sap, seeing a dark brown and ferny-green world into which only the occasional powerful ray of slanting sunlight penetrated, illuminating as if by some huge spotlight the plants in its path. In one clearing she could clearly see some beautiful lilies, yellow lilies glowing in a ray of sunlight, their slender green leaves curled protectively around the flower with its engorged brown stamen. "Look, Carlo! Lilies!" she cried out, pointing toward them. Carlo slowed the car, turned his head quickly to where her finger pointed and laughed.

"Those are skunk cabbage! They smell like skunk!" he said, concentrating once more on the road before them.

Liliana was silent, thinking he must be mistaken, continuing to peer into the forest as it passed by. The spaces between the huge trunks were tangled with vines. Moss-covered branches reached out in every direction, and below them, on the floor of the forest, dangerous-looking plants with huge thick leaves edged with long spines. The forest was different from anything she had ever seen or even imagined. It was— the word wouldn't come—it was primeval. That must be how the earth had been before man. Or at least before them. Before the Europeans. And she thought for a moment she caught a glimpse of Loretta standing there, deep among the brown moving shadows.

"We must be close now," Carlo said. The road, though rutted from frequent use, was getting narrower. It wound on, and though it was still early on a sunny August afternoon, she felt chilly. The sun was blocked out by the trees which almost met overhead. She could still hear the roar of the river, louder now, the silence punctuated only by its distant deep-voiced song and the hum of the car's motor.

And then they were there, the road widening suddenly upon a clearing into which bright sunlight streamed, glinting off the dozen or so parked cars. The ground here was hard-packed, almost shiny, separated from the picnic area by a low fence of rough poles. The picnic area, too, was illuminated by the bright sunlight, and people in colourful summer clothes stood about in groups, their laughter rising in waves through the beams of sunlight, rippling toward her. Children ran darting and laughing between them. Liliana smiled delightedly. She hadn't expected such a carefree holiday scene. This was going to be fun.

Carlo parked the car and motioned to her to follow him as he lifted the overflowing picnic basket out of the trunk and stepped over the fence, calling out to the people seated at the tables or standing about, "Here we are finally. What a long road!"

Laden with the blanket and the other things she had brought for the adventure, Liliana hurried after him. "There you are, Liliana! We thought you'd never come!"

"Hey Carlo, did you get lost? We've been wondering what happened to you two!"

Laughing and calling to their friends, they walked toward the brown-painted wooden tables with benches attached sitting randomly among the tall cedars. Grass had been planted in a roughly oval space on the bank of the river, the wall of dark forest to the left and the right. She spotted Gina and Mario at a table, with Nello sitting in the stroller beside them industriously sucking on a watermelon rind, the front of the little sunsuit that she had made for him stained pink from the juice. Gina waved and motioned them over, jumping to her feet and moving their picnic things aside so that half the table was cleared. Carlo plunked the heavy basket down on the bench, and Liliana immediately took out her tablecloth and covered her half of the table, as she saw that Gina had done, and then folded her blanket and placed it on the bench to sit on.

"Well, what do you think of this?" Mario asked, watching Liliana's face. "This is *really* roughing it, hey?'

She smiled and nodded, busy with setting out the lunch, pausing momentarily to wipe Nello's sticky hands with a napkin. Mario and Carlo wandered away, their arms around each other's shoulders, to check the condition of the coals which were being tended by Tony and several other men.

"Let's sit," smiled Gina, pouring a little of the wine she had brought into two thick glasses and diluting it with soda water. "We won't see them for a while. And you," she said, looking into Liliana's face, "how are you feeling? You seem quiet today."

"Oh, I'm fine. I feel fine. Really." She looked around, taking in the family groups gathered at tables piled high with an assortment of food, everyone dressed more casually than they ever had back home, in shorts or in jeans with the legs rolled up, the children in sunhats. There was a festive air, with much shouting and waving and loud laughter, the children running and darting between the tables. The men stood clustered about the firepit, which consisted of a square box of mortared bricks over which a metal grill had been placed. Glasses in hand, the rising smoke obscuring their faces, the men were deep in conversation. Each one had armed himself with a stick or twig and with this was poking at the fire, turning the coals over and over, his contribution to the preparation of the meal.

"What a wonderful place," Liliana went on. "That forest—it's like a jungle! But this is great." She looked around. They were enclosed by a circle of thick bush except on the river side. It felt as though they were in a private green living room, an outdoor living room filled with people. The rest of the world was far away and they were like a family, laughing, quarreling, sharing food—sharing their exile.

"Yes, it is great. The company did this for the workers and their families several years ago. It's so popular now our club has to book it well in advance. The air is much cooler and cleaner out here. And there's good fishing."

"Oh, is that what they're doing down by the river?" Liliana asked. "Let's go and see." "Sure," Gina said, scooping Nello up in her arms and starting toward the group of people on the bank. "But they're not fishing. They're watching the salmon coming home."

Liliana followed, both women calling out greetings to people they knew as they passed their tables and moved to the river's edge.

A fish jumped out of the water, its pinkish silver body arcing through the air, and then another. Suddenly she realized that the river was alive, full of fish struggling against the current, forcing their bodies against the power of the water rushing toward the ocean while they, intent on their own destruction, forged on. Going home. She had heard about this, about the salmon who returned from the ocean to their spawning grounds to die, their bodies rotting in the sun as August turned to September. She hadn't really believed it. But now, though no dead fish were yet in evidence, she knew that it was true. They glinted silver and orange and pink in the sun as they writhed and surged ahead over the rocks, sometimes stopping as if to gather their strength, mouths opening and closing as though gasping for air, until, with a mighty effort, they surged ahead again. Such a powerful urge, to return against all odds from whence you had sprung.

Liliana and Gina stood there with the others, transfixed by the spectacle, for a long time. Then, as though by some unspoken agreement, they moved further downstream, away from the others. The river, for all its noise, didn't have much water at this time of year. It was much wider and deeper in the early spring, Gina explained, because of the runoff from the melting snow on the mountains, coupled with the spring rains. Now, it ran along over its stony bed some distance from the low banks, out in the centre of a swath of pale pink and grey speckled rocks bordering it on either side. Granite, Liliana thought, granite rocks worn smooth by the action of the water running over them for who knew how many eons.

It was hard walking, the rocks were slippery, some with sharp edges where they had cracked into smaller pieces, and the sand in which they were embedded was wet, with little pools of water trapped here and there. Gina was having a hard time keeping her balance, the weight of the baby on her hip making her progress slow, and when she came to a good-sized boulder, she sat on it. Liliana sat on another beside her, facing the water. Neither spoke for some time as the sound of the rumbling river filled the air. Looking across the open expanse to the far shore, Liliana saw again the impenetrable wall of forest, glimpsing movements in its shadows. Maybe it was a bear. She had been warned sternly by Loretta and by Margie about the danger of bears, but she had not yet seen one.

"I've got to put him down, he's just too heavy," grunted Gina, struggling to hold her wriggling child on her lap. "He'll get dirty, but so what?" She plunked him down on the sand between the rocks near their feet. Immediately he began splashing in a little pool that lay within his reach. Liliana bent over and dangled her hand in the clear warm water, noticing the tiny shells and pebbles at the bottom, the sand ridged as though from waves, like a miniature ocean.

Gina too had been staring off across the river to the wall of forest growth on the other side, and now she spoke, as if to the trees. "It's so strange—to be here—to have a life here. Sometimes when I wake up in the morning I forget where I am. I think I'm back home." Her voice trailed off and they sat in silence. Then she spoke again, eyes still on the far shore. "Mario says we can't go home for good for at least another five years. Too long. It's too long." Her voice cracked. "And I'm pregnant again."

Liliana sat up straight, withdrawing her hand from the pool where Nello still splashed. "Pregnant? Oh, Gina. Aren't you happy about it?"

"Yes, and no," said Gina ruefully. "We wanted another child, but not yet. And it just makes it harder to save enough money to go home. We won't even be able to go for a holiday next summer like we'd planned." She stopped. Liliana waited. "But Mario is happy, really happy about it. I was surprised. I think he's proud—you know—of his virility." She paused. "He says he'll work lots of overtime now. Says we'll need the money." She continued to stare off across the river.

"You know," said Liliana thoughtfully, "it's not just about virility. It's more than that. Carlo's the same. They believe in family, and they want to create a family as soon as they possibly can. It roots them. It makes them like their fathers."

"I suppose so," Gina replied, turning to look at Liliana. "You and I, we're pioneers. Did you ever think of that? Our families are going to be the first ones here from the old country. And our children will have children here." Her voice faltered. "If we don't go home." And she picked up her son and started back toward the picnic grounds.

Liliana didn't even try to answer. Those last words spoken by Gina had hit her in the stomach. "If we don't go home." But she would. She knew *she* would go home.

Later, after each family had cooked its meat on the grill—steak or chops or garlicky home-made sausages—and every family had eaten, passing around bowls of salad and offering each other pieces of some special cheese or home-cooked delicacy, a lull fell over the crowd. The children were playing quietly now, the toddlers sleeping, and several of the adults too had spread their blankets on the grass in the shade of the big cedars and succumbed to sleep. Others sat playing cards or talking quietly as the sun, lowering now, created diffused halos in the tops of the trees and cast their shadows like long grey stripes across the clearing. Nello had fallen asleep in his stroller, and Gina and Mario lay side by side on their blanket nearby, her dark head resting on his shoulder. Liliana saw from where she sat at the picnic table leafing through her magazine that though he was tanned and muscled, he was quite slight in build. *They work too hard— and in such unhealthy conditions. They grew up running and playing, working and resting outdoors. In sunshine. In clean air.* In her mind's eye she saw again the men and boys, backs bent, shirts off, straining to lift the slabs of broken concrete from the airplane runway, saw them resting in the shade of an upturned chunk before returning to their labours. All that to build a church.

She lifted her head, her eyes scanning the clearing until she spotted Carlo where he sat at a table near the firepit with Tony and Anna. She stood and walked toward them.

Tony had brought his guitar. It lay on the bench near him, and she remembered that he had been one of the musicians at her wedding. Carlo greeted her arrival by slipping one arm around her waist as she sat close beside him, continuing his conversation with Tony.

"It's true," he was saying. "It's stupid to put a lot of money into these houses. We'd be better off to buy a lot and build a new one. And sell it. That way, we could earn enough to build one for ourselves."

Liliana listened carefully. She had never heard Carlo talking business before, and she felt quite proud as he spoke. He made good sense. And Tony was listening intently, nodding his head in agreement.

"You know," Anna interrupted, "you two should do that. You could work together. You could start in the spring. You'd be finished by fall." She turned to Liliana and lifted her eyebrows questioningly.

"Well, sure," Liliana added quickly. "That's a great idea. You both know enough about building, don't you? And you could sell it and make a profit."

"That's the idea," laughed Tony. "That's the idea all right. But enough business talk! Who knows *La Montanara?*" He picked up his guitar and began to strum the opening chords of this most beautiful folk song, about a mountain woman who sang to her secret lover, her voice echoing through the snowy peaks. Peaks like those Liliana could see rising above the trees, and she smiled and began to hum. She hadn't heard that melody for years. Carlo too hummed, and

Anna. Then Tony threw back his head and began to sing full-voiced. She was astonished by his clear true tenor, and one by one or two by two the others walked toward them, humming and singing, some with tears on their cheeks. They stood now in a circle two-deep around the table, every one of them singing. They all knew the words, all of them. Some had beautiful voices, and those who didn't were drowned out. Without a break in the music other tables were dragged nearer the fire until they were all able to face it, backs to the black trees which surrounded them. They began to harmonize, drawing out the last note in each phrase, turning and singing into each other's faces, eyes glowing. They sang as if their lives depended on it, as if they had been storing up this music, these joyous sounds, forever. They sang until long after the sun had set, until their voices were hoarse, until they shivered with cold and wrapped the blankets around their shoulders. And still they sang. All the songs of their youth, stored up all these years. Their voices soared to the tops of the silent trees, across the river and into the dark forest, and Liliana lifted her head and looked straight up into a canopy of cobalt velvet in which stars, more stars than she had ever seen at once, glittered down on them like blazing holes in the sky.

Liliana was tired this morning. She had difficulty pulling herself out of sleep, rising only slowly to consciousness even when she felt Carlo leave the bed. What day was it? Oh, yes, it was Monday, and Carlo had to go to work. They had stayed at the picnic much too late last night, leaving with the last stragglers. They had sung until they were hoarse and could not think of another song that they hadn't already done at least twice. When they finally stopped, the couples wandered off to their cars, blankets draped over their shoulders to protect them from the chilly night air.

Remembering, Liliana allowed herself to sink down and pull the covers up to her chin, her arm across her eyes to keep out the insistent light of morning. Carlo would get himself off to work, he didn't mind. He had told her last night, when at last they had turned away from each other to sleep, to stay in bed as long as she could this morning.

She kept her eyes closed, and soon she knew with one part of her mind that she was dreaming. Or was she dreaming that she was dreaming? Was it a dream about a dream? *The velvet blue sky is undulating, swooping down to touch the tops of the trees, then flowing away and up again. She feels herself moving with it, moving into the sky, past the blazing stars, and away.*

Sometimes lately, when she was awake, she had the most powerful feeling about the baby that was sleeping inside her. She could see him plainly, curled around himself, his eyes closed, his tiny fists under his chin, a peaceful look on his round little face, his head covered with long silky black hair. Once, she had dreamt that she felt his silky head between her thighs as he entered the world, and she knew what he looked like. What he felt like. She tried once to tell Carlo about the baby, about the realness of him, but she couldn't. She couldn't find the words. It would have to be her secret, one that she found it impossible to share. Carlo would have to find out for himself about the beauty of the baby when he arrived. There was no way she could make him understand now.

The next Sunday, one week after the picnic, would be her first wedding anniversary, and when Carlo came home from work that Monday evening, she brought the subject up. Should they 'make a fuss', have a party, or celebrate it quietly, just the two of them?

"I don't know. I'd rather just have a quiet day together," Liliana said, scraping the plates and stacking them in the sink. "We've had quite a few social events lately, don't you think?"

"I know, it's true," Carlo replied, drinking the last of his coffee.

She sighed. She was still feeling tired from her late night. "Let's talk about it tomorrow. I've got to get out and water my geraniums. I didn't do it yesterday."

"I'm feeling a little tired myself tonight," said Carlo, pushing back his chair and standing. He stretched, lifting his arms above his head and letting out a deep moaning sound. "And I've got work to do too. We'll see. Let's just see how we feel tomorrow."

Liliana sighed as she stood at the sink slowly washing the plates and glasses and cutlery, the warm suds frothing around her wrists. She had always liked washing dishes. She remembered Nonna telling her as a young girl how fortunate she was to have food, to have dishes that needed to be washed. Nonna had told her that she herself had always liked this task, even as a young bride. It gave her a peaceful pause in the busy day, a time, she said, when she could think or remember or pray. Liliana had been surprised then and a little disbelieving. But now she often thought of this as she stood at the sink, sometimes not even looking at the dishes as she washed them, her eyes instead on the Mountain Ash outside the window or the tall cedars at the corners of the yard, or across at Margie's house. She too loved the quiet, contemplative time that this task afforded her. Like Nonna. Like Mama.

She began to think about Luisa, who was never far from her thoughts these days. She had phoned again. Still no word about when Olivo was coming back from Argentina. But at least she was receiving letters from him regularly now. Letters full of promises. Liliana remembered receiving those crisp blue envelopes herself. She could still feel them in her own hand, feel again the butterflies in her stomach as she tore one open and extracted the folded blue pages covered with closely written spidery words. And suddenly she remembered her anger, like an old acquaintance about whom she had not thought in a very long time. She remembered it as though through a veil. It had been so long ago. It had happened to another person, in another world. The preparations, Rome, the trip, the few anxious days before the wedding, the day itself, all as though it had happened to someone else. Not her.

Luisa had never let on to any of them what she was feeling all those years when she was betrothed to a phantom. Never cried in front of them, railing at the fates for the injustice of it all, as Liliana was sure she would have done, never berating Olivo for his treachery, never expressing her shame, her sorrow. Never. But she must have felt these things. Must have been angry, embarrassed, full of puzzled sadness. And now, there must be fresh anger, knowing he had chosen to be lost and then had chosen to be found. Luisa was like a puppet, dancing at the end of long strings that Olivo pulled at will. That was certainly how Carlo had reacted. She felt anger again, anger on behalf of her silent sister. She must call her tomorrow when she felt better. Call her and tell her to be strong, to be firm, not to let him toy with her any longer. She wouldn't tell Luisa that Carlo had said that he had never liked Olivo.

The week went by slowly. It seemed to Liliana that the late night of singing at the Cedar River park had left her totally enervated. She was having difficulty getting through her housework, getting up the energy to go outside and water the geraniums. She had told Margie about it the other day, and Margie, ever cheerful, had said, "Oh, it's just your condition. Pregnancy always makes you moody. I sure was. Poor Mike never knew *what* to expect when he came home at night. It'll pass. You'll see." Liliana hoped she was right. And she *was* worrying about Luisa.

All that week she could not shake off the lethargy that settled over her, making the simplest tasks seem gargantuan. She couldn't even be bothered to phone anyone, and no one called her either. It was as though all her friends, except Margie, were feeling as debilitated as she was. Carlo was somewhat surprised when no one phoned to say they were on their way over for the usual Saturday-night bocce game, but they didn't mind. "It's time we had a weekend off to just putter around the place. We need that," they told each other, sitting at the table in the back yard watching the garden grow. It had flourished, and the tomato plants were laden with fruit, the swiss chard needing cutting again, the green beans needing picking. "What a lot of work," sighed Liliana. "I guess we didn't know what we were in for when we planted so much."

"I'll help," Carlo said. "We'll get started Monday after work. I'll pick the tomatoes and some basil and we can make a big pot of sauce. We can freeze it for winter."

"Yes, we'll get started on Monday," she said. "Not tomorrow."

They went to church early the next morning, as they always did on Sundays. Liliana spent longer than usual on her knees. She had much to be thankful for. And much to pray for. It was their first wedding anniversary. They had remembered as soon as they woke, and she prayed for forgiveness for all her pettiness, all her anger, her lack of gratitude. She prayed for strength, for acceptance, for peace. She prayed for Carlo, for their baby, for Luisa, for everyone at home, for her friends. And Carlo was beside her, on his knees, his head bent over his folded hands. She wondered briefly if he was praying for the same things. But she was sure he was.

After church they drove down to the beach again, wanting to sit on the big rock. But the beach was crowded with young people splashing and shouting, and without a word Carlo turned the car around. They drove up the highway and parked on the shoulder of the road. They got out and stood at the foot of the waterfall, looking down into the deep pool below into which the funnel of water roared, then looking up to the top where it first appeared between the trees to begin its furious descent. It was so powerful, so beautiful, the splashes of spray catching the light and glistening like diamonds. They stood in silence for a long time, holding hands, before turning and getting back into the car.

Liliana had decided that although they would not mark the day in any special way, they would at least have a proper multi-course mid-day meal, and she served it at one o'clock promptly, as was done back home every Sunday.

"Marvellous, Lili. A marvellous meal! You've come a long way. As good as any I've ever had."

"Well, I thought we ought to have something a little special today, don't you?"

"Yes, I thought so too," he replied, and left the room for just a minute, returning with a small white box which he handed to her. Without a word she opened it, her eyes widening when she saw the narrow silver bracelet with its fine engraving. A match for her earrings.

"Oh, Carlo, I do love you!" she exclaimed, jumping to her feet and throwing her arms around his neck.

"And I love you, my darling Lili. I love you too!" he replied, returning her embrace. They lingered in each other's arms for what seemed like a very long time, standing there beside the kitchen table covered with the remnants of their meal. *I must be the happiest woman alive.*

Chapter 22

It was a year and a month since her wedding day, her second September in Canada. The time had gone slowly, she reflected as she put the last of the swiss chard into plastic bags and placed them in the small freezer, their latest acquisition from the Eaton's catalogue. It stood against the wall in her sewing room, the only place they could find where it would fit and not look too out-of-place. Margie had taken a good deal of time to show them how to clean and blanch the vegetables for freezing, which bags to buy, how to label and store them and keep a record of what was consumed. She had offered to teach Liliana how to preserve vegetables and fruits in glass jars, and make pickles and relishes and sauces—canning—as she called it. "We did everything up in jars back home," she said, "but it's a terrible lot of work." Liliana wondered why these methods of food preservation had not been utilized in Italy, where produce that couldn't be dried or preserved in oil had gone to waste. A pity. But she had demurred. "Next year, I'll learn to can next year. I'll be feeling better then."

Liliana stood in front of the freezer now, its lid open, and noted the neat piles of plastic bags and containers filled with the food they had produced, harvested, and stored away for winter. A veritable bounty. Another sign of their transition from their possession-less state to this settled domesticity. So many belongings. She sighed. A large white chest filled with food. How much would it weigh? She couldn't imagine. Its heaviness burdened her. She closed the lid and turned away.

It had begun to rain earlier in the month, catching her unawares one afternoon as she bent over the green beans that would not stop producing. The first few drops tickled her cheeks and arms, and she brushed at them, unheeding, as if they were bothersome insects. At last she stood, realizing that she was beginning to get wet, and looked up at the sky. It had darkened all at once without warning, huge blackish clouds rolling across its grey expanse. It was as though someone had turned off the light, turned off the sun, and she shivered and went into the house, carrying her bucket of beans. She stood at the sink heading and tailing them without looking as she watched the sky. The clouds rolled and shifted as the rain began pelting down diagonally, streaking across the windows in a pattern of rivulets that obscured her vision. And it had been raining ever since.

"We'll have to pay now. Pay for the beautiful summer we had."

"It's all over. It'll rain now until it snows."

Liliana had a feeling that this was true. Everyone was saying so. But she hated to hear it. Hated to see the end of the glorious days of sun. She would be forced to remain indoors once more, she and the baby she was increasingly aware of. He had begun to move ever so slightly, so that she thought she had only imagined it. The first time it happened she was frightened—something was wrong. And then, realizing what it was, waited, willing it to happen again. It felt like the fluttering of a wing, of a moth or a butterfly inside her. But the feeling didn't return for several days, and she put it out of her mind. Then one day as she stood in front of her mirror he had given her a good thump, and she had seen the front of her nightie, pulled taut now over her belly, move, a small bump surging out at one side and then back in. It was the baby! He was kicking her, just as Margie and Gina had said would happen. He was alive. He was real. She knew she probably shouldn't be so sure he was a boy, but after the dream when she had seen him clearly she couldn't convince herself otherwise. It didn't really matter, they had told each other, a little girl would be every bit as wonderful.

Liliana and Carlo saw little of their friends now, all of whom, it seemed, were as busy preparing for winter as they were. And the weather was depressing in its greyness, its wetness precluding any chance of back-yard bocce games. The rain had continued unabated throughout the month, and desperate for something to occupy her time once the garden was finished, Liliana had begun sewing a layette for Gina's new baby, having long ago finished one for her own. She lost herself in the work, cutting out the tiny pieces—pale yellow or white or soft green—fitting and sewing them together on the machine and then hand-stitching the details, adding some dainty embroidery at the neck and sleeves of each little garment. It was mindless work like washing dishes, and she was lost in her thoughts as she sewed.

She often felt very sleepy after lunch, and on the days when Carlo was at work would allow herself the luxury of a nap. After all, she was an expectant mother. Mama had urged her in their last phone conversation to take very good care of herself. Carlo was solicitous, treating her with a new gentleness that touched her profoundly, though neither spoke of it. They were never very good about expressing their deepest feelings in words. She must try harder—and try to help Carlo, too, in his struggle to do so.

It was early afternoon, the middle of the first week of October, and Liliana had lain down on the sofa in the living room to the sound of the rain pelting on the windows and drumming on the roof as it had that first September so long ago. She would just let herself drift off. There was nothing to prevent her from taking her afternoon nap out here, though it would have been unheard of to nap in the living room in Nonna's house. And then, as though from a great height, she sees her own house, this house, surrounded by a few streets of small wooden houses just like this one and then abruptly, the forest. A wall of dark impenetrable forest on three sides and on the fourth, the ocean.

She is alone, walking in the forest, and she is lost. And frightened. Not knowing which way to turn she presses on, sobbing, the branches slapping her in the face, cutting her skin like needles, like knives, the vines reaching out to entwine her, the snake-like roots catching at her feet, tripping her. The rough black trunks grow closer and closer together, the spaces between them darker and more ominous. There are movements in the shadows, there are creatures there. Her heart is beating so that she can barely breathe, the air becoming thick and fetid with the smell of decay, of dank rotten wood, of stagnant water in which huge overblown yellow lilies wave and writhe as she skirts the black pools in which they stand. She can hear the roar of water, tumbling water, raging water, and she falls and gets up and falls again in her rush to escape. She can hear herself panting, whimpering, as she stumbles on, dirty, bleeding. And then a sound, an insistent sound—she struggles against the blackness, the smothering blackness, and suddenly she is awake. Where is she? What is it? The telephone!

She swung her legs over the edge of the sofa and sat up, then stood, all in one motion. Lurching, trying to shake off the leaden sense of dread, she grabbed the black receiver from its cradle on the wall.

"Hello?" There was no time to say anything else. As though from a great distance she heard a strangled cry.

"O-o-o-h, Li—li. Come. O-o-o-h, ple-e-ase come."

And then a drawn-out howl.

"Who is it?"

"Help me—help me!"

"Gina? Is that you? What is it?"

"Lili— *sì*—it's me—please—come." And then another drawn-out howling sound.

"All right, Gina. I'm coming. I'll be right there."

It sounded as though Gina had dropped the phone. Liliana stood for a moment, barefoot, her heart pounding, wild thoughts rushing through her head. What? A miscarriage? Something wrong with Nello? Stepping into her shoes and grabbing a jacket from the back of a chair, she ran out, slamming the door behind her and pounding down the middle of the road as fast as she could, the jacket over her shoulders streaming out behind her as she clutched it with one hand at her neck, her other hand under her swollen abdomen, the rain pelting into her face. Up Gina's driveway she ran, and through the open kitchen door. She could hear Nello's wailing coming from the bedroom. Gina was sitting at the kitchen table holding onto its edge as if to stop it from moving, her eyes wide open, staring in shocked horror at the wall opposite her where the telephone receiver dangled by its cord. Tears were coursing down her cheeks and she was breathing in choppy gasps.

Liliana approached her gingerly, seeing that she was almost in shock. She didn't want to startle her, but she needed to know what the trouble was. Gina did not acknowledge her presence.

"Gina, what's wrong? What is it? Tell me." There was no response. Liliana grabbed her shoulders and shook her. "What? What is it? Gina! Answer me!"

Turning her blotchy face toward her, Gina's mouth opened in a soundless O. Then she spoke, her words emerging raggedly from between sobbing gasps. "It's Mario! Some—body just—just phoned—from the plant—Mario's hurt! Hurt bad! I—I need—go to—hospital. He's there, in the hospital. Oh God, G-o-o-o-d." Her voice became a wordless wail.

At that moment they heard the squeal of brakes and a car door slammed. Margie came running up the driveway and entered the kitchen as Liliana quickly replaced the receiver in its cradle on the wall.

"I saw you run by just as I was getting into the car. What is it? What's wrong?"

Gina was sobbing, unable to answer. Nello's howling continued unabated from the bedroom.

"It's Mario, he's hurt. He's at the hospital. Gina needs to get there." Liliana heard her own voice, calm and capable, explaining to Margie. "You take her. I'll stay here with the baby."

"Come on, Gina. Let's go. I'll get your coat."

Liliana and Margie got Gina, still huddled at the kitchen table, to her feet and into her jacket and shoes, moving her as though she were a stuffed doll out of the house and into the car.

As Margie roared off down the street, Liliana ran back inside and down the corridor to the bedroom. She scooped a red-faced Nello into her arms, nestling his head in the crook of her neck and rocking from side to side. He was big now, and heavy, but he still responded to the comforting rhythm and soon a few last sobs dwindled down to nothing. Liliana walked with him through the house, from the bedroom to the living room and into the kitchen, then back again, swaying her body back and forth and murmuring, "Hush now, hush. There, there, baby. It's all right. Everything's all right. Hush. Hush."

But she knew it wasn't. Her knees were trembling and she was aware of the quavery feeling in the pit of her stomach. She felt her baby move inside her, as if protesting at the weight of the other child upon him, protesting the noise, the anxiety felt by his mother. She tried to calm herself, telling herself that it was a good hospital, good doctors, modern equipment. Mario would be all right. He would be fine. Her job was to keep things together here. She wished she could contact Carlo but he wasn't due home from work for another two hours or so.

When Nello finally quieted she was able to put him down on the living-room rug near the kitchen doorway where she could keep an eye on him as she made a pot of coffee. She couldn't think what else to do. She wished they would come home. What was happening? Anxiously she peered out the kitchen window, watching the end of the street, hoping to see Margie's car returning. Nothing. She paced, squatting every now and then to wiggle a toy in Nello's face and talk to him, thinking at least she could do that much. Keep him content until his mother and father came home. She wouldn't let herself think of any other possibility.

A car! She could hear it before she could see it. Margie was at the wheel, and she was alone. This time she drove right up into the driveway, parking the car a few feet from the house. Liliana ran and stood on the step to watch Margie as she walked quickly toward her, searching Margie's face intently as she approached.

"What is it? What's happened?"

Margie came into the kitchen, closing the door quietly behind her. She turned a chair away from the table and sat down carefully. Quickly Liliana turned another chair and sat facing her.

"Tell me," she pleaded. "What is it?"

"He's dead. Mario's dead." Margie's voice was flat. Without emotion. Without inflection.

"No-o-o-o! Oh, no-o-o-o! Not dead! Are you sure? Oh, G-o-d!"

Taking a deep breath and sitting up straighter, Margie reached out and took both Liliana's hands in hers. Nello crowed and gurgled, talking to himself as he played on the floor in the living-room doorway. Margie looked into Liliana's eyes.

"Mario was very badly hurt. They couldn't save him." She shuddered. "There were doctors and nurses everywhere, and the First-Aid guys from the plant. They'd brought him in to Emergency. But they couldn't—couldn't—he was gone when we got there. Oh God. Poor Gina." And she began to cry quietly, her face crumpling slowly as her hands twisted in Liliana's.

"Where is she? Where is Gina?"

"I left her there. She told me to come back here and tell you. And to help you look after Nello. The priest was already there. Thank God for that. She just fell apart—sobbed—fell to her knees beside the bed—it was horrible. Just horrible." She lifted one hand and rubbed the tears from her cheeks. "But she wanted to stay."

"God. What are we going to do? There's nobody—only us to help Gina. And another baby coming—oh it's too—too awful. I can't believe it." She put her head down on her arms and gave way to the sobs that shook her body. Margie stood then, bending over her, patting her head and back while she murmured words of comfort. But there was no comfort. Liliana grieved for the terrible waste, the terrible loss that Gina and her children had suffered, and she grieved for Carlo. Nothing would ever be the same.

The sound of another car door slamming out in the driveway made them both stop sobbing. Liliana turned toward the door as Margie opened it. There was Carlo, his face ashen as he walked toward them, still in his dirty work clothes. Liliana ran out to meet him and threw her arms around his neck, sobbing, saying over and over, "Oh God, oh God. Poor Mario. Oh, God!" Carlo stood absolutely still, his arms dangling at his sides, his face like a marble carving, his eyes looking past her as she writhed and sobbed. Finally, he reached up and disentangled her arms from around his neck, so that she walked quietly at his side as he moved woodenly up the driveway. Margie backed up silently and sat again on her chair as Carlo and Liliana came into the room.

"How did you hear?" It was Margie's voice, hoarse, flat.

"News spread fast at the plant. And I've just left the hospital." He sat down across the table from Margie. Liliana sat beside him, one hand on his arm as it lay on the table, her eyes never leaving his face. Suddenly, without warning, he moaned, the sound coming from deep inside him, forcing itself out as though overcoming great resistance, and Carlo's shoulders shuddered as he dropped his head onto his arms. The two women were silent, struck dumb at the sight of such wanton emotion as his body shook. It terrified Liliana. With one part of her mind she watched him as though from a distance, shaken by his total abandonment to grief, while with another she grieved too, for him and for Mario, gone too soon. And for Gina and the babies, alone now. Tears streaming down her face, she stood behind Carlo's chair so that she could lean over his body protectively, holding him, stroking his hair, rubbing his back as she sobbed. Margie too was crying softly as she sat across the table from them. The sound of their cries mingled and became as one, until they heard the baby wailing in the background, the sadness of the moment affecting him so that he too wept.

The double doors of the church stood open to the foyer, the interminable rain falling in sheets outside. Liliana and Carlo were standing on one side of Gina, with Anna and Tony on the other in a sort of bizarre reception line just inside the foyer. The closed coffin was across from them, a black-suited attendant standing silently beside it, a photo of a much-younger Mario in a silver frame almost buried in the masses of flowers atop it. Liliana couldn't bear to look.

Each person who entered the foyer from outside, shaking and closing black umbrellas, avoiding eye contact, had stopped short at the sight of the coffin to their left, then had moved to the right where Gina stood, her friends flanking her on either side. Liliana could see each one take a deep breath before solemnly approaching to shake hands or to offer a word of comfort before entering the church itself. A stone-faced Gina offered a white cheek to be kissed, dutifully turning her head from side to side, her eyes downcast. She did not speak, though every now and then Liliana or Anna would murmur a word of encouragement to her.

"Hang on, Gina. It's almost over," Liliana whispered. Gina gave no sign that she heard.

"*Corraggio,* dear Gina. *Corraggio,*" murmured Anna.

"He was a good man. We'll miss him."

"So sorry for your loss."

The cloying perfume of the masses of flowers on top of the coffin and inside the church, together with the smell of hot wax from the tall white candles and the incense permeating the air was nauseating. Liliana was afraid she might faint, fall to the floor and retch, but she knew she mustn't. If Gina could remain standing there, so straight, so silent, so could she.

Finally, Carlo and Tony, along with several other men, lifted and carried the polished wooden coffin up the aisle toward the front, leaving the three women to follow. At a nod from the tall, thin man who seemed to be directing proceedings, Liliana stepped out and offered one arm to Gina as Anna did the same on the other side. Holding tightly to each other, the three women stood facing the second set of open doors which led into the church itself, watching the black-clad backs of the pallbearers moving toward the altar with slow, measured steps. Somehow now Liliana and Anna had to propel Gina up the centre aisle to their seat at the front of the church, following Mario's body in its burnished casket.

Squaring their shoulders and pressing Gina's elbows into their sides to steady her, they walked behind it until finally they could lower themselves into the front pew. They were so close they could have reached forward and put their hands on the polished wood, but they didn't. Carlo took his seat then beside Liliana and Tony sat next to Anna, Gina sitting rigidly between the two couples.

The priest, his purple vestment hanging in crisp folds over the white robe that hung on his slight figure, stepped toward the pulpit, clearing his throat, his diminutive pink hands appearing from his wide sleeves, palms pressed together, pointing upward toward his nose. Liliana's eyes went to the little curtained box on the altar, the Tabernacle. God was in there. *God. How could you do this? Why? Why such a random, cruel act. Why?* Quickly she averted her eyes. She mustn't think like that. There had to be a reason. The priest began to speak in a tremulous voice, his quavering sing-song notes spreading out above their bowed heads.

She stood in stocking feet in the kitchen, her good black shoes, muddied from the cemetery, beside Carlo's on the mat behind the door. Her coat was thrown over the back of a chair, with Carlo's on the chair beside it. Her hair, still wet, clung to her head and dripped onto her shoulders. She looked disheveled, she knew, like a wild woman, but she didn't care. Carlo sat at the table, his shoulders hunched, forearms resting on either side of the glass of brandy, largely untouched, which sat in front of him.

It had taken forever it seemed, the funeral, the slow procession behind the hearse to the cemetery, the sandwiches and coffee served in the basement of the church by anonymous, solicitous women—then getting Gina home, getting her and the baby settled. Anna and Tony would stay the night with them and then Liliana would go over in the morning and spend the day. They had it all mapped out so that Gina would never be alone. Not for a while. And through it all, Liliana had remained calm. Competent. She, along with Anna and with a lot of help from Margie, had made all the arrangements during the preceding days. Interminable days. Gently questioning Gina as to her wishes, Liliana would then consult the other two women as to how best to carry them out. Often Liliana would need Margie to make the phone calls, to answer the questions, to explain options to her, so that she could tell Gina.

Carlo had been unable to help. He had moved through the past week like a man in a trance, speaking rarely, looking off into space, not seeming even to notice when she put her arms around him or caressed his arm or cheek. There was simply no response. He had spent most of the week sitting on the sofa in the darkened living room, visited sometimes by one or another of the men who would sit quietly beside him, both of them at a loss for words. It didn't anger her that he sat there so woodenly. It didn't surprise her either. She understood that he was having a dreadful time coming to terms with Mario's death, with the unthinkable. The unbelievable which had happened. But the anger, that old insidious feeling, had been gathering slowly again in her. Where was the God who was supposed to be so benevolent? Where was her husband who was supposed to be her steadfast support in times like these? She was experiencing again that sense of abandonment—there was no one to turn to. No one who really knew what she was feeling, no one to comfort her, to give her strength. She had walked like an automaton through the preceding week, doing alone what needed to be done. No one had comforted her, no one had offered her a hand, a shoulder, a word of appreciation. All this—and fear. Fear that the same thing would happen to her —to her husband. All the grief, all the fear held in— unexpressed.

But the dam burst when finally they returned to their own house from Gina's, closing the kitchen door firmly behind them and taking off their muddy shoes and damp coats.

"That's it!" she screamed suddenly, taking Carlo by surprise. He whirled and looked wide-eyed into her face, the most emotion he had shown in a week.

"I can't stand this any more! We're leaving. We're going home. That's it!" Her voice rose to a crescendo and her breath came in gasps. "I hate this place! I hate everything about it! I can't stand it any more!"

Carlo walked calmly to the kitchen counter, not answer- ing, carrying his now empty glass and taking the brandy bottle from the cupboard, pouring himself a shot of the amber liquid. He stood with his back to her and tipped the glass toward his mouth. His Adam's apple bobbed as he swal- lowed and he gave a little shudder. Then he turned and started toward the table, bottle and glass in hand, and slowly sat.

"I hate you! I hate you!"

Carlo sat silently at the table, his face turned away. Silent.

"Say something! Answer me!" She couldn't believe the harsh sound of her own voice. "I knew it! I knew something awful would happen! You see! You see! Mother of God! He's dead! Dead!" But he only ducked his head at the words coming from her mouth, as if they were stones raining down upon him. Something else to be endured stoically.

She whirled, pacing the length of the kitchen and then back toward him. "And you just sit there! Say something. For God's sake, say something!" He remained silent, staring into his glass.

"That's it. We're leaving—before something awful happens to you! I've had enough! Enough of this God-forsaken place."

Stopping in the middle of her rant, she turned and stared out the window above the kitchen sink. It was pouring rain, sheets of it cascading off the eaves and falling in a curtain of grey outside the glass. "And this god-damned rain! This everlasting god-damned rain! I can't stand it! I can't stand it!" She burst into tears, her words coming out in chunks between the sobs. "Why—why did you—bring me—here? I h—hate you! I hate you!"

He lifted his head then, as if realizing for the first time that she was speaking to him. He turned his head to look at her, still silent, his white face pierced by the dark eyes. But still he didn't speak.

"Carlo, please!" Her voice took on a pleading tone. "Please, let's go home. Before it's too late. Let's go home. Before the baby comes. Please!"

She quieted then, her sobs diminishing, and they looked silently at each other. She dropped her gaze and wordlessly turned and walked out of the kitchen and down the corridor toward their bedroom, staggering slightly as she went.

Taking off her wrinkled dress and peeling off her stockings, she left them where they lay on the floor and lowered herself onto her bed, giving way again to the tears she had been so proud about withholding all that week. She lay on her back at the edge of the bed, one forearm over her eyes.

When she came to, the room was in semi-darkness and she knew that she was no longer alone. She turned her head. Carlo knelt on the floor beside the bed, his forehead resting on its edge. As soon as he sensed that she was awake, he lifted his head and looked at her, and she saw the pain, the misery that he was unable to express. She remembered her words. "I hate you!" she had said, and she had thought she meant it. Wordlessly she reached out and touched his cheek, caressing his hair with her other hand, like a mother.

The next day was Sunday, and by some unspoken agreement they did not even discuss going to church. They had been there only yesterday, had received communion in front of Mario's coffin and there was no need to go today. They had not spoken much last night after she had awakened to find him kneeling beside her. They were exhausted, depleted from the emotion of the preceding week and the scene in the kitchen. Liliana knew they had to talk, had to have some sort of rational conversation. She wasn't sure herself how much of what she had said—screamed—last night she had really meant.

They sat silently across the kitchen table from each other, drinking their coffee, stirring the sugar into it with unnecessary care, trying not to rattle their spoons when they returned them to their saucers, avoiding each other's eyes. Liliana fingered the neck of her nightie. Carlo looked past her to the window, to the mountain ash with its few orange and russet leaves and its pendulous clusters of orange berries. Then his eyes went to her swollen abdomen and up again to her face. She returned his gaze, her sleep-swollen lips trembling, one hand resting now on the shelf of her stomach. "I'm sorry, Carlo." She paused. He waited. "But I worry—I worry about you working in that place. And I was just so tired and miserable last night."

"I know…," he said finally, his voice coming from deep in his throat. "I know." He sighed, exhaling his breath in a protracted shudder. "And I wasn't much help this past week. I'm sorry, Lili… I'm sorry." There was another silence. The kitchen clock ticked on the wall, the rain lashed at the windows. Then he spoke again, struggling, as though the words were painful to utter.

"Lili, I brought you here because I need you. You are my life. I love you. And the baby." Silence. And then in a pleading tone, "Don't you know that?"

She smiled at him, her face pale in the morning light, her hair tousled. Then, in a quieter voice, looking off again to the tree outside the window, he said, "Everything was going so well—I can't believe Mario's gone." He shook his head back and forth, his voice cracking.

"I know… and though I don't even want to think about it, I guess Gina will go now—back home, I mean." She took a sip of coffee, a look of distaste on her face. It was cold. "It's going to be hard—without Gina… I suppose she'll go as soon as things are tidied up here. Nothing to keep her," Liliana said, her voice fading.

"It's been a hard week for everybody." He got to his feet. "Come on," he said, "we'd better get over there like we promised. Give Anna and Tony a break." He picked up their cups and carried them to the sink as Liliana preceded him to the bedroom, her hand still resting lightly, protectively, on the front of her nightie.

The little group huddled together in the rain next to the wire fence that separated the parking lot from the tarmac. Holding black umbrellas above their heads, their shoulders hunched inside their jackets, they peered upward into the moving grey sky at the spot where the silver plane carrying Gina and her children away had disappeared. She was returning to her homeland, a widow, carrying one child in her arms and another in her womb.

They had taken Gina and Nello to the airport in Edgeton, the town before Cedar Ridge where the Lombardos had left her so long ago. Four couples had driven in a caravan— Carlo and Liliana leading, with Gina and Nello in the back seat, then Mike and Margie, then Anna and Tony riding in Aldo and Loretta's car, which brought up the rear.

One by one the others turned away and walked slowly back to their cars, but Liliana's tear-streaked face was turned upward long after the plane had been enveloped by the moving grey clouds, until Carlo tugged at her arm. They had been through so much during the past month, arranging the funeral, helping Gina sell her house, sell the furniture, make travel arrangements, pack. Their own lives had been on hold, all their energies directed toward assisting poor Gina, who moved white-faced through the days and lay sleepless, staring up at the ceiling through the nights. Someone was with her always, and occasionally she would fall asleep sitting bolt upright on the sofa. They would tiptoe away and leave her, hoping she would sleep for a few hours. Nello had become accustomed to their presence and allowed himself to be cared for by whoever was there. He was a sweet little boy, no trouble at all, they said. He wouldn't even remember his father, they thought sadly.

Slowly Carlo and Liliana turned away from the fence and went back to their car, shaking and folding their umbrellas before getting in. One by one the other cars turned and headed back along the narrow tree-lined highway toward Cedar Ridge, the rain drumming on the roofs, the wipers keeping up their insistent rhythm. They drove past the cemetery, and Liliana averted her eyes. Carlo too looked straight ahead. As they turned the corner and entered the town, Liliana saw that it was at its worst, the small nearly-identical houses huddled together in the pouring rain, their colours dulled, the tall dark cedars enclosing them, the mountains obscured once more by the fog. Not even the plumes of grey smoke from the plant could be seen today, their yellowish-grey colour blending in with the clouds and the fog and rolling together out across the dark Pacific.

Chapter 23

She struggled against rising to consciousness, against enduring yet another dark day of isolation in the house with the rain drumming on the roof. It had been raining the entire time since the funeral. And then, just before she opened her eyes, she knew. The rain had stopped. Her eyes flew open and she saw that there was bright light in her room. The other side of the bed was empty. Carlo had gone to work without waking her. It must be late. She hadn't slept that well since— for a long time.

She dressed and moved down the hallway toward the kitchen. All her movements were slower and more deliberate. She felt heavy, and she rubbed her protruding abdomen in a circular motion, as if to calm her baby. *Poor Gina.* Liliana missed her and hoped that she was settling in at home.

The sunlight streaming in the kitchen window startled her. How could the sun be shining today? She had thought it would never shine again, at least not until the winter was over. But looking out at the mountain ash and behind it the blue sky studded with puffy white clouds she realized that it was still autumn. *It's not winter yet!* Her spirits lifted. Perhaps she would go for a walk later. But first she would make a cake, a surprise for Carlo. She hadn't baked since before—but she would try not to dwell on that. She would make a cake and then she would go for a walk. It would be good for her. Margie had told her she should exercise every day.

Stepping out of her kitchen, redolent with the sweet smell of baking, she drew in a deep breath and exhaled slowly. She looked up. The sky was a startling blue, the clouds bright white against it. Her eyes were drawn to the birch tree and she was amazed. Its leaves were a luminous yellow, standing out in sharp contrast to the dark green of the cedar behind it. When had that happened? She looked up and down the street and saw that in all the yards and on the boulevard there were trees and shrubs dotted with leaves in brilliant hues of flame and gold, ochre and apricot, moving and dancing in the sunlight. The brilliance and clarity of the light made each colour more vivid than she had ever seen it—the deep cerulean of the sky, the smoky blue of the mountains with the leaves ablaze against them.

Slowly she began to walk down the middle of the road, turning her head from side to side to take in this unexpected and powerful beauty, and tears stung her eyes. It was glorious, but Gina was gone. And Mario. They had missed this. Brushing her cheeks with the backs of her hands like a child, she lifted her head and went resolutely on down the street, turning in the opposite direction from Gina's now-empty house—the house she had come to at the beginning of her life. You have to keep on living, you cannot die, too. She remembered her mother saying this when her father had died so unexpectedly. You must simply keep on. There is no other choice.

Amazingly, the sun shone all that week, and Liliana went for a walk every day. Whenever Margie saw her setting off, she would rush out, her jacket thrown haphazardly over her shoulders. They would walk together, talking quietly as their feet shuffled in the crispy leaves. Sometimes they cried a little. Liliana told Margie of her attempts to talk to Carlo about losing Mario and about the future.

"But he just won't talk—about how he feels. It's like he can't." They walked in silence. Then, "Maybe if I'd had a brother—or if my father had lived longer—maybe then I'd know better how to talk to men." Liliana sighed. "And I need to talk about things myself."

"I know," Margie said, looking off into the distance. "It's always harder for men to come to terms with their feelings—never mind expressing them. Mike still can't talk about Mario's death either. It's like he's spooked."

Liliana was comforted to hear that Margie too had trouble talking to Mike, that they didn't communicate any more easily than she and her husband. She had thought earlier in her marriage that it must be a problem specific to Carlo, perhaps because they had been apart for two years before they married, and that when she had a little more experience navigating through the relationship, she would figure out how to help him—help them. Sometimes she had caught herself thinking, *When I grow up. When I grow up I will know how to fix this problem. I just have to wait. He will change, he will begin to talk.* But she knew now that this was not likely to happen, that here was one more way in which men were apparently all alike, and in which women had a common bond. She tried to remember if she had ever heard her mother and father discussing their feelings. No. Not that she could remember. In fact, the very idea seemed ludicrous. He had been a straight-backed, silent man who rarely smiled, who seemed always to be worried, a perpetual frown between his eyes. Perhaps that was why Liliana worried so much. She was like him.

On Friday morning Loretta phoned.

"Liliana? How are you doing? Haven't seen you since the funeral."

"I know. But I haven't been doing much. I try to get out every day to walk. That's all."

"Yes, it's beautiful weather. Indian Summer, they call it." Loretta laughed. "I thought we could go for a drive after lunch. There's something I want to show you."

"Oh, I'd love to."

"Great. I'll pick you up in a couple of hours."

They drove slowly along the narrow road, the forest on either side as dark and forbidding as Liliana remembered it—as it had been in the dream. She saw again the menacing-looking large-leaved plants that grew by the side of the road in front of the tall trees, and then farther down in the ditch the odd yellow lilies, like calla lilies, their feet in a pool of brackish brown water.

"Tell me," she said, turning her head toward Loretta, who drove with the same intensity as Carlo, eyes never leaving the track. "Tell me what those big ugly plants are—

the ones with leaves like big maple leaves, with the spiny stalks."

"Devil's club," Loretta replied, glancing quickly toward the ditch. "Don't ever touch one or you'll be sorry. It'll give you a burning rash even if you just barely touch it. And the prickles are hard to get out. They get infected. Hurt like hell."

"I'll be careful. They look like something in a nightmare."

"Yes, but they do have a use. My people dried the roots and pounded them into a powder—for medicine."

"What for?"

"Can't remember." Loretta looked straight ahead. Liliana didn't believe her, but she changed the subject. There were times, like now, when she felt Loretta shutting her out. But she wasn't offended. She knew how stupid, even prying some of her questions must seem—how ignorant she was.

"And what are those things that look like yellow lilies down in the ditch?"

Loretta laughed. "No, not lilies. Skunk cabbage. I'm surprised you don't know that yet. I heard about a woman from somewhere else who picked a bunch and took them to a friend—for a gift." She laughed quietly to herself.

"Well, why not?

"Because they stink—like skunk. You know, the black animal with the white stripe up his back—the one who keeps his enemies away by his awful stink."

"Oh, *moffetta*," Liliana said half to herself. Then, "I thought I really was smelling skunk when we were here at the picnic."

Loretta smiled. "No, it was them."

"I know," Liliana acknowledged with a grin. "Actually, Carlo told me the same thing you just did—but I didn't believe him."

"They were used as medicine in the old days too. Everything has its place, my mother always says. Nothing in nature is evil."

They drove on in silence through a tunnel of jungle-like growth until at last they emerged at the Cedar River picnic area where they had all sung their hearts out that beautiful summer night. It seemed impossible that it had been only two months earlier.

Loretta stopped the car as soon as she turned into the parking area, so that they were a good long walk from the river's edge across the clearing. Threading their way between the brown picnic tables dotted now with bird droppings that marked the surfaces like chalk, Loretta leading and Liliana walking carefully behind her, they arrived finally at the grassy edge and then onto the large flat stones nestled in the grainy yellow sand that bordered the water. The river was calmer now than it had been in the early summer. There was much less water and it flowed quite peacefully toward the ocean, making only gentle gurgling sounds. Across the moving green water, Liliana saw leaves in fall colours standing out against the cedars on the far bank like flames glimpsed here and there.

"Such a warm sun. I can't believe it," Liliana said, walking carefully over the river stones with both arms raised straight out from her shoulders, balancing her misshapen body.

"Yes," said Loretta, lifting her face to the sun. "It's really warm. But there's often a week like this before the rains set in. I guess the Creator thinks we need it to give us courage."

Liliana glanced quickly over to see if Loretta was joking but saw immediately that she was not. So even she thought it took courage to endure the long winter—or did she mean life itself?

"Come on. I'll help you over the rough spots," Loretta said as Liliana lumbered along. "We have to walk a little farther downstream, to where the river empties out into the ocean, but there's something I really want you to see."

Liliana remembered how the river had been filled with dead and dying salmon, orange bodies and greenish heads, when she had been here last, but now there was only the occasional decayed carcass to be seen, evidence of the failure of some to reach their final destination, though not their death. They, too, had died before they got home.

"Just a bit further," Loretta said. "We're almost at the mouth of the river where it empties out into the ocean. The delta, they call it." She continued to lead the way, walking slowly so that Liliana could keep up. "I want you to see this from the beach."

Liliana didn't understand, couldn't imagine what Loretta wanted to show her, but she followed obediently and soon they stepped out of the trees alongside the river and onto the beach, the dark blue of the Pacific murmuring beside them. Liliana saw that the river had separated into narrow rivulets here, some forked, with swatches of fine silt between them. Some of the channels were much deeper than others, and Liliana knew that she'd never be able to cross the river here if that's what Loretta had in mind.

304

Carefully the two women picked their way over the smooth pink and grey speckled granite rocks embedded in the pale ochre sand along the beach, walking in silence toward the delta, concentrating on their footing, until they could walk no further without getting their feet wet. At this point Loretta stopped and touched Liliana's arm, then pointed. "Look," she said quietly. "Look–over there."

At first, her eyes searching the thick forest on the far shore, she didn't see them, partially hidden as they were among the trees, but then she gasped in amazement. A few huge cedars had grown up between them so that their boughs in places obscured the carved figures sitting one on top of the other, but she could see enough. Tall and grey, unpainted, weatherbeaten and rain-streaked, some broken off jaggedly, others leaning. She knew immediately what they were. Totem poles. She had seen some on the tv, and had wondered about them. But she was quite unprepared for the power of their silent beauty, wings spread, beaks jutting, eyes staring out over the navy white-capped water as they had done for countless years. Like sentinels.

Neither woman spoke for several heartbeats, until Liliana expelled the breath she'd been holding. "Oh, Loretta. Oh, my God. They're so. . .so beautiful. How old. . .?"

Loretta shrugged. "They looked exactly like this when I was a child. No one knows when our people carved them and erected them here. My mother and my grandmother both said that they were just like this when they were girls."

Liliana tore her eyes away from the totems. Behind them, through the bushes and trees, she could just make out the shapes of buildings, perhaps two, standing side by side, almost completely obscured by the forest. She could see that they were long and narrow, with wide open entrances just behind the totems, but almost completely hidden by the cedars. She knew that she would never have noticed them if Loretta hadn't pointed them out. Even someone passing by in a boat would not likely see the grey poles or the low buildings behind them, hidden as they were at the forest's edge.

She turned and looked questioningly at her friend.

"But what is this place, Loretta?"

"It is what is left of our ancient summer camp. Our people have always come here when the salmon were running. At least they used to. My parents would bring me and my brothers and sisters here every year. We'd all work together, along with all the other families. We shared the work and we shared the salmon. There were plenty of fish in those days. That's where we used to stay—in those long-houses. We'd all sleep in there on ledges that run along the inside walls, several families in each one. But we'd cook outside, on campfires."

It was clear that the underbrush and fringe of alder in front of the weatherbeaten buildings had grown up since they had been abandoned. The ochre and rust of the leaves on the lower bushes stood out in sharp contrast. Behind the buildings was a seemingly impenetrable backdrop of dark trees that had been standing there for who knew how many generations—since the beginning of time, Liliana thought.

The open entryways at the front of each of the long-houses were flanked by carvings, as though a shorter totem pole had been sliced in half vertically and affixed to either side. Again, the beaks, the wings, the sightless staring eyes.

"Our ancestors had a weir across the river just over there." She pointed to the far bank and Liliana saw again the remains of dark posts sticking out of the sand. "We trapped the fish here when they tried to go upstream. It was our way. Our people built latticework between the stakes, and when they had enough fish, they'd remove the lattice so the salmon could go upstream. So others could have some, too." She stopped, and Liliana knew enough now to wait. "Then we'd smoke them in pits. It was a good time. There were lots of fish then. The river was teeming with them. We'd get enough in a month to feed the whole village for the winter."

The two women, standing shoulder to shoulder on the estuary, their eyes fixed on the remains of the summer camp, were silent.

Then Loretta resumed. "The elders were with us too. At night, we'd sit outside around a fire and they would tell us stories…of when they were young. And they would sing old songs… in our language, and teach them to us. Sometimes I remember them."

Liliana looked in awe at the sightless poles across the river, at the empty falling-down wooden buildings behind them which were almost part of the forest again, hearing the voices of children playing, smelling the smoke rising from the pits, hearing the elder's chants. This communal way of life reminded her of back home in the cortile, an old woman on every stoop, children playing, smoke rising from the chimneys. She was very grateful that Loretta had allowed her to see this secret sight, which she would never forget. It occurred to her that it was like her own family going to see ancient archeological sights where ancestors had lived.

"When?" she asked at last. "When was that?"

"I guess I was ten the last time. Me and all my brothers and sisters—together." Loretta paused, eyes straight ahead. "That was before they came and built the townsite and the plant."

"Do very many people know about this?"

"No, only my people. We don't talk about it much. This land still belongs to us, not to the company. But we know that someday they'll try to get these away from us....take them to some museum in the city."

The two women were silent. That would be wrong, Liliana thought. These precious old artifacts should be allowed to remain where they were placed by the ancestors. They'll rot though. Soon they'll fall down and rot. And disappear into the earth.

The words of the priest came to her—*to the earth you shall return.* She shivered.

"We'd better go now, you'll catch a cold," Loretta whispered. "Come on," and she tugged at her arm. "Now be careful," she said, and Liliana saw that there were tears glistening on her cheeks.

They turned and started back, Loretta leading, and began their slow passage along the river stones single file, back toward the picnic area. Liliana had the strangest feeling that she was being watched. Was there something there, some creature? She stared hard at the dark spaces between the trees on her left. Was that an animal shape she could just make out? Frightened, she moved a bit faster so that there was less space between herself and Loretta's back. Suddenly Loretta stopped short and threw one arm out to block Liliana's path, at the same time turning her head and putting a finger to her lips. She nodded toward the river's edge a few hundred yards ahead and pointed. There, upstream, stood a large black bear, his front feet in the water, blocking their way. He had been chewing on a salmon corpse. His head was turned toward them and he appeared to be looking at them, his eyes glinting in the sunlight. He dropped his massive head and peered carefully into the water, then lifted it and looked at them again. Liliana's legs turned to jelly. He was huge, shaggy and matted. He seemed to be deciding what to do. They had stumbled upon his fishing territory, and she knew he was hungry, fattening up for his long winter sleep, and would brook no interference. Loretta turned her head and whispered quietly, her words slow and measured.

"I want you to do exactly as I do. Don't speak. Don't look at him. Don't make eye contact. Follow me and be very quiet."

There were eight or ten more stones to traverse before they could step up onto the edge of the bank on their left, and Liliana's legs were shaking so hard she was afraid they'd fail her and she would fall into the water. She concentrated on following Loretta. Moving in single file toward the low grassy bank, Liliana realized that while she was watching her feet, Loretta was sneaking little glances at the bear, who appeared not to be leaving his fishing, only lifting his huge head every now and then to watch their progress. When they reached the edge of the clearing the bear was slightly behind them to the right and out of their sight unless they turned their heads. Liliana was too frightened to look. Loretta glanced swiftly back.

"He's not following us. Now walk as fast as you can, but don't run," she whispered.

They made a bee-line for the car, walking as quickly and quietly as they could between the picnic tables. Loretta reached the car first and had the passenger door open and herself in the driver's seat before Liliana reached her side of the car, sliding in and slamming the door. They leaned back against the seat, their chests rising and falling as their hearts pumped furiously. Then they looked over toward the river. There was no sign of the bear.

"He's too busy feeding to bother about us," Loretta said, "but you can never be sure. They don't like to be disturbed. Yet you can't stay out of the forest because of them. You just have to be careful. He's not the first one I've seen. Or the biggest."

"Let's go," gasped Liliana. "That's enough nature for today. But thank you, Loretta, for showing me that old camp," she said, remembering her manners, "that place where your family went when you were a child. It was wonderful to see and I will never forget it."

"Yes," sighed Loretta. "Funny how a place gets in you. You're a part of it." Silently she steered the car back along the nearly-overgrown road toward town, through the tall shadows cast now by the huge old trees as the sun slid down toward the tops of the mountains, both of them lost in thoughts of childhood.

The nights were getting longer or the days shorter, whichever way you wanted to look at it, Margie said. Liliana hated to see the greyness of the late fall days turn to blackness in the afternoon, so that the windows became mirrors reflecting her as she passed, and she would catch a glimpse of her profile and be astonished at her size. Sometimes she would turn on the overhead lights before lunch, going from room to room in her private rebellion at the tyranny of the hydro bill, ignoring Carlo's frowns.

Once summer ended, the rain had started again in earnest. Whenever the clouds were oppressively low over-head, moving and re-forming like sly grey amoeba, the fumes from the plant were pushed down toward the townsite, and despite the best efforts of the women to keep them out, would reach their putrid tentacles into the houses, creeping insidiously around the tightly closed windows and doors and entering the farthest corners of the rooms. There was nothing you could do, Margie had told her when Liliana complained. It was the low pressure. It would pass. Some days the nauseating smell of the plant permeated even the bedroom where she lay in the afternoons, exhausted from carrying her heavy body through the house. She would spray cologne on her pillowcase and on her wrists before she lay down each afternoon on her back, one arm thrown across her eyes, the mound of her belly obscuring her feet from view.

Mario's death had caused the re-arrangement of the men's work schedules, and Carlo now worked an afternoon shift every second week. This meant that he left the house around two, carrying his lunch box, and did not return until sometime after midnight, creeping into the bed so as not to disturb her. She feigned sleep and turned away. He still smelled faintly of the plant.

Liliana didn't mind this new arrangement, it meant that she could rise and have her morning coffee alone, sitting on the sofa with one foot tucked under her, balancing her saucer on her belly as she watched the news on TV, not caring so much anymore if she didn't understand everything. Carlo rose later, and she had his company as she moved slowly from stove to counter to table, preparing a proper noon meal like back home. He sat at the table with his coffee as she worked, their conversation fitful, interspersed with stretches of silence. She knew that this was her fault. Carlo couldn't fill the spaces, and she had stopped trying. She felt again as she had when she first arrived, as though she were observing the scene from afar, watching herself and this man engaged in this very domestic scene as though she were watching strangers in a pantomime. She couldn't help it. He would just have to understand. The baby rolled and stretched inside her and nothing else was immediate.

As soon as Carlo had left, pressing his cheek to hers in the doorway but foregoing the hug—impossible now to achieve anyway—she would walk down the hallway to the bedroom, hoping she would sleep, hoping she would dream.

The forest is all around, all around the little group of brown cabins, pushing up against them, and she is inside peering out the window, watching the rain dripping off the lower boughs of the cedars so close that she could reach out and touch them. She sees animals between the trees, big matted animals, small shaggy animals, so dense a brown that they look like vacant animal-shaped spaces in the forest, each one moving along beside its young. There is no sound. The babies stay close, their silky little bodies rubbing up against their mothers. And then, as though at some unheard

signal, the mother animals begin to fade, to sink into the ground. Slowly they disappear into the earth, their brown bodies melting, decomposing, until there is no sign of them. They have vanished into the earth. Only the dry bed of cedar needles on which they had lain is visible. The smaller creatures have not moved from where they stood beside their mothers, but they begin to grow, almost imperceptibly at first, then more rapidly, until they have enlarged to fill the newly vacant animal-shaped spaces. Liliana is comforted.

The snow didn't come until mid-December. She and Margie had been talking about it, dreading it, but when she woke one morning and saw the white light that entered her bedroom window, the reflection of the whiteness outside, she was delighted. She padded through the house to the kitchen window. Every twig, every bough was laden with the remarkable whiteness of the snow. The branches of the mountain ash were traced against the sky, the lonely clump of shrivelled orange berries capped with little mounds of white. The sidewalk, the roadway, Margie's and Darlene's front yards, all had disappeared, blanketed in mounds of undulating pristine snow. She had forgotten how beautiful it was, how silent. It muffled the world and turned it into another place.

"Well, it's started. Better get out the shovel." Carlo's sleep-gravelled voice behind her broke her reverie. "Hope the snowblower comes before I have to get the car out to go to work."

It did, roaring down the street like some great snow-breathing dragon. Liliana watched it move, watched its funnel blast a stream of snow first on one side of the road and then on the other. In each driveway stood a man, jacket open, high boots splotched with clumps of snow, leaning on a shovel watching its progress. The driver had better have good aim, she thought. These men had just spent several hours clearing their driveways and would be enraged if the machine were to deposit a fresh mound of snow on the newly-shovelled area.

She smiled to herself, remembering a funny story Carlo had told her last year when she had been looking out in amazement for the first time at the volume of snow. About a man who had run out and lain in his driveway just as the snowblower passed, hoping some of the extruded snow would land on him so that he could sue the municipality. He had, indeed, been covered by the blast from the snowblower, but several neighbours had reported having seen him lie down in its trajectory, and his histrionics were in vain. She had since learned more about this old fellow and his antics from all her friends, stories about how he ate the fruit in the supermarket, grazing along its counters as though in his private garden, despite the admonitions of the clerks. And how he took back old milk claiming it was bad when he bought it, in order to have it replaced with fresh for free. They were appalled and ashamed by his actions, embarrassed that he was Italian and thus was branding them all as untrustworthy and sly. Yet not one of them challenged him. He was an old man. She shook her head and turned away from the window. She remembered old Lazaro at home, who was regularly found next-to-dead in the ditch beside the bar, and who, like his Biblical namesake, rose again. Every town had its eccentrics, its lunatics. This one was no better and no worse.

A letter came from Gina finally, the first one, though she had phoned to say that she had arrived safely, her voice sounding thin and faraway. Liliana's hands trembled slightly as she opened the envelope and unfolded the pale blue pages covered with tiny round writing. She carried them into her bedroom and lay on her back to read, her forearms resting on her breasts as she held up each crisp page.

Gina wrote that while everyone was good to her, it was very difficult to be back in her parents' house, subject once more to their constraints, their ways, after having been mistress of her own home. Nello was impossible, whining and crying, resisting all attempts to distract him, and she was miserably sick with this pregnancy. What would she do, she wrote, when she had two children to feed? She thought she'd have to get a job to help out at home. The insurance money from the company wouldn't last long, and the pension was meager because Mario hadn't worked that long.

"I can't believe this has happened. It seems as though God has abandoned me. I say this to you, dear Lili, but I cannot say it out loud here. I muffle my tears in my pillow at night and wonder what will become of us. I am a burden to my parents. They are old now and shouldn't have to worry about me and my family. It's not right to be bringing up my children without a father in this house of old people. But they tell me things will look brighter after the baby is born. I hope so. I think of you so often, Lili, and miss our times together with you and Carlo. We were happy then, but I didn't know it. Only now do I see what I had, and it is gone forever.

I'm sorry to go on like this, please excuse me. And please write to me soon and give me all the news about everybody. I hope you are feeling well.

With affectionate love, Gina."

Poor Gina, with her old parents. Probably like Carlo's—poor, silent, dressed all in black. Not at all like Liliana's. Her family would welcome her home, would rejoice in having her back. Mama and Nonna would gladly help her with her child and all the aunties and uncles and cousins would gather round, delighted that she was home again and thrilled to have a new baby to fuss over. How wonderful it would be to be back in the bosom of her family. She folded the letter and put it out of sight in her top dresser drawer.

Margie didn't drop in for coffee on the days that Carlo was home in the mornings, but hardly a day went by when she didn't run over to check on Liliana after supper. And Anna phoned her frequently to be sure she was all right during the long lonely evenings. Thankfully neither woman indulged too much in the harrowing stories of childbirth that had been so common in their conversations last summer.

They knew that Liliana would soon find out for herself. What she needed was courage.

"You'll be fine. You're young and strong, and it's a good little hospital."

"And you forget about the pain as soon as you see your baby."

"Now you be sure to call me if you need me. I'm right across the street."

A few days before Christmas, with the large soft flakes falling slowly in the darkness outside the kitchen window, Liliana and Anna had just finished making a huge batch of *tortellini*. It had been Anna's idea, and Liliana had gone along with it because she simply didn't have the strength or the will to protest. So Anna had collected the ingredients for the meat filling, and had arrived at Liliana's door even before Carlo had left for work. Laden with parcels, the flakes that sat on her head melting and running slowly down her face, she smiled broadly at them, and as Carlo grabbed his lunch box and headed out the door, he seemed quite pleased, not so much at the prospect of *tortellini* in his Christmas-day broth as at the sparkle he saw in Liliana's eyes. Making *tortellini* was traditional, it was appropriate, but it hadn't happened last year. She couldn't remember why.

Later that afternoon, sitting at last to share a cup of coffee, the two women surveyed with pride the hundreds of *tortellini* that lay like little puffed-up navels on the tea-towels spread on every square inch of surface in the kitchen. After they had taken their break, they packaged them and placed the plastic bags in the deep freeze in the sewing room, alongside the cookies Liliana had made earlier. They had been Margie's idea. She said that lots of women made cookies together for Christmas, several different batches, sharing recipes and dividing the finished product. It had seemed like a good idea, and she was tired of spending the long afternoons and evenings alone. She needed the company of women.

She and Carlo had decided to invite Anna and Tony with their two boisterous children for Christmas dinner. They had been alone last year, not realizing that here in Canada a great deal more was made of Christmas than they were used to. Margie and Mike and their two children were going "home" for the holidays this year, back east, and Liliana envied Margie more than she dared say. She would miss them. But it would be good to have Anna's children around to distract her—or to remind her and Carlo of things to come. "Good practice for you." Anna laughed. "But I'll help you with the dinner. You mustn't do too much."

On Christmas day they set the table with the good dishes, the ones with the bright roses on them, and her best crystal, and Liliana surveyed it with pleasure. It looked quite festive. Carlo had helped, but it had taken a very long time. She could only lumber about, swaying from side to side, and he didn't know where things were or where to place them, but they had worked companionably until it was done to her satisfaction. The turkey was in the oven, Margie having given Liliana detailed instructions on how to do this, writing them down. Liliana had never seen an entire bird stuffed and cooked, but she had been determined to try after Margie had told her that this was the Canadian custom, that everybody did it. Everything else for the meal was either ready and sitting on the counter, or would be brought over by Anna, so Liliana lowered herself to the sofa beside Carlo, their feet on the coffee table, the lights on the tree glowing, to have a quiet break before the onslaught. His arm was around her and she rested her head on his shoulder. She loved the tree. And this year there were lights on the house, under the eaves and all around the windows. Just as he had promised.

"Mmm, smells good in here!" Tony shouted as he and Anna and the children burst through the door, each one carrying a pile of wrapped parcels or a dish of food covered with aluminum foil. There was much stamping of feet and hugging and laughing and teasing as coats and boots were taken, food placed on the counter, parcels under the tree. The children were noisy and excited, chasing each other, whining for a cookie, a drink, and Liliana revelled in it, loved having her house filled with the good smells from the kitchen, the voices, the laughter. It had been too long.

The meal was a great success, the stuffed turkey tasting as good as it smelled, and Anna and Tony were suitably impressed. Everything had been delicious, though Liliana felt uncomfortably full despite having eaten sparingly. As soon as the others had gone, Carlo flopped exhausted onto the sofa and Liliana emitted a groan as she carefully lowered herself down beside him. Thank heaven Anna had helped her clear the table and do the dishes before rounding up her brood and departing. Liliana sighed. I can't wait, she thought, tired but excited, I can't wait.

It was a snowy night in February when her time came. As soon as she rose to consciousness, she knew. There were bands tightening across her lower abdomen as though she wore an invisible girdle and something was tightening it, tighter, tighter, then stopping. She waited. Stay calm. Don't make a fuss. Don't wake Carlo until you're sure. She turned her head so that she could see the luminous dial of her bedside clock. 3:10. Eight minutes since she had first looked at it. Another surge of tightening, tighter, tighter, then stopping. She watched the clock. Eight minutes, perhaps a little less, and then the tightening, a bit stronger this time, but bearable. She remembered Margie's words: the most important thing is to stay calm. If you panic, it'll be much worse. And don't, whatever you do, wait too long. Get to the hospital, they'll take you in no matter how soon it is, and you'll have time to get settled before it gets too strong. She waited, breathing slowly, calmly. Again. She turned. "Carlo —Carlo. Wake up. It's time."

Carlo's feet hit the floor and he was getting into his pants before he spoke. "I'll take your case out and start the car." Then, glancing out the window, "Oh damn, it's been snowing. I'll have to shovel. Get dressed, get dressed!"

"It's all right, Carlo. I'm sure there's plenty of time. I'll get dressed, and you look after the car. Don't worry, it'll be fine."

She couldn't believe that she was reassuring him, keeping him calm. That's exactly how Margie had said it had been with Mike, that he was the one who was flustered. "Nervous as a cat," had been her words. Carefully, methodically, she went about getting ready as she had rehearsed in her mind so many times, everything laid out carefully for just such an eventuality. But it was as though she was watching herself put on her clothes, pack her toiletries, put on her heavy coat and sit on the kitchen chair while Carlo helped her on with her boots, watched herself get into the car and be driven down the silent dark street, the tires crunching on the snow, down the hill toward the hospital.

It was a long night. Carlo came and went from her room, wanting to help, but helpless, useless, in the way, being shooed out, then when she opened her eyes, sitting beside her again, peering anxiously into her face. Once she heard a voice whimpering and knew that it was hers. When she could, when she could think, she felt proud of herself. Margie had coached her well. She was managing through some great feat of will—will she didn't know she had—to keep the panic at bay until finally she was wheeled across the hall to the delivery room.

They placed his bloody, pasty little body on her suddenly flat abdomen and the hot sweet weight of him was the most wonderful sensation she had ever known. "A boy!" everyone shouted, and she smiled weakly as the doctor rushed out to tell Carlo, who had been hovering in the hallway, tormented by the sounds. But now she heard him give a whoop of joy and suddenly he was in the room. Their eyes met, and she saw the tears on his cheeks as he bent over her white face and kissed her on the forehead. "It's a boy," he whispered, as if she wouldn't know—hadn't known. "A boy!"

Chapter 24

"Carlo, we need to go home." She hated the pleading, whiny tone she heard in her own voice, but she felt unable to change it. "We need to go—to see our parents—to show them the baby! Please! We have to." Liliana stood in the kitchen that chilly spring morning, the front of her nightie damp and stained with her milk. "Why can't we go?" She had been thinking about this for the three months since the birth of the baby, thinking that surely Carlo would bring it up. Surely, he was feeling the same desire to see his parents, to show off his son. But he had never mentioned it, and she could bear the silence no longer. "We can save enough before the summer, and Daniele will be old enough to travel by then. Please!"

Carlo sat dejectedly at the table, almost wincing at her words, his head down. There was a silence, her voice hanging in the air.

At last he spoke slowly. "No, Liliana, we can't go now. Maybe next year."

"But why?" she wailed, "Why not?"

"Because I don't get any more holidays. I took those two weeks when Mario died, and then one when the baby was born, and that's it—I don't get any more until next year. The company is very strict about that." His own voice had taken on a pleading tone, wanting her to understand, to acquiesce. But she was undeterred.

He's just saying that to shut me up, I know. Doesn't want to give in to me even if he wants to go home as much as I do. "Well then, I'll go. I'll take your son home to see our parents! I'll go by myself! You can't stop me! I need to go!" And then, her voice quieter, trembling, "Don't you want your mother and father to see him—to see Daniele?"

He shook his head mutely.

"Don't *you*? Don't *you* want to go? How can you not want to go?"

Carlo said nothing, his head lowered, his shoulders sagging under the onslaught of her words.

"What kind of man are you?" she screamed, her voice breaking, and she turned and stomped off to the bedroom where the baby slept in his bassinette beside their bed. She knew she was being unreasonable, springing the idea on Carlo like that. She should have known better—should have found a better way to broach the subject. She had allowed her silent yearning to reach a crescendo during the preceding weeks until she screamed it out. How childish. Would she never learn? She was as angry at herself as she was at him.

Damn him—he's just so stubborn! Has to be the boss! Has to win!

She sat on the edge of the bed, her head down, her arms wrapped around herself, tears on her cheeks. Feeling shaky and sticky and ugly. She was trapped, trapped by her body and Daniele's demands. She hated her body. She had never paid much attention to it before the pregnancy. It had been attractive enough and had always served her well, but now it behaved as if it were a separate entity, soft and white and spongy, responding to the demands of the child, of Carlo. And she felt trapped by the house, by the garden, by their friends, by the very fabric of their lives which she had tried so hard to stitch together.

Three months before, when she had first come home from the hospital, her legs like jelly, her face pale, tendrils of hair sticking to her cheeks and forehead with the sweat of her body, carefully holding the bundle which contained their son, there had been no thought in her mind except to make it through that day, then the night, then the next day. She thought often of how she had handled Nello without fear, rocking him, changing him, dressing him, but this was different. She couldn't go home after Daniele had been attended to, she couldn't just hand him over to his mother and go off. She was the mother. Everything depended on her, and she was so tired she just wanted to lie down on the floor and not get up for a month. But she couldn't. She stumbled through the first few weeks from one feeding to the next, and her universe had dwindled to this scrawny, demanding little creature in whose thrall she was. Completely. She carried him about on her shoulder, rubbing and patting his little back as his head, covered with silky black hair just as she had dreamt, wobbled about on his thin little neck. Sometimes she gave him to Carlo, who was quite happy to have him if he was quiet, satiated after a feeding, but at the first tiny squawk he called out to Liliana, who came running and took him. After all, the baby didn't need him—she was the mother. Even during the night when Carlo and Daniele were both asleep, she would wake and rise to stand over him, checking to be sure he was breathing, holding her own breath so that she could hear his. She thought often of her mother, picturing her bending over the little bed of her child in the darkness of night, wondering how she had managed. Had she, too, been exhausted to the point of tears, feeling overwhelmed by these new demands? But there had been Nonna. She had not been alone.

Eventually the time had lengthened between feedings, and Danny, as they had taken to calling him, began to smile and coo and talk to them, and they were entranced. He made eye contact and responded with a deep little chuckle when Carlo held him up in the air over his head or tickled him under the chin. Liliana suddenly realized one day that their only conversations had become those about the baby, what he had done that day, his growing awareness of his surroundings. Liliana didn't ask Carlo any more about how his day at the plant had gone, and he didn't tell her. And she hadn't brought up her wish to go home either. He knew, didn't he? But he never mentioned it either.

"My God, I can't believe the size of him," Margie said one day in late May. "He can't be just three months old. He's too big."

"I know, but he is," replied Liliana, stuffing him into a bright blue outfit that Loretta had knit. And to the squirming baby, "Come on now, be still. You have to wear these little shoes, too. You can't come out with Mama and *Zia* Margie and *Zia* Anna unless you're wearing shoes."

Anna and Liliana had agreed that if Margie drove, because neither of the other two had a car to use, they would show her how to recognize wild *chicoria,* which they assured her made a most delicious salad, a real treat after the long winter—the first of the fresh spring greens.

"Gosh, I've never heard of it," protested Margie, "but it's a good excuse to get out of the house while the kids are at school. I'm game." And so it was decided.

Margie drove slowly along the highway toward Edgeton, so slowly that cars honked and passed them with a roar. "Not to worry, let them go," she said when she noticed Liliana's frown. Meanwhile, Anna was concentrating on watching the ditches on either side for the elusive chicory, until finally she called out, "Here we are. This is the spot. Turn up this side road and stop." Margie obeyed and the three women got out of the car, Liliana struggling with a squirming Daniele. Anna went ahead, the intrepid chicory stalker, until she squatted on the ground in a patch of grass and yelled, "Come on. Over here. Bring the knives, and the bags."

Quickly Liliana and Margie joined her, squatting on their haunches under a cornflower blue sky, the salmonberry bushes on either side of them dotted already with ripening berries.

"There, see it?" said Anna, pointing.

"What?" screamed Margie, "Is that it? Is that chicory? Oh, for God's sake, that's dandelion! Dandelion greens, like my Mom used to pick in the spring." She sat back down on the grass, laughing, her head thrown back, while the other two watched in puzzled bemusement. "It's dandelions! And here I thought we were looking for some exotic rare plant. I ate these every spring when I was growing up back East." Laughing now, they set to work digging the tiny white roots out of the ground and putting the green plants with their zig-zag leaves into the brown paper bags they had brought. As she worked, Liliana thought about herself and her mother picking and washing these same greens every spring back home, just as Margie and her mom had done, just as she was doing now with Daniele. Small world.

Suddenly Anna pointed to a spot behind Margie's back, and they turned their heads and saw, peeking out at them from between the bushes, a little brown bear.

"Quick!" Margie said, her voice dropping to a whisper, "Let's get back to the car. Momma Bear is somewhere close by, and she's dangerous."

Liliana was in the back seat with the door closed and the window rolled up, clutching Danny to her chest, almost before Margie had finished speaking, with the other two jumping into the car a second later. They knew that a mother bear's maternal instinct was not to be trifled with. Margie drove off without a backward glance, and no one spoke as she turned the car back onto the highway and headed home. "Man, that was a close call," she said at last. "I'll bet the mother was watching us all the time we were digging up the damned dandelions." She laughed nervously. "I guess we were in their berry-picking area."

"Serves us right," Anna said. "Next time let's bring Loretta with us for a lookout."

Liliana didn't mention their close call to Carlo, only washed and served the delicate greens, accompanied by hard-boiled eggs, without comment, though he did say how nice it was to eat them once more. A sure sign of spring, he said. She didn't answer.

On the days when Carlo didn't go to work until the afternoon, things went along smoothly enough. She didn't have to make conversation, and neither did he—except about the baby. Daniele had to be bathed and fed and diapered, and between these events, Carlo held him so that Liliana could make the noon meal. After Carlo had gone, she put the baby down in his crib and let him fuss while she tidied the kitchen. She couldn't just let him cry himself to sleep when Carlo was home because he would go and get him up immediately if he heard a sound, looking accusingly at Liliana. But she knew that she mustn't give in so easily and she had inured herself to his pre-nap howls, which soon dwindled down to occasional squawks, and then silence.

Sometimes in the afternoons after the house was quiet, she allowed herself the luxury of a long bath with scented soap, luxuriating in the hot water, in the perfumed steamy air, and in the solitude. A brief reprieve from the constant demands of the baby, the house, her husband. She tried not to think about anything bad—about what was troubling her. It only made her feel hopeless—and angry.

The dangerous days were those when Carlo came home from work around four in the afternoon, just when Daniele was at his most inconsolable and she was feeling frazzled. It was hard to hold her tongue when Carlo looked around frowning at the messy kitchen, the piles of baby laundry waiting beside the washer, the bread crumbs on the counter from her hastily-grabbed lunch. She would thrust the baby into Carlo's arms as soon as he had bathed and changed his clothes, the stubborn black grime from the plant still under his fingernails.

"Here, take your son," she would say curtly, as if he had never acknowledged paternity. "I just can't get anything done during the day."

She felt as though she was always on the brink of a major hysterical outpouring of something—anger, regret, accusation. She waged a silent war with herself—not to lash out, not to scream in rage, tear her hair, throw herself on the floor. Not to give in to her childish inclinations, which she thought she had long ago overcome. But most of all she had to push down the feelings of guilt. How could she be so ungrateful? Such a beautiful baby. No worries about food, about safety, about shelter. What was the matter with her? Sometimes she thought she'd be better off dead. And then she'd writhe inwardly at her cowardice, at her ingratitude. What an awful thing to think! How sinful! She had heard of a young woman who had killed herself and her baby during the winter. Unthinkable! Who could imagine such desperation? Carlo didn't know anything about what she was feeling, it seemed, didn't notice, didn't care. Thought everything was good. Normal. Didn't he? He had always been the silent one, and by his silence now he was simply reacting, or not reacting, to her moods. Maybe it was only she who was on the brink, teetering, trying not to fall.

She was in the waiting room of the doctor's office on the third floor of the big pink hospital she had seen on her first drive through town. The hospital where Mario had died. Where her baby had been born. Carlo was at work and since she couldn't have the car, Margie had dropped her off and would pick her up in an hour.

The baby struggled in her arms, perhaps knowing what was coming—another innoculation, another prodding of his abdomen, peering into his ears, down his throat. Just a regular checkup, and Liliana was very grateful for the good and free medical attention. But she had another purpose in her visit today—to ask the doctor for the birth-control pill that Margie had told her was now available. No use taking any chances, Margie had said. "You sure don't want another one so soon."

"But Carlo—I'm not sure what he'd think."

"Well, it's your body," Margie had said firmly. And Liliana had decided.

It was tiring holding Daniele, trying to keep him quiet as he writhed and struggled in her arms. A woman sitting across the room was doing the same thing, holding on her knee a struggling child all dressed in pink who appeared to be about the same age as Daniele.

She looked over at Liliana. "You'd think my little girl would be quieter than your boy, wouldn't you?"

"I guess they're the same at this age," Liliana replied. "She's so pretty."

"And your little fellow is very good looking," the other woman said, smiling. "But it's hard work, isn't it?"

"Yes, I had no idea," Liliana said. "You have. . . only one?"

"No, I have two older ones–in school."

"He. . .Daniele. . . is. . .our only one."

"You're Carlo's wife, aren't you?"

"Yes," Liliana replied, shifting the baby on her knee so that she could see the face of the woman who had addressed her. "Do you know him?"

"No, not really. But my husband pointed you out at church. He works with Carlo. How's he doing?"

Liliana wasn't sure what the woman meant. "Doing?"

"Yes. . .after that man. . .Mario was it. . .was killed? How is he?"

"Oh, Mario," Liliana breathed. The woman was asking about the accident. "My. . .Carlo is okay. He's. . . getting over it." She paused, searching for the right words. "But he. . .he misses his friend."

The other woman shifted her baby on her knee and, leaning forward and lowering her voice conspiratorially, said, "My husband told me. . .Isn't that awful, falling into the machinery!"

Liliana felt her stomach lurch. What did that mean? And then she suddenly remembered something Margie had told her last summer, about a man who had fallen into some big machine several years before. Into her mind shot the horrible, the unspeakable image from that day. No, it couldn't be. No one had said that Mario had fallen into a machine.

"Wha. . .at? Mario fell. . .into some machinery?"

"Oh yes, into the machinery. Not much left of him."

"Oh, my God," Liliana breathed. "I didn't. . .I didn't know."

"Uh-huh. And it was a close call for your Carlo, too."

"Wh. . .at? What do you mean?" She was afraid she would throw up right there on the floor of the waiting room.

"Well, he was, hanging there over the machinery by his fingertips. The foreman saved him."

Another wave of nausea washed over Liliana and the bitter gall rose in her throat. She felt the blood drain from her face.

"You didn't know?" the woman said shrilly, her eyebrows raised. "You mean your husband didn't tell you?"

"No," Liliana whispered, her voice quavering. "He didn't." Her eyes welled up and tears spilled down her white cheeks.

"Oh, I'm sorry, honey–I thought you knew–I'm so sorry," the other woman babbled apologetically, shifting uncomfortably in her chair.

Liliana realized she had been holding her breath as the woman spoke, holding her breath so as not to scream. It felt as though her heart had stopped beating. Time was suspended. No one had ever told her that she, too, had almost been widowed. The horrible image rose again in her mind's eye.

Just then the receptionist entered from the back room and called out, "Mrs. Pellegrino please," but Liliana had already risen, and clutching Daniele to her chest, his blanket trailing, was heading out the door.

"Why didn't you tell me?" She still had her jacket on, still held the struggling child in her arms. Ignoring the wails of the baby, she screamed at Carlo, her face drained of colour, her heart racing. "Why in God's name didn't you tell me? Why did I have to hear it from a stranger?"

Carlo turned toward her, his lunchbox still in his hand. He had arrived home just as Margie was dropping Liliana off in the driveway, entering the kitchen ahead of her. His jaw dropped, a stunned look on his face. "What? What are you talking about, Liliana?"

"A woman—a stranger—told me in the doctor's office. That you almost fell into the machinery too, when Mario died. That you almost died, too!"

Understanding dawned on his face. "But I didn't. Look, I'm fine," he said, spreading his arms and looking down at his body as though to reassure himself that it was all there. "I didn't want to worry you, that's all. That's why I didn't tell you."

"Oh God! That damned place! I don't want to be a widow, too, like Gina!"

Daniele was howling inconsolably now, but Liliana screamed over his voice. "That's it! We're going home! All of us. Quit your job—we're leaving!"

His face was ashen. "Liliana…I can't. I can't go home."

"Why? Why can't you?"

"What would I do there? I'd have to work in the fields for the rest of my life…for someone else."

"I don't care!" she screamed back. "We're going!"

"No, no, we can't…we can't go back," he answered, his voice firm but beseeching, his eyes looking directly into hers, willing her to understand. "We'd be poor, Liliana, poor forever. We could never build a nice house…like your uncles…like you deserve." He slammed his lunchbox down on the table. "No. We can't!"

And they stood there, both of them trembling.

Daniele's howls reached a crescendo, making it impossible to go on, and Liliana's voice broke as she pushed past her husband to take the baby to the bedroom. "Well, I'm going. I gave up my family for you! I'm going home. You can't stop me!"

The words were flung over her shoulder, choked out between the sobs, hers and Daniele's. Carlo remained standing, mute, staring at her retreating back. She stumbled down the hallway and slammed the bedroom door behind her.

I'll go by myself! I'll get there somehow. Why stay here and wait to be widowed? My son will be fatherless anyway. I might as well bring him up back home with my family. I can't live like this any more, waiting.

Faintly, as if from a great distance, she heard the telephone ringing. Who could be calling at this hour? Maybe Carlo had to go in to work early. That happened sometimes. The foreman had singled him out for this honour as a precursor to offering him a promotion, Carlo had said. Then she heard his voice calling her, and her heart thumped. She rolled out of bed and rushed into the kitchen. He handed her the phone.

"Lili? Oh, Lili, I'm sorry to wake you, but I have some wonderful news!"

"Luisa? Is that you? What is it?"

"Olivo's home! He's home for good, and we're going to get married at the end of August!"

That night Liliana and Carlo lay in bed, both awake, without speaking. Their movements and voices had wakened Daniele, whose crib was still in their room, but she had rubbed his back until he had fallen asleep again, without nursing him. Carlo pretended to be asleep, but she could tell by his breathing that he was not. Finally, when she could hold it in no longer, she whispered, "Carlo, I must go! She's my sister." There was no reply, but she knew he had heard her. "And the timing is perfect. Don't you see? We can save enough money in three months—and I have time to get ready. Oh please, Carlo, please."

He sighed then, and turned toward her. His voice sounded deeper, worried. "We'll see, Lili. We'll see. It's a lot of money."

"It's not about money!" Her anger choked her, the sobs robbing her of the ability to sound rational. She tried again. "I want to see them—to show them our baby. I won't be gone long." She was crying hard now, the bed vibrating with her sobs.

What is it, she wondered, what is it that makes it so difficult for him to let me go? It's not really the money. Is he afraid I won't come back? And as soon as the thought rose from her subconscious, she knew that it was true. He was afraid she would take his son and never return. And he couldn't express it, of course. Couldn't or wouldn't. Wouldn't tell her how much he needed her. Wanted her back. Her sobbing increased.

"Settle down, Liliana. Don't get hysterical—you'll wake Daniele. We'll talk about it in the morning."

Oh God, he's treating me like an unreasonable child—patronizing me. That's it. I'll find a way to go, and maybe—maybe I won't come back. Surely there's more to life than this. If I stay here, I'll just end up like Gina anyway--alone.

But they didn't talk about it in the morning, and as the days went by the silence grew, like a tangible thing between them. She couldn't trust herself to open the conversation lest she blurt out what she had been thinking more and more since Luisa had called—her secret vow to go without him. Carlo couldn't open it, she knew, because that was his way—don't talk about it and it doesn't exist. And above all, don't tell her what he was really feeling. Oh, no. Never.

Secretly she began ferreting away any money she could, anything she managed to save from the household expenses. She had a leather change purse under her folded sweaters in the middle drawer of the bureau, and every day she counted out the money. Carlo hadn't missed it. He trusted her completely. But how much would she need for a ticket? A great deal more, she thought despondently. Still, she began separating her clothes and Daniele's into piles in the sewing room, where Carlo almost never went—everyday things for now and good things, things to be left unused, washed and ironed and placed carefully in the bottom drawer. She eyed her maroon leather luggage, those pieces her uncles had given her which had been used only that once. They sat now on the floor of the closet in the sewing room, which she had thought would one day be Daniele's room. The suitcases would hold a great deal if one took only clothes.

No mention was made by either of them of Luisa's phone call, or Lili's tearful pleading, so that as the weeks went by she began to think she would burst, shatter into a thousand fragments. How could Carlo stand it, this silence? But apparently, he just didn't care. He seemed to like things this way.

That leaden sense of dread never left her. But she said nothing, only hurrying down to the bedroom as soon as Carlo had gone to work to count the money she was secretly putting away. How much would it take for a ticket? She had no idea. A great deal more than this, probably. She would think of an innocent way to ask Margie how much it would cost. She'd know.

One afternoon after counting the money, surprised at the sum, she reached into the back of her closet and took out her good wool suit, the one she had worn on the train coming out. She tried it on. The skirt was too tight, pulling over her hips, and she could not button the jacket over her enlarged breasts. But there was extra fabric at the seams, she saw, and when Carlo was at work and Daniele was asleep, she took the suit into her sewing room and managed to alter it so that it fit. Barely, but it would do. A good pressing and it would be fine. A thought struck her. What would Mama and Nonna think if she showed up wearing the same clothes she had left in? They would think she was admirably frugal, not wasting her husband's money. Wouldn't they? And she did have some new things, dresses and skirts and blouses she had made. And slacks. No. She wouldn't take those.

It was a beautiful mid-July day, the sun shining hot and clear, so that she had to leave the kitchen door open. The geraniums that she had managed to over-winter on the sill in the sewing room were outside now, on either side of the walkway, and as she passed the open door their musky perfume struck her like a blow in the pit of her stomach, and she felt a surge of nostalgia so strong she stopped dead in her tracks. She had to go. But she would never be able to save enough herself. She would broach the subject again after supper, when Carlo was showered and fed and playing with the baby. It had been six weeks since Luisa's phone call.

Carlo had probably been thinking about it all this time too, assessing the risk. She would have to reassure him. She moved to the sink and looked out to see his car rolling up into the driveway. He was a little late.

Carlo's face was serious when he walked in. Putting his lunchbox down on the kitchen table, his eyes never leaving hers, he put his hand into his breast pocket and extracted a long glossy envelope with red and blue stripes on it. He held it out toward her. "Here you are, Lili. Take it."

"What? What is it?" She watched his face closely and saw that his eyes were sparkling as he broke into a broad grin.

"It's your ticket."

She gasped. She couldn't breathe. Her legs were trembling. Shakily she reached out and took the envelope from his hand and stared at it, uncomprehending.

"Go ahead, open it. It's for six weeks. You'll get there two weeks before the wedding and stay for a month after! Go ahead. Open it."

But she didn't open it. She staggered two steps forward and threw herself into his arms as the tears sprang to her eyes. She should have known. Should have known he would come through.

"Oh, Carlo, oh darling, I can't believe it! You did it! You really did it!" She covered his face with kisses and he laughed and hugged her, dancing her round and round. "Oh, thank you. Thank you!" Then she turned in his arms. "Danny, Danny! We're going to see Nonna!" she screamed, so that the baby looked up in surprise from his playpen on the living room floor. "We're going home! We're going home!" She stopped, sensing a stiffening of Carlo's arms, a straightening of his back. "To Nonna's home," she quickly amended. "Our other home. To see both your Nonnas." Her voice was frantic.

Gradually he lowered his arms and moved over to the playpen and she knew instantly that he was afraid—afraid that he would lose both his wife and his child. She could almost sense him willing himself not to betray his fear. Leaning down, he scooped the baby up in his arms and kissed him repeatedly on his head and on his upturned face, then placed him back in the playpen. Without speaking he turned and walked out the door, and she heard the roar as he started his car and backed out of the driveway and down the road.

She stood there silently, clutching the envelope to her chest.

I am going, Carlo. I am going home and I don't think I will be coming back.

She didn't know what time it was when he finally returned, but she heard him stumbling about, bumping into furniture, swearing, and she knew he'd been drinking. He must have slept on the sofa because she didn't ever feel him getting into the bed, and when she got up in the morning, his lunchbox and the car were gone. They didn't ever speak of it.

Now the weeks dragged by. The rest of July passed, then the first weeks of August, as she sewed and ironed and packed, but she noticed that Carlo rarely laughed, that their exchanges became even less frequent. She guessed that he was feeling left-out, shut out and afraid. But that was his own fault. After all, she had begged him to go home, too.

So she cared for Danny, she looked after the house and the garden, she prepared for the trip, she laughed and talked with her friends, and she supposed that he felt unnecessary. And worried. Would she come back? Some days she was positive she wouldn't, others she vacillated. Carlo had been a good husband, loving, a good provider. How could she just leave him here? But then, he was happy here, happier than she could ever be. He had his work and his friends. He rarely seemed to need her. Rarely even spoke to her these days. It would be so lovely just to be living again in her own home—her childhood home—surrounded by the love and attention of her family, without the constant worry about Carlo's safety, the constant stress of their relationship. The numbing silences wore her down. She couldn't bear it any longer. And after all, it wouldn't be as it was for Gina—not with her family. They would be so happy to have her back and with such a beautiful little son. She could see herself in her mind's eye laughing and talking with Mama and Luisa as she moved through the spacious, cool rooms of the old stone house. It occurred to her that if she had her own money, she wouldn't need Carlo at all—ever. She would be just fine without him—she and Daniele.

It was the August evening before the day of her departure, and the maroon suitcases sat, their sides bulging, just inside the kitchen door. Aldo and Loretta, Anna and Tony and Margie and Mike were sitting with them in the back yard, as they had done so often on these beautiful summer nights after the kids were in bed. It was hard to get them to sleep when it stayed light so late, but it made for beautiful long evenings. Her friends had come over tonight to wish her bon voyage, and she and Carlo had served cool drinks in tall frosted glasses—Margie had shown her how to frost the glasses. Toasts had been drunk to her trip and to her happiness, and no one had noticed that she smiled only slightly in response, and Carlo not at all. They were sitting now in companionable quiet, almost ready to go home.

"Look, look!" Margie called out suddenly, her head tipped back, one hand raised, finger pointing to the sky. "Look! The Northern Lights!"

"Aurora Borealis—Northern Lights!" exclaimed Carlo. "I've never seen them."

"Neither have I—how beautiful! Look! How beautiful!"

"Look at that—amazing!" They were all standing now, heads thrown back, mouths open in wonder as the shimmering bands of green and white and pink rolled across the velvet sky, moving as though to silent music, making a sound like the rustling of taffeta, like the swishing of many skirts. The colours rippled and surged, now separating into glowing bands, one colour distinct from the other, then merging, then separating again, until at last they faded and the sky returned to indigo, pierced by a million glowing stars.

"That was for you, Lili," Loretta said. "A farewell gift for you." Everyone nodded.

"Yes," said Anna, "A beautiful one. To be sure you come back."

She felt Carlo's eyes on her, but she didn't return his look, didn't acknowledge Anna's comment at all.

"Oh, she'll come back," said Mike jovially. "How could she leave a place like this?"

They all laughed then, still not noticing her silence, and hugged her and kissed her and wished her a good trip and told her to get to bed. Tomorrow was a big day. And waving and blowing kisses, they turned and disappeared into the night.

Chapter 25

Liliana peered out the window beside her seat, the weight of Daniele's body sprawled in sleep across hers. She was looking down at the blue-green ocean and the silver and white towers of Vancouver spread out below her, its irregular contours bordered here and there with stands of dark trees, fingers of blue water in serpentine threads encroaching into it. She was amazed. It was huge, a big, beautiful city just an hour and fifteen minutes south by plane. Carlo had told her it was a thousand miles by car, and that made it seem impossibly distant, but it wasn't. Cedar Ridge wasn't at the end of the world after all—you could get to the city in a relatively short time if you flew. She felt as though she had just boarded the plane and managed to get her child to sleep when she had begun to see the outskirts of Vancouver. She had no idea—no idea that it was so near, so big, so sparkling and modern, nestled between the snow-tipped mountains at its back and the green Pacific at its feet. Bottle-green water, just as she had seen in her dream.

Waiting in the lounge to which she had been directed by a courteous and smiling hostess—a contrast to the aiport in Rome—her hand luggage at her feet, she stood Daniele on her lap facing out, his chubby fists grasping her hands on either side for balance, so that he could be amused by watching the passing crowd. She had only a brief wait between flights, this one to Amsterdam, the next one to Milano, and then to Venezia, where she would be met. It would be a long day and night, she knew, but she was so happy, so excited, that nothing mattered. She was proud, too, proud of herself—she was managing this long trip with a squirming, demanding baby, tickets and boarding passes and passports, even reading signs in English, and she wasn't a bit frightened. She knew what she was doing, where she was going, what to expect when she got there. She relaxed, fascinated by the colourful multi-national crowd flowing in waves past her, all races, all manner of dress, everyone seeming to be happy, chatting, laughing. It was a pleasure to watch them, and every now and then someone would stop for a moment and say something silly to Daniele, who crowed in response. He was an unusually beautiful child, she knew, with his dark sandy hair and startlingly blue eyes, like Nonna's. She could hardly wait for them to see him.

The Fiat roared into the *cortile*, spraying gravel, the two uncles in front, Liliana and Daniele in the back seat packed in with their luggage. It was evening, dark already. She had forgotten how early it got dark over here. She felt as though she had been up for at least a week. She was disheveled, her skin sticky, her eyes gritty with lack of sleep, her hair flattened and dull, but Daniele was fine. He had slept almost constantly, thank God, the noise of the engines and the motion keeping him lulled both on the plane and on the drive from the airport in Venice. Only the waits between flights in

Amsterdam and Milano had been hell, sitting in crowded lounges, trying to feed the baby or get him back to sleep, trying to keep him and herself clean.

Peering out the window as the car braked to a noisy halt, Liliana could just make out the group of dark figures waiting on the portico, the light from the kitchen window behind them glowing onto their shoulders, surrounded by the shadowy pots of geraniums and the leggy oleanders that she had known would be in bloom. But the house looked smaller than she remembered it. Probably because of the dark. She felt nauseous from fatigue, from nervousness, and from an excess of joy. She wished she had been able to fix herself up a bit, wash her face and change her blouse, but she hadn't. They would just have to overlook her appearance. This was how women looked when they had been travelling for thirty hours with a baby. But none of them had ever experienced that.

And then she was out of the car and into the familiar scents of the night air, staggering forward toward them, propelled by the weight of the child into the collective arms of Mama and Nonna and Luisa and all the aunties and even some neighbours, all anxious to touch her, to take Daniele's face in their hands and peer into it as though trying to recognize him, to pinch his chubby arms and legs and remark on how sturdy, how *bello* he was—*che bello! Madonna, è bellisimo!*

The next morning when Liliana woke from a fitful sleep, not sure where she was, she heard rain hitting the closed shutters of the room where she lay, her girlhood room. The shutters had to be kept closed because the night air was bad for you, Nonna always said, and Liliana had obediently closed them before getting into the bed, despite the oppressive heat which had been building up in the room all day. She had wakened often, feeling as though she were suffocating, the air heavy with the scent of living things. She had forgotten that smell, which crept into the room despite the closed shutters—the smell of sun-warmed fields, of hay and animals. Daniele lay beside her in the bed, his face flushed. He had kicked and thrashed all night—too hot for him too, she thought, and longed momentarily for the luxury of her own cool bedroom, with her child nearby but in his own bed. Thank God, it would be cooler today.

She lay not moving, delaying the moment when she would have to rise and take the baby downstairs with her. She didn't know what time it was, but she was still tired. She could hear the sounds of footsteps, pots clanging, laughter coming up from the kitchen below. It must be mid-morning. The baby's schedule was disturbed. He wouldn't ordinarily be sleeping this late, but he would need several days to adjust to the time difference. And so would she. She had tried to explain to them last night about that and had given up. She stretched. How unburdened she felt, here in her mother's house. All she had to do was care for herself and her child, and she had seen last night that there would be no shortage of women to fuss over him. What luxury. No responsibility, no worry, no Carlo to appease. No heavy silences to be endured. Peace.

She turned her head and was startled momentarily at the sight of herself and her child reflected in the long mirror on the wardrobe, the mirror in which she had watched herself grow from childhood to womanhood in this beloved room with the same chintz spread on the bed, the same lace curtains at the windows. The room, too, was smaller than she remembered it, the ceiling lower, and it smelled faintly of mothballs. She could hardly believe that she was really back here. But she must go downstairs—there was much yet to be done in preparation for Luisa's wedding, only two weeks away, and she had promised to help. It would be hard for Mama and Nonna after Luisa left. The house would seem so empty with only the two of them. But she and her baby would be here to fill their days.

The following afternoon, though Liliana still felt tired and disoriented and Daniele was cranky and difficult, Luisa announced that Olivo would be coming over to welcome her home. She could barely remember him except that he was taller and darker-skinned than Carlo. The other thing she remembered was that he had never paid the slightest attention to her, the younger sister, treating her as though she were invisible. Of course, she had been a child then, back when Olivo had asked Luisa to marry him, and then had gone off to South America with solemn promises to return soon. Liliana had listened to Luisa crying in the night, trying to stifle her tears in her pillow, and she had felt anger at the man who had left her sister in such pain. And then the letters had started arriving, letters that left Luisa happier until they had begun to dwindle, first to one every month, then every two months, then every six, then, eventually, none.

And now, after so many years of shame and misery, of anger and hopelessness, he had returned and they were all supposed to act as if nothing had happened–to welcome him back with open arms. Well, she couldn't. She would be polite, for her sister's sake, as she was expected to be, but she was not going to welcome him unreservedly. Too many tears had been shed because of him.

Although she would have figured it out had she given it any thought, Liliana had been shocked to learn that first evening back that Olivo would move into the big house with his bride after the wedding–into her house! Things would never be the same. It was true that her father Pietro had moved here when he married Amelia, but there had been no choice back in those days.

Still, Liliana was having a hard time coming to terms with this turn of events. There was certainly plenty of room, she thought. Olivo would simply move into Luisa's big bedroom upstairs. He would, of course, be sharing expenses, so it would make things a bit easier for Nonna and Mama, who lived on their pensions. At last, a man under the roof! But his having to move into their home meant that he had nothing to show for all those years away, that he, unlike her uncles, had not saved enough to build a new house for his bride. How shameful. Of course, she could understand why Luisa had refused to move in with his elderly parents, who lived in an old farmhouse in the countryside.

Liliana didn't really like the idea of sharing her home, to say nothing of her mother and grandmother, with this stranger. But her happiness at being back in the bosom of her family and the excitement surrounding the wedding preparations overshadowed her discomfiture at the thought of Olivo living with them, though that certainly hadn't been in her plan, and it changed everything. Nothing would ever be the same in her home again.

Liliana and Mama stood one on either side of the big table where they usually ate in the main downstairs room.

They had commandeered this surface today because what they were doing–icing and decorating trays of tiny cookies –took more space than the little table in the actual kitchen could offer. It was cooler here as well, and Liliana was immersed in her job, carefully placing the cookies in rows onto a tablecloth, when without warning the door opened.

She looked up, startled, as Olivo entered the shadowed room, redolent with the smells of baking, without knocking. "*Buongiorno. Buongiorno*," he called out. He was so confident of his welcome! He was taller than Carlo but not as tall as she remembered, and the hair above his ears was beginning to silver. She supposed he was good-looking in a wolfish sort of way.

Luisa came running downstairs at the sound of his voice and embraced him fervently. Nonna, who had been working in the kitchen, came into the room and greeted him quietly, gesturing toward a chair, inviting him to sit. Instead, he began to walk toward Liliana.

"There she is–my future sister-in-law back from Canada," he said jovially as he got nearer, "Good to see you again, Liliana," obviously expecting to be hugged and kissed on each cheek. But Liliana only stuck out her hand to be shaken, thus preventing him from embracing her, and walked around to the other side of the table, where she sat between her mother and her grandmother.

"Well, Liliana. I suppose you've heard the news. Luisa and I are going to be living here. Right, Amelia?" There was a silence.

Nonna nodded, and Amelia only said, "Sì, Olivo. Sì. That is true. We'll all be together under one roof." It was clear that while they were polite, they were not overjoyed, and Liliana suspected that Olivo was perfectly aware of their reticence but was determined to bluff it out. He was not being treated just yet as a member of the family. Liliana kept remembering Carlo's words. "I never liked him–never trusted him, you know." And now he was going to live here, in her home, with her family. She struggled to keep her face expressionless. Not to let her mouth turn down or her forehead to wrinkle in distaste. What would Carlo say when she told him about this, she wondered.

For the rest of that week, as the sun resumed its place high overhead each day, the women worked in the kitchen, the air heavy with heat from outside and from the ever-busy oven from which tray after tray of exquisite little cakes and cookies appeared, to be cooled and decorated. The wedding supper would be held in a restaurant, but these were to serve to the many guests who would come to the house bearing wedding gifts. Luisa appeared and disappeared, coming and going with last-minute arrangements for her wedding, which was to be, in Liliana's opinion, unnecessarily elaborate and expensive. But that was how it had to be, they explained to her as if she was from another planet—the family had to maintain a *bella figura*—keep up appearances. She had forgotten how important that was—above all else, it seemed. She thought of her own wedding. Rustic, perhaps, but everyone had fun. And perhaps her family was overdoing it just a bit because of the shame that Luisa had endured–that they had all endured–to show everyone that all was well now.

At the end of her fifth full day back home, Liliana sat with Mama and Nonna outside on the portico in the cool of the evening. The two older women sat on the same low, rush-seated chairs that had always been there, and Liliana sat on the cement step, her arms hugging her drawn-up knees. Daniele was asleep at last, upstairs on his little cot beside her bed. Uncle Tony had brought it over for the baby on her second day home, knowing that she would not be accustomed to sleeping in the same bed as her child. Dear Uncle Tony. So wise.

She bent her head back and looked up at the stars. It was so wonderful to be here with her family, so comfortable, sharing the homely duties once again. Aunties and neighbours came and went constantly, hugging her and the baby and remarking on how well she looked. Telling her how good it was that she had come home at last. Everything was so familiar that Liliana felt as though she had never left. Smiling, she sipped her tall glass of lemonade.

Her mind travelled to yesterday, and the smile left her face. Uncle Tony had driven her and the baby to the nearby town where Carlo's parents lived. She barely knew them, she had visited them rarely before going to Canada to marry their son. Liliana closed her eyes. The memory of their poverty had never left her since that first visit. Nor had the memory of their silence. Carlo was one of a family of four brothers, three of whom were settled with their families in the same town, so the old people were kept busy with their many other grandchildren. But it was only proper that they see this new grandchild, and she knew she was expected to make the visit.

Liliana had been surprised at their age. She had forgotten how much older they were than her own parents. And she was shocked again at their obvious poverty. Their house was small and shabby, though spotlessly clean, and the two old people, bent and dressed all in black, had been quietly hospitable though awkward and shy, the visit punctuated with long silences which Uncle Tony had tried valiantly to fill. Their eyes told her that they were glad to see her and their grandson, but they had no words. No wonder Carlo was so uncommunicative, she had reflected as she was being driven away. The old couple had both wept when she left, wetting Daniele's face with their tears. But she thought perhaps old people wept easily. She was relieved to be leaving, going back to her own family's comfortable home, guilty though that made her feel. Still, she understood better now why Carlo rarely communicated with or even mentioned his parents. She promised to return, as they asked, so that they could see their grandson again, though it was the last thing she wanted to do.

Yesterday's visit had clarified what she should have seen before. Carlo's silence was like that of his parents, who could not find words to express their feelings and therefore avoided doing so. They had probably been brought up like that themselves—in silence. Carlo's face appeared in her mind's eye. Some people were just like that, struggling for the right words, she reflected, and who knew at what cost? How painful to be unable to say what was in your heart. What sorrow to be silent.

"Liliana, where are you going?" It was Nonna's voice calling her from the doorway where she stood holding Daniele in her arms.

"Just down the road to the little store—we've run out of butter. I'll only be a minute," Liliana replied, turning and walking backwards toward the entrance of the cortile.

"In that low-necked blouse? And without stockings? You can't go out like that—barelegged! What will people say!"

Liliana stopped dead in her tracks. She couldn't believe her ears. Here she was, a grown woman with a child, who had flown halfway around the world by herself, being chastised about her immodesty. She opened her mouth to reply and closed it. What was the use? She would only anger the old woman. Without a word she returned to the house and went up to her room to change. Just like before, she reflected. Nonna was still in charge.

It was Saturday, a week to the day before the wedding, and Liliana had been invited to join a group of Luisa's friends at a restaurant for a luncheon in the bride's honour. She was excited. She couldn't remember having been any-where without the baby. She would be able to dress up, to fix her hair and makeup and wear the pretty mauve flowered dress that she had made for just such a pre-wedding occasion. Carefully she examined her reflection in the long mirror, turning this way and that to check her hem. Satisfied, she ran downstairs, high-heeled white sandals in her hand, to kiss Daniele goodbye and dash out to where Luisa waited for her at the wheel of the little red Fiat. It had been a very long time since she had felt young and pretty.

The afternoon passed all too quickly as they talked and laughed and drank white wine, sitting at a round table under the arbor of wisteria, its grape-like clusters of hanging mauve blooms casting dappled shadows on their faces. The women pelted her with questions about her new life so far away in America. They complimented her and paid so much attention to her that at one point she glanced over and saw Luisa sitting silently, a slight frown between her eyes.

"A toast! A toast to the bride!" Liliana cried, and they all raised their glasses toward Luisa and clinked them noisily. The chatter went on until Luisa rose, and she and Liliana, thanking them for the wonderful afternoon, left, roaring off in the little red car. There was still much to be done.

It was late the next morning, Sunday, and Luisa had gone out on some errands. Nonna was dozing on her bed as they had all gone to mass very early that morning, and Liliana and her mother worked side by side in the kitchen. The roast was in the oven and the sugo—a pan of tomato sauce for the gnocchi—was simmering on the stovetop, redolent with the perfume of basil.

They were making potato gnocchi, and though the dough had been made, the rolling and cutting of each individual little dumpling was a tedious job that required their full attention. Amelia prided herself on the perfection of each intricately fashioned gnocchi, and particularly so today. It was to be a special meal because Uncle Tony and his family as well as Olivo and his parents were joining them for Sunday dinner, which would be served as always at one o'clock.

Liliana thought that Amelia had been very quiet since they had come back from early mass, a distant look in her eyes.

"Mama, what is it?" Liliana asked finally. "Is something wrong?" She had noticed her mother and the priest deep in whispered conversation after mass, in the doorway of the church.

Edging closer and lowering her voice, her mother said, "I was talking to the priest this morning. He told me that. . ." She stopped.

"What? What did Don Paolo say?" Liliana asked, sensing that Amelia was troubled. "Is it about Olivo?" she guessed.

"Yes, it is about Olivo," Amelia replied, moving closer. "He. . . Oh, God! I probably shouldn't say anything, but apparently he. . .he has a family over there."

"A family? What do you mean—a family?" Liliana felt a thud in her chest.

"Well, he was living with a woman. And he. . ."

"With a woman?" Liliana's whisper crackled, her voice breaking. "You mean he was married?"

"No, no. Not married. Don Paolo wouldn't marry them if he'd been married already. But. . . he left a woman there. . . and three children!"

"He left three children behind?" Liliana stopped, her voice catching in her throat. Children! Olivo had children over there? He abandoned three children! "How could he?" she gasped, standing open-mouthed, her hands to her face.

Amelia brushed tears from her cheeks. "Yes. It's true," she said, collapsing onto the low rush-seated chair beside the stove where Nonna always sat. "But you mustn't tell Nonna. Promise me." The words came out of Amelia's mouth as though they were choking her. "If she knew she would. . .

make a scene. . . in church. . . maybe stop the wedding. . . and poor Luisa's life would be hell–again."

Liliana was still in shock. How could anyone do such a thing–abandon three children? She glanced over to where Daniele lay kicking his legs and cooing, his blue eyes seeking hers. How could you?

"But what about Luisa? Oh, Mama! She doesn't know, does she?"

"No, no. The priest said he doesn't think she knows. He says it's up to Olivo to tell her. Oh, my poor Luisa," she whispered, a sob catching in her throat. "Why did it have to be like this?"

Liliana knew that Carlo had been right about Olivo. He had said he'd never liked him, that he couldn't be trusted. Carlo had been a better judge of character than any of the others. And what would he think if he knew about this? She would have to tell him eventually.

"Don't worry, Mama, I won't tell her. But how awful. How could he?"

"I don't know, cara, I don't know. But let's not speak of it again. There is nothing we can do. We just have to try. . .try to get through the days." Amelia heaved a great sigh and stood then, stirring the sauce absentmindedly.

Liliana thought with despair about the guests who would be arriving momentarily–Olivo and his parents and Uncle Tony and his family. She knew that if her uncle found out he would react with rage. . .maybe even violence. And who could blame him? And what about Olivo's parents? What would they think if they knew about those three far-away abandoned grandchildren? Wouldn't they be inconsolable?

Furious with their son? Uncomprehending? It was all too much. Too much to come to terms with.

At this moment Olivo entered from the cortile, holding back the curtain that hung in the doorway for his parents, who came into the room and stood uncertainly behind him. "*Buongiorno*, everybody!" Olivo called out. "Here we are! We're here!"

Glancing quickly at each other, both pairs of eyes mirroring the other's despair, the two women smoothed their hair, squared their shoulders, and went to greet their guests.

Now Liliana dreaded the wedding more than ever. She worried that she would not be able to hold her tongue, that somehow she'd reveal the terrible secret. That she'd call out in the middle of the vows, "Liar!" No, she wouldn't do that. She had promised her mother not to let on to anyone about Olivo's awful secret, and she wouldn't, though he deserved to be betrayed in front of everyone. So they would all know what kind of man he was.

But she worried, too, about how she would maintain her dignity watching her sister marry in the little church that her father and her uncles and all the men had built after the war. The church in which she had always thought she herself would be married. She was afraid she would call out, "Why not me? Why not?" Or disgrace herself with a fit of angry weeping. She was afraid she would spoil things for her sister, would shame them all. She scolded herself—don't be silly. Be strong. You're a grown woman with a child. You must stop looking back. Be happy for your sister–she doesn't know about Olivo's treachery. Allow her this happiness. Be glad that you're here with your family where you belong.

When the hour arrived to go to the church, after she had stuffed herself and Daniele into their very best immaculately pressed clothes, mopping her brow in the stultifying heat of the bedroom as she struggled with the cranky, squirming child. She just wanted it to be over. She heard her mother calling her name.

"Liliana, come here. Come and help your sister."

She hurried into Luisa's bedroom and stood transfixed at the beauty of her sister, who was standing in front of the windows in her white lace dress, its full skirt accentuating the narrowness of her waist, its chaste white collar framing her face. *She's beautiful!* Liliana thought. *Olivo doesn't deserve her!* Mama was fussing with her veil, adjusting the seed-pearl tiara which held it to her dark hair, and Liliana felt a lump in her throat. This was what had been missing at her own wedding–her mother and her sister helping her to get ready, fussing over her, being there in the church. And then she remembered the look on Carlo's face when he had turned from the altar to watch her progression up the aisle. The love on his face. And she knew that there had never been anyone else for him. She was, she knew, the lucky one.

She sat stiffly in the front pew with the rest of her family, jiggling the baby on her knee, conscious of the eyes on their backs as she watched her sister and this deceitful stranger saying their vows. She closed her eyes and said a silent prayer for Luisa, who had waited so long for this day.

Afterwards, Nonna took Daniele home while the others piled into cars and were driven out of San Michele and down a narrow, twisting road bordered by fields of grapevines to the site of the wedding supper. Liliana could see, in the back window of the car in front, the white-veiled head of her sister

358

resting on the shoulder of her new husband. Luisa was happy on her wedding day, innocent of any reason why she should not be.

The wedding reception was held in an elegant restaurant in a restored villa in the countryside not far away, and Liliana thought she had never seen such extravagance. She knew her uncles were helping with the expenses, but still, things must have improved a great deal since she had left home—this much money had never been spent on anything before. On foolishness—on huge arrangements of flowers and a string quartet and a multi-course meal fit for the princes of the Medici—course after course, all served by dark-suited waiters with white gloves who deftly changed glasses and poured wines and liqueurs without end. The guests, dressed in the height of fashion (whether they could afford it or not), laughed and talked animatedly throughout the endless meal, and Luisa and Olivo circulated among the round tables where the guests sat, each table centred by an enormous arrangement of flowers in a tall vase, flanked by white candles in crystal candelabra. Luisa's voluminous white lace dress was crushed between the tables as she moved, bending over each guest to distribute the *bomboniere,* a little bundle of candied almonds tied to a miniature crystal cupid. How long would it take her family to pay this off? And then there was the expense of the honeymoon trip to Rome, though they'd be staying with Aunt Melania.

Finally, when the last course had been served, the last toast drunk, the last of the *bomboniere* distributed, the dance band took its place on the dais, replacing the string quartet that had played softly throughout the meal. It struck up the first chord and Luisa and Olivo rose and waltzed sedately around the floor as the guests cheered and clanked their cutlery against their wine glasses. Liliana saw that Luisa had a look of utter joy on her face, and it was all she could do to stop the tears. Luisa would surely learn the secret Olivo kept from her sooner or later. And then how would she feel? Betrayed. Her marriage was tainted.

Following the proper order of things, the next dance was Luisa and her eldest uncle, who had given her away in lieu of her father, and Olivo with Amelia. Liliana watched her mother waltzing sedately with her new son-in-law and she hoped her face betrayed nothing.

Now it was time for the bride to be waltzed around the room by each of her uncles in turn, as Olivo headed across the floor toward Liliana. Oh no! She was going to have to dance with him. There was no avoiding it, distasteful as it was to her. She was his bride's sister, after all. His new sister-in-law. She stood, moving reluctantly into his arms, and was immediately assailed by the overpowering stench of his alcoholic breath. He pulled her to him, too closely, so closely that she could feel the entire length of his body against hers, and try as she might, she could not move back. He held her tightly in his grip and then, almost before she knew it had happened, for only a brief moment, his hand dropped to caress one buttock. She felt a rush of anger and her face flushed.

Finally it was over and she could resume her seat beside Mama. Liliana felt unclean and somehow guilty. She prayed that no one had noticed. But now she knew for sure what kind of man he was.

Everyone was up and dancing now, except for Liliana and her mother, neither of whom had a husband there. Nor ever would, she thought, glancing at Amelia. Always sitting on the sidelines, always alone.

Fervently she wished she were back home with Nonna and Daniele. Her feet were burning, squished into the high-heeled shoes with the impossibly pointed toes. The girdle she had worn to flatten her tummy had prevented her from enjoying the plentiful food, and she just wanted it to be over. What if Olivo wanted to dance with her again?! Besides, she felt alone and even out-of-place. All she wanted was to go home, take off her tight, hot clothes, cuddle her baby, and fall asleep in her own bed to the regular sounds of Nonna's snoring in the bedroom next door. Funny, she thought, Carlo never snores.

She is sitting in the sun, on the doorstep of her little wooden house, and the geraniums in their pots on either side of her are moving, swaying back and forth rhythmically. She is alone, surrounded by a sea of waving green grass bordered in the distance by tall dark trees. She hears voices, the voices of children calling and laughing, though she cannot see them. The scent of the geraniums is overwhelming.

Liliana sat up in bed. Where was she? Peering into the darkness, she made out the familiar shapes of the furniture in her girlhood room, the dark shutters closed across the windows. Then she remembered. The wedding. Luisa's wedding. She moaned.

It was so close in the room, the night air so heavy. She knew she wouldn't be able to go back to sleep, she hadn't slept well since she had arrived, and tonight, exhausted and upset, it was impossible. Quietly, so as not to waken the baby who lay in his cot beside her bed, his covers kicked off as usual in the heat, she crept over to the windows. Carefully, trying not to let the hinges squeak, she opened first one set of shutters and then the other, reaching her bare arms out into the black night to fold the slatted wood back against the outside wall of the house. She knelt on the floor and rested her head on the broad stone windowsill as the blessedly cool air entered her room. She looked out and up at the black sky punctuated by a thousand tiny stars, and saw the silver moon riding high in the velvet darkness—the same moon that shone in the window of her bedroom at home—shone on the face of her sleeping husband. Liliana got up from where she knelt and went to cover her baby. His long dark lashes lay feathered on his cheeks as he slept, and she saw that his face in the moonlight coming from the opened shutters looked startlingly like Carlo's.

Gina had phoned several times since Liliana had arrived, and now that the flurry of activities surrounding the wedding were over and Luisa and Olivo were still away on their wedding trip, Liliana begged Uncle Tony to drive her to the village a few hours away where Gina lived with her parents. She had to see her old friend, whose voice on the phone was so little and distant even now that she was near.

The day dawned hot and bright, as usual, and although Liliana was anxious to see Gina again, in some recess of her mind she dreaded it, too. But she wanted to show off

Daniele. And she knew that Gina would be asking about all their friends back. . .over there.

She was waiting on the stoop as they drove into her cortile, much like Liliana's own, except that there were fewer flowers, a dustier, shabbier look to the place, the surrounding buildings less well-kept. Gina's black dress, her widow's weeds, hung crookedly on her gaunt frame. Nello, a sturdy toddler now, peered out from behind her skirt, his thumb in his mouth, and her second baby, a girl that she had called Maria, of course, was in her arms. The baby was small and pale, though Liliana thought with a start that she must be about four months old by now.

Gina stood there, unmoving, as Liliana, in her light flowered dress, carrying Daniele in a little white sailor's suit, walked toward her. She stood immobile as though she knew what a pitiful sight she was, as though by holding the tableau she was signalling the message, preparing Liliana for the hopeless sorrow that she could not hide. Liliana's legs were trembling as she moved toward the little group standing in the glaring sun, and she wanted to bolt. Wanted to clutch her baby to her and turn and get back into the car, to leave, to return to the laughter and comfort of home. But she could not, she knew. This, too, had to be endured. Selfish, stupid, she told herself as she turned and thrust her child into her uncle's arms so that she could embrace Gina, who cried now quite openly, her tears rolling down her perspiring face. Liliana stepped toward her and enclosed both Gina and her baby in her arms.

"Oh God, I thought I'd never see you again," sobbed Gina, her tears wetting Liliana's neck. Gina's face and body were damp with perspiration and Liliana was secretly ashamed of the distaste she felt at the faint smell coming from Gina's trembling body.

"Oh Liliana, I'm so miserable." And then, "I'm sorry, I told myself I wouldn't cry, I'm sorry," as Liliana patted her consolingly on the back. What could she say, she thought despairingly, what could she do? Gina was trapped—there would be no reprieve. She was doomed to live on in poverty and loneliness with only her few memories of a far-off place and an absent husband for comfort.

That night after the cousins and their mothers had gone home, Liliana lingered at the table with her uncles and her mother and grandmother, telling tales of Canada, drinking glass after glass of mineral water with just a touch of wine. She was so thankful to be back in her mother's house. Secretly she was glad that Luisa and Olivo were still off on their honeymoon trip to Rome–it would be hard for everyone to get used to a strange man living among them.

And poor Gina. There is no escape for her, Liliana thought. It didn't bear thinking about—there was nothing to be done. There was no way she could change things for Gina. She could only thank God that it wasn't her in that position. She had almost been widowed at the same time, but at least her family wanted her, was overjoyed to have her back.

Looking around the table at the beloved faces, animated with laughter, eyes sparkling just like old times, she thought of Carlo. How different his upbringing must have been. His parents were more like Gina's than hers. She could not imagine his family like this, gathered together around the table long after the meal was finished, enjoying each other, teasing, reminiscing, wiping a tear when they spoke of their departed loved ones, then laughing gently as they remembered other times. No, life in Carlo's family had always been a dour struggle, unleavened by laughter, and she marvelled at his ability to be light-hearted even occasionally. He would never change, but she now understood that he had come a long way.

Yawning, she pushed back her chair and after kissing everyone goodnight, slowly mounted the stairs to the room where her child lay sleeping, the shadow of his father on his face.

She is lying on her back in the sea of waving green grass, and the sound of the rustling of a thousand taffeta skirts is all around her. The lights, the Northern Lights, undulate above her, merging, separating into bands of green and rose and lilac and white, then merging again as if to the rhythmic strains of far-off music, and she hears Loretta's voice. "This place is in you. You are in it, and it is in you."

Liliana opened her eyes. Quietly, by the light of the moon streaming in through the opened shutters, she crossed the room and took out the airplane ticket she had buried deep in the top drawer and checked the return date. Three weeks. A long time to wait.

THE END